Resounding praise for Elizabeth Peters,
Amelia Peabody, and
LION IN THE VALLEY

"This author never fails to entertain."
Cleveland Plain Dealer

"A decided treat."
Booklist

"A writer so popular that the public library needs to
keep her books under lock and key."
Washington Post Book World

"Amelia is one of the most interesting and delightful
characters in the mystery genre."
St. Paul Pioneer Press

"A new Amelia Peabody mystery is like
visiting old friends."
USA Today

"Let Miss Peters and Amelia guide dedicated mystery-
lovers to their own special heaven of delightful
characters, convoluted and engrossing plot, and
writing of the highest caliber."
Washington Times

Books by Elizabeth Peters

ELIZABETH PETERS

Lion in the Valley

AN AMELIA PEABODY MYSTERY

AVON BOOKS
An Imprint of HarperCollinsPublishers

The lines quoted on pages vii and 151-152 are from the Battle of Kadesh Inscriptions of King Ramses II; translation by Miriam Lichtheim, in *Ancient Egyptian Literature*, Vol. II, *The New Kingdom* (Los Angeles: University of California Press, 1976).

AVON BOOKS
An Imprint of HarperCollins*Publishers*
10 East 53rd Street
New York, New York 10022-5299

Copyright © 1986 by Elizabeth Peters
Inside cover author photo by Osmund Geier
ISBN: 0-380-73119-3
www.avonbooks.com

First Avon Books printing: July 2001
First Avon Twilight Printing: September 1999

Avon Twilight Trademark Reg. U.S. Pat. Off. and in Other Countries, Marca Registrada, Hecho en U.S.A.
HarperCollins® is a trademark of HarperCollins Publishers Inc.

Printed in the U.S.A.

10 9 8 7 6

TO DR. ANN KING
A.K.A. MY FRIEND PENNY
WITH LOVE AND RESPECT

•

Lord of fear, great of fame,
In the hearts of all the lands.
Great of awe, rich in glory,
As is Set upon his mountain. . . .
Like a wild lion in a valley of goats.

•

Foreword

In this, the fourth volume of the memoirs of Amelia Peabody Emerson (Mrs. Radcliffe Emerson), the editor once again deems it expedient to explain certain anomalies and obscurities in the text. Mrs. Emerson was not as careful as she might have been about noting the dates of her entries. She seems to have picked up the current volume of her journal and scribbled away until something happened to distract her. However, from certain internal evidence, it seems likely that the current volume concerns events of the 1895–96 season. (Egyptologists tend to use this method of dating, since the archaeological "year" runs from late fall until early spring, the climate of Egypt making summer excavations extremely difficult.)

As the editor has had occasion to mention, the names of most of the persons involved have been changed, in order to spare the feelings of descendants of said individuals. The informed reader will recognize some names as those of well-known archaeologists, who appear only peripherally. Mrs. Emerson seems to have been fairly accurate in describing their activities; however, it would be a serious error to assume that she was equally accurate in reporting their conversations with her, for, like her distinguished husband, she had a decided tendency to attribute to other people opinions of her own.

Another obscurity in the ur-text (if the editor may so describe the journals themselves) arises from the fact that at some point Mrs. Emerson apparently decided to edit them for eventual publication. (See her remarks on p. 73) Since she was as inconsistent about her revision as she was about dating her pages, the result is sometimes a peculiar blend of journalistic and novelistic styles.

In other words, none of the eccentricities of the present volume are the responsibility of the editor. She has done the best she could and would suggest that complaints, criticisms, and other pejorative comments be addressed to the heirs of Professor and Mrs. Emerson, not to her.

One

"My dear Peabody," said Emerson, "pray correct me if I am mistaken; but I sense a diminution of that restless ardor for living that is so noted a characteristic of yours, particularly upon occasions such as this. Since that happy day that saw us united, never a cloud has dimmed the beaming orb of matrimonial bliss; and that remarkable circumstance derives, I am certain, from the perfect communion that marks our union. Confide, I implore, in the fortunate man whose designated role is to support and shelter you, and whose greatest happiness is to share your own."

I felt certain Emerson must have worked this speech out in advance. No one talks like that in the course of ordinary conversation.

I knew, however, that the formality of his speech failed adequately to express the sincere devotion that had inspired it. My dear Emerson and I have been of one mind and one heart ever since the day we met in the Egyptian Museum of Boulaq. (In actual fact, our first meeting was distinctly acrimonious. I was a mere tourist at that time, on my maiden visit to the land of the pharaohs; and yet, scarcely had I set foot on that fabled soil than the bright flame of Egyptological fervor was kindled in my bosom, a flame that soon became a roaring conflagration. Little did I suspect, that day in the museum, as I energetically defended myself against the unwarranted criticisms hurled at me by the fascinating stranger, that we would soon meet again, under even more romantic circumstances, in an abandoned tomb at El Amarna. The setting, at least, was romantic. Emerson, I confess, was not. However, a subtle instinct told me that beneath Emerson's caustic remarks and black scowls his heart beat only for me, and, as events proved, I was correct.)

His tender discernment was not at fault. A dark foreboding did indeed shadow the joy that would normally have flooded my being at such a time. We stood on the deck of the vessel that had borne us swiftly across the broad Mediterranean; the breeze of its passage across the blue waters ruffled our hair and tugged at our garments. Ahead we could see the Egyptian coast, where we would land before the day was over. We were about to enter upon another season of archaeological investigation, the most recent of many we had shared. Soon we would be exploring the stifling, bat-infested corridors of one pyramid and the muddy, flooded burial chamber of another—scenes that would under ordinary circumstances have inspired in me a shiver of rapturous anticipation. How many other women—particularly in that final decade of the nineteenth century—had so many reasons to rejoice?

Emerson—who prefers to be addressed by his surname, since he considers "Radcliffe" affected and effeminate (his very words)—had chosen me as his equal partner, not only in marriage, but in the profession we both have the honor to adorn. Emerson is the finest excavator of Egyptian antiquities the world has seen. I do not doubt his name will be revered as "The Father of Scientific Excavation" as long as civilization endures upon this troubled globe. And my name—the name of Amelia Peabody Emerson—will be enshrined alongside his.

Forgive my enthusiasm, dear Reader. The contemplation of Emerson's excellent qualities never fails to arouse emotion. Nor is his excellence restricted to his intellectual qualities. I feel no shame in confessing that his physical attributes were not the least of the elements that made me decide to accept his proposal of marriage. From the raven hair upon his broad brow to the dimple (which he prefers to call a cleft) in his chin, he is a model of masculine strength and good looks.

Emerson appears to be equally appreciative of my physical attributes. Candidly, I have never fully understood this attitude. Mine is not a type of beauty I admire. Features rather less pronounced, eyes of a softer and paler hue, a figure greater in stature and more restrained in the region above the waist, locks of sunny gold instead of jetty black—these are my ideals of female loveliness. Luckily for me, Emerson does not share them.

His large brown hand lay next to mine on the rail of the vessel. It was not the hand of a gentleman; but to me the callouses and scars that marked those tanned and stalwart members were badges of honor. I remembered the occasions on which they had wielded weapons or tools in the course of his labors; and other occasions on which they had demonstrated a delicacy of touch that induced the most remarkable of sensations.

Emerson has many admirable qualities, but patience is not one of them. Lost in my reveries, I failed to respond at once to his question. He seized me by the shoulders and spun me around to face him. His blue eyes blazed like sapphires, his lips curled back from his white teeth, and the dimple in his chin quivered ominously.

"Why the devil don't you answer me?" he shouted. "How can you remain unmoved by such an appeal? What ails you, Peabody? I will be cursed if I can understand women. You ought to be on your knees thanking heaven—and *ME*—for the happiness in store for you. It wasn't easy, you know, persuading de Morgan to give up the site to us; it required all the subtle tact of which I am capable. No one but I could have done it. No one but I *would* have done it. And how do you repay me? By sighing and moping!"

It would have been immediately apparent, to anyone familiar with the circumstances he described, that Emerson was again engaging in his endearing habit of self-deception. The Director of the Antiquities Service, M. de Morgan, *had* yielded to us the archaeological site at which he himself had worked the previous year, and which had already produced a number of remarkable discoveries. However, Emerson's subtle tact, a quality that exists only in his imagination, had nothing to do with it. I was not precisely sure what had produced M. de Morgan's change of heart. Or, to be more exact, I had certain suspicions I preferred not to think about. It was a natural progression from those suspicions to the excuse I now uttered to account for my somber mood.

"I am distressed about Ramses, Emerson. To have our son misbehave so badly, just when I had hoped we might get through one voyage without incident. . . .

How many boys of eight, I wonder, have been threatened with keelhauling by the captain of a British merchant vessel?''

''That was merely the captain's bluff, maritime exaggeration,'' Emerson replied impatiently. ''He would not dare do such a thing. You are not concerned about Ramses, Peabody; he does this sort of thing all the time, and you ought to be accustomed to it.''

''This sort of thing, Emerson? Ramses has done a number of unspeakable things, but to the best of my knowledge this is the first time he has instigated a mutiny.''

''Nonsense! Simply because a few ignorant seamen misunderstood his lectures on the theories of that fellow Marx—''

''He had no business lecturing the crew—or being in their quarters in the first place. They gave him spirits, Emerson, I know they did. Even Ramses would not have spoken back to the captain in such terms had he not been intoxicated.''

Emerson looked as if he wanted to protest, but since he obviously shared my opinion he found himself with nothing to say. I went on, ''What is even more incomprehensible is why the crewmen should endure Ramses' presence, much less share their cherished grog, as I believe it is called. What possible pleasure could they find in his company?''

''One of them told me they enjoyed hearing him talk. 'Wot a mouth that nipper 'as' was the exact phrase.''

A reluctant smile touched his lips as he spoke. Emerson's lips are among his most admirable features, chiseled and flexible, shaped with precise delicacy and yet not lacking in fullness. I felt my own lips respond with an answering smile. The untutored sailor had hit the nail on the head, so to speak.

"Forget Ramses," Emerson said. "I insist, Amelia, that you tell me what is worrying you."

Despite his smile he was not in good temper with me; his use of my proper name indicated as much. "Peabody," my maiden name, is the one he uses in moments of marital or professional approbation. With a sigh, I yielded.

"A strange foreboding has come over me, Emerson."

Emerson's eyes narrowed. "Indeed, Amelia?"

"I am only surprised you do not share it."

"I do not. At this moment my heart is suffused with the most agreeable sensations. Not a cloud—"

"You have made your point, Emerson. And if you will forgive my mentioning it, that particular metaphor—"

"Are you criticizing my rhetorical style, Amelia?"

"If you are going to take offense at the least little thing I say, Emerson, I cannot confide in you. I didn't want to cloud your happiness with my worries. Are you certain you want me to tell you?"

His head on one side, Emerson considered the question. "No," he said.

"You mean you are not certain, or—"

"I mean I don't want you to tell me. I don't want to hear about your foreboding."

"But you asked—"

"I have changed my mind."

"Then you share the sense of impending—"

"I didn't until this moment," Emerson snarled. "Curse it, Amelia—"

"How strange. I was certain the sympathy between us was complete."

The expression on Emerson's handsome countenance might have led an observer to suppose it was not sympathy but rising fury that caused his brows to lower and his eyes to snap. Since I had a few doubts on that subject myself, I hastened to satisfy the curiosity he had expressed some minutes earlier.

"Naturally I look forward to the work of this season. You know my enthusiasm for pyramids, and one could hardly find finer specimens than at Dahshoor. I particularly anticipate investigating the burial chamber of the Black Pyramid under more auspicious circumstances than those that surrounded our initial visit. One's critical faculties are not at their best after one has been dropped through Stygian darkness into a flooded subterranean pit and left to perish there."

Emerson had released his hold on my shoulders and turned back to the rail. His eyes fixed on the horizon, he said rapidly, "We will have to wait until later in the season to explore the Black Pyramid, after the inundation has receded to its lowest point. If the chamber is still flooded, perhaps a pump—"

"I have also considered that problem, my dear Emerson. However, that is not the issue at the present time."

"A hydraulic pump, with a hose—"

"Have you forgotten, Emerson, the circumstances under which we first made our acquaintance with the interior of the Black Pyramid?"

"I am not so elderly that I suffer from lapses of memory," Emerson replied waspishly. "Nor have I forgotten your response when I expressed my intention of dying in your arms. I confess I had expected a trifle more appreciation."

"You misunderstood me, Emerson. As I said at the time, I would be happy to have that arrangement prevail should the inevitability of doom be upon us. I never doubted for a moment, my dear, that you would find a way out. And I was quite correct."

I moved closer and leaned against his shoulder.

"Well," Emerson said gruffly. "We did get out, didn't we? Though if it had not been for Ramses—"

"Let's not talk about Ramses or the circumstances of our escape. You know what is on my mind, Emerson, for I am certain that it haunts you in equal measure. I will never forget our final encounter with the villain who was responsible for our near demise. I can still see his sneering smile and hear his contemptuous words. 'This, then, is farewell. I trust we shall not meet again.' "

Emerson's hands clenched on the rail with such force that the tendons stood out like whipcord. However, he did not speak, so I continued, "Nor can I forget the vow I made at the time. 'We will meet again, never fear; for I will make it my business to hunt you down and put an end to your nefarious activities.' "

Emerson's hands relaxed. In a querulous tone he remarked, "You may have been thinking that at the time, Amelia, but you certainly didn't say so, not until that young whippersnapper from the *Daily Yell* interviewed you this past July. You deliberately deceived me about that interview, Amelia. You never told me you had invited O'Connell to my house. You smuggled him in and smuggled him out, and instructed my own servants to keep me in the dark—"

"I was only trying to spare you, my dear, knowing how you dislike Mr. O'Connell. After all, you once kicked him down the stairs—"

"I did no such thing," said Emerson, who honestly believed this. "But I might have done, if I had caught him in my drawing room smirking and leering at my wife and getting ready to print a pack of lies about me. His story was absolutely embarrassing. Besides, it was inaccurate."

"Now, Emerson, I must differ with you. I am certain one of us hurled that challenge at the Master Criminal; perhaps it was you who said it. In the interview I may have omitted a few of Ramses' activities, for I thoroughly disapprove of giving children too high an opinion of themselves. In every other way the report was entirely accurate, and it certainly did not embarrass ME. What, am I not to praise my husband for his courage and strength, and commend him for rescuing me from certain death?"

"Er, hmmm," said Emerson. "Well, but Peabody—"

"Mark my words, Emerson, we have not seen the last of that villain. He managed to escape us, but we foiled his plot and deprived him of his ill-gotten treasure. He is not the man to accept defeat without an attempt at revenge."

"How can you say that? You don't know a thing about the fellow, not even his nationality."

"He is an Englishman, Emerson. I am convinced of that."

"He spoke Arabic with as much facility as English," Emerson pointed out. "And you never saw his face when it was not swathed in hair. Never in my life have I seen such a beard! Would you know him if you saw him again sans beard?"

"Certainly."

"Humph." Emerson put his arm around my shoulders and drew me closer. "Well, Peabody, I admit that nothing would give me greater pleasure than to punch that swine on the nose, and if he intrudes into our affairs I will deal with him as he deserves. But I have no intention of looking for trouble. I have better things to do. Promise me, Peabody, that you will leave well enough alone."

"Oh, certainly, my dear Emerson."

"Promise."

"I promise I will not go looking for trouble."

"My darling Peabody!" Emerson drew me into a fond embrace, careless of the watching sailors.

I had every intention of keeping my word. Why look for trouble when trouble is certain to come looking for you?

After disembarking at Alexandria, we boarded the train for Cairo. The journey takes a trifle over four hours, and it is considered somewhat tedious by most travelers, since the route crosses the featureless alluvial plains of the Delta. To the trained eye of an archaeologist, however, each mound, or "tell," indicates the presence of a buried city. Ramses and Emerson were constantly arguing about the identification of these sites, an argument in which I took no part since I do not see the sense in debating matters concerning which so few facts are known. As I told them, only excavation will determine the truth.

Not until we were within a few miles of our destination was the view enlivened by the sight of the Giza pyramids in the purple distance, framed by the low Libyan hills. It was always at this point, and not on the crowded quay at Alexandria, that I felt I had really arrived in Egypt.

Emerson smiled at me in silent sympathy before turning back to feast his eyes upon the glorious vision. He had profanely consented to put on his new gray suit, and was looking particularly handsome—though I confess that Emerson's splendid physique shows to best advantage in his working costume of shabby trousers and a rumpled shirt open at the throat, with rolled sleeves baring his muscular forearms. He was not wearing a hat because Emerson consistently refuses to wear a hat even when working under the baking sun, and it is beyond my powers of persuasion (extensive though they are) to overcome this prejudice of his.

The elegance of his appearance was only slightly marred by the great brindled feline perched on his knee. The cat Bastet was staring out the window of the train with an interest as keen as Emerson's, and I wondered if she realized she had returned to the land of her birth. Ramses would have claimed she did, for he had an exaggerated opinion of the creature's intelligence. She had been his constant companion ever since she had joined our family several years before, and was now an experienced traveler, since Ramses insisted on taking her with him wherever he went. I must say she was far less trouble than her youthful master.

Ramses—ah, Ramses! My eloquent pen falters when I attempt in a few words to convey the complex personality contained in the body of the eight-year-old boy who is my only child. Some superstitious Egyptians actually claimed he was not a child at all, but a jinni that had taken up its abode in Ramses' meager frame. There are good jinn and evil jinn (the latter being commonly called efreets), for this class of mythological beings is morally neutral in origin, an intermediate species between men and angels. I had not chosen to inquire to which class Ramses was commonly believed to belong.

Ramses was grubby and disheveled, of course. Ramses is almost always grubby and disheveled. He is drawn to dirt as a crocodile is drawn to water. He had been (for Ramses) relatively tidy when we got on the train. An hour or so after we left Alexandria I looked around and found him missing from our compartment. This did not surprise me, since Ramses had an uncanny knack of disappearing when the spirit moved him to do so. It was a particularly disconcerting talent in a boy whose normal progression through a room was marked by a singular degree of clumsiness, owing in large part to his propensity to undertake tasks beyond his ability.

At Emerson's insistence I went looking for the boy and found him in a third-class carriage, squatting on the floor and engaged in animated conversation with a woman whose flimsy and immodest attire left no doubt in my mind as to her profession. I removed Ramses and returned him to our compartment, placing him in a seat next to the window so he could not elude me again.

He, too, had turned to admire the pyramids. I could see only his filthy collar and the tumbled mass of tight black curls that adorned his head; but I knew his saturnine countenance betrayed no emotion to speak of. Ramses' countenance is habitually impassive. His nose is rather large, and his chin matches his nose. His coloring is not at all English; one might easily mistake him for an Egyptian youth, and it was this resemblance, in addition to his regal manner, that had prompted Emerson to give him the nickname of Ramses. (For I hope the reader knows, without my telling him or her, that I would never agree to have a British infant christened with such an outlandish appellation.)

Since the heads of Ramses and Emerson, not to mention the cat, blocked my view, I leaned back and relaxed—without, however, taking my eyes from the back of my son's head.

As was my custom, I had engaged rooms at Shepheard's. Emerson complained bitterly about staying there. He complains every year, so I paid no attention. Some of the newer hotels are as comfortable, but in addition to offering all the amenities a person of refinement can expect, Shepheard's has the advantage of being the center of the haut monde of Cairo. My reasons for preferring this hotel are the very reasons why Emerson complains of it. He would much prefer lodgings in the native quarter, where he can wallow in the genial lack of sanitation that distinguishes lowerclass hotels and pensions. (Men are by instinct untidy animals. Emerson is one of the few who has the courage to state his sentiments aloud.) Now I can "rough it" with the best of them, but I see no reason to deny myself comfort when it is available. I wanted a few days to recover from the crowded and uncomfortable conditions on board ship before retiring to the desert.

A most reasonable attitude, I am sure all would agree. Emerson's claim, that I stay at Shepheard's in order to catch up on the gossip, is just one of his little jokes.

I have heard people say that it is difficult to get accommodations at Shepheard's during the height of the season, but I have never had the least trouble. Of course we were old and valued clients. The rumor that Mr. Baehler, the manager, is in mortal terror of Emerson and fears to deny him anything he asks is, of course, ridiculous. Mr. Baehler is a tall, sturdy gentleman, and I am sure he would never be intimidated in that manner.

He stood on the terrace waiting to greet us—and, naturally, the other guests who had arrived on the Alexandria train. His splendid head of silvery-white hair stood out above the crowd. As we prepared to descend from our carriage, another conveyance drew up behind. It would have attracted our notice, if for no other reason, because of the effect it had on the guests sitting at the tables on the terrace. A kind of universal stiffening ran through them; all heads turned toward the newcomers, and a moment of breathless silence was succeeded by an outbreak of hissing, whispered conversation.

The open carriage was drawn by two perfectly matched grays. Scarlet plumes adorned their harness, and they tossed their handsome heads and pranced like the aristocratic beasts they clearly were.

The driver jumped from his seat and handed the reins to the groom who had been mounted behind. The former was tall and thin, lithe as a panther in riding costume and polished boots. His black hair looked as if it had received a coating of the same boot polish; his narrow black mustache might have been drawn in India ink. A monocle in his right eye caught the sunlight in a blinding flash.

Emerson exclaimed aloud, "By the Lord Harry, it is that villain Kalenischeff!"

Emerson's accents are not noted for their softness. All heads turned toward us, including that of Kalenischeff. His cynical smile stiffened, but he recovered himself almost at once and turned to assist the other passenger from the carriage.

Jewels shone at her throat and on her slender wrists. Her frock of gray-green silk was of the latest Paris mode, with balloon sleeves bigger around than her narrow waist. A huge cravat of white chiffon was pinned by a diamond-and-emerald brooch. Her parasol matched her frock. Under it I caught a glimpse of a lovely, laughing face with cheeks and lips more brilliant than Nature had designed.

The dashing couple swept up the stairs and into the hotel.

"Well!" I said. "I wonder who—"

"Never mind," said Emerson, taking me firmly by the arm.

We had our usual rooms on the third floor, overlooking the Ezbekieh Gardens. After we had unpacked and changed our attire, we went down to take tea on the terrace. Emerson grumbled less than usual at the performance of what he terms "an absurd social ritual," for we were all thirsty after the long, dusty ride.

Tea on the terrace of Shepheard's is certainly one of the popular tourist activities, but even old hands like ourselves never tire of watching the vivacious procession of Egyptian life that passes along Ibrahim Pasha Street. The environs of the hotel teem with crowds of beggars, vendors, donkey boys and carriage drivers, all vying for the custom of the guests. Once we had seated ourselves and given the waiter our order, I took a list from my pocket and read it to Ramses. It was a list of things he was forbidden to do. It began, as I recall, with "Do not talk to the donkey boys," and ended, "Do not repeat any of the words you learned from the donkey boys last year." Ramses' Arabic was fluent and unfortunately quite colloquial.

We saw a number of acquaintances pass in and out of the hotel, but none came to speak to us, and there were none with whom we cared to speak; not an Egyptologist in the lot, as Emerson put it. I was about to suggest that we retire to our rooms when another oath from my outspoken husband warned me of the approach of someone who had inspired his disapproval. Turning, I beheld Kalenischeff.

He wore his fixed smile like a mask. "Good afternoon, madame—Professor—Master Ramses. Welcome back to Cairo. May I . . . ?"

"No," said Emerson, snatching the chair from Kalenischeff's grasp. "How dare you address Mrs. Emerson? Your very presence is an insult to any respectable woman."

"Now, Emerson." I raised my parasol to indicate another chair. Kalenischeff flinched; he was remembering,

no doubt, another occasion on which I had been forced
to jab the point into his anatomy in order to prevent a
rude encroachment upon my nether limbs. I went on,
"Let us hear what he has to say."

"I won't take much of your time." Kalenischeff decided not to sit down after all. He lowered his voice. "I
would like to come to an agreement with you. A bargain—"

"What?" Emerson shouted. "A bargain? I don't enter into agreements with murdering, thieving—"

"Hush, Emerson," I implored. The people at the adjoining tables had abandoned all pretense of good manners and were eavesdropping as hard as they could.
"Hear him out."

Kalenischeff's smile stayed glued in place, but drops
of perspiration stood out on his brow. "I know your
opinion of me," he hissed. "No bargain, then, only a
promise from me. I am about to leave Cairo—to leave
Egypt, in fact. Only give me a few days to wind up my
affairs—don't interfere with me—and I swear you will
never see or hear from me again."

"Where are you going?" I asked curiously.

"That need not concern you, Mrs. Emerson."

"You will have to travel to the ends of the earth to
escape the long arm of your former master," I said sig-
nificantly.

The man's lean face paled visibly. "Why do you
mention . . . What makes you suppose . . ."

"Come, come, Kalenischeff. It is only too obvious.
Something, or someone, has frightened you badly
enough to induce you to flee. Who else could it be but
that genius of crime, that diabolical Master Criminal?
We could not prove you were one of his gang, but we
knew it to be true. If you mean to betray that all-seeing,
all-knowing individual, you would do better to cast

yourself into the arms of the police—or even better, into our arms. I speak figuratively, of course.''

"You are mistaken," Kalenischeff muttered. "Quite mistaken. I would never . . . I have never been involved with . . .''

Emerson's brows drew together. He spoke in a soft growl that was—as Kalenischeff knew—more menacing than any shout. "It is you who are mistaken, you villain. Your protestations of innocence do not convince me in the slightest. Tell your master, when next you speak with him, to stay out of my way. The same goes for you. I want nothing to do with either of you, but if you interfere with me, I will squash you like a beetle. Have I made myself plain?''

This was not at all the approach I wanted to take. I said quickly, "Think what you are doing, Kalenischeff. Confide in us and let us save you. You take a dreadful risk just by talking with us. The spies of your dread master are everywhere; if one should see you—''

My approach was no more successful than Emerson's had been; Kalenischeff paled with horror. "You are right," he muttered. And without further ado or further speech, he went with stumbling steps toward the door of the hotel.

"Ha," said Emerson, in a satisfied voice. "Good work, Peabody. That got rid of the fellow.''

"Such was not my intention. Emerson, we cannot allow that rascal to make good his escape; we cannot permit him to delude the young lady who is obviously his latest victim!''

Emerson seized my arm as I started to rise and returned me to my chair with a force that drove the breath from my lungs. By the time I had freed myself, the carriage with the matched grays had drawn up before the steps, and the young lady had come onto the terrace.

Kalenischeff hastened to hand her into the carriage. The gapers were treated to a view of a dainty buttoned boot and a flash of ruffled petticoats as the lady mounted the steps. Kalenischeff swung himself into the driver's seat, snatched the whip from the groom, and cracked it. The horses were off as from a starting gate, at a full gallop. Pedestrians and peddlers scattered. One old fruit vendor was a little slow; his sideways stumble saved his old bones from injury, but his oranges and lemons went flying.

I shook my head at Ramses as he started up.

"But, Mama, I hoped I might be of assistance to the old gentleman. As you see, his oranges—"

"I do not question the purity of your intentions, Ramses. They do you credit; but they almost always end in disaster, not only for you but for the object of your good will."

"But, Mama, dat man dere—"

His gesture indicated one of the ragged bystanders, who had come to the aid of the vendor—a tall, well-built fellow in a ragged robe and a saffron turban. He had picked up three of the oranges and had sent them spinning into the air in a fairly creditable juggling act. At the moment I took notice of him he turned away; two of the oranges fell neatly at the feet of the lamenting vendor, and the other vanished, presumably into the folds of the juggler's filthy robe.

"You are lapsing again, Ramses," I said sternly. "How often have I told you I will not tolerate your mispronunciation?"

"Quite a number of times, Mama. I am chagrined to have erred in that direction; but as you may have observed, I am inclined to forget myself when under the effect of some strong emotion or when taken by surprise, as in—"

"Very well, very well. Be more careful in future."

The vendor had changed the tone of his lament upon recognizing Emerson, who was leaning over the rail. "It is Emerson Effendi," he cried. "O, Father of Curses, see what they have done to a poor old man! They have ruined me; my wives will starve, my children will be homeless, my aged mother—"

"Not to mention your extremely aged grandmother," said Emerson, in extremely colloquial Arabic. The adjectives he used carried an implication that caused the listeners to burst into howls of laughter.

Emerson grinned. He does enjoy having his witticisms appreciated. Dropping a handful of coins into the vendor's tray, he went on, "Buy a new *gibbeh* (robe) for your great-grandmother, that she may flourish in her profession."

More raucous male laughter followed this improper remark. Emerson resumed his seat. Catching my eye, and hastily straightening his countenance, he exclaimed, "I told you we should not have come here, Amelia. What sort of hotel is this, to allow a criminal like Kalenischeff on the premises? I have half a mind to leave at once. Baehler! Herr Baehler!"

It is said that a good hotelier has a sixth sense for impending trouble. It is also said by ill-natured persons that Baehler expects trouble from Emerson and is constantly on the watch for it. Be that as it may, the manager appeared as if from thin air and made his way to our table.

"You called me, Professor Emerson?" he murmured.

"What are you whispering for?" Emerson asked curiously.

"He is attempting, by example, to persuade you to moderate your voice," I said.

Baehler gave me a look of grateful acknowledgment,

Emerson an outraged stare. "What the devil are you implying, Peabody? I never raise my voice. I would like to know, Herr Baehler, what you mean by letting a rascally reprobate like that in your hotel. It is an outrage."

"You are referring to Prince Kalenischeff?"

"Prince? Ha!" Emerson exploded. "He has no right to the title, or to that of archaeologist. He is a thief and a villain, a member of the ring of antiquities thieves Mrs. Emerson and I unmasked last year—"

"Please, Professor." Baehler wrung his hands. "People are staring. You are overheard."

"Well, I mean to be overheard," Emerson declared. "That is the function of speech, Baehler, to be heard."

"All the same, Herr Baehler is right, Emerson," I said. "You and I know the man is guilty, but we could not find legal evidence. We cannot expect Herr Baehler to evict him on those grounds. What I would like to know is the identity of the unfortunate young woman he was escorting. She appears to be very young. What is her mother thinking of, to allow her to appear alone in public with such a man?"

Baehler hesitated. From his untroubled brow and pleasant half-smile one would have supposed he was unconcerned; but I knew that he yearned to confide in a sympathetic and understanding person. He began cautiously, "The lady is an orphan. Perhaps you have heard of her. She is a countrywoman of yours—a Miss Debenham. The Honorable Miss Debenham, to be precise. Her father was Baron Piccadilly, and she is his sole heiress."

"An heiress," I said meaningfully.

Emerson grunted. "That explains Kalenischeff's interest. No, Baehler, we are not acquainted with the young woman; we do not concern ourselves with the empty-headed upper classes. I don't want to hear anything more about this Miss Devonshire, or whatever her name may be. Mrs. Emerson does not want to hear about her either. Mrs. Emerson has no time for such people."

"Hush, Emerson. Mr. Baehler knows I never interfere in other people's affairs; but I feel an obligation in this case, knowing what I know of Kalenischeff's true character. The young lady should be warned. If I may be of any assistance . . ."

Baehler was only waiting for the opportunity to speak out. "I confess, Mrs. Emerson, that the situation is—er—uncomfortable. Miss Debenham arived in Cairo quite unaccompanied, even by a personal servant. She soon took up with the prince, and their behavior has become an open scandal. You are not the first to mention it to me. Reluctant as I am to offend a member of the British upper class, I may be forced to ask Miss Debenham to leave the hotel."

I also lowered my voice. "Do you mean that they— that they are . . ."

Baehler leaned forward. "I beg your pardon, Mrs. Emerson. I can't hear what you are saying."

"Perhaps that is just as well." I looked at Ramses, who stared back at me with the owl-eyed blankness that indicated an intense interest in the conversation. I had long since abandoned hope that Ramses was ignorant of matters no eight-year-old boy should concern himself with, but I tried to maintain an appearance, at least, of decorum.

"Emerson," I said, "take Ramses upstairs and wash him."

"He doesn't need washing," said Emerson.

"He always needs washing. You know we are dining at Mena House this evening, to see the full moon over the pyramids. I would like to get an early start."

"Oh, very well." Emerson rose. "Don't think I am unaware of what you are planning, Peabody. Watch yourself."

When the two of them had gone off, I turned back to Baehler. "Speak candidly, my friend. Does Kalenischeff share Miss Debenham's room? You cannot shock me."

I had shocked Herr Baehler. "Mrs. Emerson, how can you suppose I would allow such a thing in my hotel? The prince has his own room, some distance from Miss Debenham's suite."

I permitted myself a small ironic smile, which Baehler pretended not to see. "Be that as it may, I cannot watch unmoved the headlong rush of a fellow creature to destruction, particularly when the fellow creature is a member of my own oppressed sex. We women are constantly taken advantage of by men—I except my husband, of course—and we have a moral obligation to stand by one another. I will speak to Miss Debenham."

Mr. Baehler appeared to have had a change of heart. That is so typical of men; they are always asking for something and then deciding they don't want it after all. "I am not sure," he began.

"But I am." I smiled and poked him with my parasol. "Have no fear, Herr Baehler. I will approach the subject with the utmost delicacy. I will simply point out that Kalenischeff is a cad, a thief, and possibly a murderer. I fancy that will convince Miss Debenham."

Baehler's lips quivered. "You have your mind made up? Nothing I could say would dissuade you?"

"Nothing," I assured him.

Baehler went off, shaking his head, and I finished my tea. It did not take long, for Ramses had eaten all the sandwiches.

When I returned to our rooms, prepared to assist Em-

erson in his toilette, a process that is often unnecessarily
prolonged because of his extreme reluctance to assume
formal evening dress, I found to my annoyance that he
and Ramses were gone. So was the cat. How they had
eluded me I could not imagine; they must have crept
out the back entrance.

They did not return for over an hour. Emerson's coat
and collar had been unbuttoned and the cat Bastet,
perched on his shoulder, was nibbling disinterestedly at
the dangling ends of his cravat. Ramses' tumbled curls
were gray with dust; his boots left green footprints on
the floor.

"You have been in the bazaar of the dyers and ful-
lers," I exclaimed. "Why, in heaven's name?"

"Ramses had a fancy for a fez," Emerson explained,
stooping so that the cat could step down onto the bed.

"Where is it?"

Ramses gazed round the room as if he expected to
find the headgear in question had moved under its own
power and arrived before him. "It appears to have been
misplaced," he said finally.

I groped for words. "Wash," I said.

"Yes, Mama."

Followed by the cat, Ramses went into his room,
which adjoined ours. Sounds of splashing ensued, accompanied by the tuneless humming with which
Ramses enlivens his ablutions. Under cover of the sound
I addressed my husband.

"Well, Emerson?"

"Well, Peabody. We must make haste; I had not
meant to stay so long in the *sûk*, but you know how
these negotiations go, talking and drinking coffee and
exchanging compliments. . . ." He stripped off his coat
and tie and shirt as he spoke, flinging them in the gen-

eral direction of the bed. I picked up each article as it
fell to the floor and hung it on a hook.

"I do know, I had planned to spend the day tomorrow
doing just that."

"Now you won't have to." Emerson turned to the
washbasin. "I have taken care of everything. We can
leave for Dahshoor first thing in the morning."

"Tomorrow morning?"

Emerson splashed and sputtered and shook himself
like a large dog. "Ah, most refreshing. Won't it be
wonderful to be back in the desert, Peabody? Sand and
stars, peace and quiet, solitude, no confounded distractions . . ."

I was extremely vexed with him, but amusement tempered my annoyance. Emerson is as transparent as a
child. Also, the ripple of muscle across his back distracted me. I picked up the towel and assisted him to
dry himself.

"I see through your scheme, Emerson. You want to
get me away from Cairo. Very well. Naturally I share
your enthusiasm for sand and stars, solitude, and so on.
But there are a great many things I must attend to before—"

"Not at all, Peabody. Abdullah and our men have
been at Dahshoor all summer; we decided it was inad-
visable to leave the site unguarded, if you recall. I don't
doubt that by this time they have selected a proper
house and arranged it for us, removing to it the posses-
sions we left at Dronkeh last spring."

"Abdullah's idea of a proper house is not mine. I
will need—"

"Whatever you need can be procured after you ascertain what it is you need." The words were a trifle
slurred and the speech lacked Emerson's usual precision

of syntax. I saw that he was watching me in the mirror with an expression I knew well.

"Need I shave, Peabody?" he inquired.

"Of course you must, Emerson. Your beard is heavy, and—"

He turned and wrapped his arms round me, pressing me and the towel to his breast. His cheek brushed mine. "Need I shave, Peabody?" he repeated hoarsely.

"Emerson," I began, but I got no further for reasons which should be apparent to any reader of sensibility. Since my normal intelligence becomes somewhat muddled under the circumstances that then prevailed, I do not know how long it was before an uncomfortable prickling sensation at the back of my neck made itself felt. Freeing myself from Emerson's hold, I turned to see Ramses standing in the doorway. The cat was in his arms and both were staring unabashedly.

"Ramses," I exclaimed somewhat breathlessly. "Are you smiling?"

"My expression was one of affable approbation," Ramses protested. "It pleases me to see you and Papa engaging in demonstrations of that nature. I cannot as yet explain why that should be the case, but I suspect it may indicate some deep-seated need for—"

"Ramses!" Emerson had got his breath back. "Return to your room at once. And close the door."

Ramses promptly vanished, without so much as a "Yes, Papa." But the mood had been broken. With an embarrassed cough Emerson reached for his shaving mug. "We must do something about a bodyguard for Ramses," he said. "Or rather, I meant to say, a companion, an escort—"

"The first word was appropriate," I replied, attempting to smooth my ruffled hair. It was futile, for the strands clung to my fingers with a kind of physical electricity, induced, no doubt, by the dry heat. I sat down at the dressing table in order to construct my evening coiffure.

"I wanted to bring a manservant with us," I continued. "But you said no."

"We could hardly ask poor John to abandon his new bride," said Emerson, briskly whisking the soap into foam. "Once we reach Dahshoor, Selim can take up the duties he performed last season."

"Selim was perfectly useless, Emerson. I didn't say so, for I would not hurt the lad's feelings for the world, but he proved incapable of preventing Ramses from doing anything. Indeed, he became Ramses' accomplice in crime rather than his guard.

"What he really needs is a tutor," I went on. "His education has been extremely one-sided, to say the least. He can translate hieroglyphic Egyptian as easily as most children of his age can read English, but he has only the feeblest acquaintance with the sciences, and none whatever with the history of his great nation."

"He has a good working knowledge of zoology, Peabody. He is always picking up stray animals."

"Physics, astronomy—"

Emerson snorted so vigorously that foam flew all over the mirror. He wiped it off with his arm. "What difference does it make whether the earth goes round the sun or vice versa? It is an inconsequential piece of information."

"It seems to me, Emerson, that that sentiment has been expressed by someone else."

"No doubt. It is the sentiment of any reasoning individual. Never mind about Ramses' education, Peabody. He will do well enough."

He fell silent as he drew the shining blade of his razor across his cheek. Though unconvinced, I refrained from further comment for fear of causing a serious accident. When he had completed the delicate operation, I felt it safe to refer to another grievance. "So we are to leave in the morning?"

"If that is agreeable to you, my dear."

"It is not at all agreeable to me. There are several tasks I had meant to complete—"

Emerson whirled, brandishing the razor. "Such as interfering in the private affairs of that Miss Devonshire."

"Debenham, Emerson. The lady's name is Debenham. I had meant to speak a kindly word or two—the advice her mother would give her, were she still alive. I will simply have to find an opportunity tonight, that is all."

"Curse it," Emerson said.

"Do hurry, Emerson. Mena House will be crowded; the pyramids by moonlight are a popular excursion. No," I went on, winding my braided hair into a neat knot. "The tasks I referred to were those of shopping. I feel sure you did not get all the articles I need."

"Yes, I did. I even bought a load of those cursed medicines you are always inflicting on people. Ipecacuanha, rhubarb, calomel, blistering plaster—"

"You didn't get a set of communion vessels, I suppose?"

"Communion . . . Peabody, I didn't object when you set yourself up as a physician, but I will be forced to protest if you begin administering the sacraments. Not only does that offend my principles—for I consider such activities the grossest kind of superstition—but it is sure to get you in trouble with the authorities of the Church of England."

"I presume you jest, Emerson. You know perfectly well why I want the vessels. They are to replace the ones the Master Criminal stole from the church at Dron-

keh last year. The distress of the poor Sheikh El Beled
touched my heart; we cannot restore the originals, so I
thought I would get him another set. I don't suppose
you even looked for one."

"Antique Coptic religious objects are not easily
found, even in the bazaars of Cairo," Emerson retorted.
"It is all a ridiculous waste of time anyway. Why didn't
you just bring along a set of bathroom utensils from the
Penny Bazaar?"

I ignored this churlish remark, being accustomed to
Emerson's unorthodox religious views. However, when
he reached for his trousers I was moved to remonstrate.
"Not those trousers, Emerson. I have laid out your evening clothes. A tweed suit is—"

"The only attire appropriate for climbing the Great
Pyramid, Peabody. You wouldn't want me to spoil my
only set of evening clothes, would you?"

"Climb the pyramid? In the dark?"

"The moon is at the full, as you know. There will be
adequate light, I assure you, and the view from the top
of the Cheops Pyramid is an experience not to be
missed. I had planned it as a treat for you, my dear, but
if you prefer to deck yourself out in a regalia like the
one that young woman wore today . . . On my word, she
resembled nothing so much as a pouter pigeon, and I
fully expected her to flap up into the air."

Having recognized the logic of his argument, I prepared to assume one of my working costumes, a tasteful
ensemble of purple tweed trousers and a lavender-and-
white-checked jacket, with a matching parasol. I am seldom without a parasol. It is one of the most generally
useful objects an individual can possess, and I knew I
would be glad of its assistance in the capacity of a walking stick that evening, for the terrain surrounding the
pyramids is quite uneven. However, I felt obliged to

protest Emerson's assessment of Miss Debenham's gown.

"Like all men, Emerson, you have no sense of style. I admit the gown was a trifle extreme, but it was lovely. I must ask Miss Debenham—"

Emerson interrupted my speech by planting his lips firmly on mine, removing them to murmur, "You require no such artificial adornments, Peabody. You never look lovelier to me than in your working trousers and shirtwaist, with a strip of sunburn across your nose and your hair straggling out of its net. No, allow me to revise that. You are even lovelier when you are not wearing—"

I placed my hand over his mouth to prevent the completion of the sentence, for I felt again the tingling that preceded Ramses' advent. Sure enough, I heard the familiar voice: "May I come in now, Papa?"

"Yes, come in," I replied, stepping away from Emerson.

"I wished to ask, Mama, what I should wear," said Ramses.

"I had intended you should wear your black velvet suit."

Ramses' countenance, which seldom displayed emotion of any kind, darkened visibly. The wearing of the black velvet suit was one of the few things that stirred him to open rebellion. I could not imagine why the boy felt so strongly about it; with its pretty lace collar and ruffled shirt, it was a perfectly appropriate costume for a lad his age. (Though I must admit it did not suit Ramses' swarthy, aquiline face and black curls as it would have done had his coloring been more typically English.)

I was forced to give way on this occasion, since the havoc that would have been wreaked on black velvet by an ascent of the pyramid would ruin the suit. A thoughtful expression crossed Ramses' face when I expressed this opinion, but he did not, as I had half-expected, offer to wear the suit after all.

Two

Mena House, at the foot of the Giza plateau, had been open only a few years, but its exceptional location had made it one of the most popular hotels in the environs of Cairo. It had been designed to look like an old English manor house on the outside, but the Oriental style prevailed within. A web of soft lights, suspended from the high domed ceiling of the dining salon, created an aura of mystery and magic. Mr. and Mrs. Locke, the owners, had purchased a number of the beautiful antique mashrabiya screens, which added appreciably to the charm of the room.

We were the only guests not in full evening dress, and several people stared rudely as we were escorted to our table by Mr. Locke himself. "Good Gad, how people gape," Emerson remarked. "I don't know what has happened to good old-fashioned manners. One would

33

think there was something peculiar about our appearance.''

"You and Mrs. Emerson are well known," Mr. Locke said tactfully. "People always stare at celebrities."

"Ha," said Emerson. "No doubt you are right, Locke. But it is still bad manners."

I had hoped we might encounter some of our archaeological friends, but I saw no one we knew. Not until I was studying the menu in order to select a sweet for Ramses did I hear a diffident voice murmur my name. I looked up to see a familiar face smiling down at me. It was young Howard Carter; he was happy to accept my invitation to join us for coffee. After greeting Ramses and paying his respectful homage to Emerson, he explained that he had come to Cairo on business and had taken the opportunity to run out to Giza in order to enjoy the moonlight over the pyramids.

"Don't tell Professor Naville," he added, with his amiable grin. "I am supposed to be working."

"Are you still at Thebes with Naville?" I asked. "I thought the excavations at Hatasu's temple were finished."

"The excavations, yes. But we have a good deal of recording and restoring yet to do."

"I can well believe that," said Emerson. "By the time Naville finishes an excavation, it would require a psychic to make sense of the mess."

"You sound like my old mentor Petrie," said Carter with a smile.

From the chagrin on Emerson's face I could see he had forgotten the feud between Naville and Petrie. Emerson had been in a quandary as to which side to take (it would have been against his nature to remain neutral). He

shared Petrie's poor opinion of Naville's qualifications,
but he hated to agree with his chief rival. He subsided,
scowling, as the young Englishman rattled on cheerfully,
"Petrie is a splendid teacher, and I will always be grateful to him, but he is too hard on M. Naville. The latter's
methods are sometimes a trifle hasty—"

Emerson could contain himself no longer. "Hasty!"
he cried. "Is it true that he has used the old quarry as
his dump site? Well, he is a bloo—er—blooming idiot,
then, for there are undoubtedly tombs in the quarry
which he has buried under tons of dirt."

Mr. Carter thought it advisable to change the subject,
a decision with which I heartily concurred. "Congratulations on obtaining the firman for Dahshoor," he said.
"It was the talk of the archaeological community when
de Morgan gave it up to you. Petrie has speculated endlessly as to how you accomplished it; he tried several
times to get Dahshoor, but was not successful."

I carefully avoided looking at Ramses. Emerson
stroked his chin and smiled complacently. "All that was
required was the application of a little tact, my boy.
Petrie is an admirable fellow in some ways, but he lacks
tact. He is at Sakkara this year?"

"His assistant, Quibell, is there, copying tomb inscriptions," Carter said. He smiled at me. "There are
several young ladies on his staff this year. You will have
to share your laurels with others of your delightful sex,
Mrs. Emerson. The ladies are coming into their own at
last."

"Bravo," I cried heartily. "Or, to be more precise,
brava!"

"Quite so," said Carter. "Petrie himself has gone on
to Karnak, where the others will join him later. I saw
him before I left; and I am sure he would have sent his

regards had he known I would have the pleasure of en-
countering you."

This polite statement was so patently false, it failed
to convince even the speaker. He hurried on, "And Mr.
Cyrus Vandergelt—he is another of our neighbors. He
often speaks of you, Professor, and of Mrs. Emerson."

"I am sure he does." Emerson shot me a suspicious
glance. Mr. Vandergelt's roughhewn but sincere American gallantry toward members of the opposite sex (opposite to his, I mean) had always annoyed Emerson. He
suspects every man who pays me a compliment of
having romantic designs upon me. I cannot disabuse
him of this notion, which has, I admit, its engaging
qualities.

"Perhaps you ought to consider working for Mr.
Vandergelt, Howard," I suggested. "He is a generous
patron."

"He did approach me," Carter admitted. "But I
don't know that I would like to work for a wealthy
dilettante, however keen his interest in Egyptology.
These fellows only want to find treasure and lost
tombs."

Carter refused our invitation to join us in climbing
the pyramid, claiming he had work to do before retiring.
So we bade him good night, and, leaving the pleasant
gardens of Mena House behind, we started up the slope
toward the pyramids.

Words fail me when I attempt to describe the grandeur of the scene. The swollen orb of the full moon
hung in the sky, resembling the disks of beaten gold
that had crowned the queens of this antique land. Her
radiance flooded the landscape, silvering the mighty
pyramids and casting eerie shadows over the enigmatic
features of the Sphinx, so that he seemed to smile cyn-
ically at the insignificant human creatures crawling

around his base. The sand lay white as fallen snow, broken only by ebon shadows that betokened the presence of a vandalized tomb or sunken shrine.

Unfortunately this magnificent spectacle was marred by the presence of the vociferous insect Man. Flaring torches and crawling human bodies spotted the pale sides of the Great Pyramid, and the night echoed with the shouts of travelers who ought to have remained reverently silent in the presence of such wonders. The voice of one visitor blessed with a mighty set of vocal cords rang out above the rest: "Hey, Mabel, looka me!"

Mabel's response, if any, was lost in the night, but there came a peal of scornful laughter from near at hand. A carriage had drawn up—the same open carriage I had seen leave Shepheard's earlier. Miss Debenham had changed to an evening frock of white satin. Her bare arms and breast glowed like ivory in the moonlight, and as she turned to address her companion, diamonds flashed in the ebony darkness of her hair. Kalenischeff was a study in black and white. The ribbon of some (probably apocryphal) order, cutting across the front of his shirt, had been robbed of its color by the moonlight, and looked like a bar sinister.

Impulsively I started toward them, but before I had taken more than a few steps Kalenischeff whipped up the horses and the carriage continued along the dusty road toward the top of the plateau.

"Imbeciles," said Emerson. "I am sorry we came, Peabody. I might have known every ignorant tourist in Cairo would be here tonight. Shall we make the attempt, or return to the hotel?"

"We may as well go on now we are here," I replied. "Ramses, you are to stay with us. Don't stir so much as a step from my side."

The self-styled guides, antiquities peddlers and mis-

cellaneous beggars were out in full force. They came
pelting toward us with offers of assistance, and of du-
bious scarabs. The usual ratio of assistants is three to
each tourist—two pull from above and one pushes from
below. It is an awkward and quite unnecessary procedure, since few of the steplike blocks are as high as
three and a half feet.

The assault halted as soon as the sheikh in nominal
charge of the horde recognized Emerson, whom he
greeted with the *"Essalâmu 'aleikum"* generally re-
served by Moslems for others of their faith. Emerson
replied in kind, but refused Sheikh Abu's offer of men
to drag him up the pyramid. He was quite capable of
giving me a hand whenever necessary, but we did hire
two men to hoist Ramses from step to step, his short
legs making such an expedient advisable.

After a lazy summer doing little except riding, gar-
dening, hiking and bicycling, I was a trifle out of condition, and was glad of Emerson's strong hand from
time to time. Although it had appeared from below that
the slope was crowded with people, it was not really a
populous thoroughfare. We passed one or two other
groups, several of whom had paused to rest along the
way. From time to time I heard the voice of Ramses,
carrying on an interminable, if breathless, conversation
with his guides.

The pyramidion and the upper courses of the monument have been removed, leaving on the summit a flat
table some thirty feet square. Upon the blocks scattered
here and there, a number of the successful climbers
sprawled in various positions of collapse. Instinctively
avoiding them, we moved to one side.

I had climbed the pyramid before, but never at night.
The view, spectacular at any time, is simply magical
under the spell of moonlight. To the east, the Nile glim-

mered like a ribbon of dark crystal beyond the still
meadows, where the silhouettes of the palms stood
black against the sky. Far beyond sparkled and flickered
the myriad lights of Cairo. But it was southward that
our eyes turned, to see beyond the snowy stretch of
silent sand the remains of the ancient cemeteries of the
once mighty capital of Memphis. There lay our season's
destiny—two tiny points of pale stone, marking the pyramids of Dahshoor.

Such emotion filled me that I was incapable of
speech, a condition assisted by a distinct shortness of
breath—for Emerson's strong arm clasped me tightly.
We stood in silence, ensorcelled by the magic of the
night.

I lost all track of time as we gazed. It might have
been ten seconds or ten minutes before I let out my pent
breath in a long sigh, and turned to address Ramses.

He was gone.

My first reaction was to doubt the evidence of my
senses. Ramses excels in losing himself, but it hardly
seemed possible that he could have vanished off a small
platform four hundred and fifty feet in the air without
some sort of commotion. Emerson noted his absence at
the same time and was unable—or, what is more likely,
disinclined—to repress a bellow of alarm.

"Peabody! Where is Ramses?"

"He must be here somewhere," I began.

"I thought you were watching him. Oh, good Gad!"
He threw his head back and shouted at the top of his
lungs. "Ramses! Ramses, where are you?"

When pronounced in such peremptory tones, Ramses'
name never fails to attract attention, particularly in
Egypt, where it inevitably suggests the summoning, not

of a small disobedient English boy, but of the ghost of
the most famous of ancient Egyptian pharaohs. One of
the stouter ladies fell off the block on which she was
sitting, and several others sprang to their feet with cries
of alarm and outrage. Emerson began dashing around
the platform, looking behind blocks of stone and ladies'
skirts, to the increasing annoyance of the persons concerned.

One gentleman had the courtesy to approach me and
offer assistance. He was a portly, round-cheeked American with a bristling white mustache and hair of the
same shade, as the prompt removal of his hat disclosed.

"I can't quite make out what it is you're after,
ma'am," he said politely. "But if Caleb T. Clausheimer
can be of any assistance—"

"What I am after, sir, is a small boy."

"A small boy name of Ramses? Thunder and lightning, ma'am, but that's a curious name for a youngster!
Seems to me I did see a boy here a while back. . . ."

I thanked him abstractedly and hastened to Emerson,
who was peering over the edge of the platform. "He
has fallen off, Peabody. Curse it! Curse it! I will never
forgive myself. I should have tied him to me with a
rope as I usually do; I should have—"

"Emerson, calm yourself. He can't have fallen off. It
is not a straight drop; we would have heard him bounce
from step to step, and surely even Ramses would have
emitted a cry on finding himself falling. No, he has
started down by himself, heaven only knows why. I
strictly forbade him to leave us—"

Emerson rushed to the north side of the platform and
looked down that face of the pyramid. It was deep in
shadow, but Emerson's eyes, keen as an eagle's, were
further strengthened by the desperation of paternal affection. He let out a hoarse shriek. "There, Peabody—

there, do you see? Two thirds of the way down, on the left. Are those not Ramses' guides? And does not one of them appear strangely hump-backed?''

I could only make out the glimmer of the white robes the Egyptians wore. They resembled a patch of moonlight that was gliding down the weathered stones. There was certainly a group of people there—how many, I could not make out—and they were the only climbers on that side of the pyramid, since for obvious reasons the others preferred the lighted sides.

''I can't tell who they are, Emerson, nor can I determine—''

But I addressed empty air. Emerson had flung himself over the edge and was bounding down the giant staircase like a man possessed. I immediately hastened to follow him, though at a more discreet pace.

By the time I reached the bottom and found myself ankle-deep in sand, Emerson was nowhere to be seen. I consoled myself by the fact that his body was nowhere to be seen either, so I could assume he had reached the bottom unharmed.

It may seem to the reader that I was more concerned for my spouse than for my son and heir. This was indeed the case. I had long since given up worrying about Ramses, not because of lack of affection (my feelings for the boy were those of any mother of an eight-year-old son), but because I had worn out my stock of worry on that subject. By the time he was five, Ramses had been in more scrapes than most people encounter over a long lifetime, and I had expended more nervous energy over him than most mothers expend on a family of twelve. I had no more to give. Furthermore—though I would be ashamed to confess such irrational thoughts except in the pages of my private journal—I had developed an almost superstitious confidence in Ramses' ability not only to survive disasters of truly horrendous proportions, but to emerge from them undamaged and undaunted.

Not knowing what direction Emerson had taken, I set off toward the northeast corner of the pyramid. There was no one about; tourists and guides alike preferred the lighted areas. I had almost reached the corner when a cry, faint but pervasive, echoed through the night: "Ra-a-a-mses!"

"Curse it," I thought. "He has gone the other way." Instead of turning, I continued on the same path, for we would inevitably meet in the course of time, and in the process we would have circled (if such a word can be used of a structure whose base forms a perfect square) the pyramid.

The Giza pyramids are only the most conspicuous of the ancient tombs that honeycomb the surface of the plateau. The sand around me was dimpled and scarred by traces of the underlying structures. It was necessary to pick one's way carefully for fear of tumbling into an open tomb chamber or tripping over a fallen block of stone, so my progress was somewhat deliberate. As I was running over in my mind the things I would say to Ramses when I found him—and I had no doubt I would eventually—I heard the sounds of an altercation. At first I could not make out whence came the thumps and grunts and muffled cries, for such noises carry quite a distance in the clear desert air. Not until I looked back did I see a telltale flutter of draperies. The wearers seemed to be in rapid retreat, and they soon disappeared behind one of the small subsidiary pyramids—appurtenances of the Great Pyramid near which they are situated.

I set out in pursuit, my parasol at the ready, though I feared I had slight chance of catching up with the guides, if indeed that was who they were. Nor was it at all certain that Ramses was with them. However, the most logical theory was that, for reasons known only unto himself, he had persuaded the men to take him back down the pyramid in pursuit of heaven only knew what objective. Ramses always had reasons for his actions, but they were seldom readily perceptible to rational persons.

My progress was impeded by frequent falls, for I was still in the shadow and could not make out the outlines of objects scattered about. Picking myself up after one such tumble, I beheld a sight both alarming and astonishing, and yet one that was not without a degree of reassurance. The white-robed form some little distance ahead looked spectral in that eerie ambiance, but I knew it must be one of the guides. In its arms, held close to its breast, was a small, darker form. The limbs of this latter being were in agitated motion and my ears made out the unmistakable tones of Ramses, demanding, with his usual prolixity of speech, to be put down.

With the instantaneous mental agility on which I pride myself, I revised my earlier theory of the reason for Ramses' failure to obey my orders. It now seemed clear that he was being held against his will. Perhaps that condition had prevailed from the first—though how the guides had whisked him away without causing some comment from Ramses or from the tourists, I could not imagine. However, that was a matter best left for later investigation. Ramses' liberation was the first thing to be attended to, and I proceeded to attend to it, raising myself to my feet and rushing forward at considerable speed.

The man who held Ramses was, as I assumed, struck motionless with terror at the sight of me. He made no attempt to flee. I brought my parasol down on his head as hard as I could.

The kidnapper gave an anguished cry and clapped both hands to his head, dropping Ramses, who fell face-down in the sand. Realizing that the folds of the turban had lessened the effect of the blow I intended, I quickly shifted my grasp on the handle of the parasol and rammed the steel tip into the fellow's midsection. He toppled over onto his back. I was stepping briskly forward to administer the coup de grace when two small hands wrapped round my ankle and sent me staggering. Only the deft reversal of the parasol and its forward thrust against a rock outcropping kept me on my feet.

I turned on Ramses with a reproachful cry. "Curse you, Ramses, what are you doing? This wretch abducted you—at least I hope for your sake he did, for if you went with him of your own free will—"

"I was attempting to prevent you from an action you would most assuredly regret, Mama," said Ramses. He paused to spit out a mouthful of sand before continuing, "Dis man—"

"Watch your diphthongs, Ramses." His adversary appeared to have been rendered unconscious, for he lay quite still. I kept a watchful eye on him, parasol raised, while Ramses went on with his explanation.

"Yes, Mama. This man was not my abductor but my rescuer. It was he who saved me from the persons who carried me off from the top of, and down the side of, the pyramid, with, I might add, some risk to himself, for both my assailants were armed, one with the long knife that is locally known as a *sikkineh*, and the other—"

"Never mind all that. Hmmm. Are you certain that . . . But I suppose you could hardly be mistaken. Why were you struggling then? I would not have been so precipitate had I not feared for your safety, since it certainly appeared you were attempting to free yourself from a captor's grasp.''

"I wanted him to put me down," said Ramses.

"I see. Well, that makes sense.'' I stopped to look more closely at the recumbent man. I could make little of his features in the dark, but my nostrils caught traces of an odd smell, sweet and cloying. I stepped back in instinctive disgust. "Opium! The man is a drug addict!''

"One might reasonably draw that conclusion," said Ramses judiciously. "Is he dead?''

"Certainly not.''

"I am glad of that," Ramses remarked. "It would be a poor return for his services to me; and his personal habits are not a matter of concern to us, particularly in view of—''

"Do hush for a moment, Ramses. I hear your father approaching. He certainly sets a rapid pace! Call out to him, if you please, or he will go on circumnavigating the pyramid indefinitely.''

Ramses obeyed. The far-off wails of Emerson, repeating Ramses' name in mournful accents, took on new poignancy. Ramses called again. The two of them exchanged outcries until Emerson burst upon the scene and flung himself at his son. I heard the breath go out of Ramses' lungs in an explosive whoosh as his father seized him, and knowing that Emerson would be incapable of reasoned speech for several moments, I turned my attention back to Ramses' presumed rescuer.

The sickening smell of opium again assailed my nostrils as I bent over him, but I conquered my repugnance and reached down to remove his turban that I might better ascertain the extent of the damage I had done the fellow's head. As my hand went out, the man started convulsively, flinging his arms over his face.

"Mâtekhâfsh, habîb," I said reassuringly. "Do not be afraid. It was in error that I struck; the child has told me of your courage."

At first there was no reply. Then from under the ragged folds of cloth came a muffled voice. "Let me go, sitt. I did nothing. I want nothing, only to be left alone."

"Wallahi-el âzîm, by God the great, I mean you no harm. Indeed, I wish to reward you. Come out into the moonlight that I may see if you are injured." The man did not move and I went on impatiently, "Come, you are safe with us. This is the great, the famous Emerson Effendi, Father of Curses, and I am his wife, sometimes called the Sitt Hakim."

"I know you, sitt," came the reply.

"Then what are you cowering there for? If you know my name, you know its meaning; I am somewhat skilled in the art of medicine—"

As I might have expected, this statement caught the ear of Emerson, who seldom misses an opportunity of jeering at my medical qualifications. However, on this occasion he refrained from his customary caustic comment; Ramses had evidently explained the situation, and gratitude prevailed over irony. Seizing the fallen man by the arm, he hauled him vigorously to his feet and began wringing his hand. "A father's blessing be upon you," he began in sonorous Arabic, but before he had got any further, the savior distracted him by dropping to his knees, his head bowed.

"You need not kneel, my good fellow," Emerson said graciously.

"I believe, Papa, he is not paying his respects but fainting," said Ramses coolly. "As I informed you, one of the men had a knife, the type that is known as—"

"Bless me," said Emerson in mild surprise. "I believe you are right, Ramses. Yes, this sticky substance on his fingers seems to be blood.''

"So long as you have hold of him, Emerson, you may as well drag him out into the moonlight," I suggested. ''Though a less painful hold, one that does not put such a strain on his presumed wound—''

"Hmmm, yes, quite right, my dear," said Emerson. He transferred his grip to the man's shoulders and with a heave of his mighty arms pulled him across the sand until the bright rays of the moon illumined his body.

A crowd of curiosity seekers had collected. The non-Arabs among them soon turned away in disgust upon seeing that the object of attention was only a ragged beggar. The Egyptians recognized Emerson and promptly squatted in a circle, waiting to see what would transpire, for, as one of them remarked to a friend, "The Father of Curses is a great magician. Perhaps he will bring this dead man to life."

Some of the onlookers carried torches and lanterns. Among them was Sheikh Abu, who hastened to Emerson with ejaculations of relief and congratulation. "Your son has been restored. Praise Allah!"

"Yes, quite," Emerson replied. "No thanks to the guides you assigned to us. See here, Abu—"

"First things first, Emerson," I interrupted. "Abu, please bring the lantern closer. And lend me your knife."

In the warm yellow glow of the lantern the inky stains on the man's sleeve sprang to ominous life. I seized Abu's knife and prepared to cut the cloth away. The crowd, which resembled nothing so much as an assortment of laundry bags fallen haphazardly from the back of a cart, squirmed closer, and the same commentator remarked, "It is the Sitt Hakim. No doubt she will cut off the man's arm," to which his companion replied eagerly, "Lean back so that I may see better."

The knife wound was on the outside of the man's arm, from just above the wrist almost to the elbow. Fortunately it had not touched any of the major muscles or blood vessels, but it was still oozing the roseate ichor of life, so I bound it up as best I could. My patient lay quiet, his eyes closed, but I suspected he had regained consciousness, and this suspicion was confirmed when, upon my again attempting to remove his turban, my hand was pushed away.

I repeated my reassurance, adding, "I must see your head, friend, to determine whether you suffer from . . . Curse it," I added in English, "what is the Arabic for concussion?"

"If such a word exists, I am not acquainted with it," said Ramses, squatting beside me with the same boneless ease Egyptians demonstrate in assuming that awkward position. "But you need not tax your knowledge of Arabic, Mama. The gentleman is English."

"Courtesy is a quality I always commend, Ramses," I said. "But the word 'gentleman,' when applied to this no doubt honest but somewhat disreputable . . . What did you say? English?"

"Unquestionably," said Ramses. "I thought as much yesterday, when I saw him juggling the oranges the fruit vendor had let fall. There are certain idiosyncratic structures of face and body found only in the members of the Celtic subrace, and the stubble of beard on his face, though darkened by prolonged abstinence from the means of ablution, had a reddish tinge. Should there be any doubt in your mind, Mama, as to the extent of my anatomic expertise or the accuracy of my observations, let me add that I distinctly heard issue from his lips, when one of his assailants attacked, the word 'Damn.' "

The word was repeated, just as distinctly, by the same

lips. The closed eyes snapped open. The irises were a bright, fiery blue—not the deep sapphire of Emerson's eyes, but the identical shade of the turquoise used so often in ancient Egyptian jewelry.

I sat back on my heels. "Nonsense," I said. "You will find high cheekbones and blue eyes among the Berber tribesmen to the north. A splendid race of men, true sons of the desert; it is a pity to find one of them in such a state of degradation—"

"But it would be an even greater pity, would it not, to find a member of the superior British race in that condition?" The words, couched in the purest English, came from the fallen man. His lips writhed in a sardonic smile, and he went on, "I regret to disappoint you, madam. I thank you for your attentions. And I beg you will allow me to return to my gutter in peace."

He attempted to rise, but sank back, swooning. I took advantage of his helpless state to pluck the filthy turban and the underlying brown felt *libdeh* (cap) from his head. No wonder he had resisted my attempts to remove them! I had known Berbers with blue or gray eyes, but never one with hair of that peculiar red-gold that is the hallmark of the northern peoples. Strands of silver intertwined with the gold. Yet as I examined the sun-browned countenance, further darkened (as Ramses had said) by a layer of grime, I realized it was that of a young man. What terrible tragedy had rendered him prematurely gray? Or was it the result of dissipation and drugs?

My cogitations were rudely interrupted by Emerson, who had concluded his discussion with Abu and appeared in excellent spirits. This is often the case with Emerson after he has scolded someone.

"So Ramses' hero is an Englishman? A Scot, rather, I think. He would not thank you for the error, Ramses."

He bent over the young man. "You had better return with us to the hotel, my friend."

The gentleman—for such he must be, from his educated accent—glared malevolently and impartially upon us all. "If you wish to repay me for any fancied service, you can do so by leaving me at liberty to do as I like."

"I am in complete sympathy with your desire for privacy and independence," Emerson said. "I do not wish to reward you; I wish to offer you a position."

"What?" Astonishment smoothed the scowl from the young man's brow and gave his countenance an ingenuous look that made me yearn to assist him. What he needed was a woman's firm and compassionate care, and I was about to say so when Emerson nudged me with such force that I was caught off balance—squatting being a position I never assume with ease—and toppled gently onto my side. While I was endeavoring to reassume an upright position, Emerson continued.

"I have been searching for a muscular and dependable person to take charge of my son. My name is Emerson, and this lady—"

"I know who you are, sir."

"Then you may also know that Mrs. Emerson is my professional associate as well as my wife. (Do get up, Amelia, you look very unprofessional squirming on the ground like an overturned beetle.) She has not the time to give Ramses the attention he requires—"

"I would say that Master Ramses requires a good deal of attention, if the events of this evening are typical." A faint smile accompanied this comment.

"This evening's events are not..." Emerson stopped. "Er—be that as it may, we are leaving tomorrow morning for Dahshoor, in order to begin our excavations. You would do us a favor if you would consent to take the position, for which you have already proved yourself so admirably qualified.''

I fancy the young man's surprise at this offer was scarcely less than my own. His response was a sardonic laugh. ''You are out of your head, Professor. Would you entrust your son to a renegade, a beggar, a smoker of opium, a hashish-eater?''

''As to that,'' I began, but did not finish the sentence because I saw Emerson's elbow jut out, and my balance was still precarious.

''So long as you refrain from indulging in drugs while on duty, your habits are not my concern,'' said Emerson.

''Well . . . Why not? It would be a new experience, at any rate.''

''Then let us return to the hotel,'' I said, rising.

''I will not go with you,'' said the young man firmly.

''In heaven's name, why not?''

''Because . . . I choose not to,'' was the sullen reply.

''You may choose to go to Shepheard's or to the devil,'' snapped Emerson, whose patience was at an end. ''Do I understand that you have refused my offer, Mr.—''

''Call me Nemo.''

Emerson raised his eyebrows. Before he could comment, the young man continued; ''I do not refuse. But I have certain personal matters to attend to before I leave Cairo. I will be at the hotel tomorrow—at what hour?''

''Seven A.M.''

''Seven,'' Nemo repeated. ''Until then, Professor.''

Disdaining my offer of a supporting hand, he rose and walked away without a backward glance.

We returned to our waiting carriage. Several other equipages were also waiting; the one Kalenischeff had driven was not among them. When our vehicle was underway, Emerson said, "Well, Peabody?"

"Well, Emerson?"

"I am awaiting your remarks concerning our new servant. I am surprised you have not expressed your opinion before this."

"Why, really, Emerson, I consider this an excellent idea. I would have suggested it myself had you not anticipated me."

"Oh, indeed," said Emerson.

"We have an obligation," I continued, "to assist unfortunate fellow creatures, particularly those of our own nation. I don't doubt that the young man has met some crushing disappointment—in love, most probably—which has reduced him to his present plight. I hope you will not think me boastful if I assert that my advice and experience have often proved beneficial in such cases."

"Bah," said Emerson. "My motives are less altruistic, Amelia; I simply want someone to watch over Ramses while we are—while we are otherwise occupied. I know full well the futility of asking you not to attempt to reform the young man's habits, but I beg you will not irritate him to such an extent that he quits our service. That is all I have to say on the subject, and there is no need for you to comment. Well, Ramses, you are unusually silent; what do you think?"

Ramses cleared his throat. "Thank you, Papa. I was waiting for someone to ask my opinion, for after all I am the one most immediately concerned. Aside from the fact that I do not feel myself in need of a nursemaid of either sex—"

"You were certainly in need of someone or something tonight," I said critically. "How could you be so careless as to allow yourself to be abducted practically under our noses?"

Ramses opened his mouth to reply; Emerson, who knew his son's tendency toward unnecessary loquacity as well as I did, replied for him. "From what I have been able to ascertain, from Ramses himself and from Abu, the thing was rather neatly done. It was not the guides originally assigned to Ramses who carried him off. Abu questioned these fellows after I reported that Ramses was missing, and they told him they had been dismissed by an American gentleman who said he was a member of our party. An extravagant amount of baksheesh removed any doubts they may have had, nor would they be inclined to question the command of an effendi."

"But that is an astonishing development, Emerson," I exclaimed. "I had assumed this was a simple, vulgar attempt at extracting money, or possibly a trick of Kalenischeff's, to render us impotent while he carries out the nefarious scheme in which he is presently engaged—whatever that may be."

"Neither is likely, Peabody. Kalenischeff knows better than to interfere with *me*."

His white teeth closed on the last word as if he were biting into Kalenischeff's jugular, and I was forced to admit that his reasoning was convincing.

"Then who could it have been? Who would have designs on Ramses, or on . . . Good Gad, Emerson!"

Emerson raised his hand. "Please, Peabody. Don't say it."

"Who else could it have been?" I cried. "Who else but that genius of crime, the Master Criminal?"

I see no sense in repeating the conversation that ensued. Emerson's remarks were incoherent in the extreme, and he never allowed me to complete a sentence. I presume

Ramses attempted to interject his opinions, since he usually did, but he made no headway. Emerson was still fuming when the carriage drew up before the hotel, and I abandoned the discussion, since it would have been vulgar to go on shouting at one another as we passed through the lobby.

The safragi on duty in the corridor outside our rooms informed us that a number of parcels had been delivered during our absence. Emerson nodded and flipped the fellow a coin. "It will be the merchandise I ordered this afternoon," he said. "At least one thing has gone right today."

The parcels were stacked in a corner. Atop the pile sat the cat Bastet, straight and alert, as if on guard. In fact, she was useful to us in that capacity, since the hotel servants were decidedly in awe of her. Her resemblance to the hunting cats depicted in ancient tomb paintings and her doglike devotion to her young master had convinced the superstitious fellows that she was not an ordinary feline.

She and Ramses greeted one another affectionately, but when he offered her the scraps of chicken he had brought, she refused the treat, politely but decidedly.

"Curious," said Ramses. "Very curious."

I was forced to agree. Ordinarily the cat Bastet was passionately fond of chicken. "Could there be something wrong with the food?" I asked uneasily. "Poisoned, or drugged?"

"If there had been anything wrong with it, we would all be writhing in agony or comatose by now," snarled Emerson. "I have had enough melodrama tonight; I can endure no more. Ramses, go to bed. Amelia—"

"Yes, Ramses should retire at once, since we must make an early departure. In view of what happened this evening, Ramses, you had better leave your door open."

Emerson turned a reproachful look on me. "My dear Peabody," he began.

"I see no help for it, Emerson."

"Bah," said Emerson. "Yes, very well. You should sleep soundly tonight, Ramses, after your adventures. Very soundly. If you should waken and hear—er—hear anything at all, pay no attention."

"Anything, Papa?"

"Anything, my boy. Er—Papa will attend to it, whatever it is."

"Yes, Papa. But if I were to hear you or Mama cry out for help—"

This innocent question made Emerson blush like a schoolboy. I was amused but not inclined to intervene; as the Scripture so eloquently puts it, he had dug a pit into the midst whereof he had fallen; and it was up to him to climb out of it.

"Papa will explain," I said. "I must just step out for a moment. There is a matter I must attend to."

The flush on Emerson's bronzed cheeks turned from the scarlet of embarrassment to the crimson of rising suspicion. "What matter?" he demanded.

"I will be back shortly."

"Peabody, I absolutely forbid . . ." My expression warned Emerson of the error of this approach. "I *request* that you refrain from interfering in matters that are none of your concern. The hour is late. You cannot wake people up in the middle of the night to lecture them about their personal affairs."

"I had intended to speak to Miss Debenham on the morrow, Emerson. It was your decision to leave Cairo at once—made, I might add, without the courtesy of consulting me—that forced this expedient upon me."

I slipped out before he could reply.

The safragi outside Miss Debenham's suite informed

me that she had not yet returned, so I went downstairs to search for her in the lobby and on the terrace. It was not so late as I had supposed; our evening had been so fraught with interesting incidents that it seemed to have lasted longer than was actually the case. The terrace was crowded with guests sipping refreshments and watching the jugglers and snake charmers performing on the street, but Miss Debenham was not among them. I thought I saw a flutter of saffron cloth among the entertainers, but when I looked over the rail, there was no sign of the renegade Englishman. I concluded that my eyes had deceived me. Saffron turbans, though uncommon, were not unique to that individual.

It was with a sense of deep frustration that I finally decided to abandon my quest for the time being. There was no way of knowing when the pair would return, or if indeed they would return that night. Kalenischeff had once told me in the course of that rude encounter I mentioned earlier, that he had a pied-à-terre in Cairo. He might have taken the girl there.

This thought made me all the more determined to warn Miss Debenham of the moral and spiritual dangers that threatened her. I was equally determined to have a quiet talk with Kalenischeff. I felt certain that the proper mixture of persuasion and intimidation would convince him to confide in me, and the events of the evening made it imperative that I learn all I could about the mysterious individual who was Kalenischeff's employer. I had left Egypt the previous year with the firm determination of bringing this miscreant to justice. His attempt to abduct Ramses proved beyond a doubt that he was equally determined to revenge himself on me and my family. It was no longer only a question of justice; it was a question of self-defense. Why Emerson failed to see this I could not imagine.

I proceeded to the writing room, where I inscribed two letters. The first, to Kalenischeff, was brief. I merely requested the pleasure of an interview at the earliest possible moment, adding that it would be useless for him to deny my request since I was determined to see him. The letter to Miss Debenham took longer, since I had to identify myself and list my qualifications for presuming to address her. I added a brief account of Kalenischeff's unsavory history, assured Miss Debenham of my (and Emerson's) willingness to assist her, and ended with a powerful and moving appeal to reconsider her actions and halt her downward progress on the path that could only lead to shame and sorrow.

After leaving the letters with the safragis, I sought my own room with a satisfying sense of duty done. I had accomplished all I could; I could accomplish no more. Not at the moment, at any rate.

Emerson had left a night light burning. It had become a habit of ours, since we were so frequently disturbed by burglars and assassins. He was in bed. The artificial evenness of his breathing indicated that he was awake, though pretending not to be. He did not move or speak even when I joined him in the connubial bed, so I concluded I was in disfavor. Just as well, I thought. Ramses would be on the alert for the slightest sound from our room.

If Miss Debenham did return to the hotel and read my letter, she would undoubtedly attempt to speak to me in the morning. I had informed her of the hour of our departure. The opportunity of reasoning with her was not lost, only postponed, and as sleep brushed me with her shadowy wings I promised myself the satisfaction of a useful interview the following morning.

Alas, it was not to be. We were awakened at dawn by the shrieks of the hotel servants. The safragi had discovered the body of Kalenischeff lying on Miss Debenham's bed in a welter of bloody sheets. He had been stabbed to the heart; Miss Debenham had vanished from the room, and from the hotel.

Three

The sun was approaching the zenith before we boarded the train that was to take us to Dahshoor. Emerson was muttering like a volcano in danger of eruption, but, as I had been careful to point out, he could hardly blame me for the tardiness of our departure. All the guests had been delayed by the uproar, and we were among many whom the police had interviewed.

"You need not have volunteered to be interviewed," Emerson insisted. "To question the guests was a waste of time, since the murderer undoubtedly left the hotel long before the body was discovered."

"If you mean Miss Debenham, Emerson, she did not commit the crime. I felt it my duty to explain that to the police officer in charge."

"She has disappeared, Peabody. If she is innocent, why did she flee?"

"Emerson, how can you be so dense? She did not

flee, she was abducted by the same person or persons who murdered Kalenischeff.''

Emerson settled himself more comfortably on the cracked leather seat of the carriage. The pyramids were visible on the right, but for once Emerson was not distracted by archaeological objects. He pretends to resent the interruptions of a criminal nature that have so often marked our excavations, but wifely intuition assures me that he is as keen on the scent as any sleuth. This was the first opportunity we had had to discuss the murder; I could tell by the gleam in his bright blue eyes that he was as interested as I.

"If your theory is correct, Peabody, it means that Kalenischeff was slain in an attempt to defend his in-amorata. The heroic role is not one I would have expected from him.''

"It is a difficulty," I admitted. "Whatever else he may have been, Kalenischeff was no hero.''

"But he may have been a member of a conspiracy directed against the lady," said Ramses, from his window seat next to Emerson. "Assuming for the sake of argument that the object of that conspiracy was the extraction of money by one means or another, Kalenischeff may have decided to betray his confederates by marrying the lady instead of assisting in the original scheme. He would gain sole control of her fortune by that means instead of—''

"I was about to propose that theory, Ramses," I said severely. "Look out the window. There is the Step Pyramid of Sakkara.''

"I am doing so," said Ramses. "The cat Bastet also appears to appreciate the aesthetic qualities of the view, but I assure you it does not interfere in the slightest with my ability to join you in—''

"Miss Debenham must have been taken by force," I

insisted. "No properly brought-up Englishwoman would run away—"

"Her conduct makes it fairly evident that she was *not* properly brought up," said Emerson.

I ignored this remark. "She would have remained, chin up and shoulders squared, to face the music. And I feel I am safe in asserting, Emerson, that she would have come to me. She had received my letter; it was found, open, on her dressing table."

"That is a point against the lady," Emerson said stubbornly. "It proves that she did return to her room last night. It places her at the scene of the crime, Peabody, a scene from which she has disappeared. According to the police, she also changed her clothing."

"But they don't know which garments are missing from her wardrobe. She may have been carried off in her night-clothes, Emerson. The horror of it!"

"Along the corridors of the hotel, down the stairs and out into the street?" Emerson laughed disagreeably. "No, Amelia; not even your favorite Master—"

He stopped himself, pressing his lips together and scowling at me.

"Now it comes out," I exclaimed. "I did not want to accuse you unjustly, Emerson, but you force me to be blunt. You are determined to blame poor Miss Debenham for a crime she did not commit because of your unaccountable reluctance to face the truth. How you can be so stubborn, after your own encounters with the man—"

"I warn you, Peabody," Emerson snarled.

"Who attacked us and harassed us at Mazghunah last year? Who organized the inefficient amateur tomb robbers of Egypt into a great professional conspiracy? Who is a master of disguise, as was proved by his appearance in the role of Father Girgis, priest of the church at Maz-ghunah? Who, Emerson?''

Emerson, breathing furiously through his nose, did not reply. ''The Master Criminal,'' piped Ramses.

Emerson turned an awful glare upon his son. Unper-turbed, Ramses went on, ''I share your dislike of that sensational and ambiguous appellation, Papa, but I am forced to agree with Mama that no more appropriate name comes readily to mind. We have good reason to suspect that Prince Kalenischeff had fallen out with his master; his decision to leave Egypt, suddenly and se-cretly, suggests as much. And I am inclined to agree with Mama's belief that this mysterious personage was the one behind the attempt on me last night. The crim-inal mind is a fascinating study; it may well be that the person in question harbors some resentment toward me because I—with your assistance, of course—foiled his attempt to steal the Dahshoor treasure.''

Emerson acknowledged the reasonableness of this as-sessment with a muffled ''Curse it.'' He said no more, because I spoke first.

''Ramses is correct, Emerson. The guides who were with him said they were dismissed by an American gen-tleman. There were a number of tourists atop the pyr-amid last night. In fact—in fact, I may have spoken to the man! Who else could he have been but a confederate of the Master Criminal?''

''Why not the Master Criminal himself?'' Emerson tried to speak sarcastically, but he was half convinced by my irrefutable logic, and his doubt showed in his voice.

''Because the Master Criminal was lying in wait at the foot of the pyramid! And I know who he is. We thought he might be an Englishman—''

''Oh, come, Amelia, that is really going too far, even

for you," Emerson shouted. "Not Ramses' rescuer? Why would he arrange for the boy to be kidnapped, and then save him?"

"Don't forget that it was my intervention that saved Ramses. My first impression, that the man was carrying him off, was undoubtedly correct. Once captured by me, he talked his way out of the situation with the ingenuity one might expect from such a clever man. And the proof, Emerson—the proof is that he never turned up this morning, as he promised he would."

Nemo's failure to keep his appointment was an additional cause of Emerson's ill humor. He is accustomed to having people do as he tells them.

"He was alarmed by the presence of the police, I expect. A man of his antecedents—"

"My dear Emerson," I said in a kindly manner, "such wild rationalization is unworthy of you. Every fact leads to the same conclusion—my conclusion."

Emerson did not reply. It was Ramses who cleared his throat and remarked, "If you will excuse my mentioning it, Mama, that is not strictly accurate. Several facts contradict your assumption, and one, I fear, is insuperable."

Emerson looked hopefully at his son. "And what is that, my boy? Something you observed while you were alone with the young man?"

"No, Papa, you and Mama observed it too. I do not refer to Mr. Nemo's struggle with the men who carried me off, which might conceivably have been staged—though I must say it was done with a degree of verisimilitude few actors could have achieved—for I can think of several reasons why the Master Criminal might have arranged such a misleading performance, in order to—"

"Ramses," I said.

"Yes, Mama. The fact that demolishes your otherwise intriguing theory is that my rescuer's physical attributes were not those of the man we knew as Father Girgis."

"He is a master of disguise, Ramses," I said. "The black beard and wig he wore were false—"

"But the black eyes were not," said Ramses. "We had ample opportunity to observe their color, did we not? The eyes of the Englishman—or, as Papa observed, the Scot—are blue."

It was a cruel blow. I tried to rally. "The scientific achievements of master criminals often exceed those of scholars. A method of changing the color of the eyes—"

"Exists, I fear, only in fiction," said Ramses. "I have made some study of the matter, Mama, and I know of no method of dying one's irises."

Emerson began to laugh. "A hit, Peabody—a palpable hit! Talk your way out of that one."

I did not deign to reply. Though admitting I may have been in error on one small point, I could not see that Ramses' statement had affected the essential issue. The poor young English lady was innocent; and if the renegade Englishman was not the Master Criminal himself he was surely one of the latter's lieutenants. I felt certain he had been involved in the abduction of Ramses, and that we would never see him again.

There is no railroad station at Dahshoor, which is almost equidistant between Medrashein and Mazghunah. Rather than have our extensive baggage transported by donkeyback from either of those locations, Emerson had requested that the train stop briefly at the point nearest the site. I daresay that this favor would not have been accorded anyone else; but Emerson's reputation is so well known and his powers of persuasion, particularly of a vocal variety, are so emphatic, that the engineer of the train did as he was asked, and the complaints of the other passengers were ignored by the porters.

A party of our loyal men awaited us. They had been there for five hours, since we had been unable to notify them that we had missed the early train. They were not put out by, or worried about, the delay; when we first caught sight of them they were sprawled in a patch of shade, smoking and *fahddling* (gossiping). The Egyptian temperament accepts delay with a shrug and a murmured reference to the will of Allah. This attitude exasperates Europeans and Americans (especially the latter), who complain that the most frequently used word in the Arabic vocabulary is *bokra* (tomorrow). Emerson says the Egyptian approach is much more intelligent than our own constant bustle and fuss, but although he may be correct in his judgment, he is the first to fly into a rage when his plans are thwarted.

Be that as it may, as soon as the train slowed, the brave fellows got to their feet, and when one of them saw Emerson descend from the carriage, the whole group erupted into wild gesticulations of welcome. Outstanding among the men in physical stature as in dignity was the reis, Abdullah, who had served as our able foreman for many seasons. He immediately enfolded Emerson in a fraternal embrace, the voluminous folds of his robe billowing around my husband like a sudden snowstorm. Emerson suffered this gesture stoically, and sent the rest of the men scampering off to assist with the removal of our baggage.

I received Abdullah's respectful and affectionate salutation somewhat distractedly, for, to my utter astonishment, there before me was the man who had called himself Nemo.

He made no attempt to conceal his presence. He stood aloof from the other men, his arms folded across the breast of his ragged robe. He was bareheaded, and the noonday sun turned his red-gold hair to flame.

Abdullah's eyes followed the direction of my gaze. "I hope I did not err in allowing him to remain here, sitt. He is dressed like the lowest beggar, but he said Emerson had hired him, and when we saw he was an Inglizi . . ."

"Yes, quite right, Abdullah." So that was why the fellow had abandoned his disguise. Our loyal men would have driven him away otherwise.

Nemo strolled toward me. "Good morning, Mrs. Emerson. Or should it be good afternoon? I am a trifle out of practice with expressions of polite usage."

The fellow had the effrontery to be sarcastic. His drawling voice and educated accent, the courteous inclination of his head (in lieu of removing his hat, of which he had none) were in the best manner. He had even shaved. I must confess that the countenance thus displayed would have prejudiced me in his favor had I not had reason to suspect him of the most appalling duplicity. It was no wonder I had taken him for a Berber. His high cheekbones and hawklike nose, his broad brow and thin lips were characteristic of that race.

"How is your arm?" I inquired.

"I beg you will not mention it." The scowl that accompanied this courteous disclaimer turned the statement into a demand.

"It is necessary for me to mention it in order to ascertain whether you are fit for the duties for which you have been employed," I declared. "I do not allow anyone on my expeditions to suffer from an ailment I can relieve. That includes the donkeys. Abdullah—''

"Yes, sitt," Abdullah said resignedly. "The donkeys have been washed."

"Good. You see, Mr. Nemo, I am showing you the same concern I would show a donkey—an animal which in many ways you resemble. If you are not ready to accept this, you can take yourself off."

A spark of emotion that might have been amusement or anger warmed the sea-blue depths of Nemo's eyes. They were clear; apparently he had not recently indulged in drugs. "Very well, Mrs. Emerson. I will demonstrate my ability to carry out my duties, and I think I had better begin at once. Young Ramses is about to be flattened by that packing case, which is too heavy for him."

So saying, Nemo departed. His leisurely stride was deceptive; he covered the ground at quite a rapid pace, arriving on the scene he had described just in time to lift the case under whose weight Ramses was slowly sinking to his knees.

"Well, Abdullah," I said. "What do you think?"

I had the greatest regard for Abdullah, whom I had known for many years. He was a splendid specimen of manhood, almost as tall as Emerson; and though his hair and beard were snowy white, he had the strength of a man half his age. He and his group of associates had been trained by Emerson in the methods of proper excavation, so that many of them were better qualified than the majority of European archaeologists. They were in great demand by other excavators, but their loyalty to Emerson—and, I think I may say, to me—was paramount. I would have trusted Abdullah with my life; Emerson trusted him with his excavations, which was as high a mark of favor. Indeed, Abdullah's only weakness (aside from his extensive collection of wives) was an irradicable and deep-seated superstitiousness. He had never abandoned his belief in efreets and demons, although on innumerable occasions he had seen us tear the veil from seemingly supernatural terrors and expose the ordinary human villains behind the mystery.

Abdullah also prided himself upon the imperturbability of his countenance. This characteristic seemed more marked than usual that day; his thin, well-cut lips scarcely moved as he replied stiffly, "Think, honored sitt? I do not permit myself to think, unless ordered to do so by yourself or Emerson."

I understood the reason for his ill-humor. "It was not because of dissatisfaction with your son Selim that we employed the Inglizi to act as guard to Ramses," I assured him. "Like all your people, Selim is too valuable to be wasted as a nursemaid. Besides, we hoped to do a charitable action in helping the Englishman."

Abdullah's rigid face relaxed. "Ah. I understand, sitt. Charity is pleasing to Allah, and your kind heart is well known. But, sitt, do you know that the man is a smoker of opium?"

"I intend to break him of that vile habit, Abdullah."

"Ah," Abdullah said again, stroking his silky beard. "It is not easy to do that. But if anyone can break a man, it is you, Sitt Hakim."

"Thank you, Abdullah. Will you please explain to Selim, so he won't be disappointed?"

"Disappointed," Abdullah repeated thoughtfully. "No, sitt, I do not think Selim will be disappointed."

"Good. What I meant, Abdullah, by my question, was whether the Englishman looked familiar. Think carefully, Abdullah. Have you ever seen him before?"

Abdullah did not stop to think at all. "No, sitt. Never."

Thinking back over the events of the not-too-distant

past, I realized that Abdullah had not beheld the Master Criminal in his final apotheosis, for he had been drugged at an early stage in the proceedings and had slept through the whole exciting denouement. However, he had seen the Master Criminal in his role as Father Girgis on a number of occasions.

"Are you certain, Abdullah? Do you remember the priest of Dronkeh?"

"Yes, how could I forget him? He . . ." Abdullah's mouth remained open; his eyes emulated his mouth, widening till the whites showed around the dark centers. Then his shoulders began to twitch and strangling noises issued from his parted lips. A casual observer might have mistaken his reaction for amusement; but of course I knew better.

I hastened to reassure him. "There is nothing to be alarmed about, Abdullah. I have the matter well in hand. I am glad you were also sharp enough to penetrate the villain's disguise—"

"No, sitt, no." Abdullah regained control of himself. "You mistake me, sitt. A slight coughing spell . . . The dust in my throat . . . Perhaps my ears deceived me, or my aging brain failed to understand what you meant. Are you saying that this Inglizi is the—the same person as the—the . . ."

"You had better let me give you some medicine for your throat affliction," I said. "Your ears did not deceive you, Abdullah, and your brain is as good as ever. Better than the brain of a certain person who ought to be wiser. I mention no names, Abdullah."

"No, sitt, of course not. But, sitt, it cannot be. This is not the same man."

"The huge black beard and the long black hair were false—"

"The priest had black eyes, sitt. This man's eyes are blue."

I should have known better than to depend on Abdullah. He was, after all, only a man. "I have no time to explain," I said. "Just watch the fellow, Abdullah. It is better to have him with us, under our eye, than lurking in the desert plotting against us. But don't trust him."

"I hear and will obey," said Abdullah, his lips twitching.

"I have the most implicit confidence in you, Abdullah. But I cannot stand around chatting any longer. We must get underway."

The donkeys had been loaded, but it was necessary for me to greet each of the men individually, or their feelings would have been hurt. They were all old friends, and most were sons of Abdullah (I have already referred to his proclivities toward procreation). Selim was the youngest of his offspring, a lad of fifteen with an almost Grecian beauty of feature. I congratulated him on his recent marriage, for the proprieties had to be observed even though I deplore the horrid eastern custom of sending boys and girls into the hazards of matrimony at such tender ages. Then I explained to him, as I had to his father, why we had found someone else to look after Ramses.

Selim assured me that he was not at all distressed at being replaced, and I must say that he concealed his disappointment very well. He helped me to mount and walked beside me as we started forward, laughing and chatting cheerfully about John, our footman, who had been with us the year before. John had made himself quite popular with the men, and Selim was pleased to learn that his friend had also taken a wife in the interval.

Our little caravan proceeded along the path leading west. The inundation had receded from the fields, after depositing its annual layer of rich fertile mud, and the green sprouts of the new crops could be seen against the black earth. Our road led along one of the dikes raised above the fields, toward the village of Menyat Dahshoor, which stood on the edge of the cultivated land at the point where the earth turns abruptly to desert sand.

Emerson led the way as was his habit, perched on a minuscule donkey. If he had straightened his legs and stood up, the donkey could have walked right through them, but Emerson pictures himself on such occasions as mounted on a fiery horse leading his troops into battle. I would not for all the world have spoiled his innocent pleasure by pointing out that a man of six-foot-odd looks ridiculous on donkeyback.

Ramses rode behind him, engaged in animated conversation with Nemo, who had refused a mount and was walking alongside the boy, his long strides easily matching the plodding pace of the donkey. I wondered what they were talking about. Not that there was anything unusual in Ramses' talking.

Not for long was my attention held by those in my immediate vicinity, for my eyes were drawn to the splendor of the view beyond. The two stone pyramids of Dahshoor loomed on the horizon. The brilliance of the midday sun was reflected by the white limestone blocks of their sides and they shone as if silver-plated. They are among the oldest funerary structures in Egypt, predating even the mighty tombs of Giza. The larger of the two is exceeded in height only by the Great Pyramid. The excavations of M. de Morgan had proved that it was built by King Sneferu of the Fourth Dynasty. (Emerson and I had suspected this all along, of course.)

The name of the builder of the second stone pyramid was still unknown. That was one of the mysteries we hoped to solve that season. But only one of the mysteries—for this second stone structure has a number of curious features not found in other pyramids. Most conspicuous is its shape. A sudden change in the degree of the slope, from approximately fifty-four degrees in the lower section to a more abrupt forty-two degrees fifty-nine minutes (if memory serves me) in the upper section has bestowed upon it the appellation of the Bent or Blunted Pyramid. Why this anomaly? And, even more thrilling in its implications, what was the cause of the strange winds that occasionally swept through the dark and stifling interior passageways?

I particularly dote on the interiors of pyramids. There is some strange fascination in the awesome darkness, the airless silence, and the flapping of bat wings. Though I had promised myself many hours of delightful exploration within the Bent Pyramid, seeking the source of the uncanny and intermittent winds, I knew I could not count on much help from Emerson. He sympathizes with my passion for pyramids, but he does not share it, and he had always pooh-poohed the theory that there were hidden openings and chambers within the Bent Pyramid, even though I had myself felt those eerie winds. "Bats, Peabody. Dozens of bats flapping their leathery wings and blowing out your candle. I do not deplore your imagination, my dear, for indeed it is one of your more charming qualities. But . . ."

It is a waste of time to talk to Emerson when he has made up his mind about Egyptological matters; but I privately vowed he would experience the phenomenon himself—if I had to hold him prisoner inside until it happened.

His main concern that season was to identify the owner of the Bent Pyramid. The burial chambers of the Sixth Dynasty pyramids are covered with texts identifying their owners, but, strange as it may seem, none of the earlier tombs has a single inscription inside or on it. The only way of ascertaining the names of the kings to whom they belonged is from the associated structures—temples and subsidiary tombs, enclosure walls and causeways.

(In revising these journals for eventual publication I have added a few paragraphs for the edification of readers who do not share my expert knowledge. Edification, not entertainment, is my aim, as it should be the aim of any intelligent reader. I have no intention of succumbing to the numerous requests I have already received to permit my personal diaries to be published in my lifetime, but my high regard for science demands that the interesting and useful information contained in these pages be one day disclosed to the world. Wishing to spare my heirs the painful labor of revision—and also wishing to do myself justice, which no one else can do as well—I have undertaken a few modest changes.)

Our path led past the village, whose small flat-roofed houses and minareted mosque we could see among the palms and tamarisk trees. I wondered what sort of home Abdullah had found for us. My expectations were low. When I first met Emerson, he had set up housekeeping in a tomb, and experience has taught me that members of the male sex have very peculiar standards of comfort and cleanliness. I wished we could have returned to our headquarters of the previous season. The abandoned monastery had proved a commodious and comfortable residence, once I had it remodeled to suit my requirements. But though Mazghunah was only a few miles to the south, it would have been a waste of valuable time to transport ourselves and our gear that distance daily.

Modest though my hopes were, I felt a distinct sense of depression when we reached our destination. It was

on the outskirts of the village, on the west side, nearest
the desert. A mudbrick wall enclosed a courtyard of
beaten earth. Within the compound were several structures, some no more than one-room huts or sheds. One
was a house, to use that word loosely. It was built of
the ubiquitous unbaked brick coated with mud plaster,
and was only one story high; on the flat roof were some
miscellaneous shapes that might have been rotted
screens. Some hasty efforts at repairing the crumbling
walls had been made, and that recently; the rough plaster patches were still damp.

Abdullah had drawn ahead of me. When I dismounted he was deep in conversation with Emerson,
and he pretended not to see me until I tapped him on
the shoulder.

"Ah, sitt, you are here," he exclaimed, as if he had
expected I would be lost on the way. "It is a fine house,
you see. I have had all the rooms swept."

I did not reproach him. He had done his best, according to his lights; Emerson would have done no better.

I had come prepared. Rolling up my sleeves, literally,
I put everyone to work. Water was fetched from the
well—its proximity was, I admit, a point in favor of the
location—and some of the men began mixing more
plaster, while others sprinkled the interior of the house
with disinfectant. (Keating's powder, I have discovered,
is one of the most effective.) The house had four small
rooms. After one look at the high, narrow windows and
floors of dirt, I decided Emerson and I would sleep on
the roof. The debris I had observed there was the remains of plaited screens; once they were replaced, the
flat surface would serve as an extra chamber, as was
often the case. I assigned two of the rooms in the house
to Ramses and Mr. Nemo. The latter's supercilious

smile vanished when I handed him a broom.

By evening the place was fit for human habitation. A quick visit to the village market had procured the screens for the roof and a few other necessities. As the day wore on, we had a constant stream of visitors offering "presents" of food—eggs, milk, bread, chickens—for which we were, of course, expected to pay. At dusk I ordered the stout wooden gates closed. Naturally we were objects of curiosity to the village people, but we could not have them wandering in and out, especially if we were fortunate enough to discover valuable antiquities.

Thanks to our location on the west of the village, we had a splendid view of the pyramids from our doorstep, and when we settled down to our evening meal, we saw them silhouetted against one of the glorious sunsets for which the region is famous. We dined out-of-doors; though the smell of donkey was somewhat pervasive, it was preferable to the even more pervasive odor of Keating's powder that clung to the interior of the house.

Nemo had accepted my invitation to dine with us, not so much because he enjoyed our company as because the men had indicated they did not enjoy his. He refused a chair; squatting on the ground with his dirty robes wadded under him, he ate with his fingers and then wiped the grease off on his skirts. I felt sure he did it to annoy me, so I said nothing.

Conversation lagged at first. Emerson was preoccupied with the next day's work, Nemo was determined not to be affable, and even I was a trifle weary. But Ramses was never too tired to talk, and the monologue was his favorite form of discourse. First he brought us up to date on the activities of the men. We heard all about Selim's wedding and Abdul's divorce and Yusuf's twins and the three-headed goat that had been born in a neighboring village. (Such wonders are always to be found in a *neighboring* village, and are known only through *reliable* reports from people whom no one happens to know personally.)

Moving from the specific to the general, Ramses went on to summarize Abdullah's report on the summer at Dahshoor. Though I do not as a rule encourage Ramses to talk, I did not interrupt him on this occasion, since the exigencies of domesticity had prevented me from hearing this news firsthand. We had expected there might be trouble at the site of the excavations. During the previous season a gang of professional thieves, under the direction of that desperate and enigmatic person I have mentioned, had attempted to loot the tombs around the pyramids. We had foiled their dastardly deed, but I feared they might be tempted to try again during our absence, and there were the village amateurs to contend with—if any tomb robber in Egypt can be said to be an amateur. The fellahin have been at it for generations, clear back to the time of the pharaohs, and many of them are more skilled at finding hidden tombs than are professional archaeologists. Wretchedly poor, and lacking any national pride after centuries of Turkish rule, they see no reason why they should not profit from the riches of their ancestors.

However, according to Abdullah, there had been no sign of illicit digging. He and his sons had taken it in turn to guard the site, traveling back and forth from their village south of Cairo.

As Ramses meandered endlessly on, I noticed that Nemo was listening with an interest the personal lives of the men had failed to inspire. I broke into Ramses' discourse.

"You appear intrigued, Mr. Nemo. You are not familiar with the prevalence of tomb robbing in Egypt?"

"One can hardly remain ignorant of the practice if one lives for any time in Cairo," was the bland reply. "Every antiquities dealer in the city sells such merchandise."

"Have you never been tempted to join in the trade?"

Nemo smiled insolently. "Digging requires effort, Mrs. Emerson. I am opposed to physical effort. Forgery, now . . . There is a chap in the Shâria 'Kâmel who manufactures fake antiquities, and I have sold my share of imitation scarabs to tourists who don't know better."

The word "scarab" had roused Emerson from his meditations. Instead of expressing outrage at this callous speech, he chuckled. "Don't try salting this site, Nemo. You would not deceive me."

"I have better sense than that, Professor."

"I hope so. Er—speaking of the site, I think I might just take a stroll and refresh my memory of—er—the site. Care to join me, Peabody?"

I was sorely tempted for several reasons, not the least of which was Emerson's meaningful smile. Before long the silvery globe of the moon would hang low above the Libyan hills, and as our national poet Shakespeare so nicely puts it, "such a night as this" was made for affectionate exchanges. However, I knew I ought not to yield. Ramses would want to go with us, and I had no excuse for refusing such a request, since it was still early; but if Ramses went with us, there would be no point in our going. (If the Reader follows me, which I am sure he or she does, assuming he or she has the slightest trace of romantic sensibility.) Naturally I could not explain my reasoning aloud, so I sought refuge in a (quite valid) excuse.

"How can you suggest such a thing, Emerson, when we still have hours of work ahead of us? There are boxes to be unpacked, your notes to set in order, my medicine chest to arrange—"

"Curse it," said Emerson. "Oh, very well, I don't suppose you need me—"

"I could certainly use—"

"In that case, I will just run along. Ramses?"

"Thank you, Papa. I was in hopes you would proffer the invitation and in fact I had determined I would ask permission to accompany you if you did not see fit—"

"I did see fit," said Emerson. "Come, then."

Nemo got to his feet. "You needn't come," Emerson said amiably. "I can watch after Ramses."

"I would much rather—" Nemo began.

"I require your assistance," I said.

"But, Professor—"

"No, no, young man, I don't need you and Mrs. Emerson does. Duty before pleasure, you know, duty before pleasure."

Nemo sank down again, glowering. I waited until Emerson and Ramses had left before I spoke. "I believe I would like a whiskey," I said musingly. "Will you join me, Mr. Nemo?"

Nemo gaped at me. "I beg your pardon, madam?"

"You will find the bottle and the glasses on the table in the parlor. If you will be so good as to fetch them . . ."

He did as I asked, and watched curiously as I filled the glasses. "To Her Majesty," I said, raising my glass. "God bless her."

"Uh—er—quite," said Mr. Nemo, raising his.

The appetite of an opium eater is usually poor. He had eaten very little, and the alcoholic beverage took effect quite rapidly. As I had hoped, the familiar ritual, well loved by all loyal Englishmen (and women) also had a soothing effect. Nemo took a chair instead of squatting. "This is the first whiskey I have had for—for many months," he said, half to himself.

"I am a great believer in the medicinal effects of good whiskey," I explained. "Particularly in the treatment of fatigue and minor nervous disorders. Naturally I would never condone an excessive dependence on it, but no reasonable person could possibly object to a civilized and moderate application. As compared, for instance, to opium—"

Nemo slumped forward, his head bowed. "I knew it," he muttered. "Please spare me the lecture, Mrs. Emerson. You are wasting your time and mine."

"We have yet to discuss the terms of your employment, Mr. Nemo. You can hardly suppose I would allow you to consume drugs of any kind while on duty. Watching over Ramses requires every ounce of alertness and energy a man can summon up."

The young man's tousled head sank lower. "I have neither quality left."

"Nonsense. You were alert enough the other evening; you can summon energy enough when it is needed. I am not asking you to abandon your disgusting habit altogether, Mr. Nemo, only to refrain from it at such times when you are responsible for Ramses. Is that too much to ask?"

Nemo did not reply, but I thought I detected a stiffening of his form. I went on persuasively, "I will give you one day a week to yourself. That is excessively generous, but generosity is a favorite virtue of mine. Sink yourself in a degrading stupor on that day, if you must, but remain alert the rest of the time. I will be happy to dispense a reasonable quantity of whiskey whenever—"

I broke off, for his bent shoulders were heaving convulsively and sounds like muffled sobs escaped from his lips. I had touched some tender chord; I had roused some forgotten spark of manhood! He had not fallen so low as I had feared. He might yet be redeemed, not only from his loathsome habit but from the despicable toils of the Master Criminal. What a triumph that would be!

Nemo sat up straight and raised his head. The rays of the setting sun cast his features in sharp outline and glittered off the tears that streaked his cheeks. "Mrs. Emerson . . ." But he could not master his emotion; his voice failed, and his chest heaved with sighs he could not restrain.

"I understand, Mr. Nemo. Say no more. Or rather, say only that you will try."

He nodded speechlessly.

"Would you care for another whiskey?" I asked, reaching for the bottle.

The kindly gesture was too much for the young man. With a broken cry he rose and fled into the house.

I had another small whiskey. I felt I deserved it. The interview had gone much better than I had expected. In judging the young man I had forgotten to take into account the well-known habits of master criminals. Their evil webs snare rich and poor, guilty and innocent in their tangled strands (as I had once put it, rather neatly, in my opinion). In the case of young Mr. Nemo, some relatively harmless escapade might have rendered him vulnerable to blackmail and enabled the M.C. (if I may be permitted to use that more convenient abbreviation) to entwine him in his toils. Perhaps he (Mr. Nemo) yearned to free himself and return to decent society.

Lost in such delightful thoughts, I sat musing until the sudden night of Egypt eclipsed the dying sun and the moonlight crept crepuscularly across the courtyard. Lamplight and the sound of laughing voices issued from the hut in which our men had taken up their abode.

Reluctantly I rose to return to the duties I had mentioned.

I had selected the larger of the two front rooms to serve as our sitting room and office. Our camp chairs and little stove had been set up, and a few oriental rugs on the floor added a colorful note; but there were still half a dozen boxes to be unpacked. I set to work arranging my medical supplies, for I knew the first light of dawn would bring the usual pathetic sufferers to our door. Doctors, much less hospitals, were almost unknown outside of the large cities, and the villagers naively assumed all Europeans were physicians. In my case, at any rate, their hopes were not disappointed.

Ramses and Emerson finally came in, both wanting to tell me about the site. I cut their raptures short, for there was really no sense to be got out of them, and sent Ramses to bed. The cat Bastet seemed disinclined to join him, but when Ramses lifted her off the packing case she was sniffing and carried her away, she did not resist.

"Drinking again, I see, Peabody," said Emerson, inspecting the remains of my whiskey. "How often have I warned you about the evils of the demon rum?"

"You will have your little joke, Emerson. It was an experiment, in fact, and one that succeeded brilliantly. Mr. Nemo is a cashiered army officer! He was once in the service of Her Majesty—"

"Calmly, Peabody, if you please. What did you do, get him drunk and induce a confession?"

I explained. Emerson was in an excellent humor; for once he listened without interrupting. Then he said, "You deduced Mr. Nemo's entire military history solely from his response to your toast?"

"No, no, that was merely the final proof. Everything

points to it, Emerson—the young man's carriage, his manner, his speech."

"Well, you may be right, Peabody. I had begun to wonder about that myself."

"Ha," I exclaimed.

Emerson grinned. "I know, I know; I always claim to have anticipated your deductions—and you do the same to me, Peabody, admit it. But this time I was not trying to do you in the eye. It was the most obvious conclusion. Such cases are, unhappily, not infrequent. And no wonder! Take a young man with no experience of the world, thrust him into an alien land filled with exotic temptations, fill him full of a lot of bilge about his superiority over lesser breeds of men—and all women!—segregate him from everyone except members of his own sex and social class . . ."

He went on for some time. I let him get it out of his system—for the time being. It was one of Emerson's chief aggravations and the subject would certainly arise again, as it had done often before. He had refused to allow Ramses to attend school, and in this case I had to agree with him. Any educational system that separates the sexes and denies women equal intellectual opportunities is obviously a poor system.

Finally Emerson wound down. He gave himself a shake and mopped his perspiring brow. "At any rate, Peabody, I am glad to see you have given up your nonsensical notions about master—er—about Mr. Nemo's criminal associations."

I smiled to myself but did not reply. Emerson enjoys our little arguments as much as I do; they are, if I may invent a striking metaphor, the pepper in the soup of marriage. However, I felt he had had enough excitement for one evening and I was anxious to finish and get to bed.

His thoughts had turned to the same subject. After a moment he said, "I found a very pleasant little pit in the rock, Peabody. With a bit of canvas for a roof and a trifle of the sweeping and scrubbing you women seem to consider necessary, it would make a most agreeable sleeping chamber."

"For whom, Emerson?"

I had my back turned, but I heard the creak of his chair and the elephantine tread of Emerson trying to tiptoe. His arms stole around my waist. "Whom do you think, Peabody?"

I felt a warm moist touch on my neck, just under my ear. Much as I would have liked Emerson to pursue this interesting course, I forced myself to be firm. "All in due time, Emerson. I have two more boxes to unpack."

"Leave them till morning."

"They may contain articles we will need first thing in the morning. I have not yet found the teakettle . . . Do stop it, Emerson. I cannot concentrate when you . . . Oh, Emerson! Now, Emerson . . ."

Nothing was said for some time. Eventually a persistent sound, like that of a file rasping on wood, penetrated my absorption. Emerson heard it too; his grasp on my person loosened, and I attempted, not entirely successfully, to straighten my disheveled attire before I turned toward the door. No one was there. I felt certain, however, that Ramses had been watching. The purring of his feline companion had given him away and had forced him to beat a hasty retreat.

It seemed pointless to pursue the matter, or Ramses. Silently I turned back to the labors Emerson's affectionate demonstration had interrupted. As is occasionally his habit, Emerson turned his annoyance at the disturbance, not on the perpetrator, but on the nearest object—me.

"It has taken you a devil of a time to unpack," he grumbled.

"If you had condescended to stay and help, I would be done."

"Then why didn't you say so? That is just like a woman. They always expect a fellow to read their minds—"

"The most rudimentary intelligence would have made it evident—"

"And then they whine and complain when—"

"Whine, indeed! When have you ever heard me—"

"I admit the word is inappropriate. Shout would be more—"

"How can you—"

"How can *you*—"

We were both out of breath by then and had to pause to take in oxygen. Then Emerson said cheerfully, "You were quite right, Peabody; this parcel is one I remember and it does indeed contain a new teakettle, which I purchased in the sûk. I seemed to recall that the kettle of last season had become sadly dented after I used it to kill a cobra."

"It was clever of you to think of it, Emerson. I confess that the incident of the cobra had quite slipped my mind. What is in this last parcel?"

"I have no idea. Perhaps it contains some of the things we left Abdullah to pack and bring here from Mazghunah."

He had taken out his pocket knife and was cutting the cords binding the parcel that contained the kettle. The merchants in the bazaar knew only two styles of packing—one used no string at all, so that the parcel fell apart in transit; the other employed vast quantities of heavy rope even when the parcel was only to be carried a few yards. The package I was inspecting was of the second variety, and I had to borrow Emerson's knife to undo it.

He unpacked the kettle and some pots and pans, and turned to put them on the table.

"Emerson," I said. "Look here."

In a flash Emerson was at my side. He knows every tone of my voice, and on this occasion the few simple words quivered with the intensity of the inexpressible sensations that filled me.

"What is it, Peabody?" He looked into the box. I had pushed aside the top layer of straw. The curved sides of the vessel within gleamed in the lamplight with a soft luster.

Emerson reached for it. With a shriek I caught his arm and clung to it. "No, Emerson! Watch out!"

"What the devil, Peabody, it is only an old pot. A pot made of . . ." His breath caught. "Silver?"

"It is not the vessel itself I fear, but what may be concealed in the straw. A scorpion, a snake, a poisonous spider . . . Where are your gloves—the heavy work gloves?"

For a wonder they were where they were supposed to be, in the pocket of his coat. When I started to draw on the gloves, he took them from me, and performed the task himself. I was in a perfect quiver of apprehension until he had removed the last of the objects from the container. He then overturned it, spilling the packing material onto the floor.

"No spiders, no snakes," he remarked, shoving the straw about with his booted toe. "Obviously you are in possession of information I lack, Peabody. Would you care to explain why you expected a shipment of venomous animals, and how you came into possession of what appear to be antique vessels of . . . antique vessels . . . No. No! I don't believe it. Don't tell me—"

"Obviously I needn't tell you," I replied. Normally I am tolerant of Emerson's little fits of temper, for they relieve an excess of spleen; but this situation was too serious for theatrics. A sense, not of fear but of awe, as in the presence of something larger and more powerful than myself, stole over me. "These are indeed the communion vessels stolen from the church of Sitt Miriam at Dronkeh. Stolen by that villain, that wretch, that consummate master of evil, that genius of crime . . ."

I waited for him to voice an objection to the words he knew I was about to use, but he was incapable of speech. Flushed of countenance, bulging as to his eyeballs, he continued to stare at me in silence, and I concluded, "None other than—the Master Criminal!"

Four

Emerson had never seen the famous communion vessels, since he has a constitutional aversion to organized religion and refuses to enter a church, mosque, or synagogue. He had to take my word for it, but even if he had presumed to doubt my identification, the conclusion would have been forced upon him. The vessels taken from the church at Dronkeh had been valuable antiques, centuries old. There could not be many such sets of objects hanging about, as Emerson glumly and vulgarly expressed it.

"But why return them?" he demanded. Then his expression lightened. "Wait—wait, Peabody, I have it. The thief was not your cursed Master Criminal, but an amateur who yielded to a sudden temptation, hoping the theft would be blamed on the Master Criminal. He has repented, and has returned them."

"To us? Were that the case, Emerson, the repentant

thief would have returned the objects to the church. It is a challenge from our old adversary, Emerson; it can be nothing else.''

"Peabody, I thoroughly dislike your trick of selecting one theory out of a plethora of them and loudly proclaiming it to be the only possible solution. My explanation makes as much sense as yours."

Upon further discussion, Emerson was forced to agree that the parcel must have been among those brought with us from Cairo. Its neat style of wrapping would have stood out like a sore thumb in the things Abdullah had caused to be transported from Mazghunah, for Abdullah's notion of packing was to throw everything into a sack and toss it over the back of a donkey.

We further agreed that it would be the simplest thing in the world for someone to slip the parcel in among the others Emerson had ordered from the bazaar. One of the hotel safragi's duties was to take deliveries and place them in our room, and there was no reason why he would have taken special notice of any particular parcel.

"Quite true," I said thoughtfully. "And yet, Emerson, I have a strange feeling about that parcel. I cannot tell you how I know, but I am convinced that the Master Criminal delivered it himself. That we were under observation all that day; that our departure from the hotel was noted; that had we been present, we would have seen a man stroll calmly along the corridor, parcel in hand, eluding the safragi—who is, as you know, sound asleep most of the time—entering our room, placing his parcel among the others—pausing to gloat over our discomfiture and our bewilderment . . .''

"Your intuition tells you so, I presume," said Emerson, with a halfhearted sneer.

"Something other than intuition. What it is I cannot say ... Ah, I have it!" I snatched up the discarded wrappings and turned them over in my hand. Yes, there it was; I had not imagined it—a spot of what appeared to be grease or fat, as large as the palm of my hand. I raised it to my nostrils and sniffed. "I knew it!" I cried in triumph. "Here, Emerson, smell for yourself."

Emerson shied back as I held the paper to his face. "Good Gad, Amelia—"

"Smell it. Just there, the spot of grease. Well?"

"Well, it is animal fat of some kind," Emerson grumbled. "Mutton or chicken. What is so significant about that? These people are not given to the use of knives and forks, they eat with their fingers and ..." Then his face changed, and I knew that his intelligence, equal to my own, had arrived at the same conclusion. I also knew he was too stubborn to admit it.

"Chicken fat," I said. "No wonder the cat Bastet refused the meat Ramses brought from Mena House. She had been stuffed with chicken. Emerson, that villain—that remarkable, clever wretch—has seduced our cat!"

Emerson did not dispute my deduction. He ridiculed it, he derided it, he scoffed at it. He kept this up even after we had retired. Our mattresses had been placed side by side atop the roof. The cool breeze, the soft moonlight, the exquisite but indescribable scent of the desert—even the smell of donkey droppings, wafting from the courtyard below—should have induced a state of mind conducive to connubial affection of the strongest kind; and yet, for almost the first time in our marriage, Emerson's demonstrations were inadequate to the purpose. He was ridiculously upset about it.

"I keep expecting to see Ramses' head pop up over the edge of the screen," he groaned. "I cannot concentrate, Amelia. Tomorrow night we will move to the pit. Ramses will be perfectly safe here with Nemo in the next room and our men guarding the compound."

"Much as I would enjoy sleeping in the spot you describe, Emerson, I don't think it would be wise. Not after the reminder we have just received of the awesome malice and powers of the Master Criminal. We have scarcely been in Egypt three days, and already he has challenged us twice. We are in deep waters, Emerson, very deep indeed. Was the attempt on Ramses meant to succeed, or was it only a demonstration of what the man can do if he chooses? One result of that adventure, if you recall, was the advent of Mr. Nemo in our midst."

Midway in this speech Emerson had pulled the blanket over his head and was pretending to snore. I knew I still had his attention, however, for the part of his body that adjoined my own was as rigid as a board.

"Was that perhaps the Master Criminal's intent?" I went on thoughtfully. "To insert a confederate into our confidence? And the return of the communion vessels is another enigma. Why should he give up his loot? I tell you, Emerson, the subtle machinations of that great criminal brain—"

Emerson sat up with a roar whose reverberations echoed through the quiet night. As if in answer came the queer, coughing cry of a jackal prowling the desert waste.

"Hush, Emerson," I implored. "You will waken the entire village—not to mention Ramses. What the devil is the matter with you? I was speaking of the Master Criminal—"

"I heard you." Emerson lowered his voice. The blanket had fallen away, baring his body to the waist and exposing more of my own than was strictly proper. Mesmerized by the ripple of muscle on Emerson's broad chest as he struggled for breath, I did not replace it. Emerson went on in a hissing whisper, "Great mind, did you say? How can you ramble on about that—that— that creature at a time like this? And in such terms— terms almost of respect! Devil take it, Amelia, one might suppose you think I am incapable of dealing with that scoundrel! Curse it! If you believe I am not man enough—"

"My dear Emerson—"

"Be quiet, Peabody. If you have any doubts as to my fortitude, I will prove you wrong."

And he did so, with such determination and zeal that when, at a later time, he requested my assessment of the situation, I was able to reply with utter sincerity that his arguments had been entirely convincing.

I woke at dawn, as is my habit in Egypt, whatever distractions the night may bring. Our lofty perch presented me with an unexampled view of the glorious sunrise and I lay in sleepy content for a time, watching the soft shades of gold and rose strengthen in the eastern sky. Emerson's regular expiration ruffled the hair on my brow. After a time a sense of vague uneasiness penetrated the pleasant laziness of my mind, and I raised my head. Fortunately I raised no other part of my body, for the first thing I saw was the face of Ramses, apparently detached from the rest of him, solemnly regarding me. It was an uncanny apparition and I was somewhat startled until it occurred to me that everything except his head was out of sight on the stairs leading to the roof.

"What are you doing there?" I whispered.

"I came to see if you and Papa were awake. Since I

see that you are, I have brought you a cup of tea. I tried to bring two cups, but unfortunately dropped one, the stairs being extremely steep and my—''

I put my finger to my lips and pointed at Emerson, who was twitching restlessly.

Ramses' neck and narrow shoulders rose up out of the stairwell, and I saw that he was indeed holding a cup. Whether or not it contained tea was yet to be seen. I rather doubted that it did. I started to sit up and then remembered that in the extreme fatigue following the ultimate conclusion of my discussion with Emerson, I had neglected something.

I dismissed Ramses and groped for my clothes. Assuming those garments under cover of the blanket without rousing Emerson was no easy task. By the time I was finished I quite agreed with my husband that we might do well to transfer our sleeping quarters to the place he had suggested. Ramses was even more unnerving when he was not present than when he was, because one never knew when he would turn up.

There was approximately an eighth of a cup of tea in the bottom of the cup. The rest had been spilled on the steps, as I discovered when I started to descend them.

However, it had been a kindly thought, and I thanked Ramses when I found him busily burning toast over the camp stove. "Where is Mr. Nemo?" I asked.

"Outside. I offered to prepare a light repast for him, but he said he didn't want any cursed tea and toast, and—''

I went out the door, leaving Ramses still talking. Nemo was squatting on the mastaba bench. He had resumed his filthy turban and once again resembled an Egyptian of the lowest type. I never could have mistaken him for one of our men, for they prided themselves on the elegance of their attire, and their habits were as fastidious as circumstances allowed. They had finished their morning repast and there was a busy flutter of blue-and-white-striped cotton round the cookfire. Abdullah, looking like one of the nobler Biblical patriarchs in the snowy white he preferred, called a greeting and I replied in kind, adding that Emerson would soon be ready to leave for the site.

Nemo had not moved or spoken. "You had better eat something," I said.

"I am well enough as I am."

I would have continued the discussion, but a hand gripped me and drew me back into the house. It was Emerson, fully dressed and alert; in his other hand he held a piece of scorched bread, which he was chewing.

"Leave him alone," he said, after swallowing the nasty morsel and making a face. "He is obviously regretting his bargain and struggling with the desire to succumb to the temptation of the drug. He must fight it out by himself."

"If that is the case, Emerson, his need for nourishment is all the greater. The use of opium and hashish when carried to excess—"

"He has not carried it to excess." Emerson handed me the toasting fork. I took the hint, and the fork; as I busied myself with the preparation of a fresh slice of bread, Emerson went on, "In fact, I am certain he is not physically addicted to either opium or hashish. He indulges as some men drink to excess, in order to forget his troubles, and because drugs seem to the young and foolish a romantic form of escape from reality. His physical condition makes it clear that he has not indulged long or often. Those who do so exhibit a characteristic leaden pallor and skeletal thinness, along with lethargy and disinclination towards exertion. All varieties of exertion,'' he added, with one of those masculine grins.

"Humph,'' I said. ''Well, I wouldn't know about that, Emerson, but he certainly exerted himself on the night he rescued Ramses.''

"He was probably under the influence of opium at that time,'' Emerson said coolly. ''Used moderately, it acts as a stimulant.''

"You seem to know a great deal about it.'' I glanced around the room and was relieved to see that Ramses had taken himself off. ''Emerson—have you ever . . .''

"Oh yes. Only as an experiment,'' Emerson added. "I don't enjoy the sensation or the side effects. When used in moderation, however, opium appears to be no more harmful than tobacco or alcohol.''

"I believe I have heard that that is the case; also that addiction happens chiefly in individuals of weak will-power who would just as easily become the victims of intoxicating drinks and who are practically moral imbeciles, often addicted to other forms of depravity.''

Emerson had devoured the toast as rapidly as I produced it. Now he drained his third cup of tea and sprang up from his chair. ''I don't mean to criticize, Peabody, but you are taking a confounded long time over breakfast. We have work to do, you know.''

At Emerson's request, Abdullah had already hired the necessary number of workers. Emerson hates this task, as he abhors all duties that keep him from the actual digging. When we opened the gates we found a sizable group waiting for us, squatting patiently on the ground. Some were men who had worked for us at Mazghunah the year before; their somber indigo robes and turbans, the mark of the Copts, or Christian Egyptians, stood out in sharp contrast to the paler, washed-out blue and white stripes of the Moslem garb. Around the outskirts of the mass of adults, the children ran back and forth with the splendid energy of youth, playing games and crying out in shrill high voices.

While Emerson greeted and inspected the men Abdullah had selected, I set out my medical supplies on a folding table and attended to the sufferers who awaited my coming, dispensing sulphate of copper for the ever-present ophthalmia, and ipecacuanha for bowel complaints. Emerson concluded his business first and stamped up and down until I finished, without, however, complaining of the delay; for beneath his gruff exterior Emerson has the kindest heart in the world and is never unmoved by the suffering of the less fortunate. The moment the last patient was dismissed, however, he seized me by the hand and set out for the dig, calling the men to follow.

"Makes one feel like a general, doesn't it, Peabody?" he said, in high good humor.

I glanced back at the ragged crowd straggling after us. "More like a leader of one of the madder crusades. Where is Nemo?"

"Hot on the trail of Ramses." Emerson grinned. "I fancy the boy won't find it as easy to elude or corrupt him as he did Selim. I look forward to accomplishing a great deal of useful work this season, Peabody. Without interruption, Peabody!"

I knew the poor dear man was deluding himself, but I did not voice my doubts aloud. It was hard to think of murder, abduction, and assault on such a morning. The air was fresh and cool and the purity of the atmosphere strengthened every sense. Sounds carried farther, vision seemed magnified, and the surface of the skin tingled to the slightest touch. I drew in deep breaths of the salubrious air, and although Emerson set a rapid pace, I had no difficulty in matching it.

Our march was accompanied by the musical jingle of the accouterments dangling from my belt, all of them objects I find essential on a dig, such as matches in a waterproof box, small flasks of water and brandy, writing implements, a pocket knife, and so on. Emerson was not too fond of my carrying these things, for he complained that their sharp edges were an impediment to the impulsive embraces to which he was prone; but upon at least one occasion my chatelaine, as I jestingly called it, had been instrumental in saving our lives. His opinions had not altered, but he now kept them to himself.

Ever since my first season in Egypt, when I had sometimes found myself uncomfortably, not to say dangerously, encumbered by the absurd attire fashion forces upon the helpless female form, I had been refining and improving my working costume. Though I have never received credit for my innovations from the couturier establishments of Paris—and probably never shall, for envy is a characteristic of such people—I am convinced my bold ideas have had their effect on persons such as Worth and Lanvin. Only this past year I had come upon an ensemble known as a bicycle dress which incorporated many of my inventions, and which was the latest Paris mode. I had therefore caused several versions of this costume to be made for myself, not in the impractical brown velveteen of the original, but in serge and lightweight flannel. The darker colors that are more suitable in England and in Europe, matching as they do the natural shades of nasty French mud and good healthy English dirt, are not appropriate for Egypt, so I had indulged myself in cheerful shades that would not show sand and dust. In honor of our first day, I had assumed the gayest of the collection. The wide Turkish trousers, gathered in at the knee, were so full that when I remained upright and motionless, the division was obliterated. Stout boots and gaiters completed the nether portion of the costume. A short double-breasted jacket was buttoned over a white shirtwaist, collar, and tie, and a broad leather belt adorned with the aforementioned accouterments (and of course a pistol in a matching leather holster) supported the trousers. The fabric was a brilliant crimson, Emerson's favorite shade. Though some might have considered it too flamboyant for an archaeological expedition, I felt it added a colorful touch.

Though concern about my personal appearance has never been a matter of paramount importance to me, I will candidly admit that my spirits rise when I know I look my best. I fancy there is nothing wrong with that. It displays a proper self-respect without which no individual, man or woman, can achieve great things. I was conscious that morning of looking my best. Add to that the glorious promise of the pyramids, pale gold in the morning light, and the presence of the man at my side, towing me along with hearty precipitation, and I knew there was not a woman in the universe happier than I.

I realized that I would not be able to penetrate the interior of the pyramid that day. Indeed, that pleasure would be an amusement of my leisure hours instead of a duty, since Emerson had determined to begin with the remains of the subsidiary structures alongside the major monument.

Of these there were an *embarras de richesse*, so to speak. To the north stood a tumbled pile of stone that had once been a tomb of the same shape, though considerably smaller. We also expected to find next to the pyramid the remains of the funerary temple. From this building a long roofed causeway had led across the desert to the edge of the cultivation. In addition, the land near the royal tomb was filled with burials of courtiers and family members, just as people of the Christian era had caused their graves to be placed near the tomb of a celebrated saint, in the hope, one presumes, that the sanctity of the primary corpse would seep over onto the less worthy. Superstition, alas, is a basic human weakness, and not restricted to pagans.

Halting atop a ridge, Emerson shielded his eyes with his hand and gazed upon the scene. The breeze ruffled his dark hair and pressed the flannel of his shirt against his muscular breast. A thrill of (primarily) aesthetic pleasure ran through me as I watched him.

"Well, Peabody, what is it to be?" he asked.

"I am sure you have already decided," I replied. "We have debated the matter endlessly, without agreeing, and I know you will go right ahead with your plan no matter what I say."

"Peabody, I have explained on a number of occasions my reasons for postponing any investigation of the small subsidiary pyramid. I suppose, given your particular enthusiasm, even a little pyramid is better than no pyramid at all, but I believe we ought to search for private tombs and for the temple."

Before I could reply, a high, penetrating voice said, "If I were allowed to cast my vote on this matter, I would suggest we begin with the causeway. That line across the desert, which is easily discernible from this slight elevation, surely marks its original course, and were we to follow it to its ultimate—"

Emerson and I spoke at once. Emerson said, "Yes, yes, my boy." I said, "Ramses, be quiet."

Mr. Nemo laughed. "Is that how it's done?"

Pleased to see him more cheerful, I inquired, "And what is your opinion, Mr. Nemo?"

Nemo scratched his side. The gesture roused the direct suspicions; I vowed to myself that as soon as we returned to the house that evening, I would deal with him as I dealt with the donkeys. He needed more suitable attire as well.

"You cannot expect a sensible answer from me, Mrs. Emerson," he said. "I know nothing of archaeology; like all ignoramuses, I would like to see you dig up jewels and gold. The best chance of finding such things, I believe, would be in the nearby private tombs."

I gave Emerson a significant glance, or, at least, I tried to. He was not looking at me. "You are too modest, Mr. Nemo," I said. "Your remark betrays a greater knowledge of archaeology than you would claim."

"Oh, I got all that from Master Ramses here," said Nemo calmly. "As we walked he gave me a lecture on the principles of excavation. Well, Professor and Mrs. Emerson—what is your decision? And what can a mere tyro do to assist? I can wield a pick or shovel with the best of them."

Emerson fingered the cleft in his chin, as is his habit when deep in thought. Finally he said decisively, "Ramses, you and Abdullah can begin on the causeway. Stop at once if you come upon stone or brickwork. I must do a preliminary survey before we remove any object from its place, but as you have several tons of sand to shift, I should be able to finish before you achieve that end."

Ramses frowned. "There is no need for Abdullah to share the supervisory role, Papa, since I am entirely capable of managing by myself, and he might be better employed—"

"Be quiet, Ramses," I said. "Yes, yes, my boy," Emerson said. He added, "Nemo, go along with Ramses. He will tell you what to do."

"I don't doubt that he will," said Nemo.

We scattered to our appointed tasks. Mine was to assist Emerson with the surveying. To be sure, de Morgan had surveyed the site already, but Emerson had no confidence whatever in the abilities of the Director of the Antiquities Service. "These Frenchmen can't even count properly, Peabody. No wonder, with that ridiculous metric system of theirs."

Matters proceeded smoothly. As I have said, Abdullah was as capable as most trained archaeologists, and when I looked up from my own task I could see the men digging with such vigor that a fine cloud of sand enclosed them. A line of children ran to and fro, between the diggers and the distant dump site, emptying their baskets and returning to have them filled again.

We stopped for a rest and a light repast at nine-thirty, and were about to resume work when one of the men called out and pointed. Someone was approaching. The newcomer was a European, by his dress, and he was on foot, coming across the desert from the north.

Emerson said, "Curse it." He hates visitors interrupting his work. "Deal with the fellow, Peabody," he growled, snatching up his transit. "I have vowed that this season I will not suffer the constant intrusions of idle tourists."

"He doesn't look like a tourist," I said. "His gait is rather unsteady, Emerson, don't you think? I wonder if he can be intoxicated."

"Humph," said Emerson. "As a matter of fact, he looks familiar. Who is it, Peabody?"

The countenance, whose features became ever more recognizable with increased proximity, was indeed one I had seen before, but I was unable to produce a name to go with the face. He was a pleasant-looking young chap, of medium height and wiry frame. The only unusual thing about him was his complexion, which was of an odd grayish-green.

He greeted us by name, and added hesitantly, "We met last year in Cairo. Quibell is my name."

"Of course," I said. "Won't you join us, Mr. Quibell? I can only offer you hard-boiled eggs and chilly toast—"

"No, thank you." Quibell shuddered and the greenish tinge of his cheeks intensified. "You must forgive me if I come at once to the reason for my disturbing you—"

"That would be a kindness," said Emerson. "I thought you were with Petrie this year."

"I am."

"But Petrie is at Thebes."

"He began at Sakkara, and left a few of us to finish the task of recording the private tombs," Quibell explained. "When I heard you were at Dahshoor, I took the liberty of coming to ask a favor. I know Mrs. Emerson's reputation as a physician—"

"Ha," said Emerson.

"I beg your pardon, Professor?"

"Nothing," said Emerson.

"Oh. I thought you said . . . Well, not to put too fine a face upon it, we are all rather under the weather just now, and I thought perhaps I might beg some medicine from Mrs. Emerson. What I need, I believe, is a quantity of ipacanana."

"Ipecacuanha," I corrected.

"Oh. Yes—quite. Thank you, Mrs. Emerson."

"What is the nature of your complaint?" Emerson asked. A suspicion of the truth had occurred to him; the dawning delight on his face really did him no credit.

"That is evident, Emerson," I said. "Mr. Quibell's

disinclination to take food and the peculiar shade of his complexion indicate a disturbance of the digestive tract.''

''Food poisoning,'' said Emerson, choking with amusement. ''It is food poisoning, isn't it, Quibell? Petrie's people always come down with food poisoning. He opens a tin, and eats half of the contents, and leaves it standing around in some unsanitary tomb, and then expects his staff members to finish the stuff . . . Ha, ha, ha!''

''Really, Emerson,'' I exclaimed indignantly. ''You ought to be ashamed of yourself. Here is poor Mr. Quibell, pea-green with indigestion—''

''Peas,'' Emerson gasped. ''Yes, I understand Petrie is particularly fond of tinned peas. Very good, Peabody.''

Quibell came loyally to his chief's defense. ''It isn't Professor Petrie's fault. You know he operates with limited funds and he never has the slightest trouble himself—''

''No, the man has the digestion of a camel,'' Emerson agreed, struggling to control himself. ''I do beg your pardon, Quibell; my laughter was in extremely bad taste. But Petrie's eccentricities are a source of great amusement to a simple, straightforward chap like myself.''

Quibell's wide eyes shifted from Emerson, bareheaded under the baking sun, to me, and then to Ramses, who was giving the cat Bastet her daily lesson. ''Heel, if you please,'' he was saying, and the cat promptly fell in behind him.

But, as I have said, for all his blunt manners, Emerson has the kindest of hearts. After Selim had fetched the bottle of ipecacuanha, and a few other items I thought might be useful, Emerson told Quibell to call on us for anything he needed, and insisted upon lending him a donkey and an escort for the return trip. "Petrie thinks nothing of a six-mile walk," he said, slapping the young man on the back with such friendly emphasis that he tottered. "Neither do I, of course. Do it all the time. But in your weakened condition . . . Are you sure you won't rest awhile before returning? Mrs. Emerson would love to put you to bed and dose you."

"Thank you, Professor, but I must return at once. I am not the only sufferer, and the others are awaiting relief."

"Didn't I hear there was a young lady with Professor Petrie this year?" I inquired.

A blush spread across Mr. Quibell's cheeks. The addition of pink to the original green produced a remarkable tint, a sort of mottled puce. "There are three ladies, in fact," he replied. "My sister and—er—two others. It is primarily on her—on their account that I came."

Quibell trotted off, accompanied by one of our men. He really did look ill, and after he had vanished from sight I said to Emerson, "Perhaps I ought to go to Sakkara. When I think of the young ladies alone and ill—"

"Don't be such a busybody, Amelia," said my fond husband.

On the surface and in actual fact, Mr. Quibell's visit was one of those casual incidents that often befall people in our situation. Yet it had consequences of the most dramatic nature, and Quibell himself, the innocent instigator of some of them, would have been as surprised as any of us at what ensued.

The aforesaid consequences did not occur until late in the afternoon. We had finished excavation for the day. Emerson was more determined than ever that he and I should camp near the pyramid instead of staying in the house. His arguments were persuasive, and I had returned with him to the site after tea to inspect the pit he had found.

In Upper Egypt, where the river has cut a deep channel through the sandstone of the plateau, many tombs are dug into the sides of the cliffs. Properly cleansed and swept, the empty chambers make admirable accommodations. I am speaking, of course, of the upper chambers of the tombs, those that served as chapels; for the burial chambers themselves were far back in the cliffs, sometimes at the bottom of deep shafts. Here in the north, the majority of the tombs were of the type known as mastabas, after the stone benches whose shape their superstructures resembled. When the superstructures survived, they could be converted into quite attractive dwelling places, but as yet we had discovered nothing of that sort. The pit Emerson had discovered was just that—a nasty hole in the ground.

However, I enjoyed wandering hand in hand with Emerson across the barren plain. My amiable mood was only slightly marred when Emerson kept insisting that all we needed was a scrap of canvas to stretch over his wretched hole. At the least we required tents, and tents I was determined to have. If the necessary materials could not be procured in Menyat Dahshoor, I would simply have to make a trip to Cairo.

We had climbed a ridge in order to get a better view, and perhaps to discern in the shapes of the lengthening shadows some feature of the landscape that had not been visible under the direct rays of the sun. As always, my eyes were drawn to the west, where the pyramid slopes had deepened into bronze against the sunset. Nothing moved on that vast empty plain, and there was no sound to be heard except that of our voices, which had, I fear, risen to a considerable pitch during our discussion about the tents. When we stopped speaking, it was not because we had come to an agreement, but because we both realized no agreement would ever be reached. So pervasive was the ensuing silence that it was startling in the extreme to have it broken by the sound of a human voice.

We turned as one man (so to speak) and beheld, standing motionless on the level ground below the ridge, a woman's form. The gray-blue shadow blurred her features, and for one startled moment I felt as if I were seeing my own reflection in a dusty mirror. The dark mass of loosened hair was the same shade as my own; the high boots and full nether garment were like mine; the very shape of the body, belted tightly around the waist and swelling out above and below that constriction, was the image of my form.

I remembered the old legend of the doppelgänger, that eerie double whose appearance portends approaching death, and I confess that a momentary thrill of terror froze my limbs. Emerson was equally affected. A low "Oh, curse it" expressed the depth of his emotions and his arm held me close to his side, as if daring even the Grim Reaper to tear me from him.

The shadowy shape below swayed and shivered as when one tosses a stone into a pool of dark water. Slowly it sank forward and lay motionless.

The spell was broken. It was no spirit I had seen, but a living woman—living, at least, until that moment. Though how she had come there, and why, were mysteries almost as great as the ultimate mystery of life and death.

I scrambled down the slope, with Emerson close behind, and knelt beside the fallen form. The woman's costume was certainly similar to mine, but there was no other resemblance except for the color of her hair. Despite her deadly pallor, she was obviously some years younger than I—hardly more than a girl. A pair of gold-rimmed spectacles had been pushed aslant by the force of her fall, and the lashes that shadowed her ashen cheeks were long and curly.

"This is too cursed much," Emerson declared emphatically. "You know, Amelia, that I am the most tolerant and charitable of men; I don't mind lending a helping hand to the unfortunate, but two in one day is putting a strain on my good nature. Er—she is not dead, I hope?"

"She appears to have fainted," I said. "Lift her feet, Emerson, if you will be so good."

Emerson wrapped one big brown hand round the girl's slim ankles and hoisted them with such vigorous good will that her limbs formed a perfect right angle to her body. I corrected this little error, uncapped my water bottle, and sprinkled the girl's face.

"She doesn't stir," said Emerson, the tremor in his manly tones betraying the soft and tender side of his nature which few others besides myself are privileged to behold. "Are you sure—"

"Perfectly. Her pulse is steady and strong. You can let go her feet now, Emerson—no, no, don't drop them, lower them gently."

His anxiety relieved, Emerson reverted to his natural manner. "It really is too bad of Petrie," he grumbled. "He doesn't care if his subordinates drop like flies; oh no, he knows they will come running to us and interfere with *our* work. I will have a word to say to him next time we meet. Of all the infernal, inconsiderate—"

"You think this is one of Mr. Petrie's assistants?" I asked.

"Why, who else could it be? Quibell said the young ladies were ill; no doubt this girl has had second thoughts about working with that maniac Petrie. Shows considerable good judgment on her part. Why doesn't she wake up?"

"I believe she is coming round now," I said. In fact, I was certain the girl had been conscious for some time—and I had a good idea as to why she had wanted to conceal that state.

"Good." Emerson peered into the girl's face, breathing so anxiously that her spectacles misted over. I had replaced them after sprinkling her face, though it was doubtful that she could get any good from them; they appeared to be made of plain window glass.

"Naturally I am happy to assist any ill person," I said, watching the fluttering lashes and little movements of the lips that were the signs of returning consciousness. She really did it quite well; she must have taken part in a number of home theatricals. "But I hope she doesn't expect to stay on with us. Professor Petrie would probably consider we had deliberately lured away one of his assistants—"

"Since when have I cared about Petrie's absurd opinions? He thinks the worst of me whatever I do. It will be her decision, of course, but we could use an extra pair of hands. And it would be nice for you to have another woman about."

The ridiculousness of this remark made me chuckle. "I am hardly the sort that requires female companionship, Emerson. I have plenty to do as it is."

"No, Amelia, you do not. That active brain of yours is always seeking employment; that is why you keep meddling in police investigations and concocting nonsensical theories about master . . . about criminal conspiracies. Perhaps if you have a young woman to train in archaeology, you won't be so ready to go off chasing murderers. Good Gad, I have never seen anyone take so long to recover from a faint. Ought I not slap her cheeks or her hands?"

The girl took the hint. Having felt the vigor of Emerson's grasp, she was wise enough to anticipate what the effect of a gentle slap on the face would be. Her eyes opened.

"Where am I?" she said, with a deplorable lack of originality.

"Just where you hoped to be," Emerson exclaimed. "With me and Mrs. Emerson. Miss . . . What is your name?"

I waited with considerable interest for the young woman's reply. It was not long delayed; her brief hesitation would have been imperceptible to one who had no reason to suspect her motives. "Marshall. Enid Marshall."

Emerson sat down on a rock and beamed at her. "Well, Miss Marshall, you made a wise decision to leave Petrie; he is a fair enough scholar—I have known worse—but no sane person can live as he does. Though I don't think you showed good sense walking all the way from Sakkara in your condition."

"My—my condition?" the girl gasped.

"Never mind," Emerson went on. "Mrs. Emerson will fill you up with sulphur and ipecacuanha and you will be on your feet in no time. I will just carry you to our house—"

"No, thank you; I can walk perfectly well." With my assistance, Enid—to give her the name she had selected—rose to her feet. She looked a trifle dazed, and no wonder; Emerson had labeled her and pigeonholed her and explained her motives with such vigor that even a woman with less cause to conceal her true identity might have been left in doubt as to who she really was.

I, of course, knew who she was. Emerson had been misled, not only by his delight in playing a trick on Mr. Petrie, but by the pitiable inability of the male sex to see beyond a frilly frock and touch of lip rouge. The dark eyes that had snapped with laughter were now shadowed and fearful; the delicate features were drawn and colorless; but they were unquestionably those of the missing English lady, Miss Debenham.

Five

Emerson's enthusiasm faded rapidly when he realized that the arrival of his new assistant put an end to his plans for spending the night in a hole in the ground.

"Out of the question, Emerson," I said, over his querulous objections. "Miss Marshall must certainly spend the night with us, whatever she chooses to do tomorrow, and obviously she cannot be left alone in the same house with a young person of the opposite sex. You know, my dear, that no one despises meaningless social conventions more than I, but some limits of propriety cannot be ignored."

"Humph," said Emerson. "But, Amelia, Ramses will be at the house—"

"And so will we, Emerson. I promise you," I added, smiling at him over the girl's bowed head, "that first thing tomorrow I will take steps to ensure we do not spend another night at the house."

"Humph," said Emerson. But he said it more cheer-fully than the first time.

The young woman said nothing. She walked between us with drooping head, but with steps that were firm and steady. I had to commend her quickness; she must be in considerable confusion as to what her precise status was supposed to be, but she had the good sense to keep quiet and say nothing that would challenge Emerson's assumption.

Emerson is an ebullient person by nature; his fits of temper are brief, and as soon as they are over he immediately looks on the bright side. This was the case at the present moment. "Upon my word, Peabody, I am pleased about this," he declared. "In case Nemo does not suit, we have a substitute at hand. Miss Marshall surely can have no objection to giving us a hand with Ramses. It is remarkable how neatly things work out."

"I quite agree, Emerson. It is remarkable." In order to obtain tents, it would be necessary for me to make a trip to Cairo. I would then have an opportunity to make my inquiries into the murder of Kalenischeff. I had intended to do this all along, but now I had a reasonable excuse.

"Quite remarkable," I said.

The shades of night were falling fast by the time we reached the compound. The men had retreated into their hut; despite their superior education, none of them remained outside in the darkness if he could help it, for, as every Egyptian knew, night was when the demons were out in full force. We found Ramses alone in the sitting room, except for his ever-present feline companion. He had been writing at the table, but it was clear that our approach had not gone unnoticed, for he pushed his writing materials aside when we entered and rose, with no sign of surprise.

"Good evening, Mama; good evening, Papa; good evening, Miss—"

"Where is Mr. Nemo?" I asked.

"He was here a moment ago. I presume he has gone to his room." Ramses stepped forward, his hand extended. "We have not had the pleasure of meeting, I believe. Allow me to introduce myself. I am Mr. Walter Peabody Emerson."

"More familiarly known as Ramses," said Emerson, laughing. "This is Miss Marshall, my boy. She is a distinguished archaeologist, so you must treat her with respect."

"Hardly distinguished, Professor," the girl said quickly. "I am the merest beginner. So this is your son. What a fine little chap!"

She took Ramses' hand. A curl of the lip expressed Ramses' opinion of her description; feeling my gaze fixed upon him, he kept that opinion to himself, saying instead, "I was unaware of your academic qualifications, miss. May I inquire at what learned institutions you have studied?"

"No, you may not," I said. "Will you light the stove, Emerson? I am sure Miss Marshall would like a cup of tea. While the water is heating, I will show her to her room."

"I am afraid I am putting you to a great deal of trouble," the false Miss Marshall began. She broke off with a shriek and jumped back. The cat Bastet, who had been coiling her sinuous form around the girl's ankle, emitted a reproachful mew and butted her furry head against one scuffed little boot.

"It is only Ramses' cat," I said.

"The cat Bastet," Ramses elaborated. "She seems to

have taken a fancy to you, miss. That is unusual, and in my opinion you should be flattered by the attention, for animals, as it is well known, have a sixth sense that gives them—"

"Be quiet, Ramses," I said. The girl had raised a trembling hand to her brow, and I took the liberty of putting a supportive arm around her. "Miss Marshall is exhausted and can't be bothered with your unorthodox theories. Come into the next room, my dear. When you see your accommodations, you won't apologize for putting us out, I assure you."

Only a curtain separated the small adjoining chamber from the sitting room, and thus far the sole furnishings were a few empty crates. I assisted the young lady to one of them and sat her down.

"You will not be as comfortable here as in the sitting room," I said in a low voice. "But I could see your nerve was ready to give way, and believed you would be better alone."

"You are very good. Please don't let me keep you from your family—"

"Oh, I have no intention of leaving you." I took a seat on another crate. "There are a number of matters we must discuss without delay, if you expect to continue your masquerade."

The room was illumined only by the moonlight. The girl had shrunk back into the darkest shadows, but I heard her gasp sharply. She made a valiant effort to recover herself. "What do you mean, Mrs. Emerson?"

"My husband, though the most intellectual man of my acquaintance, is singularly naive about some things," I said. "But surely you did not suppose you could deceive me, did you—Miss Debenham?"

For a few seconds the silence was unbroken even by the sound of her breathing. Then a long sigh quivered through the air. "I knew I could never sustain the deception, Mrs. Emerson. I hoped only for a few days' respite, in order to decide whether to cast myself upon your mercy or take flight again. When the professor assumed I was someone else, I felt Fate had approved my venture."

Her voice was weary but calm, with no trace of the incipient hysteria it had displayed before. Obviously it was the strain of deceit that had unnerved her; her relief at finding herself free to speak candidly proved to me that she was essentially an honorable person.

"You read my letter, then," I said.

"Yes. I must admit, Mrs. Emerson, that my first reaction upon reading it was anger. I am a very headstrong and stubborn person. I was overindulged by doting parents who made no attempt to curb my faults of character; I am impatient of criticism, and too set on having my own way. It is a grievous flaw—"

"What one person terms 'headstrong,' another may call 'determined.' Strength of character is not a flaw. You sound as if you were quoting someone, Miss Debenham—no, excuse me, I must accustom myself to calling you Miss Marshall."

"Then—then you mean to allow me to continue my masquerade? You are willing to deceive your husband?"

"Oh, as to that, I would never deliberately deceive Emerson. If he chooses to deceive himself, it would be tactless in the extreme for me to correct his misapprehension, particularly since there is a distinct possibility that in the heat of the moment he might be moved to rash actions and/or expressions he would later regret. But, much as I would enjoy discussing the complexities of matrimony, a subject about which I have decided opinions, we must not stay here too long or even my dear Emerson will begin to wonder why we continue to sit in the dark. And Ramses . . . I will warn you about Ramses in due time. First it is essential that you tell me, as briefly but accurately as possible, precisely what happened on the night of the murder."

"I dined with Prince Kalenischeff," the girl said quietly. "We went to see the moonlight over the pyramids—"

"I saw you there. And afterwards?"

"We returned to the hotel. The prince said good night to me at the door of my room—"

"You did not invite him in?"

"I suppose I deserve that," she said, after a moment. "No, Mrs. Emerson, I did not."

"Continue, please. And be succinct."

"The safragi had given me your letter. I read it as I brushed my hair and, as I have said, I was angry—"

"You may omit your emotional reactions except in so far as they have bearing on the events of that night."

"Thank you. I tossed the letter aside. I prepared for bed. I went to bed. I fell asleep. Much later something woke me. Perhaps it was the sound of the door opening, or footsteps. A dark form came into the field of my vision. I recognized the prince. He moved quietly toward the bed. I got out of the bed. I fell to the floor. I lost consciousness. When I awoke the first light of dawn was brightening the window and I saw the prince lying dead across the bed. I went to my wardrobe. I took out—"

"Just a moment, if you please. I know I told you to be succinct, but that is carrying it a bit too far. Let us go back to your awakening in the middle of the night. How did you feel then? Alert and fully conscious, or unnaturally weak and drowsy?"

"I had barely strength enough to roll off the bed, away from him. How did you know?"

"I assume you were drugged, of course. Did you have anything to eat or drink before you retired?"

"I drank from the water bottle on the bedside table. The dry air makes one so thirsty. . . ."

"I thought so. Those damnable water bottles! One would think they had been invented for the convenience of burglars and murderers. Some kindly guardian angel roused you in time. . . . But it would not have mattered, you were never in any danger of *that* sort.

"Kalenischeff was lured to your room by a message purporting to come from you. He had made advances to you? No, you need not answer, I felt sure he had; he was a vain man with an inordinately high opinion of his attraction for the opposite sex. He would not be suspicious of a request for an assignation.

"The assassin was waiting for him. Fortunately for you, your awakening was brief and incomplete, for you were spared the horror of seeing Kalenischeff dispatched; and if you had seen the deed done, the murderer would have felt it necessary to dispose of you as well. Either you are unusually resistant to drugs or you did not drink much of the water; your guardian angel, still on active duty, again wakened you before you were meant to awaken. If matters had gone according to plan, you would have been discovered with the dead body of your presumed lover, and would have been placed under arrest. As it was, you had time to dress and creep out of the hotel unseen. The safragi had been bribed to leave his post, possibly by Kalenischeff himself. It was early morning, and if you avoided the public rooms, few people would see you, or recognize the frivolous, fashionable Miss Debenham in the costume you are presently wearing. You then went into hiding—never mind where, you can tell me about it later—and, remembering my offer of assistance, you determined to seek me out. I commend you on your presence of mind, Miss Marshall. Few women would have had the strength of character to behave so sensibly after such a frightful shock. Thank you. You told your story very nicely.''

''But—but—''

''Hush. We have not time for more.''

I was correct. A sound behind the curtain preceded by no more than a few seconds the appearance of Ramses. ''Papa wishes me to tell you that the water has boiled. He also wishes to know what—I omit the qualifying phrase, since it is one you have specifically forbidden me to repeat—what you are doing in here without a chair or a table or a lamp. I confess that my own curiosity on that point—''

''Will probably never be satisfied,'' I said, rising. I permitted myself that small jest, since I was in excellent humor. Matters were working out nicely. ''We are coming, Ramses.''

The girl caught my hand. ''But, Mrs. Emerson,'' she whispered. ''What am I to do? You believe me—''

''Yes.''

''How can you trust me? You don't even know me!''

''It is very simple,'' I murmured. ''I know who the murderer really is.''

''What?'' Her cry rang out. Ramses turned. Silhouetted against the light from the adjoining room, his thin limbs and mop of hair, and the inquiring tilt of his head, made him look exactly like an oversized vulture.

''Later,'' I hissed, and escorted Miss Marshall to the chair Emerson had set for her, and the cup of stewed tea he had prepared. Emerson's talents, though diverse, do not extend to the culinary arts.

*   *   *

Revising our sleeping arrangements was more complex than I had anticipated. I could not send Ramses up to sleep on the roof: he might decide to climb down the wall and go off on some peculiar errand of his own. Ramses seldom disobeyed a direct order, but he had a diabolical facility for finding a loophole in my commands.

Emerson and I could not sleep on the roof and leave the young lady and the young man down below. Emerson thought I was being uncharacteristically prudish, and said so at length. I did not bother to explain my true reasons, since they would have aggravated him even more. By a fortuitous combination of circumstances, Miss Marshall had eluded the Master Criminal. I could hardly leave her at the mercy of a man whom I strongly suspected of being the M.C.'s lieutenant.

The same objection applied to having Miss Marshall sleep on the roof. The only solution was for Emerson and me to place our mattresses in the sitting room, which adjoined the small chamber I had assigned to Miss Marshall. No one could reach her without stepping over our recumbent forms, for the only doorway opened out of the sitting room, and the window was too narrow to permit anyone to enter.

These arrangements were not concluded without a considerable amount of noise. Emerson is too well bred to swear in the presence of a lady, but his state of mind found expression in loud, broken ejaculations, and frequent cries of "Good Gad!" My first concern was to get Enid settled as soon as possible; she was clearly on the verge of total collapse, a normal reaction for one finding sanctuary after hours of nervous strain and physical exertion. A camp cot and blankets, a lamp and basic toilet articles were easily supplied (for I always equip my expeditions adequately). Not until this was accomplished and Enid was tucked into bed did I realize I had seen nothing of Mr. Nemo. A normally curious individual would have come out to see what was happening. I went to his room, but I knew in advance what I would find.

There was no lock on the crude wooden door, but Nemo had attempted to barricade it with the packing case that served as his table. People often underestimate my physical strength. I am only five feet tall and rather on the thin side (in most areas), but I keep myself fit; when I put my shoulder to the door, I had no difficulty shoving the empty case out of the way.

Nemo lay on his side, facing the door. A slight, sweet smile curved his lips; the flame of the tiny lamp on the floor in front of him was reflected in his unblinking eyes.

He had brought the vile instrument of his destruction with him. I reproached myself for neglecting to search his belongings, though in fact I had not seen that he had any. But it would have been easy for him to conceal the pipe and the opium in the folds of his robe. I found them almost at once; sunk in the euphoria of the drug, he had not thought to conceal them again. The pipe lay beside him, where it had fallen from his lax hand. Near it were a small tin box half-filled with a dark, treacly substance and a thin metal dipper, which was used to scoop up a small quantity of the opium. Dipper and opium were then held over a flame until the substance was cooked and reduced in size, after which it was dropped into the bowl of the pipe.

I knew the futility of attempting to speak to Nemo. He was far away, wandering in fields of illusion. I gathered up the tin of opium, the pipe, and the metal dipper;

blew out the lamp; and went quietly away.

The rest of the night passed without incident. Emerson snored. He seldom snores. When he does, it is usually deliberate.

I was up with the dawn, filled with my usual boundless energy. There was a great deal to be done that day, and I looked forward to it as a pugilist rejoices in the prospect of testing his strength against a worthy opponent. I moved quietly about my morning tasks, trying not to wake Emerson, for I thought it would be a good idea to have his breakfast ready when he woke. His temper would be tried often enough in the hours to come.

The absence of wooden flooring was annoying, for it enabled people to creep up on one unheard. My trained sixth sense, however, warned me that someone was watching me; expecting to see my ubiquitous son, I looked up with a frown and beheld instead the countenance of Mr. Nemo peering warily through the curtain we had rigged to give us a modicum of privacy.

He inspected the room from one corner to the other, as if he expected to see monsters lying in wait. "Will you step outside with me, Mrs. Emerson?" he asked in a whisper.

I had been about to suggest the same thing. A long, serious conversation with Mr. Nemo was high on my list of activities for the day. I was only surprised that he made no effort to avoid the scolding he must have known was coming. But perhaps instead of asking forgiveness he meant to go on the offensive and demand the return of his abominable drug apparatus. His grave expression and the firm set of his lips indicated determination rather than repentance.

Once outside, he beckoned me to follow him to the

north side of the house, where we could not be seen
from the doorway. Then he faced me.

"Mrs. Emerson, I am leaving your employ."

He had not shaved that morning, nor used a comb
and brush on his tumbled golden locks. (In fact, so far
as I knew, he did not have a comb or brush.) The effects
of the drug showed in his shrunken pupils and pale
cheeks. But months of degradation had not eradicated
all traces of the splendid young Englishman (or Scot)
he had once been. Shaved and brushed, dressed in a
proper suit, he would turn any woman's head.

"No, Mr. Nemo, you are not," I said.

His lips twisted. "How do you propose to stop me?"

"By force, if necessary." I leaned against the wall
and folded my arms. "A shout from me would bring
ten sturdy men who are sworn to obey my slightest
command. I do not include Emerson, since, although his
strength and devotion exceed all the others, he is rather
disoriented when he is suddenly roused from sleep, and
you might well elude him before he gets his wits in
order. I doubt, however, that you could fight off Abdullah and his sons. No," I went on calmly, as he took
a step toward me, his fists clenched. "Don't try to in-
timidate me, for I know you are incapable of laying
violent hands on a woman.

"You are not leaving my employ, Mr. Nemo. What—
do you suppose that, having once placed my shoulder
to the wheel and my nose to the grindstone, I will leave
the furrow unplowed? I have sworn to redeem you and
redeem you I will, with your cooperation or without it.
In principle, I am in full sympathy with the right of
every Englishman—or woman—or, come to that, any
man or woman of any nation . . . What was I about to
say?"

Nemo's frown had been replaced by a blank, almost

imbecile stare. "I haven't the slightest idea," he mumbled.

"Oh, yes. I believe firmly in the right of the individual to seek or leave employment whenever he or she chooses. Any infringement of that choice constitutes serfdom, and liberty is the inalienable right of humankind. However, in this case your right to liberty must be laid aside temporarily in favor of a higher good.

"Having made that plain, Mr. Nemo, I will proceed to the next point. Pay close attention, if you please. My determination to lift you out of the gutter was reinforced last night when I discovered you in the loathsome clutches of the devil's weed. It is not what you think," I went on, more gently, as he turned his head away, a flush of shame mantling his bristled cheeks. "That discovery proved to me that I had been mistaken in another, more important assumption. I am not often mistaken. In this case there was some excuse for me, since the circumstances were suspicious in the extreme.

"I knew full well that the man whose confederate I suspected you of being would never choose as a trusted aide any man whose loyalty or efficiency could be weakened by opium. You had said you were addicted, but in fact I had never seen you indulging in drugs. It makes a neat syllogism, you see. You are, as I know firsthand, a user of drugs. The Master Criminal does not admit drug addicts into his inner circle. (I make that assumption because only a fool would commit that error, and the Master Criminal is not a fool.) Therefore you are not—"

"The—who?" Nemo stammered.

"The Master Criminal. The mysterious individual who controls the illicit antiquities trade in Egypt. Don't tell me that during your sojourn in the underworld of Cairo you never heard of him."

"A beggar and drug addict is not taken into the confidence of a professional criminal," Nemo said thoughtfully. "But what you say is true; there is such a man. I have heard rumors of him. It was—er—the name you used that surprised me. I certainly never heard him called that."

"He has a name, then? What is it?"

"He has no name, only a variety of appellations. Those in his employ, I believe, refer to him as the Master. To others, less intimately associated with him, he is known as Sethos."

"Sethos! A curious name. You know nothing more?"

Nemo shook his head. "The men who work for the Master are the cream of the criminal crop. To be chosen by him is a mark of honor. Even those who are not in his employ are in deadly terror of him, and it is said that his revenge on a traitor is swift and horrible."

"Fascinating," I exclaimed. "I am deeply indebted to you for the information, Mr. Nemo. Please forgive me for suspecting you. Though it now appears I was, in a sense, paying you a compliment!"

Nemo did not return my smile. "You owe me no apology. What you have told me changes nothing, Mrs. Emerson. You are right, I would not touch a hair of your head, and your men could certainly overcome me; but you will have to bind me or imprison me to keep me here. I must and will go."

"I understand, Mr. Nemo. I know what has moved you to this decision. It is the arrival of the young lady."

Nemo's tanned cheeks paled. "You—you—"

"Looking from the window last night you saw her," I went on. "A flower of English womanhood, with the grace and charm that achieves its fullest perfection in our favored nation. Seeing her must have reminded you of your shame and of what you have lost."

Nemo raised a trembling hand to his brow. "You are a witch, Mrs. Emerson!"

"No, Mr. Nemo; only a woman, with a woman's heart. Our intellectual powers, never doubt it, are fully equal to those of the so-called stronger sex, but we have a greater understanding of the human heart. It was a woman who brought you to this, was it not?"

A muffled voice from the house interrupted the conversation at this interesting juncture. I took my watch from my pocket and inspected it. "Time is passing, Mr. Nemo. I must be about my business. We will discuss your situation at a future time. Until then I count on you to remain. The young lady will keep to her room today. You won't have to face her until I have spruced you up a bit and decided on a story to tell her. Have I your word not to run away?"

"You would take my word?" Nemo asked incredulously. "After I broke it?"

"You did not break it. You said you would try not to succumb." Another, more irate shout from within reminded me of my duties. "I must be off. I am going to Cairo today. I will see you this evening."

Nemo shrugged. "Until tonight, then. Beyond that—"

"That will do. Yes, Emerson. I am here; I am coming."

I hastened within.

When I set out shortly after breakfast, it was with the serene consciousness that I had dealt with all the outstanding emergencies. Enid had been warned that she must pretend weakness and keep to her room. We dared not risk her exposing her ignorance of archaeology, which would certainly occur within five minutes of her appearance at the dig. Mr. Nemo had been measured for a suit of clothes and sent off, with Ramses, to supervise the excavation of the causeway. Emerson had been soothed and fed and encouraged by my solemn promise that our bed that night would be under the open sky and the brilliant stars of the desert. (To be sure, a canvas roof would intervene between us and the open sky, brilliant stars, et cetera, but Emerson is particularly susceptible to poetic expressions of that nature. And I confess that I was myself peculiarly stimulated by the image thus evoked.)

I had sent Abdullah to hire a horse from the mayor of the village. It was the finest steed in the neighborhood, a charming little brown mare that was reported to be the apple of the sheikh's eye. Certainly the cost of her hire bore this out, as did her shining coat and the confidence with which she greeted me. I quite fell in love with her myself. Her high spirits matched my own; when she broke into a gallop I made no effort to restrain her, but abandoned myself to the joys of speed. I felt like one of the heroes of Anthony Hope or Rider Haggard, dashing to the rescue. (Their heroines, poor silly things, never did anything but sit wringing their hands waiting to be rescued.)

It seemed only a few moments before I saw the first of the monuments of Sakkara. Some energetic specimens of the tourist breed were already there, for next to Giza, Sakkara is the most popular excursion in the Cairo region. One of the guides told me where the archaeologists were working, and I was pleased to find Mr. Quibell on his feet, notebook in hand, copying inscriptions. After I had lectured him on the impropriety of standing in the hot sun too long, following his indisposition, I asked after the young ladies.

Quibell replied, with proper expressions of gratitude, that, thanks to my assistance, all were recovering. They expected to finish their work at Sakkara within a day or

two, after which they would join Petrie at Thebes. Miss
Pirie had particularly asked him to express her thanks
to me, if he should be fortunate enough to see me before
they left. (Again the young man's blush, as he mentioned the young lady's name, told me she would not
long retain it, if he had his way in the matter.)

I was relieved to hear of their imminent departure,
and pleased that I had had the foresight to stop by in
order to receive Quibell's thanks, for otherwise he might
have felt obliged to visit us again, and this would certainly have spelled disaster for Enid. I offered, in duty
bound, to examine the ladies; Quibell assured me, with
touching sincerity, that there was no need. Since I had
a long ride ahead, I did not insist.

We parted with the friendliest compliments, and I
proceeded northward to Giza, where I left the horse at
Mena House and hired a carriage for the trip to Cairo.
After completing my shopping, I arrived at Shepheard's
in time for a late luncheon, which I felt was well deserved.

Not that this pause in the day's occupations was
purely for sustenance and recreation—no, indeed. My
principal errand in Cairo was yet to be accomplished,
and as the first step, I needed to find out what the informed public knew about the murder. Even before ordering my repast, therefore, I told the waiter to ask Mr.
Baehler to join me, at his convenience, of course.

The dining room filled rapidly and I amused myself
by watching the tourists. They were a variegated
group—stout German scholars and smart English officers, shrill American ladies and giggling girls in the
custody of sharp-eyed mamas. At a nearby table was a
group of young Englishmen, and from the number of
"your lordships" and "my lords" that sprinkled their
conversation, it was not difficult to deduce that the pale,

effeminate-looking young man to whom the others deferred was a sprig of the aristocracy. Their clothing was a bizarre combination of fine English tailoring and local costumery—a striped silk *sudeyree*, or vest, with riding breeches, or a gold-embroidered *aba* over a tweed shooting suit. None of them had removed their fantastic headgear—turbans of cashmere and white silk shawls, or tasseled tarbooshes—and several were puffing cigars, though there were ladies present.

I was ashamed to share their nationality, but after they had swaggered out I was able to console myself with the thought that bad manners are not restricted to any one country; not long afterwards an elderly American lady entered the dining room, and her strident voice and loud complaints turned all eyes toward her. She was attended by a plain, timid female, apparently a maid or companion, and by a young man whose arm she held more in the manner of a prison guard than a frail woman requiring assistance. She was tall and heavy-set, and her voluminous black gown and veils were many years out of date. Her antique bonnet was trimmed with tiny jet beads; with each ponderous step a little shower of them fell, rattling like sleet on the floor.

From the celerity with which the headwaiter approached her I decided she must be very rich or very distinguished. He got short shrift for his pains; the old lady rejected the first table she was offered, demanding one nearer the window—which also happened to be nearer to me. She then criticized the cleanliness of the silverware, the temperature of the room, and the clumsiness of her attendants, all in tones that rang like a gong. Catching my eye, she shouted, ''Yes, you agree with me, don't you, ma'am?''

I turned my back and applied myself to my soup, and to the book I had brought with me—the new translation of Herr Erman's delightful account of *Life in Ancient Egypt*. Wandering through the barley fields with the happy peasants, I was soon so absorbed that Mr. Baehler had to touch me on the shoulder before I was aware of his presence.

For once, conversation with this pleasant man, who usually knew all the gossip about Cairo's foreign community, proved to be a waste of time. He knew no more than I—less, in fact, for he informed me that Miss Debenham's whereabouts were unknown. Her fiancé had arrived—

"Her what?" I exclaimed.

I am sure my voice was not raised much above its normal pitch, but for some reason all conversation in the dining room happened to stop just at that moment. The elderly American lady shouted, "What is it, ma'am? What's the matter, eh?"

"Her affianced husband," Mr. Baehler said softly.

"I know what the word means, Mr. Baehler." I picked up my spoon, which I had dropped onto the table in the stress of the moment. "I was not aware that Miss Debenham was engaged to be married."

"Nor was I, until he came here looking for a room. Unfortunately, I was unable to accommodate him on such short notice. He said he had been hunting in the Sudan and, upon hearing the shocking news, had at once hastened to the lady's side."

"Only to find she had disappeared. He must be in great distress."

"No doubt," Baehler said expressionlessly.

"But that is a curious story, do you not think? First he leaves his affianced wife to disport herself alone in Cairo while he is amusing himself in the Sudan. Then he rushes to assist her—but surely not from the Sudan. It would take weeks for the news to reach an isolated camp, and for him to make the return journey.''

Baehler looked uncomfortable. ''That had occurred to me, Mrs. Emerson. I can only assume the gentleman was on his way back, or had actually arrived in Cairo, when he learned of the murder.''

''Humph. I must speak to him. Where is he staying?''

''I sent him to the D'Angleterre. Whether he was successful in obtaining accommodations there, I cannot say. And now, Mrs. Emerson, if you will excuse me—''

''Miss Debenham is not a murderess, Herr Baehler. And I intend to prove it.''

Baehler, who had risen to his feet, took the hand I extended and raised it gallantly to his lips. ''Mrs. Emerson, if you set out to prove the sun rises in the west, you could certainly convince me. I must return to my duties now. My respectful compliments to your distinguished husband and to Master Ramses.''

After he had left the room, I thought of several questions I had meant to ask, including the name of the man who called himself Miss Debenham's fiancé. However, upon further consideration, I decided I had better ask Miss Debenham herself—and ascertain as well why she had deceived me. The young lady had a good deal of explaining to do if she wished to retain my good will.

I gathered up my parcels, my parasol, and my handbag. As I was leaving, the old American lady shouted, ''Good day to you, ma'am. It has been a pleasure talking with you.'' Realizing that she must be a trifle senile, I gave her a pleasant smile and waved my parasol.

Once outside the hotel, I bargained for a carriage and had just got in when one of the vendors accosted me. ''Flowers for the lady,'' he cried, thrusting a bouquet into my hands.

''I don't want flowers,'' I said in Arabic.

''They are for you, sitt,'' the fellow insisted. ''You

are the Sitt Hakim, wife to Emerson Effendi? Yes, yes, I know you; a gentleman told me to give these to you.''

The nosegay was a charming ensemble of red rosebuds and fragrant mimosa, framed in green leaves and tied with a silk bow. The flower seller bowed and retreated without even waiting for the usual tip, so I had no choice but to keep the flowers, which I was not reluctant to do, for I have a particular fondness for roses of that shade. I decided they must have come from Mr. Baehler—a token of friendly esteem, and an apology for his somewhat abrupt departure. It was the sort of gesture a gentleman of his refined courtesy might make.

The carriage bore me swiftly to my destination, the Administration Building on the Place Bab el-Khalk. Until recently the constabulary of Cairo had been under the benevolent supervision of a British Inspector General. It was still under British supervision; only the title of the administrator had been changed, to that of Adviser. Sir Eldon Gorst, who was a personal acquaintance, held the position; but when I asked for him I was told he was not in his office, and I was referred to one of the officers on his staff.

It was with some chagrin that I found myself in the presence of Major Ramsay, the least intelligent and most unsympathetic of Sir Eldon's subordinates. On the occasion of our last meeting, at a social gathering at the Consulate, I had taken the opportunity of correcting some of his ill-informed opinions on the subject of women, their rightful position in society, and the unjust laws that prevented them from assuming that position. I would never accuse a British officer of rudeness, but Major Ramsay's responses had come as close to that condition as a British officer could come; and toward the end of the discussion Emerson had said something about punching someone in the jaw. It was only one of

Emerson's little jokes, but Major Ramsay had no sense of humor. I was sorry to see, from the unsmiling curtness of his greeting, that he still harbored a grudge.

I explained the reason for my visit. Ramsay looked at me severely. "I had assumed you came in order to correct or amend the statement you originally made to the officer in charge of the investigation, Mrs. Emerson. Surely you know I cannot discuss the conduct of a police inquiry with a member of the general public."

I settled myself more comfortably in the hard chair and placed my parasol across my lap. "Oh, yes, Major Ramsay, that is an admirable rule so far as it goes, but it does not apply to *me*. Professor Emerson and I can hardly be called members of the public, much less the general public."

"You—" Ramsay began.

"I am certain that by now you have reached the same conclusion that was immediately apparent to me; namely, that Miss Debenham is innocent. Have you any other suspects?"

Ramsay bit his lip. His long, melancholy countenance was incapable of expressing subtle alterations in the intellectual process (assuming he had an intellectual process), but it was not difficult for me to follow his thoughts. He disliked telling me anything substantive, but hoped that by doing so he could gain information.

The latter motive triumphed over the former. Pursing his lips, as if he had tasted something sour, he said, "We are looking for a man to assist us with our inquiries. An Egyptian—a beggar, in fact. Perhaps you noticed him outside Shepheard's."

An unpleasant premonition crept over me. Naturally I did not display any sign of perturbation, for *my* countenance only expresses my intellectual process when I allow it to do so.

"A beggar," I repeated, smiling ironically. "I noticed several dozen of them."

"Taller than the average, sturdily built; wearing a pale-blue robe and a saffron turban."

"I can't say I recall such an individual. Why do you suspect him?"

"I didn't say we suspected him, only that we wish to question him."

And that, dear Reader, was all I was able to learn. Ramsay absolutely refused to elaborate or add to his statement.

Once outside the building, I found myself in a rare state of indecision. I was tempted to call on Sir Evelyn Baring, the Consul General, and request his cooperation, which I surely would have received, since we were old friends. But the afternoon was wearing on, and I had wasted too much time with the imbecile Ramsay. I would have enjoyed a delightful ride home under the desert moon, but I knew Emerson would fly into a rage if I did not return by sunset. Emerson is completely fearless where his own safety is concerned, but the mere thought of danger to me reduces the dear fellow to a positive jelly.

As I stood debating with myself, I heard a voice pronounce my name in questioning accents. Turning, I found myself face to face with a stranger. "Face to cravat" would be more accurate, for the man was eight or ten inches taller than I. Stepping back in order to see his face, I beheld a lean, hawk-nosed countenance atop a wiry body dressed rather oddly, for that climate, in a caped tweed coat. Tinted spectacles protected his eyes from the glaring sun. In his hand he held a matching tweed cap.

"I am Mrs. Emerson," I acknowledged.

His thin lips parted in a pleasant smile. "I recognized

you from the portraits which have appeared at various times in the newspapers. Though, if I may say so, they did not do you justice.''

"Newspaper photographs seldom do. Perhaps I have seen your features similarly reproduced. They seem familiar to me, Mr.--?''

"Gregson. Tobias Gregson. Yes, I have been featured in the popular press from time to time. I am a private investigator—a well-known private investigator, to quote the same source.''

"That must account for it. What cases have you investigated, Mr. Gregson?''

"Many of my cases are of the most secret nature, involving sensitive family scandals or delicate government negotiations. However, you may recall the matter of the Amateur Mendicant Society? Or the Camberwell poisoning case?''

"I can't say that I do.''

"No matter. I don't want to detain you, Mrs. Emerson; I ventured to address you only because I believe you have an interest in my present investigation.''

I looked at him more closely. "Have you been called in to assist the police in the murder of Kalenischeff?''

Gregson smiled contemptuously. "I am not on good terms with the official police, Mrs. Emerson. Professional jealousy ... But I will say no more. No, I happened to be in Egypt on another matter—a related matter, as it turned out. The case has its points of interest.''

"It does. No doubt your long experience in criminal matters has already given you some hint as to the identity of the guilty party.''

"Obviously it was not Miss Debenham," Gregson said coolly.

"Obviously. But who?''

Gregson glanced from side to side and lowered his voice. "I am endeavoring to discover the whereabouts of a certain beggar who was seen hanging about the hotel on the night of the murder."

"Ah," I said, in equally mysterious tones. "A tall, well-built man wearing a yellow turban?"

"I might have known the famous Mrs. Emerson would be on the same trail," said Gregson, with a look of respectful admiration.

"Not at all. I heard of him from Major Ramsay."

"Ramsay is an idiot. He doesn't know what you and I know."

"And what is that, Mr. Gregson?"

"That the beggar is not a beggar at all, but an emissary of that genius of crime, that master of deceit—"

"What?" I cried. "How do you know of *him?*"

"I have my methods, Mrs. Emerson. Suffice it to say that I do know of this enigmatic personage, to whom you referred, in a newspaper interview, as the Master Criminal. I have set myself the task of tracking him down."

"I have set myself the same task, Mr. Gregson."

"We must confer, Mrs. Emerson."

"I would like you to meet my husband, Mr. Gregson."

"I—I beg your pardon?"

I smiled, and explained the apparent non sequitur. "I was not changing the subject, Mr. Gregson. Emerson and I are equal partners, in our criminal investigations as in our professional and marital activities; perhaps you can convince him, as I have not yet succeeded in doing, that capturing the Master Criminal is a matter of paramount importance."

"I see. I will, of course, be honored to meet Professor Emerson."

"I must be off now, or that same Professor Emerson will be rushing to Cairo in search of me. Are you staying at Shepheard's, Mr. Gregson?"

"No. But a letter left with the concierge will reach me."

"We are at Dahshoor, should you care to call on us." I gave him my hand in farewell, but when I would have taken it back, he held on. "Please don't hurry away, Mrs. Emerson. May I not offer you a cup of tea or a lemonade?"

It was a tempting suggestion, for I was anxious to learn all I could from this remarkable individual. As I debated with myself, my wandering gaze found an object that caused me to doubt the evidence of my own eyes. I snatched my hand from the warm clasp of Mr. Gregson and started in pursuit; but my quarry mounted a horse and galloped away before I could speak to him. When I returned from a hasty investigation of the nearby streets and lanes, Mr. Gregson had also vanished. My carriage awaited; I directed the driver to take me to Mena House.

I had not got a good look at the horseman, but one physical feature had been unmistakable—the red-gold waves of hair that shone in the sun like a brazen helmet. I would not have been surprised—though I would have been deeply grieved—to discover that Nemo had broken his word. He was only a weak male creature, after all. But if he was *only* a weak male creature, a beggar and a drug taker—what was he doing outside police headquarters, wearing a suit of the best British tailoring?

Six

Despite the best efforts of my noble steed, the stars were blossoming upon the blue velvet of the sky before I reached Dahshoor. The afterglow washed the sloping sides of the pyramids in an eerie pinkish light, but the desert floor was veiled in twilight; long before I made out his form, I heard the well-loved voice: "Peabody! Peabody, is that you? Answer me, curse it!"

I urged my horse into a gallop. Emerson came running to meet me, and before long I was held in his tender embrace.

"What the devil do you mean being so late?" he demanded. "I was about to send a search party after you."

"Please, Emerson. If you must shout, wait until your lips are farther from my ear."

Emerson mumbled something unintelligible into the orifice in question. Eventually the little mare politely

requested the attention she well deserved by nudging
me with her velvety nose, and I suggested to Emerson
that we save further demonstrations of welcome for a
more suitable time and place.

"Yes, quite," said Emerson. "Come and see our new
sleeping quarters, Peabody."

"The tents have been delivered, then? I particularly
requested Ali to send them out immediately."

"I don't know whether he sent them immediately, but
they arrived a few hours ago. I had Nemo put up our
tent—"

"Nemo!"

"Yes, and he did it very deftly, too. What do you
think?"

From what I could see in the gloaming, the structure
appeared to be properly constructed. I accepted Emerson's pressing invitation to inspect the interior, and it
was only after a somewhat lengthy and thoroughly satisfactory interval that I was able to turn my attention to
a matter I had meant to pursue immediately upon my
arrival. Emerson politely held the tent flap aside for me,
and as we walked hand in hand toward the house I
asked, "When did Nemo leave, Emerson?"

"Why, not at all, Peabody, unless he has taken to his
heels within the past half hour. I left him with Ramses.
. . . What did you say, Peabody?"

"I only uttered a brief ejaculation, fearing for a moment that I was in danger of tripping over a stone."

"Oh," said Emerson. "What were we talking
about?"

"I was about to say that you should have had Mr.
Nemo erect both tents."

"Amelia, I do not intend that Ramses shall sleep in
a tent."

"It is not for Ramses, it is for Miss Marshall."

"Oh, curse it, Amelia, why the devil—"

"I told you, Emerson. It is not suitable—"

He interrupted me, of course. We continued our discussion as we walked to the house. The inevitable conclusion having been reached, Emerson shook himself and said calmly, "It is good having you back, my dear Peabody. The place is just not the same without you. I only hope I have not made a mistake in taking that young woman on my staff. Can you believe she kept to her room all day? I am afraid she is not up to the work. I am afraid she is sickly. Night air is bad for sickly persons—"

"The night air is just what she needs to complete her cure. I promise you, she will be ready for work tomorrow."

"Humph," said Emerson.

Before we left England, Ramses had informed me that he had decided to write an introductory Egyptian grammar, the volumes available being, in his opinion, completely inadequate. I agreed with his evaluation, but I would have encouraged the endeavor in any case, since I hoped it would help to keep him out of mischief. I was pleased, that evening, to find him busily scribbling, with the cat Bastet sitting on the table acting as a paperweight.

"Where is Mr. Nemo?" I asked, after greetings had been exchanged.

"In his room. I presume," said Ramses, picking up the pen he had laid aside upon my entrance, "that he is smoking opium. I asked him if I might participate, but he—"

"Ramses!" I exclaimed. "You are not to take opium!"

"I don't recall that you ever told me I must not, Mama."

"You are right. I neglected to make that observation. Consider it made now. Whatever put such an idea into your head?"

Ramses fixed me with his wide, serious gaze. "It is a question of scientific experiment, Mama. A scholar should not depend upon descriptions of results; in order fully to assess them he must have a firsthand acquaintance with—"

"Never mind; I should have known better than to ask. Ramses, if you . . . You are strictly forbidden . . . Oh, good Gad, I have no time to counter your Machiavellian arguments. I must see how Miss Marshall is getting on. But please bear in mind . . . Emerson, I leave you to talk to Ramses."

"Listen to Ramses" was more like it; the boy launched into a long speech, in which Emerson's feeble "But, my boy—" was swallowed up like a scrap of paper in a whirlpool. At least I was confident that while the discussion continued, I could talk to Enid without being overheard.

She was lying on the cot when I entered, her face turned to the wall; but when she saw who it was she leaped up with the energy and grace of a tigress.

"I am going mad with boredom," she hissed. "I would prefer a prison cell to this solitude—this suspense—and that abominable child popping in to ask me questions about the funerary monuments of the Fourth Dynasty—"

"I hope you didn't attempt to answer them?"

"How could I? I didn't understand one word in ten." After a moment, the fiery rage on her face faded and she collapsed onto the thin mattress, her face crumpling like that of a frightened child. "Forgive me, Mrs. Emerson. I owe you so much—but inactivity and ignorance of what is happening prey on my mind."

"I would feel much the same. Your inactivity is at an end. Tomorrow you will join us on the dig. Don't worry about betraying your ignorance. You will be acting as my assistant, and I will make sure you are in no difficulty. If Emerson asks you a question you cannot answer, simply say, 'Mr. Petrie is of the opinion . . .' You won't get any further. Emerson will either interrupt you or stalk off in a rage. If Ramses questions you—which he almost certainly will—you need only ask him what *he* thinks. The only difficulty then will be to get him to stop talking. Have you any questions?"

"Any? I have a hundred." Her eyes flashed. "You went to Cairo today. What has happened? Have the police—"

"The police are idiots. You must remain here until I have solved the case and made it possible for you to resume your rightful position."

"You said you knew—"

"I said I knew who the murderer of Kalenischeff is. I spoke no more than the truth, Miss Marshall. The only trouble is, I don't know who he . . . Let me rephrase that. I know who he is: but I do not know . . . Good Gad, this is more complex than I realized. The murderer is the leader of a criminal network of which Kalenischeff was a member. You follow me so far? Good. Unfortunately, although I have met the individual in question, I don't know his true identity. He is a master of disguise."

Enid looked doubtfully at me. "Do I understand you correctly, Mrs. Emerson? Are you saying that the murderer is a sort of Master Criminal?"

"Excellent," I cried. "I applaud your intelligence, Miss Marshall. I knew from the first that you and I would be in accord."

"Thank you, ma'am. Forgive me if I do not appear

to be encouraged by the information. From what I have heard about master criminals, they are geniuses of crime and are not easily brought to justice."

"Quite true. However, you may be sure that *this* genius of crime will be brought to justice and by *me*. It may take a little while, though, so you must be patient. Here are a few personal items I purchased for you in Cairo." I handed her the parcel. "I apologize for the poor quality of the garments; ready-made clothing is not of the best, but I did not feel I could march into Shepheard's and collect your luggage."

"You are more than kind," she murmured, her head bent over the parcel.

"Not at all. I have the bill and expect you will reimburse me as soon as you are able."

Enid looked up with a smile on her lips and a tear in her eye, as the poet has it. All at once she flung her arm around my neck and hid her face against my shoulder. "Now I begin to understand why people speak of you as they do," she murmured. "My own mother could have done no more for me. . . ."

My heart went out to the girl, but I knew that an overt expression of sympathy would bring on the flood of tears she was trying valiantly to repress. I therefore attempted to relieve the situation with one of my little jokes. Patting her hand, I remarked with a smile, "I doubt that even your dear mama could have been as useful in the present situation; a lady so well bred as she would not have had my extensive acquaintance with hardened criminals and their habits. Now, now, my dear, cheer up. I have a question for you. Why didn't you tell me you were engaged to be married?"

She raised her head, astonishment writ large upon her features. "But I am not. Whoever told you that?"

"Mr. Baehler, the manager of Shepheard's Hotel.

Your affianced husband is in Cairo, burning to assist you."

"I cannot understand . . . Oh. Oh, heavens. It must be Ronald. I should have known!"

"You owe me an explanation, my dear girl. Who the dev—Who is Ronald?"

"The Honorable Ronald Fraser. We grew up together, Ronald and I and . . ." Her lips closed. She sat for a moment in silence, as if thinking how best to explain. Then she said slowly, "Ronald is my second cousin—the only kin I have now. He has no other claim on me."

"Why would he call himself your fiancé, then? Or did Mr. Baehler misunderstand?"

Enid tossed her head. "He asked me to marry him. I refused. But it would be like Ronald to assume I would change my mind. He has a habit of believing what he wants to believe."

"Ah, I see. Thank you for your confidence, Miss Marshall. And now I think you had better put on the dress I brought you and join us for a cup of tea and a little conversation. Afterwards we will retire to our tents. Did I mention you will be sleeping in a tent tonight? I am sure you will enjoy it. Much more pleasant than this stuffy room."

When I returned to the sitting room, Emerson was still trying to explain to Ramses about the horrors of opium addiction. He did not appear to have made much headway. Ramses remarked, "May I say, Papa, that the poignant description you have just delivered verges on the classic? However, you will permit me to point out that there is no danger whatever that I would succumb to the temptations you have so eloquently described, since mental lethargy is not one of my—"

Emerson shot me a look of agonized appeal.

"Ramses," I said, "you are not, under any circumstances whatever, to smoke, eat, or imbibe any form of opium."

"Yes, Mama," Ramses said resignedly.

I then went to have a look at Mr. Nemo. I did not expect to find him indulging in the occupation Ramses so longed to experience, since I had his supply of opium and did not suppose he had money to buy more. I found him undrugged, and in a very bad temper. He looked up from the book he was holding and glared at me.

"I am glad to see you improving your mind, Mr. Nemo," I said encouragingly.

Nemo tossed the book aside. "I don't want to improve my mind. I had no choice. Haven't you anything to read except books on Egyptology?"

"You should have asked Ramses. He has brought along some of his favorite thrillers—a surprisingly low taste for a person of his erudition. Never mind that now, I have a task for you. The moon is still bright; can you see well enough to put up the other tent? I intend the young lady to sleep there tonight."

"I would work in total darkness if it would get her away from the house," Nemo said gruffly. "What is she doing here? How long is she going to stay?"

"She is an archaeologist, Mr. Nemo. She has come to help with the digging."

"Is that what she told you?" Nemo laughed harshly. "She has taken you in, Mrs. Emerson—you, of all people! She knows nothing of archaeology."

"Are you acquainted with the young lady?"

Nemo averted his eyes. "I saw her in Cairo—another vain, empty-headed society girl. Everyone knew who she was. Everyone saw her with that vile—that contemptible—"

"Language, Mr. Nemo. Language."

"I was not going to finish the sentence. I don't care . . . I don't care about anything. I only want to be left alone. You took my opium, didn't you? I don't blame you; you had every right. But the moment I get my hands on any money, I will buy more. I cannot trust myself. You cannot trust me. Let me go back to the gutter from which you took me."

I was not moved by his appeal, though I knew it came from the heart. The young do take themselves so seriously, poor things, and they tend to express themselves in theatrical parlance.

I sat down on the cot beside him. "Mr. Nemo, you are in deeper trouble than you know. If you return to your gutter, you will be removed from it forthwith, by the police. Are you honestly ignorant of the fact that the vile—that Kalenischeff was murdered the night before last, and that you are one of the prime suspects?"

Nemo's reaction ended my suspicions of him once and for all. His look of abject astonishment might have been feigned, but the dark blood that flooded his haggard cheeks was a symptom beyond the skill of the most accomplished thespian.

"I know you didn't kill him," I said. "I am going to take you into my confidence, Mr. Nemo. I am going to share with you a secret unbeknownst even to my husband and—and, I *hope*, my son, although with Ramses one can never be certain."

With a mighty effort Mr. Nemo got control of himself. "I am deeply honored, madam. To tell me something even the professor does not know—"

"I really have no choice, Mr. Nemo, since you already know it—the young lady's true identity. The murdered man was found in her room. Fortunately for her, she fled before the police could apprehend her, but she is also a suspect. I have reason to believe she may be in even greater danger from another source. Until I can find the real murderer, she must remain incognito and in concealment. Admittedly her relationship with Kalenischeff was indiscreet, but I am convinced it was no worse than that. She needs your help; she does not deserve your scorn. Well?''

"I am in a daze of disbelief," Nemo exclaimed. "I knew nothing of this! I *was* at the hotel that night. I followed—that is to say—I followed my own inclinations. . . . But I had every intention of keeping my appointment for the morning. However, after—after a while I changed my mind again. That is not atypical of drug users, you know. There seemed to be no sense in waiting there for hours, and I had some notion of showing my independence by making my own way to Dahshoor. . . . But if I told that story to the police—''

"It would sound very suspicious," I assured him.

"I suppose so." Nemo brushed a lock of shining copper hair from his brow. "Yet it seemed reasonable at the time. I swear to you, Mrs. Emerson, I did not kill the rascal! And how anyone could suppose that she—a girl like that—why, she is incapable of stepping on a beetle, much less murdering a man in cold blood!''

"Your incoherent exclamations testify to your good heart but are not of much assistance otherwise," I said, rising. "Our task is to capture the real murderer of Kalenischeff, thus freeing both you and Miss Debenham from suspicion. He is the genius of crime of whom we spoke earlier—the man known as Sethos. Are you with me?''

"Every step of the way!" His fists clenched, his eyes glowed. "Wherever it may take us. Into danger, into death—''

"I don't intend to let it take us that far. First I want

you to set up that tent for Miss Marshall, as she has chosen to be called."

Mr. Nemo wilted. "I dare not leave my room," he muttered. "I don't want her to see me. Not like this . . ."

"Then I suggest you creep up the stairs to the roof and lower yourself to the ground. It should be easy for a healthy young man. Once we have left the house, you can safely return. Remember, I am counting on you to watch over Ramses tonight. I doubt that our adversaries would dare enter the compound, but Ramses is apt to take it into his head to go exploring while his papa and I are out of the way. I have brought you a suit of clothing. Bathe, shave, brush your hair (the necessary implements are in this parcel), and let me see you tomorrow looking like an English gentleman."

I left him looking like a blooming idiot, as Emerson might have said (though Emerson would probably have employed a more colorful adjective). I have found that people are often struck dumb with amazement at the quickness of my intellect. However, I was confident that he would do as I had asked. By appealing to his gallantry in assisting a lady in distress I had struck at the deepest chords in an Englishman's nature, and I did not doubt he would rise to the occasion.

Enid wisely waited until she heard my voice before drawing the curtain aside and joining us in the sitting room. Emerson greeted her with hearty good will.

"I am glad to see you on your feet again, Miss Marshall. If you feel any signs of a recurrence, you must tell Mrs. Emerson at once so she can pump you full of ipecacuanha. First thing tomorrow we will begin excavating at the base of the pyramid. Perhaps you can tell me—"

I thought it wise to intervene. "First, Emerson, tell

me what progress you made today. Have you discovered any traces of the causeway?"

Emerson scowled. "Nothing but a few bricks. I don't doubt that the causeway once ran along that line, but the local looters have removed every scrap of stone. It is a waste of time to go on. Instead I will begin at the pyramid and work out from there. I want Miss Marshall to take charge of one group of diggers and—"

Consternation ruffled the serenity of the girl's brow, and again I came to her rescue. "I think it would be better for her to work with me for a few days, Emerson—to get the hang of our methods, if you will excuse the slang. I propose to have a look at the subsidiary pyramid. It shouldn't take long to determine whether there is anything left in the burial chamber. If necessary, we can hire a few more men."

"I don't know, Peabody," Emerson began. But I did not hear his objections; for, out of the corner of my eye, I had seen Ramses close his mouth. His mouth was usually open, speaking or attempting to speak; the sudden compression of his lips would have passed unnoticed by a casual observer, but years of experience had taught me not to ignore the slightest change in that impassive though juvenile countenance. I promised myself I would have a word with Master Ramses. He knew something about the small pyramid, possibly from the illicit digging he had done at Dahshoor the year before.

"Well then, that is settled," Emerson said. "Er—it is getting late, don't you think?"

"No, not really," I said absently, for I was still thinking about the duplicity of my son. "Where are the rest of the things I bought today?"

Emerson indicated an untidy heap in the corner of the room. "Well," I said with a sigh, "we had better sort them out. Some will have to be taken to the tents. I also brought a few small items with me in the saddle bags. Where . . ."

Eventually I found them on the mastaba outside, where Abdullah had dumped them before returning the mare to her owner. Shaking my head, I carried them inside. My poor little nosegay had been crushed by Abdullah's careless handling. Emerson glanced at it as I put it to one side. "Buying yourself posies, Amelia?"

"No indeed. It was a gift from a gentleman," I said jestingly. Not that I wanted to arouse Emerson's jealousy, for such tricks are unworthy of an affectionate spouse. However, a little stirring up never hurts a husband.

Emerson only grunted. "Baehler, I suppose. These Frenchmen—"

"He is not French, Emerson. He is Swiss."

"It is the same thing."

"In fact, I am not certain of the identity of the kind giver. The flowers were handed to me by a vendor as I left the hotel. Poor things, they were so pretty. . . . Here, Emerson, smell the fragrance."

I thrust them at him with playful impetuosity, so that the lower part of his face was quite smothered by the fading blossoms. Emerson's eyes bulged. With a cry he struck at my hand. The flowers fell to the floor, and Emerson began jumping up and down on them.

Miss Marshall leaped from her chair and retreated to the farthest corner of the room, staring. Knowing Emerson, I did not share her alarm, but I considered his reaction exaggerated, and I did not hesitate to say so. "Emerson, Mr. Baehler only meant to make a gallant gesture. You really must—"

"Gallant?" Emerson glared at me, and with a start of horror I saw that his brown cheek was disfigured by a creeping trail of blood. "A gallant gesture, upon my word," he cried. "Inserting a poisoned insect or an asp into a bouquet!" He resumed jumping up and down on the flowers. If a beaten earth floor could have reverberated, this one would have done so. "When my face—thump—turns black—thump—remember—thump—I gave my life—thump—for you!"

"Emerson, my dearest Emerson!" I rushed to his side and attempted to lay hold of him. "Do stop jumping; violent physical activity will increase the rapidity of the movement of the poison through your veins!"

"Hmmm," said Emerson, standing still. "That is a good point, Peabody."

My heart pounded in profound agitation as I turned his face to the light. The wound was no more than a scratch, and it had already stopped bleeding. Shallow and uneven, it did not in the least resemble the bite of a venomous reptile or insect. Yet my tender anxiety was not entirely assuaged until I heard Ramses remark calmly, "There is no animal life of any kind here, Papa. I believe this bit of metal must have scratched you. It seems exceedingly unlikely—"

Emerson flung himself at Ramses. "Drop it at once, my boy!"

Ramses eluded him with eellike sinuosity. "I am confident there is no danger, Papa. The object is—or was, until you trampled it underfoot—a trinket of some kind. The material appears to be gold."

Gold! How often in the course of human history has that word trembled through the air, rousing the strongest of passions! Even we, who had learned in the course of our archaeological endeavors that the smallest scrap of broken pottery may be more important than jeweled treasures—even we, I say, felt our pulses quicken.

Ramses held the scrap near the lamp. The sensuous shimmer of light along its surface proved him right.

"I don't like you holding it, my boy," Emerson said nervously. "Give it to Papa."

Ramses obeyed, remarking as he did so, "Your fears for my well-being are, I assure you, Papa, without foundation. Mysterious poisons unknown to science are rare indeed; in fact, I believe I am safe in asserting that they exist only in sensational fiction. Even the most virulent substances in the pharmacopoeia require dosages of several milligrams in order to ensure a fatal result, and if you will stop and consider the matter for a moment, you will agree that it would be impossible for a bit of metal this size to contain enough—"

"You have made your point, Ramses," I said.

Emerson turned the twisted metal over in his fingers. "It appears to be a ring," he said in a quiet voice.

"I do believe you are correct, Emerson. How very odd! Wait—turn it this way. I caught a glimpse of something—"

"There are a few hieroglyphic signs still decipherable," said the shrill voice of my infuriating offspring. "They were stamped upon the bezel of the ring, which had the shape of the cartouche used to enclose royal names. The alphabetic hieroglyph for *n* was at the bottom; above it you will see the form of an animal-headed god, followed by two reed signs. The name is unquestionably that of Sethos, either the first or the second pharaoh of that name, and I would surmise—"

"Sethos!" I cried. "Good Gad—can it be—but it must be! That he would dare—that he would show such consummate—such incredible effrontery—that—that—"

Emerson took me by the shoulders and shook me so vigorously that quantities of hairpins flew from my head. "You are hysterical, Peabody," he shouted.

counter with the Master Criminal during the previous season. He declined with a degree of acerbity even greater than the mention of this person's name generally produced, so I took the task on myself.

"You know, of course, Miss Marshall, about the deplorable trade in illicit antiquities. Owing to the vast number of buried tombs and cities, it is impossible for the Department of Antiquities to guard all of them, especially since the locations of many are not known. Untrained diggers, both native and foreign, lured by the high prices such antiques command, carry out digs of their own, often neglecting to keep the careful records that are essential if we—"

"If she already knows it, why are you telling her about it?" Emerson demanded. "The facts are known to every schoolchild, much less a trained excavator like Miss Marshall."

I laughed lightly. "Quite right, Emerson. I have delivered the lecture so often to tourists and other ignoramuses that I forgot myself.

"At any rate, Miss Marshall, we discovered that the illicit trade had increased a hundredfold, and deduced that some genius of crime had taken charge of the business. These deductions were triumphantly confirmed when we encountered the mastermind himself. Our investigations—the details of which I will not tell you at the present time, though they were fraught with interesting incidents—put a spoke in the wheel of this man; he had us abducted and imprisoned in a pyramid, from which we escaped by the skin of our teeth just in time to stop the genius of crime—"

"On the whole, Amelia," said Emerson in a reflective voice, "I believe I prefer even the atrocious term Master Criminal to genius of crime."

"Very well, Emerson, it is of small concern to me.

As I was saying, Miss Marshall, we robbed Sethos of his ill-gotten gains, but unfortunately he made good his escape. He is out there somewhere, lurking in the shadows of the underworld and, I do not doubt, burning for revenge. The flowers were a reminder that his unseen eyes are upon us and his unseen hand may at any moment descend.''

Miss Marshall drew a long breath of amazement. "You quite take my breath away, Mrs. Emerson. What a thrilling tale!''

I thanked her, and Emerson growled, ''Mrs. Emerson's rhetorical style, I fear, is influenced by her taste for third-rate romances. You left out all the important details, Amelia. Ramses' daring rescue—''

''I will elaborate at another time, Emerson. Here we are, at our little camp; I do hope, Miss Marshall, that you will be comfortable.''

Emerson cheered up when he saw that the second, smaller tent had been placed some distance from our own. ''Out of hearing range'' was, I believe, his precise phrase. I got the girl settled nicely and returned to my spouse, who had already retired. The interior of the tent was quite dark; but when I asked Emerson to relight the lamp, he refused in such terms that I decided not to pursue the subject.

''I cannot see a thing, Emerson,'' I said, edging toward the spot where I believed he must be.

''I can't see you either, but I can hear you jingling,'' said Emerson's voice. A hand closed over the folds of my trousers and drew me down.

''You see?'' said Emerson, after a while. ''The visual sense is not necessary for the activities I had planned for this evening. One might even argue that it is an interference.''

''Quite right, my dear Emerson. Only, if you don't

mind, I would prefer to remove the net and combs and pins from my hair myself. You have just put your finger in my eye.''

When these and other encumbrances to conjugal fraternization had been removed, Emerson drew me into his strong arms. Not wishing to discourage the sensations of intense affection that had begun to develop, I unobtrusively freed one hand long enough to draw a blanket over us. Once the sun goes down, the desert nights are chilly. Also, I had not closed the flap of the tent. However, I felt sure Miss Marshall had closed hers; Emerson had mentioned at least four times that she must be sure and do so, for fear of the night air.

As I have had occasion to remark earlier in the pages of this journal, I do not share the prudish attitude of some self-appointed guardians of righteousness concerning the relationship of married persons. I rejoice— nay, I glory in—the depth of the regard Emerson and I have for one another. The fact that Emerson is as attracted by my physical characteristics as he is by my character and my spiritual qualities should, in my opinion, be a source of pride rather than embarrassment.

I will therefore state, candidly and without reserve, that I sensed a subtle change in his behavior that night. It was more tempestuous and at the same time oddly tentative. This may sound contradictory. It *was* contradictory. I cannot account for it, I can only say that such was the case.

Sometime later, after we had settled into our usual sleeping positions—Emerson flat on his back with his arms folded across his breast like a mummified Egyptian pharaoh, I on my side with my head against his shoulder—I heard him sigh.

''Peabody.''

''Yes, my dear Emerson?''

"There is, if I am not mistaken, a foolish convention known as the language of flowers."

"I believe you are not mistaken, Emerson."

"What do red roses mean in the language of flowers, Peabody?"

"I have no idea, Emerson. Like yourself, I am sublimely indifferent to foolish conventions."

"I think I can guess, though," Emerson muttered.

"Emerson, I cannot imagine why you should concern yourself about such a trivial and meaningless matter when we have so many other important issues to discuss. Several things happened today that I want to tell you about. I met a gentleman—a very interesting and attractive individual—"

Emerson rolled over and seized me in a fierce embrace. "Don't talk to me about interesting gentlemen, Peabody. Don't talk at all!"

And he proceeded to make it difficult, if not impossible, for me to do so, even if I had been so inclined, which at that particular moment I was not.

• Seven •

When we returned to the house next day, we found another group of would-be workers patiently waiting outside the gates. Ramses advanced purposefully on Enid, and she fled into her room. Nemo was nowhere to be seen; but I had observed the flutter of a ragged robe in the doorway of the donkey shed, so I went after him.

Since part of the roof was missing, I had no trouble noticing that Nemo had obeyed only part of my orders. He was clean-shaven, and smelled of Pears soap; his hair had been combed and flattened down with water, though drying strands curled around his neck and brow. I reminded myself I must not forget to give him a haircut.

I asked why he had not put on his new suit. Instead of answering he countered with another question. "Is there any reason why I should not wear native costume,

Mrs. Emerson? I am used to it now, and it is much more comfortable.''

"You can wear anything you like, so long as it is clean. I do not tolerate slovenliness on my expeditions. Is that your only robe? Well, then, we will wash it this evening, and while it dries I will cut your hair.''

Mr. Nemo made a face, like a little boy about to be given medicine, but he had learned the futility of arguing with me. "I wonder if I might ask you for a pair of blue spectacles, Mrs. Emerson. The blazing sun is hard on my eyes.''

"Don't try to deceive me, Mr. Nemo. I know why you want the spectacles—you will find a pair in the third box on the second shelf in the sitting room. You are ashamed of having the young lady see you. Childish, Mr. Nemo. Very childish. You will have to face her sooner or later.''

"Not if I can help it," Nemo muttered. "Mrs. Emerson, all this fuss about washing and cutting hair is a waste of time. Shouldn't we be bending all our efforts to finding the criminal you mentioned? Surely we would have a better chance of spotting him in Cairo. I could return to my old haunts, and—''

"No, no, Mr. Nemo. You have not the faintest idea of how to proceed. Leave that to me, and follow my orders implicitly. Was there any disturbance last night?''

"No, all was quiet. But that news seems to disappoint you, Mrs. Emerson. Were you hoping for another attack on your son?''

"I *am* disappointed; I was hoping for an attack— though not necessarily on Ramses. Do you not see, Mr. Nemo, that we have not a hope of finding the man we want among the teeming thousands of Cairo? The fellow is a master of disguise; he might be anyone. Our best hope is to wait for him to come to us."

"You mean we must sit and wait—indefinitely?"

"Not indefinitely. Not long, in fact. Sooner or later he will visit us; he has made his interest plain; and I have a few ideas as to how to attract his attention. No, do not ask me what they are; just leave it to me. Now I must be going. Remember—watch Ramses!"

"With all respect, Mrs. Emerson, I cannot imagine why you talk about the boy as if he were some sort of monster. He seems a decent little chap—frightfully long-winded—I don't believe I have ever heard anyone use so many confounded polysyllabic words. Aside from that, he appears normal enough. Is there something you haven't told me? Does he suffer from—forgive me—fits of hereditary madness?"

"I would hate to think it is hereditary," I said. "No, Mr. Nemo, Ramses is quite sane—cold-bloodedly, terrifyingly sane. That is why he is so dangerous. Let me give you a brief summary. . . . No, I have not the time. Even a brief summary would take too long. Just watch him!"

When we set out for the dig a short time later, Nemo mingled with the men. We had taken on an additional dozen or so diggers and a like number of basket children, who were to work with me. We separated our forces, Emerson leading his crew to the Bent Pyramid, and I proceeding toward the smaller one.

This structure was some sixty yards south of its larger neighbor and was obviously part of the same complex. The precise function of the subsidiary pyramids was still being debated. There were three of them attached to the Great Pyramid at Giza, and others at other sites. For my part, I felt certain they had been built for the principal consorts of the kings who were buried in the larger pyramids. If I could find a mark or inscription mentioning a royal lady's name, I could prove my thesis.

I studied the charming little ruin, trying to decide where to begin. I could not determine its height, for not only was the drifting sand piled high around its base, but the removal of the casing stones which had once covered its surface like frosting on a cake had allowed it to slump like an overweight lady after she has removed her corsets. The first thing was to remove the sand and clear the four sides down to ground level.

Enid trailed after me like a dog who is afraid to lose his master. As I proceeded, I explained to her what I was doing and why. "I have decided to begin with the north face, since it is more likely that the funerary chapel would be on the side closest to the principal monument. That hollow to the west will be our dump site. We don't want to cover up any other tombs, and I see no evidence of such a thing there. Here, on this plan, which has been mapped and surveyed, I am indicating the area we will be excavating. It is marked out in squares of ten feet by ten. . . . Miss Marshall, you are not paying attention. You will give yourself away sooner or later if you don't learn to make noises like an Egyptologist."

"Why not sooner, then? This is hopeless, Mrs. Emerson. Perhaps the best thing for me to do is to turn myself in. What good am I doing here?"

"Faint heart never won . . . anything, my dear," I said, amending the quotation as the situation demanded. "I am surprised to see you give up so soon."

"But it is hopeless!"

"Not at all. Kalenischeff—did I mention this?—was a member of the Master Criminal's gang. He was murdered, if not by that man's hand, by his orders. All we have to do—"

"Is find this man—who, by your own admission, is

a master of disguise and whose identity is unknown
even to you—and force him to confess! You have your
own duties, Mrs. Emerson—your husband, your child,
your work—"

"My dear Miss Marshall, you underestimate me if
you think I cannot carry on two or more activities simultaneously. It is true that I am looking forward to
solving the mystery of this little pyramid, but that does
not mean I cannot at the same time put my mind to
solving a mystery of another kind. I have several
schemes in mind—"

"What?"

It was the second time someone had asked me that
question, and I had to admit it was a good question.
"The less you know, the safer you will be," I said.
"Trust me."

"But, Mrs. Emerson—"

"You had better call me Amelia. Formality is absurd
under these circumstances."

"My name is Enid. It is my real name," she added,
with a rueful smile. "When I chose my nom de guerre,
I took the chance of retaining my true first name. It is
hard to respond, with instinctive ease, to one that is
unfamiliar."

"Good thinking. You see, you have a talent for deception that is worth cultivating. But please don't employ it when you tell me about your cousin."

Enid started violently. "Who?"

"Your kinsman. Ronald—I forget his other name. Is
he the sort of person who could help us in our investigation?"

"Ronald! I beg your pardon; I never think of him as
a cousin, since the relationship is so distant. No. Ronald
is the last person on whom I would depend in time of
trouble. He is an amiable, empty-headed young man

who has never done a useful day's work in his life, or employed his brain for anything more demanding than totaling up his gambling debts."

"He sounds a most unattractive person."

"No," Enid said. "Physically he is quite handsome; he has an engaging manner and can be the most amusing companion in the world."

"But you don't want me to tell him where you are—reassure him as to your safety?"

"Heavens, no. I am sure Ronald is concerned about me—in so far as he is capable of being concerned about anyone but himself. But I am equally certain he didn't put himself out hurrying to Cairo. He has been in Egypt for some weeks, on—on business. . . . Which he abandoned in order to go hunting in the Sudan."

An indefinable but unmistakable change in her voice and look made me suspect she was holding something back. As later events proved, I was correct, but I will frankly admit—since candor is a quality I prize, and since my errors in judgment are so infrequent as to be worthy of mention—that I was mistaken as to the cause of her reticence. Young ladies often abuse a gentleman in whom they have an intense personal interest. I assumed Miss Debenham was in love with her cousin and was ashamed to admit it because she considered him unworthy of her affection.

Delicacy, therefore, prevented me from pressing the subject, and Enid made it even more difficult for me to do so by reminding me that the men were waiting for my command to begin digging.

After several hours we halted for refreshment. Sitting before our tents, we applied ourselves to eggs and tea, and fresh bread from the village, with good appetite. Emerson's humor had improved, thanks to the discovery of some blocks of cut stone which betokened the presence of some sort of structure.

Ramses, of course, had to express his evaluation. "In my opinion, Papa, we have found signs of two distinct building periods. Since the cult of Sneferu the Good was popular in Ptolemaic times, it is probable—"

"Ramses, your papa is perfectly well aware of that," I said testily.

"I only wished to suggest that extreme care must be taken in order to discover—"

"Again, Ramses, let me remind you that there is no excavator in the field today whose skill equals that of your papa."

"Thank you, my dear," said Emerson, beaming. "Are you having a good time with your little pyramid?"

"Yes, thank you, Emerson."

Before I could draw breath to continue, Ramses addressed Enid, requesting her opinion on what we had accomplished thus far. It might have been only a courteous attempt to draw her into the conversation. But I doubted that it was.

Enid distracted him by seizing the cat, who was sniffing around her ankles. I was surprised the aristocratic creature permitted the liberty. She was on good terms with me and had a certain tolerant affection for Emerson, but Ramses was the only person whose caresses she actively encouraged.

The distraction proved effective, for Ramses then asked about Enid's pets—having deduced, as he explained at length, that she must have owned a cat or she would not know the precise spots to scratch. When Enid replied that she had several dogs and a dozen cats, most of whom had been abandoned by cruel owners, Ramses' countenance took on quite a pleasant look of approval.

As he sat cross-legged beside her, his curly head tipped to one side and his black eyes bright with interest, one might have taken him for a normal little boy—so long as he kept his mouth closed.

All at once, Emerson leaped to his feet, dropping his bread and butter (buttered side down, of course) onto the rug. He shielded his eyes with his hands and looked east, toward the rising sun. "Upon my word, Amelia, I believe it is a group of cursed tourists. And they are coming this way."

"That is hardly surprising, Emerson," I replied, trying to scrape the butter off the rug, which was a handsome old Bokhara. "You know that is one of the disadvantages of working at Dahshoor. Though not so popular as Giza and Sakkara, it is mentioned in the guidebooks."

"Did you ever see such absurd figures?" Emerson demanded. "Green umbrellas, flaps of cloth about their heads . . ."

Compared to Emerson, they did look ridiculous. Hatless, his bronzed throat and arms bared, he was in tune with his surroundings as few foreigners in Egypt could be. But then Emerson is a remarkable man. He has never suffered from sunstroke or sunburn or even from catarrh, though he absolutely refuses to wear a flannel belt, which, as every physician knows, is the only certain preventative for that common affliction.

The little caravan approached us. None of the riders was accustomed to donkeyback; they bounced up and down like jumping jacks on strings. Emerson pushed his sleeves to his shoulders. "I will just go and run them off."

"Wait, Emerson. . . ." But I was too late. Emerson's long legs carried him swiftly toward the enemy.

His raised hand brought the procession to a halt. One

stout gentleman fell off his donkey and was hauled to his feet by a pair of grinning donkey boys. A lively discussion ensued. I could not make out the words, except for an occasional expletive from Emerson, but the gestures of the participants left no doubt as to their state of mind.

Enid chuckled. "I am reminded of Aunt Betsy, in Dickens' charming novel," she said.

"Like Aunt Betsy, Emerson will prevail," I said, buttering another bit of bread.

Sure enough, after a while the caravan turned away, heading for the North Pyramid, and Emerson returned, refreshed and exhilarated by the encounter. We all went back to work except for the cat Bastet, who yawned and sauntered into the tent to take a nap.

I did not expect the discoveries of that first day to be momentous, and they were not—only the usual pottery shards and fragments of funerary objects. The whole area was one vast cemetery—a city of the dead whose population far exceeded that of any metropolis, modern or ancient. I showed Enid the proper procedure for dealing with such finds, for we kept scrupulously accurate records of every object, no matter how undistinguished.

There was little going on to occupy my mind, so I was able to devote part of my attention to working out an answer to the question people kept asking me. How indeed to attract the attention of the Master Criminal? I sympathized with Mr. Nemo's disinclination to sit with folded hands until that gentleman decided to make his next move. Tactically and psychologically it would be to our advantage to take the initiative and encourage an attack. What I needed was a treasure—a cache of royal jewelry like the one that had attracted the M.C.'s interest the year before. Ramses had found one such cache at Dahshoor. (In fact, I was fairly certain he had found two; the treasure of Princess Khnumit, which M. de Morgan had produced with such fanfare at the end of the season, might have been his reward for promising to yield the site to us. I had not questioned Ramses about the matter and I had no intention of doing so, since confirmation of my suspicion would raise delicate ethical questions I was not prepared to deal with.)

Nor had I any intention of going, hat in hand, to my own son and asking him to help me find antiquities. I had even rejected the idea of interrogating the boy about the subsidiary pyramid. I meant to carry out my excavation according to the strictest scientific principles— but what I really wanted to find was the entrance. I yearned to squirm into that entrance and search for the burial chamber, and it would not have surprised me in the slightest to learn that Ramses knew precisely where it was located. He had a diabolical instinct for such things. However, great as would be the pleasure of entering the pyramid, the pleasure of finding it without Ramses' assistance would be even greater, and as the morning passed, with no sign of an opening, I began to think I had overestimated the boy. The men were still digging out sand, and not even Ramses—surely, not even Ramses?—could have located a hidden entrance buried under tons of debris.

The thought of pyramids had distracted me. I turned my thoughts back to the other problem. In lieu of a treasure, what would attract the Master Criminal? An answer soon came to me; but although I had every confidence in Ramses' ability to get himself out of ordinary scrapes, it did not seem quite right to use him as a lure to capture a murderer. There was another way, just as effective and less open to criticism on the grounds of maternal affection.

The sun climbed higher and the temperature climbed

with it. Occupied with my work and my schemes, I did not notice the passage of time or feel the heat until, glancing at Enid, I saw she was flushed and aglow with perspiration.

"You had better join Bastet in the tent," I said, taking the notebook and pencil from her. "I forgot you are not accustomed to the sun."

Courageously she asserted her willingness to remain on duty, but I overcame her scruples. She went off, and I was about to resume my labors when I saw a cloud of sand on the northern horizon. Another group of cursed tourists! Coming from the direction of Sakkara this time, and on horseback. The younger and more adventurous visitors preferred this approach.

When I saw that the riders did not halt at the North Pyramid but were coming straight toward us, I left Selim in charge of the diggers and hastened to Emerson. He had once bodily removed from a tomb a little old lady who turned out to be the former Empress of the French. The ensuing international furor had taken quite a while to die down.

He was rolling up his sleeves. I took firm hold of him and awaited the event. Before long I recognized, in the party of mounted men, the same young Englishmen I had seen at Shepheard's the day before.

They were still wearing the fantastical and inappropriate bits of Arabic costume they had purchased in the bazaars. However, they were expert horsemen—not surprising in persons who have few occupations in life other than sport and idle amusement. The guns slung from the saddles or carried over their arms were of the latest and most expensive design.

Whooping and laughing, they drew up beside the tent, and the young man in the lead prepared to dismount. Seeing me, he stopped midway, one foot still in the stirrup, the other lifted over the horse's back. The horse chose that moment to curl its lips back, and the resemblance to its rider, whose teeth were almost as prominent, was so absurd I had to stifle a laugh.

"'Pon my word, it's a lady," the young man exclaimed. "Look here, you chaps. What the devil d'you suppose she's doing out here in the middle of nowhere? How de do, ma'am."

He whipped off his turban. Emerson was not appeased by the gesture. He growled, "Watch your language, young man. Mrs. Emerson is not accustomed to vulgarity."

"Mrs. Emerson? Then you must be Mr. Emerson." The fellow grinned as if proud of this brilliant deduction.

"Professor Emerson," I corrected. "And you, sir?"

One of his companions hastened to his side. "Allow me to present his lordship Viscount Everly."

Emerson grunted. "Now that you have presented him, you may take him away. This is an archaeological expedition, not a club for wealthy idlers."

"Archaeology! Is that so? 'Pon my word! I say, Professor, you can just show us round a bit. Or better, let your better half do it, eh? Always take a pretty woman when you can get one, isn't that right, old chap?" He clapped Emerson on the shoulder and bared so many of his teeth, I was afraid they would fall out of his mouth.

I did not hear Emerson's reply, which is just as well. I had seen something that drew my attention and roused my most intense detective instincts.

Another of the viscount's entourage had come forward. When he removed his headgear, a turban of astonishing height and breath, his head looked as if it had caught fire. The features below the coppery locks were hardly less astonishing. It took a second look to convince me that they were not those of Mr. Nemo. Further examination indicated the resemblance was not, in fact, as close as I had supposed; it was the unusual hair color shared by both that gave a misleading impression. This man—undoubtedly the same person I had seen at the Administration Building—was slighter and softer, from his delicately cut features to his plump, manicured hands.

Feeling my fixed stare, the young man shifted from one booted foot to the other and smiled uneasily. "Good morning, madam."

In my surprise I had forgotten my duty to my irate husband, but fortunately Ramses had intervened in time to save the viscount from bodily harm. Apparently he had admired the latter's horse, for when I returned my attention to the others, I was in time to hear Everly giggle foolishly and remark, "Yes, young feller, he's a dazzler, all right. Want to try him out?"

"Ramses," I cried. "I absolutely forbid—"

But Ramses was already in the saddle, and if he heard me, which I rather think he did, he pretended not to.

Ramses was not an unskilled equestrian, but he looked very small perched atop the great white stallion. Emerson stood watching with a foolish look, half smile of pride, half frown of exasperation, as the boy put the animal to a walk. I caught his arm. "Emerson, stop him. Order him to dismount."

"Don't fret yourself, ma'am," said his lordship, with another imbecile giggle. "Caesar is as gentle as a kitten."

Our men had gathered around to watch. They were grinning proudly, and Abdullah said in Arabic, "He will take no harm, sitt. He could ride a lion if he chose."

The words were scarcely out of his mouth when a gun went off, practically in my ear. The stallion reared and bolted. Ramses stuck to his back like a cocklebur, but I knew he must fall; his feet were a good eight inches above the swinging stirrups, and his arms had not the strength to hold the reins.

Deafened by the sound of the shot and dazed by horror, we stood frozen for several seconds. Emerson was the first to move. I have never seen a man run so fast. It was a splendid effort, but of course quite senseless, since a man on foot could never hope to catch up with a galloping horse.

His lordship reacted more quickly than I would have expected. "Don't worry, ma'am, I'll save the lad," he cried, and ran toward the other horses, which were standing some distance away with a pair of grooms in attendance. Before he reached them, however, a flying form cannoned into him and sent him sprawling. The newcomer vaulted into the nearest saddle. With a shout, and an answering neigh, they were off, man and equine moving as one. The flying robes of the rider blew out behind him like great wings.

Our men started running after Emerson, shouting and waving their arms. After some confusion, the viscount and his followers mounted and galloped off in pursuit. The two grooms looked at one another, shrugged, and sat down on the ground to watch.

Whether by accident or because Ramses had managed to regain some control over the horse, it had swung in a wide circle. If this was indeed designed by Ramses, it was a serious error on his part; for the steed was rapidly approaching one of the wadis, or canyons, that cut through the western desert. I could not see how deep it was, but it appeared to be a good ten feet across. The horse might be able to jump it. However, I felt reasonably certain Ramses would not be able to stay on it if it did.

As the Reader may suppose, my state of mind was not so calm and collected as the above description implies; in fact, "frozen with horror" would be a trite but relatively accurate description of my condition at that time. However, I could do absolutely nothing except watch. There were already enough people running and riding wildly across the countryside.

His lordship had outstripped his men. Whatever his other failings—and I felt sure they were extensive—he rode like a centaur. Even so, he was far behind the first pursuer, who was rapidly closing in on the large horse and its small rider. As one might have expected, Emerson was a considerable distance behind, with the rest of our men strung out behind him like runners in a race.

The unknown rider—of whose identity, however, I had no doubt; it could only be Nemo—in a sudden burst of speed cut in front of the runaway horse and turned him, on the very edge of the wadi. For a few heart-stopping moments the two steeds thundered on side by side; Nemo's appeared to be galloping on thin air, so close were its hooves to the crumbling rim of the ravine. Then the courageous effort of the rescuer bore fruit. Ramses' mount turned and slowed and finally came to a stop. Ramses fell off the horse, or was plucked off, I could not tell which; for he was immediately enveloped in the billowing folds of Nemo's robe. From that distance it was hard to see whether Nemo was embracing the boy in a frenzy of relief or shaking him violently in another kind of frenzy.

By this time the other pursuers were spread out all over the terrain, in their efforts to follow the changing course of the runaway. It must have been Emerson's strong paternal instincts that led him to be first upon the scene, for no one could possibly have predicted where the animal would eventually halt. The others all converged on the spot, and before long the protagonists in the drama were swallowed up by a crowd of screaming supernumeraries and hidden by agitated blue and white draperies.

Not until that moment did I feel the hand that had gripped my shoulder, though its pressure was hard enough to leave (as I later discovered) visible bruises. The grip relaxed and I turned in time to catch Enid as, with a tremulous moan, she sank fainting to the ground.

I dragged the girl into the tent and left her there. The intensity of the drama was sufficient excuse for her re-action, but I knew Emerson would be annoyed if he discovered she had succumbed. He had a poor opinion of swooning females.

The viscount and his entourage were the first to re-turn. Most of them kept their distance, but his lordship summoned courage enough to face me. However, he was prudent enough to remain on horseback as he made his stammering apologies.

I cut them short. "I don't hold you wholly account-able, since Ramses has a habit of getting into scrapes; however, I think you had better take yourself off before Professor Emerson gets here. I refuse to be responsible for his actions when he is under extreme emotional stress, as I suppose him to be at this time."

The gentlemen took my advice. They were in full retreat when Emerson staggered up, with Ramses clasped to his bosom. After Ramses had finally con-vinced his father he was capable of standing, Emerson ran after the riders, cursing and demanding that they come back and fight like men. Having expected a dem-onstration of that sort, I was able to trip him up, and by the time he had resumed an upright position and brushed the sand from his perspiring countenance, he was relatively calm.

"No harm done," he said grittily. "But if that idiot ever shows his face here again—"

I handed him my water flask, for it was evident that his speech was encumbered by sand. "Perhaps we had better stop for the day," I suggested. "It is after noon, and everyone is tired from all that running around."

"Stop work?" Emerson stared at me in amazement. "What are you thinking of, Peabody?"

So we returned to our labors. The diggers went at it with renewed vigor; I heard one of them remark to another that he always enjoyed working for the Father of Curses, since there was sure to be something amusing going on.

Naturally we looked for Nemo in order to express our appreciation and admiration, but he was nowhere to be found. Since he was still wearing his Egyptian robes and turban, it was not difficult for him to hide among the fifty-odd diggers; and even after we had finished work and returned to the house, I was unable to locate him. I need not tell the Reader that my reasons for wishing to speak to him were not solely those of parental gratitude. I had a number of questions to ask that young man, and this time I was determined to get answers.

I had, of course, explained to Ramses that his behavior was wholly inexcusable. Not all the blame for the incident could be attributed to him, since the accidental discharge of the firearm had startled the horse into bolting. However, if Ramses had not been on the horse, the danger would not have occurred.

Remarkably, Ramses made no attempt to defend himself, but listened in silence, his narrow countenance

even more inscrutable than usual. Upon the conclusion
of the lecture I ordered him to his room—not much of
a punishment, since he usually spent the hottest part of
the day there working on his grammar.

Emerson and I had never succumbed to the lazy habit
of afternoon rest which is common in the East. There
is always a great deal to do on an archaeological expedition, aside from the digging itself. I knew Emerson
would be busy that afternoon, for as he admitted, the
stratification of the ruined buildings at the base of the
pyramid was complex in the extreme. His copious notes
and sketches would have to be sorted and copied in
more permanent form.

He was frowning and muttering over this task when
I began to set in motion the scheme I had contrived that
morning.

I found Enid lying on her cot. She was not asleep;
her wide eyes stared unseeingly at the ceiling and she
did not turn her head when I entered, after giving the
emphatic cough that was the only possible substitute for
a knock—there being, as the Reader may recall, no door
on which to knock.

I understood the cause of her lethargy, and the despair
of which it was the outward sign, and I was tempted to
mitigate it by assuring her that I was about to take action. I decided I could not risk it; she might have tried
to dissuade me from the course I contemplated. Subter-
fuge was necessary, and although I deplore in the
strongest possible terms the slightest deviation from
straightforward behavior, there are occasions upon
which moral good must yield to expediency.

"I have brought you something to read," I said
cheerfully. "It will, I hope, beguile the hours more effectively than Meyer's *Geschichte des Altertums*." For
such was the volume she had tossed aside.

A slight show of animation warmed her pale cheeks, though I fancied it was politeness rather than genuine interest. She took the books and examined the titles curiously. "Why, Amelia," she said, with a little laugh. "I would not have suspected you of such deplorable taste in literature."

"Only the book by Mr. Haggard is mine," I explained, taking a seat on the packing case. "The other belongs to Ramses—a collection of what are called, I believe, detective stories."

"They are very popular stories. You don't care for them?"

"No; for in my opinion they strain the credulity of the reader to an unreasonable degree."

I was pleased to see that our little literary discussion had cheered the girl: her eyes twinkled as she said, "To a more unreasonable degree than the romances of Mr. Haggard? I believe his plots include such devices as the lost diamond mines of King Solomon, beautiful women thousands of years old—"

"You give yourself away, Enid. You would not be so familiar with the plots if you had not read the books!"

Her smile faded. "I know—I knew—someone who enjoyed them."

Her cousin Ronald? He had not struck me, from what I had heard of him, as a reading man. I was tempted to inquire why the memory brought such a look of sorrow to her face, but decided I must postpone further questions, since I had only a limited time in which to put my scheme into effect.

"Mr. Haggard's stories," I explained, "are pure fantasy and do not pretend to be anything else. However rational the mind—and mine is extremely rational—it requires periods of rest, when the aery winds of fancy may ruffle the still waters of thought and encourage those softer and more spiritual musings without which no individual can be at his or her best. These so-called detective stories, on the other hand, pretend to exhibit the strictly intellectual qualities of the protagonist. In fact, they do nothing of the sort; for in the few I have read, the detective arrived at his solutions, not by means of the inexorable progress of true reasoning, but by wild guesses which turned out to be correct only because of the author's construction of his plot.''

Enid's abstracted murmur proved that I had lost her attention; and since the books had been only the pretext for my visit, I was quite content to change the subject to one which might appear—as I trusted it would—even more frivolous than that of literature, but which was, in fact, at the root of my scheme.

I began by telling her how much I had admired her gray-green afternoon frock, and asking where she had obtained it. Emerson has been heard to assert that the discussion of fashion will distract any woman from any other subject whatsoever, including her own imminent demise. Without subscribing to this exaggerated assessment, I am bound to admit that there is some truth in it, and this was proved by Enid's response. We discussed fashion houses and fabrics and the frightful expense of dressmaking; and then I subtly closed in upon my purpose.

''The costume you were wearing the day you arrived quite intrigued me,'' I said.

''Oh, but it is the latest mode,'' Enid explained. ''It is called a bicycling dress. Have you not heard of them? I was sure you had, since your own costume is similar in design—if not in color.''

''Oh yes, quite; I try to keep au courant with the latest styles, although practicality is a greater consideration than beauty here. That was what surprised me—that a young lady of fashion would include such a garment in her travel wardrobe."

"I am not as frivolous as my recent conduct may have led you to believe," Enid said with a wry smile. "I took it for granted that boots and short skirts would be useful for exploring ruins and descending into tombs. And indeed they were, though not in the sense I had expected. When I woke from my sleep or swoon that awful morning, my first thought was to get away. I knew what people were saying; I knew what the police would believe if I were found with the dead body of my supposed lover. To make matters worse, we had quarreled the evening before, and several of the hotel employees could have testified to the fact."

I had intended to inquire into the details of Enid's flight at another time. Here she was confiding in me voluntarily, without the firm interrogation I had thought might be necessary. The moment was not the one I would have chosen, but I feared I would lose her confidence if I put her off; so I settled myself, with a degree of interest the Reader may well imagine, to hear her story.

She continued in an abstracted tone, as if she were speaking to herself and exorcizing the anxiety of that dreadful experience by reliving it in memory. "I find it hard to believe I could have acted so quickly and coolly. Shock, I am told, does sometimes have that effect. I dressed myself, selecting a costume suited to the physical hardships I expected I would have to endure. It had the additional advantage of being one I had not worn before, so it would not be recognized. I left the room by means of the balcony outside my window, descending a stout vine that had twined up the wall. A few tourists had assembled before the hotel, though it was scarcely daybreak. Hiring a carriage, I asked to be taken to Mena House, for some of the others were going to Giza. By the time I reached the hotel, the reaction had set in; I was sick and trembling and had no idea what to do next. I knew I could not remain undiscovered for long, since an unaccompanied woman would provoke questions and—and worse.

"I was having breakfast in the dining room when a gentleman asked if I was one of the archaeologists working in the area. That gave me the idea, and also reminded me of your letter. I had no one else to turn to, and I determined to make my way to you. It was a council of desperation—"

"Not at all. It was a sensible decision. But how did you remain undiscovered that night and throughout the following day?"

"It was not easy. For, as you know, the archaeological sites are infested with guides, beggars, and the like, who follow one like a cloud of flies. I finally realized that the only persons who pass unnoticed are Arab women of the poorest class. I purchased a robe from one of them, assumed it in the privacy of an unoccupied tomb, and began walking. No one paid the least attention to me, and I spent the night huddled in a cleft in the rock somewhere between here and Sakkara. I cannot say I slept well. . . . When I reached here the next afternoon, I was on the verge of collapse. I had only strength enough to remove my disguise and conceal it, with the few small articles I had brought away with me, before I made myself known to you and the professor."

"Well," I said judiciously, "allow me to say, Enid, that you displayed a tenacity and inventiveness that do you credit. I take it that the coat to your bicycling dress was among the objects you hid?"

"Yes. The notion of disguising myself as a lady ar-

chaeologist was still in my mind; when, from concealment, I saw you talking with the professor, I tried to
adjust my dress to match yours. You were not wearing
your coat, so I removed mine. I had decided to attempt
to deceive you as well—"

"You need not apologize, my dear. I would have
done the same. I had better retrieve your belongings for
you. Can you describe the place where you hid them?"

She did so, with such accuracy that I felt sure I could
find the place. "I meant to get them last night," she
went on. "But when I looked out the flap of the tent,
the desert was so cold and eerie . . . And I heard strange
noises, Amelia—soft cries and moans—"

"Jackals, Enid. Jackals. However," I added thoughtfully, "you must promise me you will not leave your
tent at night, whatever you may hear."

When I left her, I took with me the skirt of her bicycling costume, explaining that I would have it cleaned
and brushed. Emerson was still doggedly drawing plans.
There was a great spatter of ink on the wall, so I deduced he had encountered a stumbling block and had
got over it, as he often did, by hurling his pen across
the room.

I said encouragingly, "Persevere, Emerson; persevere, my dear." Then I went up the stairs to the roof.

Behind the shelter of the screen I changed into Enid's
divided skirt, and removed my belt. It cost me a pang
to leave it and its useful tools behind, and to abandon
my parasol; but I knew I could never be mistaken for
another while I had them. After I had put on tinted
spectacles and fastened a pith helmet on my head, I had
done all I could to complete the resemblance. Rather
than pass through the parlor and prompt questions from
Emerson, I descended from the roof by means of the
holes and crevices in the wall.

Though the sun was sinking, the village yet drowsed in the somnolence of the afternoon nap. I crossed my arms casually across my chest—the dimensions of that region being the most obvious difference between Enid's figure and mine—and emulated her slower, swaying walk.

I had not gone a hundred yards from the compound before I felt eyes upon me. Nothing moved on the broken expanse of the desert slope ahead; no living creature could be seen, save the eternal vultures swinging in slow graceful circles down the sky. Yet I knew I was being observed—knew it with the certain instinct described so well by Mr. Haggard and other writers of fiction. It is a sense developed by those who are often the object of pursuit by enemies; and certainly no one had been pursued more often than I.

I went on at a steady pace, but the hairs at the back of my neck were bristling. (Emerson would probably have claimed the sensation was produced by perspiration, and I admit that the pith helmet was cursed hot. However, Emerson would have been mistaken.) The sensation of steady, watching eyes increased until I could bear the suspense no longer. I spun round.

The cat Bastet sat down and returned my look with one of amiable interest.

"What are you doing here?" I inquired.

Naturally she did not reply. I continued, "Return to the house at once, if you please." She continued to stare at me, so I repeated the request in Arabic, whereupon the cat rose in a leisurely fashion, applied her hind foot to her ear, and walked away.

The prickling at the back of my neck did not lessen as I went forward. Though I raked the landscape with

keen eyes, turning from time to time to look behind me,
I saw no living form. Bastet had abandoned her pursuit;
it had not been her eyes I felt fixed upon me. As I had
told Emerson, I felt certain that Sethos had kept and did
keep us under constant observation. That he would
strike again I felt certain; that he had selected Enid as
the scapegoat for his hideous crime and would endeavor
to deliver her to the police—I was equally certain of
that. Cheered and encouraged by the confirmation of my
suspicions, in the form of that significant prickling sensation, I proceeded on my way.

It was not difficult to find the place where Enid had
concealed her belongings. She had not buried them
deep, and in fact a fold of black fabric protruded from
the sand like a sable banner.

I dug up the parcel, glancing furtively round as I
thought Enid might do under those circumstances, and
hoping the assailant I expected would make his move
without delay. There were many places nearby where
such a person might be concealed, for, as I believe I
have mentioned, the rocky plateau was marked by innumerable ridges and crevices.

Nothing happened, however. Continuing my role, I
gathered the bundle in my arms and returned with it to
Enid's tent, where I could examine it at leisure.

The worn black *tob* and *burko* (face veil) were of the
poorest quality, and sadly worn—worn often and con-
tinuously, to judge by the odor that pervaded them.
They would have to be washed—boiled, in fact—before
they could be worn again, but I put the garments aside.
One never knows when a disguise may be useful.

The robe had been wrapped around a small handbag
within which was a pitiful collection of odds and ends,
obviously snatched up at random in the panic of that

fearful morning. A little box of pearl powder and a pot
of lip paint, an ivory-handled brush and a dainty handkerchief were objects she might have had already in the
bag. Crammed on top were a few pieces of jewelry,
including a gold watch and a locket of the same precious metal, adorned with pearls. The most interesting
item, however, was a large roll of banknotes. The total
came to over five hundred pounds.

The girl had been described as an heiress, and the
names of the couturiers she had mentioned bore out the
assumption that she had ample wealth at her command.
Yet this was an astonishing amount for a young woman
to carry on her person. Thoughtfully I returned the
money and the watch to the bag. There were unplumbed
depths in that young person; they might or might not
have bearing on her present dilemma, but I was determined to know the facts so that I might decide for myself. To that end I permitted myself another violation of
propriety. I opened the locket.

It was with a sense of inevitability that I saw a familiar face enshrined there. The frame of the locket cut
off the lower part of the chin, and the color of the hair
was reduced to sober gray. I knew the color, though, as
I knew the features.

Was the photograph that of Nemo or of the other man
who so nearly resembled him? Was one, or both, Enid's
cousin Ronald? And if one was Ronald, which one?
And which, if either, was Sethos?

I confess that for a moment my thoughts were in a
whirl. But was I distracted from my purpose by this
startling development? Never believe it, Reader! I hung
the locket round my neck. I shook out Enid's coat,
which had been wrapped around the bag. It was quite
snug across my chest—in fact, the buttons would not

fasten. That was all to the good, however, for I wanted the locket to be seen.

Settling myself atop a promontory some distance from the tents, I prepared to wait. I had no assurance that anything interesting would occur that day, but sooner or later my efforts must bear fruit. Nothing escaped the notice of that unknown genius of crime; he must know of Enid's presence at Dahshoor. He would not have been deceived by her masquerade any more than I had been. All things come to him who waits, as the saying goes, and I did not doubt that assault and/or abduction would come to me.

I felt horridly undressed without my belt and my parasol. However, the pressure of my pistol, in the pocket of the trousers, was reassuring, if uncomfortable. Once I thought I saw something move, behind a rock some distance away, and with hope rising high in my heart, I deliberately turned my back. But no one came.

I was not bored. An active mind can never be bored, and I had a great deal to think about. In between musing on the possible location of my pyramid's entrance and my plans for washing Nemo's robe (and Nemo) that evening, I considered means of keeping Enid safe that night. I was forced to admit that my initial plan, of having Enid sleep in a tent near our own, was unsatisfactory. I had neglected to consider the fact that my marital obligation (which is also, let me hasten to add, my pleasure) would distract me to such an extent that I would be unable to hear, much less prevent, an attack on the girl's person should such occur. At last I concluded that it would be better for Enid to remain at the house that night. Proper chaperonage, though important, had to yield in this case to more vital matters, such as Enid's survival and Emerson's and my conjugal felicity.

As the sun sank lower in the west, the changes of light along the sloping sides of the pyramid produced fascinating aesthetic alterations, and I found myself musing about the long-dead monarch whose mummified remains had once rested in the now desolate burial chamber. With what pomp and circumstance had he been carried to his tomb; with what glitter of gold and glow of precious stones had his petrified form been adorned! A natural progression of ideas led me to recall another Pharaoh—the one whose name had been taken by the terrible man whose emissaries I awaited even now. The tomb of the great Sethos, Pharaoh of Egypt, lay far to the south in the Valley of the Kings at Thebes. It had been discovered in 1817 and it was still among the leading attractions of the area. The magnificent carvings and paintings of that most splendid of all royal tombs suggest that Sethos' funerary equipment must have excelled all others; yet alas for human vanity! Thousands of years ago, the monarch had been robbed of his treasures and his mortal remains had been ignominiously thrust into a humble hole in the cliffs, with others of his peers, to save them from destruction. The cache of royal mummies had been found a few years before, and the remains now rested in Cairo, where I had seen them. Sethos' withered features still retained the stamp of royalty and the pride of race. In his day he was a leader of men and a remarkably handsome individual—like his son Ramses, a lion in a valley of goats. I wondered if the modern-day Sethos had ever contemplated the shrunken yet noble features of his ancient namesake. Was it that mummy that had prompted him to select his nom de guerre? Not too fanciful an idea for a man who had already demonstrated a poetic imagination and considerable intellectual ability. I felt a certain unwilling kinship for him, for I have the same qualities myself.

The lengthening shadows reminded me that the afternoon was almost spent and that Emerson would be wanting his tea. I decided to wait five more minutes, and shifted my position so that I faced the northeast. I could see the green of the cultivated fields and the trees that half-concealed the minaret of the village mosque. A haze of smoke from the cooking fires hung over the town like a gray mist.

A rumbling crash behind me brought me to my feet. Turning, I saw a cloud of dust and sand rise from the base of the small pyramid. Apparently our excavations that afternoon had weakened the crumbling stone, and part of the north face had given way.

Mercifully it had not happened when our men were working underneath. That was my first thought. My next reaction was one of excitement. Surely there was something visible on the northern face that I had not seen before—a square of shadow too regular to be anything but man-made. Had the fortuitous accident disclosed the hidden entrance?

Forgetting detective duties and marital responsibilities, I started eagerly down the slope. In the surge of archaeological fever I had forgotten my reason for being there. A herd of antelope could have swept down upon me without my noticing them.

The person who attacked me made far less noise. I was unaware of his presence until an arm, sinewy as braided leather, lifted me off my feet. A folded cloth, reeking of an odor that set my senses reeling, was pressed to my face. I fought to extract my pistol from my pocket. I could feel it against my body, but I could not reach the cursed thing. The voluminous size of the trousers defeated the attempt. However, Amelia P. Emerson does not cease struggling until comatose, and I continued to fumble through endless folds of brown velvet, though my eyes were dimming and my fingers were numb.

Eight

Suddenly there was a violent upheaval. I found myself on hands and knees, staring dizzily at what seemed to be twenty or thirty feet dancing briskly around me. A few inhalations of blessed ozone cleared my brain; the feet reduced themselves to four.

When I had gained strength enough to sit up, the combatants were locked in a close embrace. In their flowing robes they looked absurdly like two ladies performing a polite social ritual. Only the looks of agonized strain on their faces betrayed the ferocity of the struggle. One of them was Nemo. His turban had been displaced, and his bare head blazed in the rays of the setting sun. The other was a man I had never seen before. The darkness of his complexion suggested that he was a native of southern Egypt.

In a frantic flurry of fabric the men broke apart. Neither held a weapon. The hand of the Egyptian moved in a bewildering blur of motion. Nemo grunted and staggered back, his hands pressed to his midsection. It was a foul blow; but my defender was not daunted. Recovering, he knocked his opponent down with a shrewd uppercut to the jaw, and fell upon him.

The struggle was horrible to behold. I can only excuse my delay in halting it by pointing out that the fumes of the drug still clouded my mind, and that I was still trying to find my pocket. By the time I did so, Nemo was definitely in need of assistance. His assailant had both hands around his throat, and his face was turning black.

In my excitement I forgot myself, and shouted a phrase I had learned from an American friend: "Hands up, you varmint!" I doubt that the miscreant understood, but the tone of my voice was vehement enough to attract his attention, and when he glanced at me the sight of the pistol I held had the desired effect.

Slowly he rose from Nemo's prostrate form. The fury of battle had faded from his face, to be replaced by a look of quiet resignation, as lacking in character as a mummy's papier-mâché mask. There was nothing distinctive about his features or his faded cotton robe; they were similar to those of thousands of his fellow countrymen.

Nemo rolled over and staggered to his feet. He was panting heavily, in contrast to his opponent, whose breast was as still as that of a man in prayer. White patches which would shortly be bruises marked Nemo's face, and a bright stain on his torn sleeve told me the violence of the struggle had reopened his wound. He edged toward me, circling to keep out of the line of fire. "Splendid, Mrs. E., splendid," he gasped. "Why don't you give me the pistol now?"

"And risk this fellow escaping while we made the

exchange? No, Mr. Nemo. You may question my willingness to fire at a fellow human being—and my ability to hit him if I did—but I'll wager he has no doubts. You know me now, don't you, my friend? You made a mistake. I am not the lady you took me for, but the Sitt Hakim, wife to the great magician Emerson, Father of Curses, and no less dangerous to evildoers than Emerson himself. My eye is as keen as those of the vultures overhead, and like them I lie in wait for criminals."

I had, of course, addressed the man in Arabic. It is a language that lends itself to vainglorious self-applause, which is indeed a style Egyptians rather admire. The little speech had its effect. In the same tongue the man said softly, "I know you, sitt."

"Then you know I would not hesitate to use this weapon—not to kill, but only to wound. I want you to live, my friend—to live and talk to us." Unable to control my excitement any longer, I added in English, "Good Gad, Nemo, do you realize who this man is? He is the first of the Master Criminal's associates I have managed to capture. Through him we may reach his dread master. Do you approach him—carefully, if you please—and bind his arms with your turban. Are you too badly injured to do that?"

"No, of course not," Nemo said.

The man raised his hand. There was such dignity in the gesture that Nemo halted. The Egyptian said quietly, "I have failed my master. There is only one fate for those who fail him; but I feel no shame at losing to the Sitt Hakim, who is not a mere woman, but one who has the heart of a man, as I was told. I salute you, sitt." And he moved his hand from breast to brow to lips, in the respectful gesture of his people.

I was about to respond to this graceful compliment when a dreadful change came over the man's face. His

lips drew back in a hideous grin; his eyes rolled up until
only the blank white of the eyeballs showed. His hands
flew to his throat. He fell over backward and lay still.

Nemo rushed to him. "It's no use," I said, lowering
my pistol. "He was dead before he struck the ground.
Prussic acid, I suspect."

"You are right. There is a distinct odor of bitter al-
monds." Nemo straightened, white to the lips. "What
sort of people are these? He took the poison rather
than . . ."

"Allow himself to be questioned. Curse it! I should
have taken steps to bind his hands immediately. Well,
I will know better next time."

"Next time?" Nemo raised a trembling hand to his
brow. His sleeve was drenched with blood and I said,
recalling myself from my chagrin, "You are not yourself, Mr. Nemo. Loss of blood has weakened you, and
we must tend to your injuries without delay."

Dazed and shaken, Nemo allowed me to bind his arm
with a strip torn from the hem of his robe. "That will
stop the bleeding," I said. "But the wound requires to
be cleaned and bandaged. Let us return to the house at
once."

"What about—" Nemo gestured.

I looked at the dead man. His empty eyes seemed to
stare intently at the darkening vault of heaven. Already
the vultures were gathering.

"Turn him over," I said brusquely.

Nemo glanced from me to the birds circling overhead.
Silently he did as I asked.

When we got back, the gates were open and Abdullah
was standing outside. "Sitt," he began, as soon as we

were within hearing range, "Emerson has been asking—"

"So I imagine." I could hear Emerson rampaging
around the house, yelling my name. I had nurtured the
fond hope he might still be absorbed in his work; but
now there was nothing for it but to admit at least part
of the truth.

"There has been an accident," I explained to Abdullah, who was staring at Nemo's bloody sleeve.
"Please take Ali or Hassan and go at once to the
ridge behind the tents. You will find a dead body
there. Carry it here."

Abdullah clapped his hand to his brow. "Not a
dead man, sitt. Not another dead man . . ." A flicker
of reviving hope returned to his stricken face. "Is it a
mummy you mean, sitt? An *old* dead man?"

"I am afraid this one is rather fresh," I admitted.
"You had better fashion a litter or something of that
sort with which to carry him. Get on with it, if you
please; I cannot stand here *fahddling* with you, can't
you see Mr. Nemo needs medical attention?"

Abdullah staggered off, wringing his hands and
muttering. A few words were intelligible: "Another
dead body. Every year it is the same. Every year, another dead body . . ."

"Am I to understand you make it a habit to discover dead bodies?" Nemo asked.

I drew him toward the house. "Certainly not, Mr.
Nemo. I don't look for such things; they come upon
me, so to speak. Now let me do the talking, if you
will. Emerson is not going to like this."

Before we reached the door, Emerson came bursting
out. He stopped short at the sight of us. The blood
rushed to his face. "Not again!" he shouted. "I
warned you, Amelia—"

"Sssh." I put my finger to my lips. "There is no need to make such a fuss, Emerson. You will alarm—"

"A fuss? A fuss?" Emerson's voice rose to a pitch I had seldom heard, even from him. "What the devil have you been up to? You disappear for hours and then return disheveled and sandy, accompanied by a bloody—"

"Emerson! Language!"

"The adjective was meant literally," Emerson explained. "Mr. Nemo, am I to understand that once again I have to thank you for saving a member of my immediate family from doom and destruction?"

"It will all be explained to you, Emerson," I said soothingly. "Mr. Nemo does indeed deserve your thanks, and the first expression of our gratitude ought to be the tending of the wounds he courageously incurred in our service. Will you be so good as to fetch my medical equipment? I believe I will operate in the open air, where the light is better, and he won't drip blood on my carpets."

Silently, ominously, Emerson did as he was asked, and I led Nemo to the back of the house, where I had set up a primitive but efficient area of ablution. It was even possible to bathe behind a modest arrangement of woven screens, for a ditch served as a drain to carry off the water. Emerson and Ramses did so daily, Emerson of his own free will, Ramses because he was made to; but since the exercise involved having a servant pour jars of water over one from above, I did not consider it suitable for me to emulate them.

When Emerson joined me, I had persuaded Nemo to remove his tattered robe. It was beyond repair, and I directed one of the men, who had gathered round, to fetch one of his, promising, of course, to replace it. Under his robe Nemo wore the usual cotton drawers, reaching to his knees and tied around the waist with a drawstring. The bright flush of embarrassment that suffused even his bare breast assured me he had not lost as much blood as I feared.

I hastened to set him at ease. "I assure you, Mr. Nemo, bare skin is no novelty to me. I have tended many wounds and seen many naked breasts—and yours is nothing to be ashamed of. In fact, your pectoral development is quite admirable."

A growling sound reminded me of the presence of my irate spouse, and I hastened to add, "Though not as admirable as Emerson's. Now, Emerson, as I work I will inform you of the latest occurrence—"

But that offer had to be delayed. Through the ring of interested onlookers burst a slight form, wild-eyed and agitated. Nemo made a violent movement as if to turn, but stopped himself.

For a moment they confronted one another in a silence fraught with emotion, their faces matching one another's in snowy pallor. Enid raised a delicate hand to her throat. "You," she choked. "You . . ."

I said sharply, "Do not for a moment entertain any notion of fainting, Enid. I cannot attend to both of you."

"Fainting?" The hot color rushed back into her face. She darted forward. She raised her hand—and struck Nemo full across the face! "You bloody idiot!" she cried.

Even I was taken aback. Such behavior and such improper language from a young lady left me momentarily incapable of speech. It was my dear Emerson who rose to the occasion as only he can. Enid turned and ran, her hands over her face. The men gave way before her, but not Emerson; his mighty arm swept out and wound round her waist, lifting her clean off her feet. As she hung in his grasp, kicking and—I regret to say—swearing, he remarked calmly, "This has gone far enough. I have resigned myself to being the pawn of those vast impersonal powers who guide the destinies of humanity; but I am cursed if I will submit to being manipulated by mere mortals, and kept in ignorance even by that individual whom I had believed united to me by the strongest bonds of faith and affection, not to mention trust."

The eloquence of his speech—aye, and the justice of his complaint—brought an unaccustomed flush to my cheeks. Before I could respond, Emerson went on in a less literary vein. "Sit down," he bellowed. "You too, young lady—" And he deposited Enid onto the nearest stool with a thump that made two combs and a number of hairpins fly into the air. "No one is moving from this spot until I have received a full account of this astonishing affair."

"You are quite right, Emerson," I murmured. "And I will sit down—I really will—the instant I have finished washing—"

"You can wash him just as easily in a sitting position," thundered Emerson.

I sat.

Appeased by this gesture of compliance, Emerson lowered his voice to a fairly endurable level. "Pray confine your attentions to the young man's injury, Amelia. If the rest of him requires washing, he can do it himself."

"Oh, quite, Emerson. I was only—"

"Enough, Amelia." Emerson folded his arms and surveyed us with a masterful air. The men had collapsed onto the ground at the instant of his command, and now formed a fascinated audience, mouths ajar and eyes wide. Enid clutched the sides of the stool with both hands, as if she were expecting to be plucked off it; Nemo sat with bowed head, the mark of the girl's fingers printed crimson on his cheek.

"Ha," said Emerson, with satisfaction. "That is better. Now, young lady, you had better begin. I address you in that manner since I am certain your name is not Marshall."

I could not but admire my husband's cleverness; for his statement was admirably composed so as not to give away the fact that—as I firmly believed, and believe to this day—he was still ignorant of her true identity. Only the briefest flicker of his lashes betrayed his surprise when she admitted who she was, and repeated the narrative she had told me.

"Most interesting," said Emerson. "Of course I recognized you immediately, Miss Debenham. I was merely—er—biding my time before challenging you."

He fixed his stern gaze on me, where I sat next to Mr. Nemo. I started to speak, but thought better of it.

"Ha," Emerson said again. "However, Miss Debenham, you have omitted something from your most interesting story. You have, in fact, omitted everything of importance. I assume you are intimately acquainted with Mr. Nemo here, or you would not have addressed him so informally. Who is he? What is your relationship?"

Nemo rose to his feet. "I can answer those questions and others. If I can spare Enid—Miss Debenham—that shame, in recounting a history replete with—"

"Never mind the rhetoric," Emerson snapped. "I am a patient man, but there are limits to my patience. What the devil is your name?"

"My name is Donald Fraser."

I started up. "Ronald Fraser?"

"No, Donald Fraser."

"But Ronald Fraser—"

The vibration of the dimple in Emerson's chin warned me that he was about to roar. I stopped, therefore, and Emerson said, with the most exquisite courtesy, "I would be grateful, Mrs. Emerson, if you would refrain from any comment whatever—refrain, if possible, even from breathing loudly—until this gentleman has finished. Begin at the beginning, Mr. Fraser— for of your surname at least I feel fairly confident—and do not stop until you have reached the end."

Thus directed, the young man began the following narrative.

"My name is Donald Fraser. Ronald is my younger brother. Our family is old and honorable; never, until recently, did a blot of shame darken the name of Fraser—"

"Humph," said Emerson skeptically. "I take leave to doubt that. The ancient Scot was a bloodthirsty fellow; wasn't there some tale about an ancestor of yours serving up the severed head of an enemy to the widow of the deceased at a dinner party?"

I coughed gently. Emerson glanced at me. "Quite right, Amelia. I did not mean to interrupt. Continue, Mr. Donald Fraser."

"It will not take much time, Professor. The story is only too familiar, I fear." With an attempt at insouciance, the young man started to cross his arms, but winced and let the injured member fall back. For an instant the girl's face mirrored the pain on his and she made as if to rise. Almost immediately she sank back onto the stool. Ha, I thought, but did not speak aloud.

Donald—as I shall call him, in order to prevent confusion with his brother—proceeded. "Being the elder, I was the heir to the estate upon the death of our parents a few years ago. Our family was not rich, but thanks to my father's prudent management, we were left with enough to maintain us in modest comfort. I say we, because morally, if not legally, half of what I had inherited was Ronald's.

"My father had purchased a commission for me in—in a regiment of the line. . . . There is no need, I believe, to mention which one. After his death my brother nobly offered to take over the management of the estate so that I might pursue my military career. I had . . . I incurred debts. Allow me the favor of refusing to be specific about their nature; they were . . . They were not the sort one likes to mention, especially before . . ."

He gazed at Enid. I was as intrigued by the silent interchange between them as by his halting speech. She never looked at him, he never took his eyes off her; and the air between them fairly crackled with emotion. When his voice faltered, she started to her feet. Her cheeks were flaming.

"You lie!" she cried. "Despicably, stupidly—"

Emerson put one big brown hand on her shoulder and gently but inexorably returned her to her seat. "Be silent, Miss Debenham. You will have your chance at rebuttal. Sir—finish your story."

"It is quickly told," Donald muttered. "The regiment was gazetted to Egypt. Being in need of funds, I had forged a signature on a bill. My crime was discovered. The person I had attempted to defraud, a fellow officer, was generous. I was given the choice of resigning my commission and—and disappearing. I did so. That is all."

He had come to the end, but so abruptly, that Emerson and I were both left staring. Assuming my husband's prohibition ceased to have effect at that time, I exclaimed,

"Upon my word, Mr. Fraser, that is a rather curt narrative. I think, though, that I can fill in some of the details you have omitted. Your brother is in Egypt—"

"I know. I saw him yesterday."

"I presume he came to find you and extend a brother's hand in forgiveness and affection."

Nemo's drooping head sank lower. From Enid, squirming under Emerson's hand, came a scornful laugh. I turned to her. "And you, Miss Debenham, also came here on an errand of mercy and redemption, to save your old playfellow?"

"I came to tell him what I thought of him," the girl cried. She twisted away from Emerson's grasp and jumped to her feet. "He is a stupid fool who deserves everything that has happened to him!"

"No doubt," said Emerson, studying her with interest. "But if you will forgive me, Miss Debenham, I am determined to push doggedly onward—against the opposition of everyone present—to some understanding of the facts themselves. Is that how you became involved with Kalenischeff? For I do you the credit to assume you would have better taste than to take up with such a villain for his own sake."

"You are quite right," Enid said. "I had not been in Cairo two days before Kalenischeff approached me. He offered his assistance—for a price, of course—in finding Donald, who, Kalenischeff assured me, had slunk off like a whipped cur and hidden himself in Cairo's foul underworld."

Donald winced and covered his face with his hand. Enid went on remorselessly, "Alone I had no hope of entering that disgusting ambiance or approaching its denizens. Kalenischeff persuaded me that we should pretend to be—to be interested in one another in order to conceal my true purpose and lull Donald and his criminal associates—''

"That was rather credulous of you," Emerson said critically. "But never mind. I take it you did not, in fact, murder the rascal in a fit of pique or in defense of your virtue? No, no, don't lose your temper; a simple shake of the head will suffice. I never believed a woman could strike such a blow, penetrating the muscles of the chest and entering the heart—''

"Emerson, how can you!" I cried indignantly. "You told me—''

"You misunderstood," said Emerson, with such sublime indifference to truth that I was struck dumb with indignation. He compounded the insult by continuing, "Well, well, we are in a confused situation here, but that is nothing new; and at least the story these two young idiots—excuse me, young people—have produced puts an end to your theory that Sethos was responsible for Kalenischeff's death. There is no evidence—''

"But there soon will be," I assured him. "Abdullah and Hassan are bringing it—the body of one of the Master Criminal's henchmen, dead by his own hand after he had failed his dread master in the assignment of abducting me. That is to say, he did not know it was me; I was disguised as Enid, and he—''

"You were disguised," Emerson repeated slowly, "as Miss Debenham?"

I explained. Emerson listened without interrupting once. Then he turned to Nemo—or Donald, as I must call him.

"You, sir, were present, when these remarkable events occurred?"

"Emerson, do you doubt my word?" I demanded.

"Not at all, Amelia. The only thing I doubt is that

anyone could mistake you for Miss Debenham."

"Donald did," I declared triumphantly. "Is that not true, Donald? You followed me, believing I was Enid. No doubt you were trying to work up courage enough to reveal yourself."

But the untenability of this assumption was apparent as soon as I voiced it, for Nemo had remained in concealment for an hour and a half without making his presence known. The deep flush of shame that dyed his manly cheeks betrayed his true motive. He loved her—deeply, hopelessly, desperately—and his only joy was to worship her dainty form (or what he believed to be hers) from afar.

Tactfully I turned the subject. "The evidence will soon be forthcoming, Emerson. I believe I hear Abdullah coming now."

It was indeed Abdullah, with Hassan close on his heels.

"Where have you put the body?" I asked.

Abdullah shook his head. "There was no body, sitt. We found the spot you described; there were signs of a struggle, and bloodstains upon the ground. We searched far and wide, thinking the man might have recovered and crawled away—"

"Recovered from being dead?" I exclaimed. "Abdullah, do you think I don't know a corpse when I see one?"

"No, sitt. But dead or alive, he was gone. No doubt he was dead, as you say, for we heard his ghost calling in a high, thin voice, as spirits do."

Hassan nodded in emphatic confirmation. "We ran away then, sitt, for we did not want the dead man to mistake us for his murderers."

"Oh, good Gad," I said disgustedly. "That was not a ghost you heard, you foolish men. There are no such things. It must have been a bird, or a—or a—"

"Never mind, Peabody, I will conduct my usual exorcism," said Emerson. The use of that name instead of "Amelia" indicated that he had forgot his annoyance with me in the pleasurable anticipation of the theatrical performance to which he had referred. Emerson had often been called upon to perform exorcisms, Egypt being, in the opinion of its citizens, a particularly demon-ridden country. He has quite a reputation as a magician and is deservedly proud of it.

"Emerson," I said, interrupting his description of how he meant to go about the ritual. "Emerson—*where is Ramses?*"

We looked in Ramses' room, purely as a matter of form; I knew, as did Emerson, that if he had been anywhere about, he would have come to see what the commotion was, talking and interrupting and asking questions and making comments. . . .

We set out en masse for the Bent Pyramid. Emerson soon outstripped the rest of us, but Donald was not far behind him. The young man's look of haggard reproach was so poignant I had not the heart to reproach him for neglecting his duty. Love, as I reflected philosophically, has a corrosive effect on the brain and the organs of moral responsibility.

Since I had not mentioned to Emerson the collapse of the subsidiary pyramid, he had no idea where to start looking; when I arrived on the scene he was rushing around like a dog on a scent and making the evening hideous with his stentorian repetitions of Ramses' name.

"Be silent a moment," I begged. "How can you hear him reply if you keep shouting?"

Emerson nodded. Then he turned like a tiger on poor

Abdullah and clutched him by the throat of his robe. "From what direction did the cry you heard come?"

Abdullah gestured helplessly and rolled his eyes, finding speech impossible because of the constriction of the cloth around his throat.

"If you will forgive me, Emerson, that was a foolish question," I said. "You know how difficult it is to determine the origin of a faint, muffled cry in this barren region. I have, I believe, more pertinent information which I will produce as soon as you are calm enough to hear it. Look there, Emerson. Look at the small pyramid."

One glance was all that trained eye required. His hand fell in nerveless horror from the throat of our devoted reis; his eyes moved with mingled dread and deliberation over the new-fallen debris at the base of the small structure. None knew better than he the dangers of a careless attack on the unstable mass.

It was young Selim who gave a heartbreaking cry and flung himself onto the debris, where he began digging frantically. Emerson dodged a perfect rain of broken stone and lifted Selim up by the scruff of his neck. "That won't do, my lad," he said in a kindly voice. "You will bring the rest of the heap down on your head if you aren't careful."

Contrary to popular opinion, Arabs are very softhearted people and feel no shame in displaying emotion. Selim's face was wet with tears, which mingled horribly with the sand to form a muddy mask. I patted him on the shoulder and offered him my handkerchief. "I don't think he is under there, Selim," I said. "Emerson, do you call again. Just once, my dear, and then wait for an answer."

No sooner had the echoes of Emerson's poignant cry died into silence than there was an answer, high and faint and far away, quite easily mistaken by superstitious persons for the wailing of a lost spirit. Abdullah started. "That was it, O Father of Curses. That was the voice we heard!"

"Ramses," I said, sighing. "He has found the entrance, curse—I mean, bless him. Emerson, do you see that shadow ten feet above the debris and slightly to the right of center?"

A brief and, on my part, rational discussion of the situation resulted in the conclusion that the opening might indeed be the long-concealed entrance, and that it would be possible for us to reach it if we exhibited a reasonable amount of care. Emerson kept interrupting me with whoops of "Ramses!" and Ramses kept answering, in that uncanny wail. I finally put an end to the procedure by reminding Emerson that shouting used oxygen, a commodity of which Ramses might be in short supply if indeed, as one could only assume, he was shut into a place from which he could not extricate himself unaided. Emerson at once agreed, and I must say I found it much easier to cogitate without him bellowing.

Like the larger stone pyramids, this smaller version had been built of blocks that ascended like a giant, four-sided staircase. However, this structure was—as we had evidence—much less stable than its neighbor; it would be necessary to ascend with extreme caution, testing each block before putting one's weight upon it. Emerson insisted upon leading the way. As he correctly (but, I thought, depressingly) pointed out, if the block would not hold his weight, I would know it was not safe to step on it.

At last we reached the level of the opening and discovered that it was indeed the entrance—or, at least, an entrance—to the interior. Nothing but blackness showed within. Emerson took a deep breath. I stopped him with a soft reminder. "Even the vibrations of a loud shout . . ."

"Hmmm," said Emerson. "True, Peabody. Do you think he is in there?"

"I am certain of it."

"Then I am going in."

But he could not. The narrow opening would not admit the breadth of his shoulders, twist and turn them as he might. I waited until he had exhausted himself before I mentioned the obvious. "My turn, Emerson."

"Bah," said Emerson; but he said no more. An exclamation of distress came from quite another quarter. Donald had followed us; I had observed the skill with which he moved on the uneven surface, and deduced that he must have done some climbing. Now he said softly, "Professor, surely you don't intend to let her—"

"Let her?" Emerson repeated. "I never *let* Mrs. Emerson do anything, young man. I occasionally attempt to prevent her from carrying out her more harebrained suggestions, but I have never yet succeeded in doing so."

"I am narrower through the shoulders than you," Donald persisted. "Surely I am the one—"

"Balderdash," Emerson said brusquely. "You have had no experience. Mrs. Emerson has an affinity for pyramids."

While they were discussing the matter, I removed my coat and lighted a candle. After discovering that Ramses was not in his room (and before leaving the house) I had dashed to the roof to retrieve my belt and my parasol. The latter I had of necessity left below, but the belt and its accouterments had again proved their utility.

"*A bientôt*, Emerson," I said, and wriggled head-first into the hole.

There was no reply, but a surreptitious caress upon the portion of my body yet exposed was sufficient evidence of his emotions.

I found myself in a narrow passageway lined with stone. It was high enough for me to stand erect, but in view of the steep angle at which it descended I considered it better to proceed in a crawling position. I had not gone far before I saw something unusual. The darkness ahead was broken by an irregular patch of brightness. The light strengthened as I moved slowly forward, and I found that it streamed through a narrow gap in a huge fall of stone and brick which had blocked the passage. Cautiously I assumed an upright position and applied my eye to the gap.

Seated on a large block of stone, his back against the wall of the passage, was Ramses. He had stuck a candle onto the stone with its own grease, and he was scribbling busily on a notepad. Though I knew he must have heard my involuntary gasp of relief at finding him unharmed, he did not stop writing until he had finished the sentence and ended it with an emphatic jab of his pen. Then he looked up.

"Good evening, Mama. Is Papa with you, or have you come alone?"

No, dear Reader, the break in the narrative at this point is not intended to keep from your ears (or eyes) the words I spoke to my son. I did not dare shout at him for fear of disturbing the delicate balance of the stones around me. In fact, it was Ramses who spoke, describing in wearisome detail the method by which we ought to remove the fallen rubble in order to free him. He was still talking when I left.

My head had scarcely emerged from the entrance

hole when it was seized by Emerson. In between raining
kisses on my face, more or less at random, he asked
questions I could not hear owing to the fact that his
hands were covering my ears.

I was pleased but surprised; Emerson's demonstrations of affection, though extravagant in private, are not
often displayed before an audience. And indeed, if he
had seen Donald Fraser's grin, he would have desisted
at once.

Having solved the auditory problem, I explained the
situation. "I cannot shift the stones, Emerson; they are
too heavy for me. I think we will have to take advantage
of Mr. Fraser's offer after all."

"Is Ramses all right? Is the dear boy injured?" Emerson inquired anxiously.

"He is working on a manuscript which I presume to
be his Egyptian grammar," I replied curtly. "Mr. Fraser, if you will?"

Donald followed me into the passageway. At the sight
of the obstruction he let out a soft whistle. In the dim
flame of the candle I held, he resembled one of the
ancient workmen crouching on hands and knees before
the burial chamber in which he had left his royal master
hidden (as he vainly hoped) for all eternity.

I said softly, "Study the situation, Mr. Fraser, I pray,
before you touch any of the stones. A careless move—"

"I understand," Donald said.

Then we heard a thin, high voice. "I suggest, Mr.
Nemo—or Mr. Fraser, as the case may be—that you
endeavor to locate the pivotal point on which the relative mass of the rockfall is balanced; for according to
my calculations the total weight of the portion of the
pyramid over our heads is approximately eighteen and
one-third tons, give or take a hundred weight. . . ."

I find myself quite incapable of recording the rest of

Ramses' lecture. It was accompanied by a monotonous undercurrent of profanity from Donald Fraser, for which, I must say, I could hardly blame him. He performed well, particularly under those somewhat exasperating circumstances, and soon succeeded in enlarging the hole through which I had first seen the light of Ramses' candle. As soon as it was big enough, Ramses' face appeared in the opening, hideously shadowed by the candle he held. His thin face looked alarmingly like the mummy of his namesake, and he was still offering suggestions. "Mr. Nemo—if you will permit me to continue the use of that pseudonym until I am formally introduced to you under your proper name—I strongly request that you do not remove anything to the left—your right, it would be—of the present gap. My appraisal of the situation—"

The speech ended in a squawk as Donald, driven beyond endurance, snatched his charge by the throat and dragged him through the opening. It was a chancy thing to do, but it had no ill effect except on the nether portion of Ramses' anatomy, which, as I later discovered, was violently scored by the rough edges of the rocks as he passed rapidly under them.

"Precede me, Ramses, if you please," I said coldly.

"Yes, Mama. I would rather do that in any case, since I have the distinct impression, from the strength of Mr. Nemo's grip, that he is in a state of emotional excitation that makes me prefer to have some obstacle between myself and his—"

I gave Ramses a push. He said later that I had struck him, but that is not correct. I simply pushed him in order to hasten his progress. It certainly had that effect.

Our return to the house was effected in utter silence. When we arrived it was completely dark, and Hamid the cook informed us indignantly that dinner was burned to a crisp because we had not told him we would be late.

After the required repairs to our physical and sartorial deficiencies had been effected, and a distinctly inferior meal had been consumed, we gathered in the sitting room for a council of war.

Feeling that repairs to shattered nerves were also required, I offered whiskey all round, except to Ramses, of course. He and the cat had milk and Enid chose a cup of tea. The genial beverage (I refer in this instance to the whiskey) had the desired effect, though in Emerson's case the improvement of his spirits was due in large part to the relief of recovering his son more or less unscarred, and to the fact that I was about to admit him to my confidence. As he put it, during a brief moment of privacy, while I was removing my (or Enid's) disheveled costume, "Much as I deplore your insane escapades, Peabody, I resent even more being excluded from them."

Yet, as I explained once we had settled around the table in the sitting room, there was very little he did not know, now that the identities of the two young persons had been disclosed. He could not blame me for failing to inform him of Enid's real name, since he claimed to have recognized her from the start.

Ramses, of course, also maintained he had penetrated Enid's disguise. "The bone structure is unmistakable. A student of physiognomy is never misled by superficial changes in appearance such as are wrought by clothing, ornaments, or cosmetics. Which reminds me, Miss Debenham, that at some future time I would like to discuss with you the devices ladies employ in order to change their natural appearance—for the better, as they no doubt assume, or they would not resort to such things. The coloring of the lips and cheeks reminds me of the Amazulu people, who often paint broad stripes—''

We stifled Ramses, figuratively speaking—though Donald looked as if he would like to have done so literally. He had already informed me that he was beginning to understand my warnings concerning Ramses. ''The boy doesn't need a bodyguard, Mrs. Emerson, he needs a guardian angel—or possibly a squad of them.''

The young man was wearing his new shirt and trousers, and for the first time resembled the English gentleman I knew him to be. He sat with eyes downcast and lips pressed tightly together. Enid was also silent. The concerted effort both made to avoid touching or looking at one another was in my opinion highly significant.

Emerson was the first to break the silence. ''It seems that whether I will or not, I have become involved in the little matter of Kalenischeff's murder. Let me say at the outset that I cannot help but believe there is some connection between that event and the domestic matters Mr. Fraser has outlined. It is too much of a coincidence that a third party should have decided to do away with the villain—much as he deserved it—at the precise time when Miss Debenham had hired him to help find her missing kinsman.''

''Coincidences do occur, Emerson,'' I said. ''I know you would rather eliminate from consideration that individual whose name I refrain from mentioning—''

''Oh, the devil,'' Emerson growled. ''You cannot mention his name, Amelia, for you don't know what it is. Call him whatever you like, so long as it is pejorative.''

''Whatever we call him, it would be folly to deny that he is involved. He has favored us with communications on no less than four occasions. First, the attempted abduction of Ramses; second, the return of the stolen communion vessels; third, the presentation of the flowers and the ring; and last, today's attack. Only a mind hopelessly and irrevocably prejudiced''—I carefully refrained from looking at Emerson, but I heard him snarl—''would deny that all four events bear the signature of Sethos.''

"I beg your pardon, Mama," Ramses said. "I concur with your conclusions regarding the last three incidents, but in the first case—"

"Who else would want to abduct you, Ramses?"

"A great number of people, I should think," said Emerson. "Ordinarily I would agree with your premise, Peabody—that there cannot be many individuals in Egypt who yearn to make off with Ramses—but as I have learned to my sorrow, we seem to attract criminals as a dog attracts fleas. I should feel hurt if we had fewer than five or six murderers after us."

"He is speaking ironically," I explained to Donald, whose bewildered expression betokened his failure to comprehend. "However, there is some truth in his statement. We do attract criminals, for the simple reason that we threaten to destroy them and their vile activities."

"Yes, but curse it, we aren't threatening anyone now," Emerson cried. "At least . . . Ramses! Look Papa straight in the eye and answer truthfully. Are you threatening any criminals at this time?"

"To the best of my knowledge, Papa—"

"Just answer yes or no, my son."

"No, Papa."

"Have you unearthed any buried treasures or antiquities you neglected to mention to your mama and me?"

"No, Papa. If you would allow me—"

"No, Ramses, I will not allow you to elaborate. For once in my life I intend to direct the course of a family discussion and decide upon a sensible course of action.

"To return, then, to the subject of the murder. I find it difficult to believe that the police really consider Miss Debenham a serious suspect. If she were to surrender herself—"

Donald started up from his chair. "Never!" he exclaimed. "Even if she were to be cleared of the crime, the shame—the notoriety—"

"Be still a moment," I said. "Emerson, I think you underestimate the strength of the case against her. Let me play devil's advocate and state the facts as they will appear to the police. Item: Miss Debenham and Kalenischeff were intimately acquainted—lovers, to put it bluntly. (Donald, I insist that you be quiet.) They quarreled on the night of the murder. He was found dead in her bed, and she was with him in the room when the dastardly deed was done. Alone with him, mark you, and in her nightclothes. Her story of a midnight intruder who rendered her helpless by means of a drug will be dismissed as a not very clever invention. You may be sure no one else saw a sign of the fellow."

"Kalenischeff's shady reputation—his criminal connections—" Emerson began.

"His criminal connections are no more than suspicions in so far as the police are concerned. As for his reputation—don't you see, Emerson, that might work against Miss Debenham? To put it as nicely as possible, Kalenischeff was a ladies' man. Is not jealousy a motive for murder?"

Emerson looked grave. "Is there no other suspect?"

"Er—yes," I said. "As a matter of fact, there are two."

Emerson brightened. "Who?"

"Both," I said, "are in this room."

Emerson's eyes moved, quite involuntarily, I am sure, to Ramses.

"Oh, come, Emerson," I said impatiently. "If a woman could not strike such a blow, how could an eight-year-old boy? No! Who is the man with thews of steel and a formidable temper, who has been heard on numerous occasions to describe Kalenischeff as a villain and a rascal and has stated that his very presence was an affront to any decent woman?"

A modest smile spread across Emerson's face. "Me," he said.

"Grammar, Emerson, if you please. But you are correct. You are the person I meant."

"On my word, Peabody, that is cursed ingenious," Emerson exclaimed. "If I didn't know I hadn't done it, I would suspect myself. Well, but who is the other suspect?"

"She is referring to me, Professor," said Donald, carefully avoiding the grammatical error Emerson had committed. "I was at the hotel that night. You had told me to meet you there—"

"But you didn't," Emerson said.

"No. I—I was in a strange state of mind. Appreciating your trust and yet resenting your interference . . . I wandered half the night trying to decide what to do."

"I believe I can understand, Mr. Fraser. But the fact that you were in the motley crowd outside the hotel doesn't make you a suspect. You were there other evenings, you and dozens of other nondescript Egyptians. I assume you did not enter the hotel?"

"How could I?" Donald asked with a wry smile. "A ragged beggar like myself would not be admitted to those precincts."

"Then I fail to see how you can fall under suspicion."

Ramses had been trying for some time to get a word in. "Papa—were Mr. Fraser's true identity known—"

"Just what I was about to say," I remarked, frowning at Ramses. "Mr. Donald Fraser might have a motive for killing Kalenischeff that a ragged beggar would not. Furthermore, I know for a fact that he is suspected."

"Who told you?" Emerson demanded. "Baehler?"

"No, it was—"

"You went to police headquarters the day you were in Cairo," Emerson said accusingly. "You misled me, Amelia. You promised—"

"I made no promise, Emerson. And in fact the police were of little assistance. I cannot think why our friend Sir Eldon has such incompetent people as his aides. Major Ramsay is a perfect fool, and he has no manners besides. The person I was about to mention is a well-known private investigator. I started to tell you about him last night before you—before we—"

"Please continue with your narrative, Amelia," said Emerson, glowering.

"Certainly, Emerson. I only mentioned the—er—interruption because I don't want you to accuse me of concealing information from you."

"Your explanation is noted and accepted, Peabody."

"Thank you, Emerson. As I was saying, I happened to meet this gentleman outside the Administration Building. He recognized me and addressed me—most courteously, I might add—and it was he who informed me that a certain beggar in a saffron turban was under suspicion. His name is Tobias Gregson. He has solved such well-known cases as the Camberwell poisoning—"

I was not allowed to proceed. Every member of the

group—with the exception of the cat Bastet, who only blinked her wide golden eyes—jumped up and attempted to speak. Enid cried, "Ronald is behind this! How could he . . ." Donald declared his intention of turning himself in at once. Emerson made incoherent remarks about the moral turpitude of private detectives and told me I ought to know better than to speak to strange men. Ramses kept exclaiming, "But, Mama—but, Mama—Gregson is—Gregson is—" like a parrot that has been taught only a few phrases.

By speaking all at once, each defeated his (or her) purpose, and as the hubbub died, I seized the opportunity to go on. "Never mind Mr. Gregson; we won't speak of him since he has aroused such a storm. It is out of the question for Donald and Enid to give themselves up. Donald's case is as desperate as Enid's—indeed, it may be worse, for I am sure the authorities would prefer to arrest a man rather than a young lady. No; we must sit pat, as one of my American friends once said—in regard, I believe, to some sort of card game. Our game is a dangerous one, and we must hold our cards close to our persons. I have made one attempt to lure Sethos out of hiding; I propose to continue that method tomorrow—"

Another outcry silenced me, punctuated, like the monotonous tolling of a bell, by Ramses' reiterated "But Mama." Emerson won over the rest this time, by sheer volume.

"Rather than allow you to repeat that imbecile and hazardous experiment, Amelia, I will bind you hand and foot. Why must you take these things on yourself? Can't you leave it to me to smoke out the villain?"

"I cannot because I am the only one who can pass for Enid. Or do you propose to assume women's clothing and walk with her dainty, tripping steps?"

The very idea outraged Emerson so thoroughly that he was momentarily mute. It was Enid who said timidly, "But, Amelia—are you absolutely certain it was I the man wanted? Perhaps you were the intended victim all along."

"By Gad," Emerson exclaimed. "Out of the mouths of babes and . . . Hem. Excuse me, Miss Debenham. Precisely the point I would have made had I been permitted to speak without these constant interruptions."

"Nonsense," I said. "My disguise was perfect. Donald here was deceived—"

"I was not," Ramses said quickly. "I knew it was you. Mama, there is something I must—"

"There, you see," Emerson exclaimed triumphantly.

"The eyes of true love cannot be deceived," Enid said. Donald glanced at her and glanced quickly away.

Emerson's lips tightened. "That," he said, "is what I am afraid of."

Emerson refused to explain this enigmatic remark; nor, in fact, did any of us ask him to explain, for we had more important matters to resolve. We finally decided to wait upon events for another day or two, in the hope that something would turn up. I should say, "Emerson decided," for I was opposed to the idea. He promised me, however, that if nothing happened in the next two days, we would go together to Cairo in an effort to obtain information.

"Let me work for a brief time without distraction," he groaned piteously. "The stratification of the structure next to the pyramid is not clear in my mind as yet."

I knew what Emerson was up to. He had no more intention than I did of sitting with folded hands awaiting Sethos' next move. He was deceiving me, the sly fellow—trying to get the jump on me in another of our amiable competitions in criminology. Well, I thought, smiling to myself—two can play at that game, Professor Radcliffe Emerson! I had a few cards up my own sleeve.

"Very well," I said pleasantly. "That will give me a chance to explore the interior of the subsidiary pyramid."

"It will prove a wasted effort, Mama," said Ramses. "The burial chamber is empty. Indeed, I suspect it was never used for a burial, since its dimensions are only seven feet by—"

"Ramses," I said.

"Yes, Mama?"

"Did I not, on an earlier occasion, forbid you to go inside a pyramid without permission?"

Ramses pursed his lips thoughtfully. "Indeed you did, Mama, and I assure you I have not forgotten. I might claim that since you were present, though at some little distance, I was not violating the literal sense of the command. However, that would be disingenuous. In fact, my position was on the very edge of the entrance opening—technically neither in nor out—and I had every intention of remaining there, and would have done so, but for the fact that a careless move on my part caused me to lose my footing and slide down the passage, which, if you recall, had a slope of perhaps forty-five degrees fifteen minutes. It was my body striking the wall that disturbed the delicate equilibrium of the structure, whose stones had already been—"

"Ramses."

"Yes, Mama. I will endeavor to be brief. Once the passage was blocked and I realized that my strength was inadequate for the purpose of freeing myself, I took advantage of my position to explore the rest of the interior, knowing it would be some time before my absence was noted and a rescue party—''

"I think, my son," said Emerson uneasily, "that your mama will excuse you now. You had better go to bed."

"Yes, Papa. But first there is a matter I feel obliged to bring to Mama's attention. Gregson is—''

"I will hear no more, wretched boy," I exclaimed, rising to my feet. "I am thoroughly out of sorts with you, Ramses. Take yourself off at once."

"But, Mama—''

I started toward Ramses, my arm upraised—not indeed to strike, for I do not believe in corporal punishment for the young except in cases of extreme provocation—but to grasp him and take him bodily to his room. Misinterpreting my intentions, the cat Bastet rose in fluid haste and wrapped her heavy body around my forearm, sinking her teeth and claws into my sleeve. Emerson persuaded the cat of her error and removed her—claw by claw—but instead of apologizing, she chose to be offended. She and Ramses marched off side by side, both radiating offended hauteur, the cat by means of her stiff stride and switching tail, Ramses by neglecting to offer his usual formula of nightly farewell. I daresay they would have slammed the door if there had been one to slam.

Emerson then suggested we retire. "After such a day, Peabody, you must be exhausted."

"Not at all," I said. "I am ready to go on talking for hours if you like."

Emerson declined this offer, however, and after gathering our belongings we started for our tent. I was uneasy about leaving the others, but we had taken all possible precautions, requesting Abdullah to close and bar the gates and to set a guard. I felt sure I could rely on Donald, not only to watch over both his charges, but to maintain a respectful distance from one of them. Poor boy, he was so in awe of the girl, he hardly dared speak to her, much less approach her.

I promised myself I would have a little talk with him on that subject. For in my opinion (which is based on considerable experience), there is nothing that annoys a woman so much as fawning, servile devotion. It brings out the worst in women—and in men, let me add, for a tendency to bully the meek is not restricted to my sex, despite the claims of misogynists. If someone lies down and invites you to trample him, you are a remarkable person if you decline the invitation.

I told Emerson this as we strolled side by side through the starlit night. I half-expected him to sneer, for he takes a poor view of my interest in the romantic affairs of young people; instead he said thoughtfully, "So you recommend the Neanderthal approach, do you?"

"Hardly. What I recommend is that all couples follow our example of marital equality."

I reached for his hand. It lay lax in my grasp for a moment; then his strong fingers twined around mine and he said, "Yet you seem to be saying that a certain degree of physical and moral force—"

"Do you remember remarking on one occasion that you had been tempted to snatch me up onto a horse and ride with me into the desert?" I laughed. Emerson did not; in fact, his look was strangely wistful as he replied, "I do remember saying it. Are you suggesting I ought to have done so?"

"No, for I would have resisted the attempt with all the strength at my disposal," I replied cheerfully. "No woman wants to be carried off against her will; she only wants a man to want to do it! Of course, for old married folk like us, such extravagance would be out of place."

"No doubt," Emerson said morosely.

"I admit that a proper compromise between tender devotion and manly strength is difficult to achieve. But Donald has gone too far in one direction, and I intend to tell him so at the earliest possible opportunity. He adores her; and I rather think she reciprocates, or would, if he went about wooing her in the proper manner. She would not say such cruel cutting things to him if she did not—"

We had reached the tent. Emerson swept me up into his arms and carried me inside.

Nine

Neither of us slept well that night. My lecture had obviously made a deep impression on Emerson, in a sense I had not at all anticipated but to which I had no objection.

Even after the time for slumber had arrived, Emerson was unusually restless. He kept starting up at the slightest sound; several times his abrupt departure from the nuptial couch woke me, and I would see him crouched at the entrance to the tent with a heavy stick in his hands.

All the sounds were false alarms—the far-off cries of jackals prowling the desert waste, or the surreptitious movements of small nocturnal animals emerging from their lairs in the relative safety of darkness to seek refreshment and exercise. I myself was not troubled by such noises, which I had long since learned to know and recognize. But I dreamed a great deal, which is not usual with me. The details of the dreams fled as soon as I woke, leaving only a vague sense of something troubling my mind.

Despite his disturbed night Emerson was in an excellent mood the following morning. As he stretched and yawned outside the tent, his stalwart frame stood out in magnificent outline against the first rays of dawn. We had brought a spiritlamp and supplies of food and water, so we were able to make a scanty morning meal. As we waited for the workmen to arrive, Emerson said, "You were restless last night, Peabody."

"So would you have been had you been wakened hourly, as I was, by someone prowling round the tent."

"You talked in your sleep."

"Nonsense, Emerson. I never talk in my sleep. It is a sign of mental instability. What did I say?"

"I could not quite make out the words, Peabody."

The arrival of the crew put an end to the discussion and I thought no more about it. Ramses was in the van, of course, with Donald close beside him. The young man assured me there had been no trouble during the night. "Except," he added, scowling at Ramses—who returned the scowl, with interest—"I caught this young man halfway up the stairs to the roof shortly after midnight. He refused to tell me where he was going."

"I could not go out the door because Hassan was on guard there," Ramses said—as if this were an acceptable excuse for his attempt to creep out of the house.

"Never mind," I said, sighing. "Ramses, in case I neglected to mention it, I forbid you to leave the house at night."

"Is that a wholesale prohibition, Mama? For instance, should the house catch fire, or be invaded by burglars, or should the roof of my room appear in imminent danger of falling—"

"Obviously you must use your own discretion in such cases," said Emerson.

I abandoned the lecture. Ramses could always find a way to do what he wanted, if he had to burn the house down in order to justify it.

"Where is Enid?" I asked.

Then I saw her standing some distance away, her back turned. "She wanted to stay at the house," Donald said. "But I insisted she come with us."

"Quite right. She must not be left alone for an instant."

"Besides, I need every pair of hands," Emerson announced. "Listen to me, all of you. I intend to work without interruption this day. If all the powers of hell were to choose this spot on which to wage the final battle of Armageddon, I would not be distracted. If one of you feels a mortal illness come over him, pray go off and die at a distance. Come along, Ramses. You too, Fraser."

And he marched off, shouting for Abdullah.

"Well!" I said to Enid, who had approached me. "He is in a temper today! We had better humor him, my dear. I have a great treat for you—we are going to explore the interior of the pyramid!"

Instead of mirroring the enthusiasm I expected, the girl's face lengthened. "But Ramses said—"

"My dear girl, I hope you are not suggesting that a mere infant has my expertise in archaeology? There may be many important signs Ramses has missed."

I set the men to work clearing away the debris and enlarging the entrance. A closer examination of the ceiling of the descending passageway convinced me there was no danger of further collapse except in the section immediately adjoining the one that had already fallen. A few stout timbers were arranged to brace this; the fallen stones were removed; and I allowed myself the pleasure of being the first to penetrate the interior. We disturbed the usual number of bats, and the advent of these harmless creatures, squeaking and flapping, had a deleterious effect on Enid's nerves. She absolutely refused to accompany me any farther, so I went on alone.

At the end of a series of passages and corridors was a small chamber some seven and a half feet square, with a fine corbeled roof. It was entirely empty. A brief search through the debris on the floor disclosed nothing of interest, and, leaving Selim to sift through the dust to make sure nothing had been overlooked, I returned to the open air, heroically concealing my disappointment.

I found Enid outside, perched on one of the blocks on the side of the pyramid. Chin on her hands, the breeze ruffling her hair, she watched the others gather for the midmorning break. I indicated I was ready to join them, and as we scrambled down the steplike stones I remarked, "It won't do, you know. You cannot go on forever treating him like a leper."

"I can and will," Enid said hotly. "Unless he comes to his senses and confesses the truth."

"He has already confessed to such a staggering variety of sins, I can't imagine what he could be concealing," I remarked. "Unless you believe he is the killer."

"You misunderstand me." We reached the ground and she turned to face me. "It was Ronald," she blurted. "Not Donald at all. He took the blame for Ronald's fault, as he has always done."

"Losing his commission, his honor, and his fortune? Come, Enid, I can't believe any man (even a man) would be so foolish. Nobility and self-sacrifice are the highest qualities of which humanity is capable, but when carried to excess, they are not so much admirable as idiotic.''

"I quite agree," Enid said, with a bitter laugh. "But you don't know Donald. Quixotic is too mild a word for him. Ronald was always his mother's darling—the younger and smaller and weaker of the two."

"The runt of the litter," I said musingly.

"I beg your pardon?"

"It is a slang expression, and a very pithy one. How often have I seen a mother cherish some pitiful crippled infant, to the neglect of the other children in the family. Weakness brings out the best in us, Enid, and I must say—"

"Yes, I have no doubt that in the abstract it is a noble quality. But in this case it resulted in terrible harm to both brothers. Ronald was never at fault, he was never punished. Instead of resenting this unfair treatment, Donald tried to win his mother's approval by appointing himself Ronald's defender and whipping boy. When Ronald did something wrong, he blamed Donald, and Donald took the beating. When Ronald taunted a hulking bully, Donald did the fighting. Their mother's last words to Donald were, 'Always love and protect your brother.' And he has done exactly that."

"In childhood, perhaps. But how can you be certain Donald took the blame for his brother this time? A beating is one thing; to admit responsibility for a debt one has not incurred—"

"It would not be the first time," Enid said. "Donald has paid a number of Ronald's debts in the past. This time the situation was more serious. Ronald would have been publicly disgraced and perhaps sent to prison if the gentleman whose signature had been forged had decided to press the matter. He was willing to let Donald off more lightly because of the respect and affection felt for Donald by all who know him—a consideration that would assuredly not have been extended to Ronald. For that reason Donald agreed to take the blame on himself. I am as certain of that fact as I am that we are standing here, but I cannot prove it. The only ones who know the truth are the brothers themselves. Ronald won't betray himself, and if Donald is determined to play the martyr . . . That was why I had to come to Egypt. Ronald had already set out, ostensibly to find Donald and bring him home. I knew he would not press the search, and of course I was right. When I reached Cairo I learned that Ronald had gone off on some pleasure trip. It was up to me to locate Donald and beg him—threaten him—"

"Bribe him?" I inquired delicately.

A deep flush stained the girl's rounded cheeks. "He has never given the slightest indication that an offer of the sort to which you refer would influence him."

"I see. Well, men are strange creatures, Enid; it requires experience like mine, which extends over many nations and two separate continents, to understand their foibles. Did it ever occur to you that Ronald might have taken steps to prevent you from finding Donald?"

"Such a suspicion did enter my mind," Enid murmured. "I even wondered whether Kalenischeff might not have been sent to lead me astray. But I cannot believe that, even of Ronald. . . ."

"Believe it," I said firmly. "Kalenischeff was up to something; he told me he intended to leave Egypt, and he would never abandon a lucrative scheme until he had collected every possible penny first. He meant to betray someone, I am certain of that. The only question is— who? Well, my dear, you have raised several interesting and suggestive issues, which I must mull over. Now we had better join the others. I believe I hear Emerson calling me.''

There was no doubt about it, in fact. Emerson's voice, as I have had occasion to remark, is notable for its carrying quality.

Ramses was the first to greet us. He asked whether I had found anything interesting inside the pyramid.

I changed the subject.

We had almost finished our repast when the sound of voices from afar warned us that another party of tourists was approaching. The absurd little caravan came trotting toward us, and after one look at the formidable figure leading the procession, Emerson dived headlong into the trench that had been dug. After the episode with the empress, he was wary of old ladies.

I sent the others back to work and advanced to meet the intruders, hoping I could head them off and spare my poor Emerson. The rider on the lead donkey looked familiar, and I realized that it was indeed the elderly American lady I had seen at Shepheard's. Her voluminous black skirts practically swallowed up the little donkey. Nevertheless, he proceeded at a brisk trot, which caused the old lady to roll perilously from side to side. Two donkey boys took turns shoving her back into the saddle.

Seeing me, she changed course. ''I know you,'' she said, in a piercing nasal voice. ''Saw you at the hotel. Friend of Baehler's? Most improper, a lady dining alone.''

''I was not dining, I was lunching,'' I reminded her, and then introduced myself.

''Huh,'' said the old lady. ''And who's that, then?''

She pointed with her parasol. I turned. ''Allow me to present my son,'' I said. ''Ramses, go back—''

''Ramses?'' The old lady trumpeted. ''What kind of

name is that? Sickly-looking child. Not long for this world.''

''Thank you for your concern, madam,'' I said with frigid courtesy. ''I assure you it is unwarranted. Ramses, will you please—''

The old lady distracted me by dismounting. Indeed, the process would have seriously alarmed someone of a nervous temperament, accompanied as it was by infuriated screams and wild waving of her parasol. I thought she was going to topple over onto one of the small donkey boys and mash him flat. However, the action was eventually completed and the old lady, straightening her skirts and her black veil, addressed me again.

''Show me the pyramid, ma'am. I came a long way to see it, and see it I will. Mrs. Axhammer of Des Moines, Iowa, don't do things by halves. I've got a list. . . .'' She plucked it from her pocket and waved it like a flag. ''And I'm not going home till I've seen everything that's writ down here.''

''What about your companions?'' I asked. Both had dismounted. The pale young man leaned weakly against his donkey, mopping his brow. The woman had collapsed onto the ground, her face as green as the palms in the background.

Mrs. Axhammer of Des Moines, Iowa (wherever that barbaric location may be), emitted the evillest laugh I had ever heard. ''Let 'em sit. Poor weak critters, they can't keep up with me—and I'm sixty-eight years old, ma'am, not a day less. That's my nephew—Jonah's his name—I brung him along so he could tend to things, but he ain't worth a plugged nickel. Thinks he'll get cut out of my will if he ain't nice to me. Doesn't know he's already cut out of it. I hired that fool woman for a companion, but she ain't holding up either. A lady's got to have a chaperone, though. What's that boy staring at me for? Ain't you taught him any manners?''

"I venture to say," said Ramses, in his most pedantic manner, ''that most people would forget their manners when confronted with someone as remarkable in appearance as yourself. However, I do not wish any opprobrium to attach to my mama. She has endeavored to correct my behavior, and if the result is not as it should be, the blame is mine, not hers.''

It was difficult to assess the effect of this speech on Mrs. Axhammer, for the veil blurred her features. Personally, I thought it rather a handsome effort. Ramses advanced and held out his hand. "May I escort you, madam?'' he asked.

The old lady brandished her parasol. "Get away, get away, you young rascal. I know boys; trip you up, boys do, and put spiders on you."

Ramses began, "Madam, rest assured I had no intention—''

"Now how could you be any use to me?'' the old lady demanded irascibly. "Puny little critter like you. . . . Here, ma'am, I'll take your arm. You're short, but you look strong.''

She caught me by the shoulder. She was wearing dainty black lace mittens, but there was nothing delicate about her hand, which was as heavy as a man's. I permitted the liberty, however. Courtesy to the elderly is a trait I endeavor to instill in my son—and the lady's grip was too strong to be easily dislodged.

As we walked slowly toward the pyramid, Mrs. Axhammer subjected me to a searching and impertinent interrogation. She asked how old I was, how long I had been married, how many children I had, and how I liked my husband. I returned the compliment as soon as I could get a word in, asking her how she liked Egypt.

After a long diatribe about the heathen customs and unsanitary habits of the modern Egyptian, she added in an equally vitriolic tone, "Not that civilized folks act much better, ma'am. The scandals I heard in Cairo would make a lady blush, I do assure you. Why, there was a young English lady murdered her inamorato a few days ago; cut his throat ear to ear, they say, in her very room."

"I had heard of it," I said. "I cannot believe any young lady would do such a thing."

A gust of wind blew Mrs. Axhammer's veil askew, just as she bared a set of large white teeth whose very perfection betrayed their falsity. "There's no doubt in my mind," she snapped. "Women are dangerous, ma'am, much more dangerous than the male. I see you've got one out here with you. Don't approve of women taking work away from men. Ought to stay home and tend to the house."

Realizing I would get no more out of the malicious old creature except ignorant maledictions about her own sex, I determined to finish my duties and get rid of her. She paid no attention to my lecture, which, if I may say so, was of admirable quality, and resisted my efforts to lead her away from the excavations.

"There's a white man down there with all them natives," she exclaimed indignantly. "Is that your husband? Ain't he got no sense of dignity? Hi, there, you—" And she made as if to jab Emerson, whose back was turned, with her parasol.

Like lightning I brought my own parasol into play, striking up the shaft of Mrs. Axhammer's with a skill worthy of a master swordsman. The ring of steel on steel made Emerson jump, but he did not turn round.

The old lady burst out laughing and feinted playfully

at me with her parasol. "Useful instruments, ain't they?
Never travel without one. Hey, there—"

She spun round; and as her flailing draperies settled,
I saw to my consternation that they had concealed a
small kneeling form.

"Ramses!" I exclaimed. "What are you doing?"

"Looking up my skirts," the old lady howled. "Let
me at him, ma'am, let me at the little rascal. You've
been too soft on him, ma'am; he needs a good thrashing,
and Mrs. Axhammer of Des Moines, Iowa, is the one
to give it to him."

While I engaged the agitated old person in a spirited
exchange of thrusts and parries, Ramses skipped hastily
away. "I was merely examining your feet, madam," he
said indignantly. "They are very large, you know."

This remark may have been intended to soften Mrs.
Axhammer's anger, but as might have been predicted,
it had precisely the opposite effect. She set off after
Ramses, and, seeing he was having no difficulty in
keeping a safe distance from her, I followed at a more
leisurely pace. At least Ramses' dreadful lapse of manners had succeeded in drawing Mrs. Axhammer away
from Emerson, and I fondly hoped that once away, she
would not return.

Such proved to be the case. Shaking with indignation,
Mrs. Axhammer mounted her donkey and the caravan
trotted off.

When we returned to the house that afternoon, Emerson
expressed himself as satisfied with the morning's work.
"I think I have it clear in my mind now, Peabody. There
are traces of at least three occupation levels, the latest
addition having probably been made in Ptolemaic times.
The plan is complex, however, and I would appreciate

your assistance, if you are finished messing about with your pyramid.''

Overlooking the derogatory tone, I assured him that I was at his disposal. "There is nothing inside, Emerson. I doubt that it was ever used for a burial.''

"That is what I said, Mama,'' remarked Ramses.

After luncheon, Enid retired to her room with her book of detective stories. She had not spoken a word to Donald, and his gloomy look testified to his depressed spirits. I was about to suggest we have a little talk when Emerson said, "What would you think about a ride to Mazghunah this afternoon, Peabody? The communion vessels ought to be returned to the church.''

"An excellent idea, Emerson,'' I replied, wondering what was behind this suggestion.

"Shall we take Ramses?''

"I would rather not,'' I said truthfully.

"And I,'' said Ramses, "would prefer to take a little mild exercise, in the form of a stroll around the village and its environs.''

"Mild exercise indeed,'' I exclaimed. "You have had a great deal of exercise already, being chased by infuriated old ladies. Stay here and work on your grammar.''

"Never mind, Peabody,'' Emerson said with a smile. "We cannot keep an active lad like Ramses shut up in the house all the time. There is no harm in his taking a stroll so long as Mr. Fraser accompanies him.''

Neither Ramses nor Donald appeared to care for that idea. "Such an arrangement would leave the young lady unprotected,'' Ramses protested. Donald nodded vigorous agreement.

"She has stout walls and strong men to protect her,'' Emerson replied. "It is broad daylight, and we won't be long. Mazghunah is only ten kilometers from here, and our business will be easily concluded.''

So it was arranged. Taking two of the donkeys, Emerson and I rode southward. We saw no one, for at that time of day tourists and natives alike retire into the shade. I hardly need say that Emerson and I are never deterred from the path of duty by climatic conditions, and I, for one, enjoyed the ride.

The path, scarcely discernible to any but a trained eye, led across the rocky waste of the plateau, past the tumbled remains of the three brick pyramids of Dahshoor. They had been built a thousand years after their great stone neighbors, but the shorter passage of time had not dealt kindly with them. Once faced with stone, in imitation of the older and larger tombs, they had crumbled into shapeless masses of brick as soon as the facing stones were removed.

Dominating the other ruins was the great bulk of the Black Pyramid, the tomb of Amenemhat of the Twelfth Dynasty. Because of its location on the highest part of the plateau, it appears from some vantage points to be even taller than its stone neighbors to the north, and its ominous reputation is justified by its appearance. I knew the interior of that monstrous structure only too well, for it was in its sunken and flooded burial chamber that Emerson and I had been flung by the villain who assumed we would never emerge alive. Only the most heroic exploits on both our parts (with a little assistance from Ramses) had enabled us to escape from perils which would have destroyed lesser beings.

Although I would have liked to explore the Black Pyramid again, and visit the ruined monastery we had occupied the year before, we had no time for nostalgia that day. We went directly to the village.

By comparison to Mazghunah, Menyat Dahshoor is a veritable metropolis. The former village is primarily inhabited by Copts (Egyptian Christians), but except for the characteristic indigo turbans, the inhabitants are indistinguishable in appearance from other Egyptians, and the wretched little houses are like those of any Moslem village. Ancient Coptic, the last remnant of the tongue of the pharaohs, is no longer spoken except in a few remote hamlets to the south, but it survives in the ritual of the Coptic Church.

The village looked deserted. Even the dogs had sought shelter from the sun, and nothing moved except a few chickens pecking at bugs. Strangers are such a rarity in these primitive places, however, that our advent was soon acknowledged, and people began trickling out of their houses. We drew up near the well, which is the center of communal activity. Facing us was the church, with the house of the priest next to it.

The men gathered around Emerson, calling out greetings and inquiries. The women approached me, many carrying sickly babies. I had expected this and had come prepared; opening my medical kit, I began dispensing ipecacuanha and eyewash.

The Sheikh El Beled (mayor of the village) had of course noted our arrival as soon as the others, but dignity demanded that he delay awhile before presenting himself. Eventually, he made his appearance; when Emerson informed him that the lost communion vessels were about to be restored to him, tears filled the little man's eyes, and he dropped to his knees, kissing Emerson's feet and babbling thanks.

"Humph," said Emerson, not looking at me. Honesty demanded that we decline to take credit for something we had not achieved; but on the other hand, there was no need to explain a situation that was inexplicable even to us.

As the news spread through the crowd, a scene of

utter pandemonium broke out. People wept, shouted, sang, and embraced one another. They also embraced Emerson, a favor he endured without enthusiasm. "Ridiculous," he grunted at me over the head of a very fat lady, whose veiled face was pressed against his chest. She was, I believe, raining kisses on that region, while holding him in a grip he could not escape.

"You see, Peabody," he went on, "the degrading effect of superstition. These people are carrying on as if we had conferred health and immortality upon them instead of fetching back a few tarnished pots. I will never understand—er—awk—" He broke off, sputtering, as the lady raised herself on tiptoe and planted a fervent kiss upon his chin.

Eventually we quieted the crowd and, escorted by the mayor, proceeded to the church. On the step, hands raised in thanksgiving, was the priest, and very odd it seemed to behold his stout figure and genial face in the place of the great (in all but the moral sense) Father Girgis. Everybody trooped into the church, including the donkeys, and when the precious vessels had been restored to the altar, such a shout broke out that the very rafters shook—which was not surprising, since they were extremely old and brittle. Tears of joy streaming down his face, the priest announced there would be a service of thanks the following day. He then invited us and the mayor to join him in his house.

So again we entered the edifice where once we had been welcomed by the Master Criminal himself. So pervasive were the presence and the memory of that great and evil man that I half-expected to see him in the shadows, stroking his enormous black beard and smiling his enigmatic smile. It is a strange and disquieting fact that evil can sometimes appear more impressive than virtue. Certainly the Master Criminal had made a more imposing man of God than his successor. Father Todorus was a foot shorter and several feet wider round the middle; his beard was scanty, and streaked with gray.

He was a pleasant host, however. We settled ourselves on the divan with its faded chintz cushions, and the priest offered us refreshment, which of course we accepted, for to refuse would have been rude in the extreme. I was expecting the thick, sweet coffee which is the common drink; imagine my surprise when the priest returned from an inner room with a tray on which rested a glass bottle and several clay cups. After Emerson had taken a cautious sip of the liquid his eyebrows soared.

I followed suit. "It is French cognac," I exclaimed.

"The best French cognac," Emerson said. "Father, where did you get this?"

The priest had already emptied his cup. He poured another generous measure and replied innocently, "It was here in my house when I returned."

"We have been anxious to hear of your adventure, Father," Emerson said. "How well I recall the anger of my distinguished chief wife, the Sitt Hakim here, upon learning that the priest of Dronkeh was not who he pretended to be. 'What have you done with the real priest, you son of a camel?' she cried. 'If you have injured that good, that excellent man, I will cut out your heart!' "

Emerson's version was not a very accurate rendering of what I had said, but I had indeed inquired about the missing priest, and well I remembered the M.C.'s cynical reply: "He is enjoying the worldly pleasures he has eschewed, and the only danger is to his soul."

After thanking me for my concern, Father Todorus launched into his story. It was clear that he had only been waiting for us to ask, and that constant repetition had shaped his account into a well-rehearsed narrative of the sort to which Egyptians can listen over and over again. Unfortunately, there was less information than stylistic elegance in the long, rambling tale; stripped of unnecessary verbiage, it could have been told in a few sentences.

Father Todorus had gone to bed one night as usual, and had awakened in a strange place, with no notion of how he had arrived there. The room was elegantly, indeed luxuriously furnished (the description of its silken curtains and soft couch, its tinkling fountain and marble floors occupied the bulk of the speech). But he saw no one save the attendants who brought him rich food and rare liquors at frequent intervals, and since the windows were barred and shuttered, he could see nothing that would give him the slightest clue as to his whereabouts.

His return was accomplished in the same eerie fashion; he awoke one morning in the same narrow cot from which he had been spirited away, and at first he could hardly believe the entire episode had not been a long and vivid dream. The astonished cries of his parishioners upon his reappearance, and the accounts they gave him of what had transpired during his absence, proved that his experience had been real. But the innocent man frankly admitted he was inclined to attribute the whole thing to evil spirits, who were known to torture holy men by tempting them with the goods of this world.

"So you were tempted, were you?" Emerson asked. "With rich food and fine wines and liquors—"

"They are not forbidden by our faith," Father Todorus hastened to remark.

"No, but other temptations are forbidden, at least to the clergy. Were the attendants who waited upon your reverence men or women?"

The guilt on the poor man's face was answer enough. Emerson, chuckling, would have pursued the subject had I not intervened. "It would be more to the point,

Emerson, were we to ask Father Todorus for a more detailed description of the place in which he was imprisoned. He may have heard or seen something that would give us a hint as to its location."

I spoke in English, and Emerson answered in the same language. "If that swine Sethos is as clever as you seem to think he is, he will have abandoned that place long ago. Oh, very well, it will do no harm to ask."

Father Todorus was visibly relieved when, instead of returning to the awkward subject of his temptations, Emerson asked about his prison. Like so many people, the priest was a poor observer; specific questions brought out facts he had suppressed, not intentionally but because he had never thought about them. He had not been able to see out the windows, but he had heard sounds, though muffled and faraway. When added one to another, the noises he mentioned made it evident that he had been, not in a village or isolated villa, but in the heart of a city.

"Cairo, Emerson," I cried.

"I assumed that from the first," said Emerson repressively. "But where in that teeming hive of humanity?"

Further questioning failed to answer that important question. When we rose to take our leave, we were hardly wiser than when we had come. Father Todorus, who had consumed two cups of brandy, accompanied us to the door, reiterating his thanks and assuring us he would mention us in his prayers—a compliment Emerson received with a grimace and a growl.

As we walked toward the donkeys I said, "Father Todorus is certainly generous with his cognac. I suppose Sethos left in such haste, he could not carry away the comforts with which he had provided himself, but to judge from the rate at which it is being consumed he must have left a considerable quantity."

Emerson came to a stop. "Ha!" he cried. "I knew some detail was nagging at my mind, but I could not imagine what it was. Good thinking, Peabody."

Whereupon he ran back to the priest's house, with, I hardly need say, me following. When Father Todorus responded to his peremptory knock, he was still holding his cup. Seeing Emerson, he smiled beatifically. "You have returned, O Father of Curses. Come in, with the honored sitt your wife, and have—hic!—more brandy."

"I would not deprive you, Father," said Emerson with a grin. "For surely your supply must be limited."

The little man's face lengthened. One might have thought Emerson had accused him of robbery and worse, and Emerson said aside, in English, "Really, Peabody, it is too easy to confound this fellow; he has no more talent for dissimulation than a child."

"Less," I said meaningfully, "than some children."

"Humph," said Emerson. Returning to Arabic, he addressed the priest. "Your supply has been replenished, Father—is that not true? How often and in what manner?"

The priest groaned. He started to wring his hands; remembering that he still held the cup, he quickly drained it. With a glance at the curious onlookers, he muttered, "It was the devils, O Father of Curses. I beg you will not let these people know; they might appeal to the patriarch for help against the powers of evil, and I assure you, I swear to you, that I can conquer the devils, I am constantly at prayer—"

Emerson reassured him and the little man found courage to speak. There had been two deliveries of cognac by the demons since his miraculous return from imprisonment. On both occasions he had found the boxes at his bedside when he woke in the morning. He had not bothered to look for signs of intrusion, since it was well known that devils, being bodiless, do not leave footprints.

With further assurances of our good will, we took our leave. The priest disappeared into his house, no doubt in order to rid himself of the demonic gift in the most appropriate manner.

"What a curious thing," I exclaimed, as we trotted out of the village. "This man, this unknown genius of crime, is a strange mixture of cruelty and compassion. Cases of fine French cognac would not be my notion of apology and compensation for such rude handling, but—"

"Oh, do use your head, Peabody," Emerson shouted, his face reddening. "Apology and compensation indeed! I never heard such balderdash."

"Why else would he—"

"To complete the corruption of the priest, of course. A bizarre and evil sense of humor, not compassion, is the motive for these gifts."

"Oh," I said. "I had not thought of that, Emerson. Good Gad, it is no wonder, such consummate depths of depravity are beyond the comprehension of any normal person."

"They are not beyond my comprehension," said Emerson, with a vicious snap of his teeth. "Ordinary assault, abduction, and attempted murder I can put up with; but this villain has gone too far."

"I quite agree, Emerson. To play such a trick on poor Father Todorus—"

"Grrr," said Emerson. "Peabody, you astonish me."

"I don't know what you mean, Emerson. Do you think there is any hope of waylaying the deliverers of the cognac?"

"No, I do not. Sethos may tire of his joke and stop delivery, and if he continues, we have no idea when the next visit will take place. It would be a waste of time to keep the priest's house under observation, if that is what you were about to propose."

"I was not. I had reached the same conclusion."

"I am happy to hear it, Peabody."

We reached the house at teatime, and I at once set about preparing that repast, assisted by Enid. Ramses and Donald had not returned; I caught myself listening for sounds of riot and furious pursuit, such as often accompanied Ramses' departure from home. Aside from the normal noises of awakening village life, however, the only untoward sounds were those of distant gunshots. Even these were not unusual, for shooting was a favorite amusement of the more ignorant tourists, and the swampy areas between the canal and the river harbored great flocks of unfortunate birds whom these "sportsmen" liked to massacre.

The shadows lengthened, and still the wanderers had not returned. Emerson was pacing up and down the courtyard glancing alternately at his watch and at the closed gates, when at last a shout announced the long-awaited event. Abdullah opened the gates and they rode into the compound, Donald close behind Ramses.

Ramses immediately slid off his donkey and started for the back of the house, trying, I suppose, to appear as if he were anxious to wash. Donald's hand shot out and caught him by the collar. Holding him by that uncomfortable but convenient handle, he marched the boy toward us.

"Professor and Mrs. Emerson, I deliver to you your son. He has achieved a degree of dirtiness I once thought impossible, even after my own youthful experiments along that line, but he is intact, as I received him. I assure you that to keep him in that condition was no small feat."

It was evident that they had been near the river, for the substance that covered Ramses was dried mud. Parts of it had flaked off, giving him a peculiarly antique appearance, like a rotted mummy.

"I will wash immediately, Mama," he wheezed. "If you will be so good as to direct this—this person to unhand me."

But by that time I had observed the little detail Ramses was so intent on concealing from me. It was little indeed—a hole a half inch in diameter drilled neatly into the side of his pith helmet. Moving a step to the side, I observed a second hole, slightly larger, opposite the first.

Emerson observed these unusual features at the same time, and, with a shout of consternation, he snatched the hat off Ramses' head. He threw it to the ground and began running his fingers through the boy's hair, completing the total dishevelment of that area.

"It is the mark of a bullet, Peabody," he cried. "A bullet has gone completely through Ramses' hat! Ramses, dear boy, where are you wounded?"

"Oh, do stop it, Emerson," I said. "If Ramses had been wearing the hat when the shot was fired, the bullet would have gone straight through his cranium and you would have no difficulty in noticing the result."

"He was not wearing the hat," Donald said. "He was holding it in his hand. That may relieve your apprehension, Professor, but in my opinion it still calls for punishment. If this young man were my son, I would turn him over my knee and give him a good hiding.''

Ramses slowly turned his head and gave Donald a look that would have made a wiser man retract his threat. The boy's raven curls stood up in a bush like that of a Masai warrior, and his expression was no more affable.

Emerson ignored Donald's remark—it was not the first time he had heard suggestions of that nature—but Enid gave an indignant cry. ''I am not surprised at hearing so cruel a sentiment from *that* source,'' she exclaimed, putting a protective arm around Ramses. ''Poor child! After such a frightening experience, to be manhandled and cursed—''

''Confound it, Enid, I didn't swear,'' Donald protested. ''I was tempted to, but I didn't.''

Enid turned her back on him and pulled Ramses close to her. ''Come with Enid, poor lad; she will tidy you and protect you from this bully.''

Ramses' face was pressed against her impeccable shirtwaist—impeccable, I mean to say, until that moment—but I could see his cheek and one corner of his mouth. The latter feature was curved in an insufferable smirk. He allowed himself to be led away, with every appearance of enjoying the sort of embrace he would ordinarily have protested.

Displaying hands almost as filthy as those of Ramses, Donald also went to wash. If he hoped to plead his case with Enid, he was given no opportunity, for she came back almost at once, clasping Ramses' hand. His face and hands at least were clean, and realizing that only total immersion would restore him to a semblance of decency, I allowed him to take his tea with us, providing he sat some distance from the table. Owing to the nutrients contained in it, Nile mud has a particularly pungent and pervasive smell.

Nor did Donald linger over his toilette. He had been wearing Arab dress over his shirt and trousers; the removal of the robe removed the worst of the mud and he had taken time to pass a brush over his waving locks. After he had joined us I invited him to tell us what had happened and to provide us with the name of the person who had attempted to assassinate Ramses.

"As you must know, from your calm tone, Mrs. Emerson, it was an accident," he replied. "Brought on in large part by Master Ramses himself. We had gone down to the canal and were talking with the women who were washing clothes—at least Ramses was. By the way, your son has an appalling familiarity with certain Arabic idioms. . . . While we were there, we heard gunfire some little distance off. Before I could stop him, Ramses had mounted his donkey and was going hellbent for leather—I beg your pardon—riding rapidly in the direction from which the shots had come. I caught up with him after a while and explained that it was illadvised to blunder into a shooting blind. We had a little discussion. He persuaded me—fool that I am!—to go closer, in order to observe the shooting. We—er—we had made quite a lot of noise, and I did not doubt the hunters knew we were there, but in order to be perfectly safe I called out again. A great flock of pigeons were wheeling and preparing to settle; it was clear that the rifles would be aimed in that direction, and since we were approaching from the west, I thought I had taken every possible precaution—"

"It sounds as if you had," I observed, pouring him another cup of tea. "I presume Ramses ran out into the line of fire."

Donald nodded. "Shouting at the top of his lungs and

waving his hat. Naturally the birds took alarm and flew off—"

"Which was precisely my intention," exclaimed Ramses. "You know my sentiments about blood sports, Mama; killing for food or in self-defense is one thing, but the slaughter of helpless fauna for the sake of simply counting the number of the slain is a process I cannot—"

"Your sentiments on that subject are known to me, Ramses," said Emerson. "But, dear boy—"

"Don't scold him," Enid begged. "The gallant little fellow was not thinking of his own safety. His action was reckless but noble! I might have done the same thing had I been there, for I share his abhorrence of men who find a perverse pleasure in killing."

This statement was obviously directed at Donald, who flushed painfully. He got no chance to defend himself, for Enid continued to praise and admire Ramses, whose smug expression was really enough to try the patience of a saint. In a typical Ramsesian effort to show appreciation for her spirited defense, he offered to give her a lesson in hieroglyphic—the highest compliment in his power—and they went into the house, hand in hand.

Donald slammed his cup into his saucer with such force that it cracked. "I resign my position, Mrs. Emerson. I have faced armed foes and fierce savages, but Ramses has defeated me."

"Ramses? You mean Enid, don't you? Have more bread and butter, Donald."

"I don't want any cursed . . . Forgive me, Mrs. E. I only want to be left alone."

"Alone with your pipe and your opium?" said Emerson. "Give it up, my boy. You won't elude Mrs. Emerson; she has made up her mind to reform you, and reform you she will, whether you like it or not. Excuse me; I believe I will go in and work on my notes."

"Emerson is so tactful," I said, as my husband's stalwart form vanished into the house. "He knows I wanted a confidential chat with you, Ronald—I beg your pardon, Donald. No, don't go, for if you do, I will have Abdullah bring you back and sit on you until I am finished. Goodness, the stubbornness of the male sex! Enid has told me everything, Donald."

The young man sank back into his chair. "Everything?"

"Well, almost everything. She did not say in so many words that she loves you, but it was not difficult for me to see it. I am constantly astonished—"

Donald leaped to his feet. "Loves me?"

"—at the inability of men to see what is right under their noses. And you love her—"

"Love her? Love her!"

"You sound like a parrot. Do sit down and stop shouting, or you will have everyone coming round to see what is wrong."

Slowly Donald subsided into his chair, like a man whose limbs will no longer support him. His eyes, wide as saucers, and blue as the best Egyptian turquoise, were fixed on my face.

I continued, "Why else would she pursue you and attempt to persuade you to defend yourself? Why would she submit to the disgusting attentions of a man like Kalenischeff, if not to aid you? Why is she so furious with you? Mark my words, a woman does not go to such lengths for the sake of old friendship. She loves you! But she despises you too, and with reason. You do your brother no favor to take his punishment on yourself, and if you are foolish enough to submit to shame and disgrace for the sake of some absurd notion of gallantry, you have no right to make those who love you suffer. Proclaim your innocence and your brother's guilt; take the position that is rightly yours, and claim your bride!''

''I can't believe you,'' Donald muttered. ''She despises me. She—''

''Well, of course she does. That has nothing to do with her loving you. Now listen to me, Donald. You cannot desert us. I am unable to explain this to Emerson, for he is becoming so unreasonable about the Master Criminal that the mere mention of the name starts him shouting, but you, I dare hope, will understand. Enid is in grave danger, not from the police, but from that mysterious genius of crime. He meant her to be charged and convicted for the murder of Kalenischeff. Why else would he have selected her room as the scene of slaughter?''

''Possibly,'' Donald suggested, ''because Kalenischeff was on his guard at all other times and was only vulnerable to attack when he believed he had been summoned to a romantic rendezvous.''

''My question was rhetorical,'' I said sharply. ''Take my word for it; Enid is not safe. Who knows, she may have seen or heard something on that terrible night that would endanger Sethos, could she but recall it. Let her abuse you and insult you, but do not abandon her when she needs you. And, while I am on the subject of insults and abuses, let me inform you that your abject acceptance of Enid's contumely is not going to improve her opinion of you. I would be happy to give you one or two suggestions—''

Again Donald started up, so impetuously that his chair toppled over. ''I beg you, Mrs. Emerson—spare me. Your arguments have won me over; I will never desert Miss Debenham so long as she is in need of protection. But I cannot—I cannot endure—oh, God!''

Whereupon he rushed into the house.

Ten

Abdullah had neglected to close the gates. I sat in rare and pleasurable solitude, listening to the distant voices of Ramses and Enid discussing ancient Egyptian (or rather, the voice of Ramses lecturing Enid about ancient Egyptian) and enjoying the splendor of the sunset. The grand palette of the heavens was streaked with colors no earthly painter could achieve, savage-glowing bronze and gleaming crimson, indigo and rose and soft blue-gray. I knew the lurid beauty of the sky was due to the amount of sand in the atmosphere, and hoped we were not in for a storm.

One of the paths from the village passed in front of the gates, and my vigil was further enlivened by the forms of fellahin returning home from the fields, donkeys loaded with wood for the cookfires, women muffled in black and carrying heavy water jars on their heads. The procession of eternal Egypt, I thought to myself—for poetic fancies come to me at such times.

An alien shape broke into the slow-moving parade, the very speed of its approach an intrusion. The shape was that of a mounted man, who rode straight through the open gates. Seeing me, he dismounted, sweeping off his hat.

"Mrs. Emerson, I am Ronald Fraser. We met the other day—"

"I know," I said. "Are you by chance the person who put a hole in my son's hat this afternoon?"

"No, indeed! At least I hope not." His smile made him look so much like his brother, I glanced involuntarily over my shoulder. Donald was nowhere in sight, but Emerson was. His broad shoulders filled the open doorway and a scowl darkened his face.

"You hope not," he repeated ironically. "I hope not too, young man; for if you were the one who committed that little error, you would have to answer to *me*."

"It is in order to explain and apologize for the incident that I do myself the honor to call on you and your charming lady," Ronald said smoothly. "May I—"

"You may," I said, indicating the chair Donald had overturned in his hasty departure. "I would offer you a cup of tea, but I am afraid it is cold."

Ronald righted the chair and deposited himself in it. He was a graceful creature, more elegant and less manly than his brother. Knowing them as I now did, I could never have mistaken one for the other. The younger man's countenance betrayed the weakness of his character; his lips were thin, his chin was irresolute, his brow narrow and receding. Even his eyes, of the same sea-blue, were paler in color. They met mine with a clear candor I could not help but find highly suspicious.

In the most charming manner he disclaimed any intention of troubling me, even to the extent of a cup of

tea. "I came," he went on, "only to make certain that
no harm had been done the lad. He ran out in front of
our guns, Professor and Mrs. Emerson—I assure you he
did. I honestly don't know whose bullet it was that
struck the hat out of his hand. He had retrieved it and
retreated before we could go after him. Though we
searched for some time, we found no sign of him, or of
anyone else—though I thought I caught a glimpse of
another person, an Arab, by his clothing. . . ."

He ended on a questioning note, but I was not
tempted to inform him that the other person present had
been his brother. Nor was Emerson; in fact, my husband's response was direct to the point of rudeness.
There were references, as I recall, to young idiots who
could find nothing better to do with their time than blast
away at birds who could not shoot back, and to his
(Emerson's) sincere hope that the shooters would end
up riddling themselves and each other.

Mr. Ronald's fixed smile remained in place. "I don't
blame you, Professor; in your place I would say much
the same."

"I doubt that," Emerson replied haughtily. "If you
think your powers of invective can equal mine, you are
sadly mistaken."

"I will make any amends in my power," the young
man insisted. "A gift to the little chap—a profound
apology—"

I had been wondering why Ramses had not made an
appearance. It was most unlike him to refrain from interrupting. Yet even this conciliatory and tempting offer
did not bring him out of the house. The most profound
silence filled that edifice; even the murmur of Ramses'
lecture had ceased.

"That is not necessary," I said. "But thank you for
coming."

I had no intention of allowing him to leave as yet, but it was not easy to introduce the topic I wanted to question him about. "Did you forge your brother's signature?" or "Do you believe Miss Debenham is a murderess?" seemed a trifle abrupt, especially since I was not supposed to be acquainted with the persons in question. However, the young man saved me the trouble by an inquiry almost as direct as the ones I had rejected.

"I had another reason for coming," he said gravely. "May I have a word, please, with Miss Debenham?"

I rallied at once without, I am sure, indicating how surprised I was by the question. "Miss Debenham? I don't believe I know—"

"I cannot believe she has succeeded in deceiving you, Mrs. Emerson, no matter what name she has assumed. You are too astute to be gulled. Your kind heart and gentle sympathy are well known; everyone talks of it; it is impossible to spend more than a few days in Egypt without knowing your reputation—and, of course, that of your distinguished husband. You took her in, a helpless fugitive, and for that you will always have my gratitude. Do you suppose I would betray her— I, who hold her above all living creatures? Only let me see her, speak to her—assure myself she is unharmed— learn what I can do to serve her. . . ."

Unwillingly impressed by his eloquence, I listened without either confirming or denying his assumption. How long he would have gone on I cannot say, but his speech was halted by Enid herself. She had to push Emerson out of the way; he had been listening with an expression of incredulous disgust.

"You see me," she said icily. "I am unharmed. You know what you can do to serve me. That answers all your questions, I believe."

"Enid!" He rushed toward her, overturning the chair

for the second time that afternoon. I heard a crack as one of the legs gave way.

Enid waited until he was almost upon her, then raised one hand with a solemn dignity that stopped him in his tracks. "Enid," he repeated, in tones of gentle reproach. "How could you do this? If you knew what agonies I have endured, being ignorant of where you were or how you fared—"

"Always *your* agonies," she interrupted, with a curl of her lip. "I don't know how you traced me here, but we have nothing to say to one another. Unless you have decided to play the man and admit what you did."

"But I've told you over and over, Enid, that I would gladly confess to anything if it would save the dear old chap from his present plight. Heaven knows he took the blame for me often enough when we were children; the least I can do—"

"Is nobly confess to a crime you did not commit? Ronald, you are—you are beyond words." With a gesture of disgust, she turned as if to go back into the house.

"Wait, Enid. Don't leave me like this. What more can I do?"

She whirled around, her eyes flashing. "Go to Donald's commanding officer and make a clean breast of it. But you will have to be convincing, Ronald."

"My darling girl—"

"And don't call me darling!"

"I beg your pardon. It is hard to keep from one's lips the sentiments that fill one's heart. Enid, I will do as you ask—I swear. But first I must find my dear brother. I have searched for him night and day, Enid, in places I would not want to mention in your presence. But always he has fled before me. I am in terror that he may do something desperate—that any day I may hear of a body drawn from the Nile, or found in some foul den. . . .''

His voice broke. He covered his face with his hands.

Enid was unmoved. Coldly she said, "Have no fear of that, Ronald. Have no hope of that, I might say. Do as you have promised—then come to me with the papers proving your brother innocent."

"And then?" He raised his head. Tears filled his eyes. "And then, Enid?"

The color drained from her face, leaving it as white as a statue's. "I promise nothing," she said falteringly. "But . . . come to me then."

The blood that had abandoned her countenance rushed into his. "Enid," he cried. "I will! Oh, my dear—"

She fled before him, going into the house and closing the door. Ronald would have gone after her had not Emerson stepped in the way.

"No, no," he said, in the genial growl that sometimes deceived insensitive persons into believing he was in an affable mood. "In case it has slipped your mind, Mr. Fraser, a gentleman does not force his attentions upon a lady when she is unwilling to receive them. Particularly when *I* am able to prevent it."

"She is not unwilling," Ronald said. "You don't know her, Professor. She has always scolded and insulted me; we got into the habit as children. It is just her way of showing her affection."

"A most peculiar way, I must say," Emerson said skeptically. "I have never heard of such a thing."

"I appeal to Mrs. Emerson," said Ronald with a smile. He certainly was a volatile young person; all traces of sorrow had vanished, and a look of satisfaction brightened his handsome face. "Isn't it true, Mrs. Emerson, that some young ladies enjoy tormenting the persons they love? She treats Donald just the same; you must have observed that.''

"Had I had the opportunity to see them together, I might indeed have observed it," I replied shortly, for I resented his transparent attempt to trick me into an admission. "Without wishing to seem inhospitable, Mr. Fraser, I suggest you leave."

Ronald bent his earnest gaze upon me. "Now that I am at ease about Enid's safety, I have only one concern. My brother, Mrs. Emerson—my poor, suffering brother. Enid has always taken his part; she has for him the affection of a sister. He did wrong, but he has been punished enough. I want to find him and take him home. Together we will face whatever troubles the world sends us. If I could only tell him—only speak with him! I would remind him of the happy days of childhood, the hours we spent in harmless play, the reeds by the canal where we lay for hours watching the little birds fly in and out—''

"Oh, really, I cannot stand any more of this," said Emerson, half to himself. "First he bleats and sobs at the girl, now he is blathering on about his childhood days—and in the most maudlin, sentimental clichés I have ever heard. Goodnight, Mr. Fraser. Go away, Mr. Fraser."

There was no way even Ronald Fraser could turn this into a conventional and courteous farewell, but he did his best, bowing over my hand and repeating his thanks for my protection of his poor delicate darling, as he put it. The phrase was unfortunate, for it moved Emerson into abrupt action. I think he meant only to snatch Mr. Fraser up and throw him onto his horse, but Mr. Fraser anticipated him. After he had galloped away, Emerson bellowed to Abdullah to close and bar the gates. "If anyone tries to come in, shoot to kill," he shouted.

Then he turned to me. "How long until dinner, Peabody? I am ravenous."

"It has been a busy day," I agreed. "Sit down, Emerson, and have another cup of tea. I can boil more
water in an instant."

"I think I will have whiskey instead. Will you join
me, Peabody?"

"Yes, thank you. Where is everyone?"

"Fraser—our Fraser—is probably skulking around
somewhere in back." Emerson picked up the chair and
looked at it critically. "One of the legs is broken. These
young men are deuced hard on the furniture, Peabody."

"So they are, Emerson."

"The young woman," Emerson went on, "is, if I
know young women, weeping wildly in her room. That
is what young women do when they are in a state of
emotional confusion. Have I mentioned to you, Peabody, that one of the reasons why I adore you is that
you are more inclined to beat people with your umbrella
than fall weeping on your bed? The latter is a very trying habit."

"I quite agree with you, Emerson. That takes care of
Enid, then. We have only to account for Ramses before
we can settle down to a nice quiet—"

"I am here, Mama," said Ramses, emerging from the
house with the whiskey bottle and glasses on a tray.
Emerson leaped to take it from him, and Ramses continued, "I heard all that transpired through the crack in
the door. I considered that my appearance on the scene
might divert the course of the discussion, which I found
most interesting and provocative. Now that I am here,
we can talk over the possible permutations of the most
recent disclosure and their bearing on the major problem
that confronts us. I refer, of course, to—"

"Good Gad, Ramses, have you added eavesdropping

to your other misdemeanors?'' I demanded. ''Listening at doors is not proper.''

''But it is very useful,'' said Ramses, holding out a glass as Emerson poured the whiskey. He lived in hopes that his father would absent-mindedly fill it and that I would absent-mindedly fail to see him drink. The chance of both those failings occurring on the same day were slim to the point of being nonexistent, but as Ramses had once explained to me, it cost nothing to make the attempt.

It proved ineffective on this occasion. Emerson handed me my glass. ''I wonder,'' he said musingly, ''how Mr. Ronald Fraser knew the young lady was with us. He does not strike me as a person of profound mental capacity.''

''He may have caught a glimpse of her yesterday,'' I suggested.

''Possibly. Well, Peabody, what do you think? Is the guilty man Donald or Ronald?''

''How can you doubt, Emerson? Enid told us—''

''Yes, but it is the word of a young girl who admits she does not know the facts against those of both brothers. They are certainly in a better position to know than she.''

Logically he was correct. In every other way he was wrong. I had no rational arguments to offer, only a profound understanding of human nature, which is a far more reliable guide in cases of this kind than logic; but I knew what Emerson's response would be if I mentioned that.

''Interesting and touching as the personal affairs of the young people may be, Emerson, more important is our search for the Master Criminal. The revelations of Father Todorus may contain a clue after all. Or perhaps one of the villagers knows more than he or she is willing to admit.''

Ramses instantly demanded to know what I was talking about. Humoring the boy, Emerson told him about the temptation of Father Todorus—omitting, I hardly need say, any reference to other than liquid temptations.

''Hmmm,'' said Ramses, pursing his lips. ''The incident casts a most intriguing light upon the personality of the gentleman for whom we are searching, but I cannot see that it offers any useful information. Perhaps if I were to interrogate the priest—''

''You would learn no more than we did,'' I said shortly. ''In fact, Father Todorus would be even less inclined to confide in a person of your tender years. Your father is right; this genius of crime—''

A spasm crossed Emerson's face. ''Must you refer to him by that complimentary name?''

''I don't see what is complimentary about it, Emerson. However, if it disturbs you, I will confine myself to calling him Sethos. A most curious appellation, that one; I wonder what prompted him to select it.''

''I,'' said Emerson, ''could not care less.''

''But Mama has raised a point worthy of consideration,'' piped Ramses. ''We know this gentleman has a peculiar sense of humor and a fondness for challenging his opponents. What if this alias is in itself a joke and a challenge?''

''I hardly think so, Ramses,'' I said. ''It is much more likely that the name expresses the man's poetic and imaginative qualities. The mummy of Sethos the First is remarkably handsome (as mummies go) and the phrase describing Set as a lion in the valley—''

''Bah,'' said Emerson. ''What rubbish, Peabody.''

''I am inclined to agree with Papa's evaluation, though not with the language in which it was expressed, for I would be lacking in filial respect should I apply such a term to the cognitive processes of either parent, particularly—"

"Ramses," I said.

"Yes, Mama. I was about to suggest that the golden ring bearing the royal cartouche may be significant. Where did Sethos obtain such a rarity? Was it conceivably part of the loot from his first venture into tomb-robbing, and did it suggest the name by which he has chosen to be known?"

"Humph," said Emerson thoughtfully. "Quite possible, my boy. But even if you are right, the information is of no use to us. It seems to me that my original suggestion was nearer the mark. Curse it, what about the red hair? We have not one but two redheaded men. One of them must be Sethos."

Darkness had fallen. The waning moon cast a pallid light across the courtyard. In the silence that followed Emerson's statement, the cheerful voices of the men gathered around the cookfire struck strangely on our ears.

"Surely not," I said. "As a matter of fact, Emerson, you were the one who informed me, when I made that very suggestion, that Donald could not possibly be the man in question."

"It could be either of them," Emerson said. "Donald or his brother."

"The same objection holds, Papa," said Ramses. "The color of their eyes—"

"Oh, never mind that," Emerson and I burst out simultaneously.

I added, "We might question Enid, to learn whether

one or both of the brothers was away from England last winter."

"I will go and ask her now," said Ramses, rising.

"I think not, my boy."

"But, Papa, she is in great distress. I meant to go to her before this."

Emerson shook his head. "Your intentions do you credit, my boy, but take Papa's word for it: Young ladies in a state of great distress are best left alone, except by the persons who occasioned said distress."

"Is that indeed the case, Mama?" Ramses turned to me for confirmation.

"Decidedly I am of your papa's opinion, Ramses."

"Yet I would think," Ramses persisted, "that a demonstration of affectionate concern and perhaps a brief lecture on the futility of excessive emotion would have a positive effect."

A hideous premonition crept through my limbs. I had not failed to observe the tolerance with which Ramses permitted Enid to pet and caress him. It was a liberty he did not allow strangers unless he had some ulterior motive, and I had naturally assumed he had an ulterior motive with regard to Enid—that, in short, he hoped to win her confidence by pretending to be a normal eight-year-old boy. Now, hearing the earnest and anxious tone in his voice, I began to have horrible doubts. Surely it was much too soon. . . . But if Ramses proved to be as precocious in this area as he had been in others. . . . The prospects were terrifying. I felt a cowardly reluctance to pursue the inquiries I knew I ought to make, but the traditional Peabody fortitude stiffened my will.

"Why did you allow Enid to embrace you today?" I asked.

"I am glad you asked me that, Mama, for it leads me into a subject I am anxious to discuss with you. I was

conscious today of a most unusual sensation when Miss
Debenham put her arms around me. In some ways it
resembled the affectionate feelings I have for you and,
to a lesser extent, for Aunt Evelyn. There was, however,
an additional quality. I was at a loss to find words for
it until I recalled certain verses by Mr. Keats—I refer
in particular to his lyric poem 'The Eve of St. Agnes,'
which aroused—''

''Good Gad,'' I cried in agonized tones.

Emerson, naive creature, chuckled in amusement.
''My dear boy, your feelings are quite normal, I assure
you. They are the first childish stirrings of sensations
which will in time blossom and mature into the noblest
sentiments known to mankind.''

''So I surmised,'' said Ramses. ''And that is why I
wished to discuss the matter with you. Since these are
normal, natural sensations, I ought to know more about
them.''

''But, Ramses,'' his father began, belatedly aware of
where the conversation was leading.

''I believe I have heard Mama say on several occasions that the relationships between the sexes were
badly mishandled in our prudish society, and that young
persons ought to be informed of the facts.''

''You did hear me say that,'' I acknowledged, wondering what had ever possessed me to say it in his hearing.

''I am ready to be informed,'' said Ramses, his elbows on the table, his chin in his hands, and his great
eyes fixed on me.

''I cannot deny the justice of the request,'' I said.
''Emerson—''

''What?'' Emerson started violently. ''Now, Peabody—''

"Surely this is a matter more suitable for a father than a mother."

"Yes, but—"

"I will leave you to it, then." I rose.

"Just a moment, Papa," Ramses said eagerly. "Allow me to get out paper and pencil. I would like to take a few notes."

As I strolled toward the kitchen I heard Emerson begin speaking. His voice was too low to enable me to make out the words, but I thought he said something about amoebae.

The kitchen was only a cooking fire in a ring of stones, with the cook's pots and pans and jars set here and there in seeming confusion; but Hamid knew where everything was. He was a cousin of Abdullah's, and I must say his appearance would not have inspired confidence in a prospective employer, for he was cadaverously thin, with sad, drooping mustaches. In this case the prospective employer would have been misled, for Hamid's cooking was first-rate. He looked up from the pot he was stirring and told me dinner was ready. I persuaded him to put it off for a while; if Emerson was beginning with one-celled life forms, it would probably take him quite some time to work up to the hominids. Delighted at my visit, the men gathered around and we had a refreshing gossip.

Before long, however, Hamid's mustaches drooped even more visibly and his comments became brusque and sullen. I gathered that, like all great chefs, even those who wear turbans instead of tall white hats, he would do something unpleasant to the food if it were not served on time. I therefore told him we would dine, and went to collect the diners.

Emerson had vanished. Ramses was scribbling busily by the light of a candle.

"Is the lecture over?" I inquired.

Ramses nodded. "For the moment, yes. I had not finished asking questions, but Papa informed me he had no more to say on the subject."

"Do you consider that you have been properly educated?"

"I confess," said Ramses, "that I find myself unable to visualize certain of the procedures. They sound, if not physically impossible, very tiring. I asked Papa if he could draw a diagram or two, but he said no, he could not. Perhaps you—"

"No," I said.

"Papa did mention that the subject was to be avoided in conversation and that our particular cultural mores view it as taboo. I find this rather curious, since to the best of my knowledge other societies do not share this attitude. Relative cultural values—"

"Ramses," I said. "The topic of relative cultural values must be regarded at this time as a digression. Can you not turn your attention to more immediate questions?"

"For example, Mama?"

"For example, dinner. Hamid is fetching it now and he will be seriously displeased if we let the food get cold. Fetch Mr. Fraser and Miss Debenham, if you please, and I will call your papa."

I found Emerson on the roof, brooding silently in the starlight like a life-sized sphinx. I congratulated him on his efficient handling of a complex subject, to which he replied, "I beg you will not mention it again, Amelia. Ill-natured persons might view any comment whatever as tantamount to rubbing it in."

Dinner was not a social success. Ramses kept glancing at his notes and occasionally adding a word or two, a process that made Emerson extremely nervous. Enid ignored Donald, addressing most of her remarks to Ramses. The *káwurmeh* was excellent, though a trifle overseasoned.

I asked Donald why he had not made his presence known to his brother. "For surely," I added, "you must have heard his voice."

"I heard him," Donald answered shortly.

"How could you resist such an affectionate appeal?"

"You can hardly suppose I would expend so much effort in avoiding him and then change my mind."

Enid said, ostentatiously directing her comment to Ramses, "Cowardice, you know, is not always of the physical variety. Refusal to confront the truth is a form of moral cowardice, which to me is even worse."

Statements of this nature were not designed to improve the mood of the gathering.

Nor was Emerson any help. As a rule, after a successful day of excavation he is full of cheerful talk about his accomplishments and his plans for the future. I attributed his silence to resentment—unreasonable and unfair in the extreme, since it was Ramses who introduced the subject in the first place, and I only acted as any mother would have done. My attempts to woo Emerson from his bad humor by questioning him about the temple ruins won no response.

As might have been expected, Ramses was quite ready to talk, and I must say his conversation was a curious blend of his normal Egyptological interests and his new infatuation. He kept inviting Enid to come to his room so he could show her his Egyptian grammar.

At the end of the meal Emerson announced abruptly that he intended to go to Cairo next day. "It is the day of rest for the men, so I won't be losing any more time than I would in any case. I count on you, Mr. Fraser, to watch over Ramses and the ladies—''

"The ladies!" I exclaimed. "I hope you don't include *me* in that category, Emerson. Naturally I intend to accompany you.''

"I phrased it badly, Peabody. Pray excuse me. I had hoped you would also remain here, on guard. You are worth a thousand men, you know.''

This flagrant attempt at flattery was so unlike Emerson, I could only stare in silent astonishment. Donald said, "As to that, Professor, you may be sure I will do my duty with or without Mrs. Emerson's assistance. Even a moral coward may be willing to die in defense of the weak and helpless.''

This statement infuriated both Enid and Ramses. Enid suggested that they retire, to inspect the grammar, and they went off together. Bastet followed them, but not before she had indicated her loyalty to her young master by biting Donald on the leg.

It was agreed that we should spend the night at the house, in order to be ready to catch the early train. Emerson applied himself to writing up his professional journal, while I labeled and sorted the artifacts that had been found. Sometimes, though, when I looked up from my work, I saw him sitting with idle hands staring at the paper in front of him, as if his mind had wandered far from his work. I went to bed early. Emerson did not come up with me, nor did he rouse me, as he usually did, when he joined me later.

The zenith was still dark when I was awakened by a surreptitious sound below, but the faint pallor of the eastern sky showed that dawn was not far distant. Carefully I crawled to the edge of the roof and looked down.

The sound I had heard was that of the door being softly opened and closed. I expected to see a diminutive form creeping out on some unimaginable errand, but the shadow that stole toward the gate was that of a man. I had no difficulty in realizing it must be Donald.

I did not waken Emerson. When roused suddenly from profound slumber he makes loud noises and strikes people. It took only a moment to slip into the garments I had laid out ready for the morning, and to seize my trusty parasol. I did not take my belt of tools, for I feared their rattling would arouse Emerson and make the surreptitious pursuit I contemplated impossible. As it was, the parasol caught my foot as I was climbing down the wall and caused me to fall rather heavily. Luckily the earthen surface muffled the thud. I reminded myself that in future, should such a descent become necessary, I had better drop the parasol down before descending myself.

Donald had left the gate slightly ajar. Slipping through it, I looked in vain for him, and feared he had escaped me. However, I had some idea where he might be going. As I dressed I had remembered a statement of his brother's the day before. That rambling, sentimental speech had not been so pointless as I had believed; for in reminiscing about childhood days, Ronald had suggested an assignation, hoping Donald would overhear. He had obviously known Donald was among us, even as he had been aware of Enid's presence. How he had come by this information was a matter of some concern, but I did not waste time speculating on it. With any luck, I would soon be in a position to ask him point-blank, for I felt sure Donald was going to meet his brother on the reedy bank of the canal, near the place where the latter had been shooting.

The sky lightened and the rim of the rising sun

peeped over the hills. I followed the path along the dike that skirted the village, for I assumed that Donald would want to avoid being seen. Sounds of activity and the acrid smell of woodsmoke from the cooking fires were already to be discerned, for, like all primitive people, the villagers rose with the sun.

I had not gone far when I saw the young man ahead of me. A few others were abroad by then, and at first glance one might have taken him for an industrious farmer heading for the fields. It was obvious that he thought he had left the house unobserved, for he did not look back. However, I took the precaution of concealing myself behind a small donkey loaded with sugar cane, which was going in the same direction.

Finally Donald left the path and plunged into the lush green growth between the canal and the river. I had to abandon my donkey, but the reeds and coarse grass sheltered me so long as I moved with my back bent over. At last Donald stopped. I crept forward and crouched behind a clump of weeds.

Donald made no attempt to conceal himself. On the contrary, he straightened to his full height and removed his turban. The sun's brazen orb had lifted full above the horizon and its rays edged his form with a rim of gold. His sturdy shape, the sharp outline of his profile, and above all the red-gold of his hair rendered him a prominent object.

I could not help recalling Emerson's insistence on the red hair of the god Set. Had I been misled after all by a consummate actor simulating the role of an innocent, wronged young Englishman? Impossible! And yet— what if Sethos were not one brother, but both? His seemingly uncanny ability to accomplish more than an ordinary mortal could achieve would thus be explained.

Yet the other half of the persona (if my latest theory

was indeed correct) failed to make an appearance. Donald was as puzzled by his brother's absence as was I. He scratched his head and looked from side to side.

A violent agitation in the reeds made him turn. I was not the source of the disturbance; it came from some distance to my rear. However, it had the unhappy effect of turning his eye in my direction, and the screen of weeds proved too frail a barrier for concealment. In two long strides he had reached my hiding place and plucked me out of it. He had not expected to see me. Astonishment contorted his face, and his hand fell from my collar.

"Mrs. Emerson! What the devil are you doing here?"

"I might ask you the same thing," I replied, tucking my waist back into the band of my shirt. "At least I might if I did not know the answer. Your brother's message was heard and understood by me. However, it appears that he has been delayed. What was the hour of the rendezvous?"

"Sunrise," Donald replied. "That was the hour at which we were accustomed to go to the marsh to shoot. Please go back, Mrs. Emerson. If he wants to speak privately with me, he won't make his presence known so long as you are here."

I was about to acquiesce, or appear to—for of course I had no intention of leaving until I had heard what the brothers had to say to one another. Before I could so much as nod, a disconcerting thing happened. Something whizzed through the air a few inches over my head with an angry buzzing sound. A split second later I heard the sound of the explosion. A second and third shot followed.

With a stifled cry Donald clapped his hand to his head and collapsed. So startled was I by this untoward event that I failed to move quickly enough, and I was borne to the ground by the weight of Donald's body.

The ground was soft, but the impact drove the breath from my lungs, and when I attempted to free myself from the dead weight upon me I was unable to move. I hoped the figure of speech was only that, and not a description of fact, but the utter inertness of his limbs aroused the direst forebodings. Nor was my apprehension relieved by the sensation of something wet and sticky trickling down my cheek. I felt no pain, so I knew the blood must be Donald's.

I was trying to turn him over when I heard the rustling of foliage. Someone was approaching! I feared it was the murderer, coming to ascertain whether his foul deed had been accomplished, and I struggled to free myself. Then the weight holding me down was removed, and I heard a voice cry out in extreme agitation.

"Donald! My dearest—my darling—speak to me! Oh God, he is dead, he is slain!"

I raised myself to a sitting position. Enid sat on the ground, all unaware of the mud that soaked her skirt. With the strength of love and desperation she had lifted the unconscious man so that his head lay on her breast. Her blouse and her little hands were dabbled with his blood, which was flowing copiously from a wound on his forehead.

"Put him down at once, you ninny," I said.

For all the attention she paid me, I might not have been there at all. She went on moaning and showering kisses on his tumbled hair.

I was still short of breath but I forced myself to crawl toward them. "Lower his head, Enid," I ordered. "You ought not to have lifted him."

"He is dead," Enid cried repetitiously. "Dead—and it is all my fault. Now he will never know how I loved him!"

Donald's eyes flew open. "Say it again, Enid!"

Joy and relief, shame and confusion stained her lovely, tear-streaked face with a glory as of sunrise. "I—I—" she began.

"Say no more," Donald exclaimed. With an agility that belied his encrimsoned visage, he freed himself from her embrace, and took her into his. She made but a feeble attempt to resist; his masterful manner overcame her scruples, and when I left them—as I did almost at once—I had no doubt that he would prevail. I also had no doubt but that my lecture on the subject of firmness had had the desired effect, and I congratulated myself on bringing this romantic confusion to a satisfactory end.

I had not gone far before I heard sounds indicative of haste and alarm. The sounds of haste were produced by a heavy body crashing through the reeds; the sounds of alarm were those of a well-loved voice raised to its fullest extent, which, as I have had occasion to remark, is considerable.

I answered, and Emerson soon stood face to face with me. He had dressed in such haste that his shirt was buttoned askew and hung out of his trousers. Upon recognizing me, he rushed forward, tripping over his dangling bootlaces, and lifted me in his arms.

"Peabody! Good Gad, it is as I feared—you are wounded! You are covered with blood! Don't try to talk, Peabody. I will carry you home. A doctor—a surgeon—"

"I am not wounded, Emerson. It is not my blood you see, but Donald's."

Emerson set me on my feet with a thud that jarred my teeth painfully together. "In that case," he said, "you can damned well walk. How dare you, Peabody?"

His angry voice and furious scowl touched me no less

than his tender concern had done, for I knew they were prompted by the same affection. I took his arm. "We may as well go back to the house," I said. "Donald and Enid will follow at their leisure."

"Donald? Oh, yes. I assume he is not seriously wounded, for if he were, you would be dosing him and bandaging him and generally driving him out of his mind."

"I suppose you followed Enid," I said. "And she followed me, and I followed Donald. . . . How ridiculous we must have appeared!"

"You may call it ridiculous," Emerson growled, holding my hand tightly in his. "I would call it something else, but I cannot find words strong enough to express my opinion of your callous disregard for every basic marital responsibility. How do you suppose I felt when I woke to find you gone, and saw a female form slip out of the gate? I thought it was you. I could not imagine why you should creep from my side unless— unless . . ."

Emotion overcame him. He began to swear.

"You must have realized that only the sternest necessity could have moved me to such a step, Emerson. I would have written a note, but there was not time."

"There was time to wake me, though."

"No, for then explanations would have been necessary, delaying me even longer."

I proceeded to render the explanations. Emerson's face lightened a trifle as he listened, but he shook his head. "It was extremely foolhardy of you, Peabody. For all you knew, you were walking into a conference of desperate criminals. You did not even take your belt of tools."

"I had my parasol, Emerson."

"A parasol, though an admirable weapon—as I have

been privileged to observe—is not much defense against a pistol, Peabody. Those were pistol shots I heard.''

"They were, Emerson. As you know, the sound is quite different from the report of a rifle or shotgun. And Donald may thank heaven it was a hand weapon, for at such close range only a very poor shot could have missed with a rifle.''

Emerson stopped and looked back. "Here they come—positively intertwined, upon my word. I take it an understanding has been arrived at.''

"It was most touching, Emerson. Believing him dead or mortally wounded, Enid confessed the profound attachment she had kept hidden—though not, I hardly need say, from me. It is a great relief to have it all settled.''

"I would say it is far from settled,'' remarked Emerson. "Unless you can clear the young lady of a charge of murder and the young man of embezzlement or fraud or forgery, or whatever it may have been, their hopes of spending a long and happy life together do not appear prosperous.''

"But that is precisely why we are going to Cairo today. Do hurry, Emerson, or we will miss the train.''

Thanks to my organizational talents we did not miss the train, but it was a near thing, and not until we had settled ourselves in the carriage did we have a chance to discuss the morning's interesting events. To my astonishment I learned that Emerson did not share my belief as to the identity of the concealed marksman.

"But there is no other possible explanation,'' I insisted. "The Master Criminal is still seeking a scapegoat for the murder of Kalenischeff. Furthermore, Donald has on several occasions foiled his attacks on us. Naturally, Sethos would resent his interference. Or—here is another attractive idea, Emerson—perhaps it was not Donald but my humble self at whom the bullet was aimed.''

''If that is your notion of an attractive idea, I shudder to think what you would call horrible,'' Emerson grumbled. ''You were not the target of the assassin, Amelia. In fact, the whole business is unaccountable. It makes no sense.''

''Aha,'' I exclaimed. ''You have a theory, Emerson.''

''Naturally, Peabody.''

''Excellent. We have one of those amiable little competitions of ours, to see who can guess—deduce, I meant to say—the solution to this most perplexing mystery. For I feel sure,'' I added, with an affectionate smile, ''that our opinions do not coincide.''

''They never have yet, Peabody.''

''Would you care to disclose to me your reading of the matter thus far?''

''I would not.'' Emerson brooded in silence, his rugged profile reminding me of the Byronic heroes so popular in some forms of literature. The dark hair tumbling on his brow, the lowering frown, the grim set of his mouth were extremely affecting. At least they affected me, and had there not been a dour old lady sharing the compartment with us, I might have demonstrated my feelings. As it was, I had to content myself with looking at him.

Emerson went on brooding and finally I decided to break the silence, which was getting monotonous. ''I don't understand why you find this morning's events puzzling, Emerson. It is obvious to the meanest intelligence that the—that Sethos used a pistol instead of a rifle because he hoped to make Donald's death look like suicide. Donald would have been found with the

weapon in his hand, and a suicide note in the other—
for I have no doubt that the genius of crime could re-
produce his handwriting.''

"Oh, yes," Emerson said bitterly. ''You wouldn't be
surprised to see him sprout wings like a bat and flap off
across Cairo, spouting lyric poetry as he flies.''

"Lyric poetry?" I repeated, genuinely perplexed.

"Merely a flight of fancy, Amelia. Your theory of a
false suicide falls apart on one simple fact. You were
there.''

"Suicide and murder, then," I said promptly. ''Sethos would not be balked by a little matter like that, and
I am sure he would shed no tears over my demise.''

Again Emerson shook his head. "You astonish me,
Peabody. Can it be possible that you fail to see . . . Well,
but if the truth has not dawned on you, I don't want to
put ideas into your head.''

And he would say no more, question him as I might.

Eleven

Emerson was more forthcoming when I asked precisely what he intended to do in Cairo. "For it is all very well," I added, "to talk vaguely of getting on the trail of Sethos, but without any notion of where to start, it will be difficult to find a trail, much less follow it."

My tone was somewhat acerbic, for Emerson's refusal to confide in me had wounded me deeply. He appeared not to notice my annoyance, but replied amicably, "I am glad you raised that question, Peabody. I have two approaches in mind. First, we must inquire of official sources what they know of this villain. We have a legitimate reason to demand information, since we have cause to suppose ourselves threatened by him.

"I have greater hopes, however, of my second approach—to wit, my acquaintances in the underworld of Cairene crime. I would not be surprised to discover that even Sethos' chief lieutenants are unaware of his true identity; however, by putting together bits and scraps and odds and ends, we may be able to construct a clue."

"Good, Emerson. Precisely the approach I was about to suggest."

"Humph," said Emerson. "Have you any other suggestions, Peabody?"

"I could hardly improve on your ideas, Emerson. However, it has occurred to me to start from the other end, so to speak."

"I don't follow you, Peabody."

"I mean that instead of gathering more information, we should pursue the few facts we already have. I am convinced it was Sethos himself who brought the communion vessels to our room. And we know that he or one of his hired assassins was in the hotel on the night of Kalenischeff's murder. I propose to question and, if necessary, bribe or threaten, the servants who were on duty upon those occasions."

"Of course you know the police have questioned them already."

"Oh yes, but they won't have told the police anything. There is a reluctance among people of that class in all countries to cooperate with the police."

"True. Anything else?"

"Yes, one other thing. Has it occurred to you that if Ronald Fraser is not Sethos himself, he may be involved with the gang?"

"Oddly enough, that had occurred to me," Emerson replied, fingering the dimple in his chin. "Or, if not Ronald, then Donald. Curse these people," he added, "why can't they have distinctive names? I keep mixing them up."

"I am sure we can eliminate Donald, Emerson. He was with me this morning, and it was a miracle he was not killed."

"What better alibi could there be?" Emerson demanded. "If he is Sethos, he could instruct a confederate to fire at him and miss—as indeed he did."

"He couldn't know I would awaken and follow him, Emerson."

"That isn't why you want to eliminate him, Peabody," Emerson grumbled. "You have a pernicious weakness for young lovers."

"Nonsense, Emerson. I eliminate Donald on purely logical grounds. We both heard Ronald Fraser ask his brother to meet him; as Donald explained to me, the reference was to a place where they had been accustomed to meet as children. How did Ronald learn the whereabouts of his brother, and of Enid, unless he is in touch with that mysterious personage who knows all and sees all? And how did Sethos know Donald would be by the river at dawn unless Ronald told him?"

"Curse it, Peabody, you have a positive genius for overlooking the obvious! It is because you are obsessed with this villain. You see him everywhere and credit him with well-nigh supernatural powers!"

"Really, Emerson—"

"The simplest and most obvious explanation," Emerson continued angrily, "is that Ronald tried to kill his brother. An act of purely private villainy, Peabody, with not a Master Criminal in sight! Why Ronald should hate Donald I do not know, but there are several possibilities—an inheritance, or rivalry for the hand of the young lady, for instance. People do kill people for the most ridiculous reasons."

"In either case," I replied with equal heat, "it behooves us to learn more about Ronald Fraser. At least I can ascertain whether he was in Egypt last winter. He would have to enter the country in his true name, and he would probably have stayed for a time at Shepheard's.

Mr. Baehler can tell me whether this was the case."

"Your sweeping generalizations are, as usual, unfounded; but it can't do any harm to ask," Emerson grunted. "Here we are, Peabody; get your traps together."

The train pulled into the main station. Emerson opened the door of the carriage and turned with a benevolent smile to assist the old lady who had been our sole companion during the journey. She was sitting at the extreme end of the seat watching us with wide eyes, and when Emerson offered his hand she let out a scream.

"Get away!" she shrieked. "Murder—assassins—bats—leave me, monster!"

My attempts at reassurance only maddened her more, and we were forced to abandon her. She appeared, poor creature, to be rather lacking in her wits.

We went first to police headquarters, on the Place Bab el-Khalk. Major Ramsay was rude enough to keep us waiting a good ten minutes, and I daresay it would have been longer had not Emerson, with his habitual impetuosity, brushed the protesting clerk aside and flung open the door to the inner office. A brisk exchange followed, in which I did not interfere since I felt Emerson's criticisms to be fully justified. During the discussion Emerson held a chair for me and sat down himself, so Ramsay finally resigned himself to the inevitable.

Emerson wasted no more time in compliments. "You are of course familiar, Ramsay, with the matter of the antiquities thieves Mrs. Emerson and I apprehended last season."

"I have your file here before me," Ramsay replied

sourly, indicating a folder. "I was perusing it when you burst in; had you given me time to study it—"

"Well, the devil, man, how much time do you need to read a dozen pages?" Emerson demanded. "You ought to have known all about it anyway."

I deemed it appropriate to calm the troubled waters with a soothing comment. "May I suggest, Emerson, that we save valuable time by avoiding reproaches? We are here, Major Ramsay, because we want you to tell us all you know about the Master Criminal."

"Who?" Ramsay exclaimed.

"You may know him as 'the Master,' which is one of the names his henchmen call him. He is also known as Sethos."

Ramsay continued to stare at me with a particularly feeble-minded expression, so I tried again. "The head of the ring of antiquities thieves. If you have indeed read the report, you know that he unfortunately eluded us."

"Oh! Oh yes." With maddening deliberation Ramsay turned over the pages. "Yes, it is all here. Congratulations from M. de Morgan of the Department of Antiquities, from Sir Evelyn Baring—"

"Well, then," I said. "No doubt the police have been actively engaged in attempting to identify and locate this mastermind of crime. What progress have you made?"

"Mrs. Emerson." Ramsay closed the file and folded his hands. "The administration and the police are grateful to you for your efforts in closing down a ring of local thieves. All this talk of master criminals with outlandish aliases is absurd."

I put a restraining hand on Emerson's arm. "They know of Sethos in the bazaars," I said. "They whisper of the Master, and the dreadful revenge he takes on traitors to his revolting cause."

Ramsay raised a hand to conceal his smile. "We pay no attention to the gossip of natives, Mrs. Emerson. They are such a superstitious, ignorant lot; why, if we followed up every idle rumor, we would have no time to do anything else."

From Emerson's parted lips came bubbling sounds, like those of a kettle on the boil. "Please don't say such things, Major," I implored. "I cannot guarantee your safety if you continue in that vein. Since we arrived in Egypt less than a week ago, we have been several times attacked by this man, whose existence you deny. There was an attempt at abducting our son, and only this morning a shot fired from ambush narrowly missed me, and actually wounded Don—er—one of our assistants."

Ramsay was too obtuse to notice my momentary confusion. The smile had vanished from his face. "Have you reported these crimes, Mrs. Emerson?"

"Why, no. You see—"

"Why not?"

Emerson leaped to his feet. "Because," he bellowed, "the police are consummate fools, that is why. Come along, Amelia. This jackanapes knows less than we do. Come, I implore you, before I kick his desk to splinters and perpetrate indignities upon his person which I might later regret."

Emerson was still seething when we emerged from the building. "No wonder nothing is being done to stop the illegal trade in antiquities," he growled. "With a fool like that in charge—"

"Now, Emerson, calm yourself. The major has nothing to do with antiquities. You said yourself, you had no great hopes of learning anything from him."

"That is true." Emerson wiped his perspiring brow.

"I wish you had not been so hasty, Emerson. I wanted to ask how the investigation into Kalenischeff's death is progressing."

"Quite right, Peabody. It is all the fault of that cursed idiot Ramsay for distracting me. Let us go back and ask him."

"Emerson," I began. "I don't think—"

But Emerson had already started to retrace his steps. I had no choice but to follow. By running as fast as I could, I caught him up outside Ramsay's office. "Ah, there you are, Peabody," he said cheerfully. "Do try to keep up, will you? We have a great deal to do."

At the sight of Emerson the clerk fled through another door, and Emerson proceeded into the inner office. Ramsay jumped up and assumed a posture of defense, his back against the wall.

"Sit down, sit down," Emerson said genially. "No need to stand on ceremony; this won't take long. Ramsay, what is the state of the investigation into the murder of that villain Kalenischeff?"

"Er—what?" Ramsay sputtered.

"The fellow is very slow," Emerson explained to me. "One must be patient with such unfortunates." He raised his voice and spoke very slowly, as people do when they are addressing someone who is hard of hearing. "What—is—the—state—"

"I understood you the first time, Professor," Ramsay said, wincing.

"Speak up, then. I haven't got all day. Is the young lady still under suspicion?"

I think Ramsay had come to the conclusion that Emerson was some species of madman, and must be humored for fear he would become violent. "No," he said, with a strained smile. "I never believed she was guilty. It is out of the question for a gently bred lady to have committed such a crime.''

"That isn't what you told my wife," Emerson declared.

"Er—didn't I?" Ramsay transferred his stiff smile to the madman's wife. "I beg your pardon. Perhaps she misunderstood."

"Never mind, Major," I said. "Whom do you suspect, then?"

"A certain beggar, who was often outside Shepheard's. One of the safragis claims to have seen him inside the hotel that night."

"And the motive?" I inquired calmly.

Ramsay shrugged. "Robbery, no doubt. I haven't much hope of finding the fellow. They all look alike, you know."

"Only to idiots and ignoramuses," said Emerson.

"Oh, quite, quite, quite, Professor. Er—I meant to say, they all stick together, you know; we will never get an identification from the other beggars. One of them actually had the effrontery to tell me the fellow was English." Ramsay laughed. "Can you imagine?"

Emerson and I exchanged glances. He shrugged contemptuously. "And what of Miss Debenham," I asked. "Have you found no trace of her?"

Ramsay shook his head. "I fear the worst," he said portentously.

"That she is dead?"

"Worse than that."

"I don't see what could be worse than that," Emerson remarked.

"Oh, Emerson, don't be ironic," I said. "He is referring to the classic fate worse than death—an assessment made, I hardly need add, by men. Major, are you really naive enough to believe that Miss Debenham has been sold into white slavery?''

''Slavery has not been stamped out,'' Ramsay insisted. ''Despite our efforts.''

''I know that, of course. But the unfortunates who suffer this fate—and I agree, it is a ghastly fate—are poor children of both sexes, many of whom are sold by their own families. The dealers in that filthy trade would not dare abduct an Englishwoman out of the very walls of Shepheard's Hotel.''

''Then what has become of her?'' Ramsay asked. ''She could not remain concealed for long, a woman with no knowledge of the language, the customs—''

''You underestimate our sex, sir,'' I said, frowning. ''Next time we meet you may have cause to amend your opinion, and I will expect an apology.''

After we left the office I heard the key turn in the lock.

''So much for that,'' said Emerson as, for the second time, we emerged into the street. ''Not very useful, was it?''

''No. Well, Emerson, what next?''

Emerson hailed a carriage and handed me into it. ''I will meet you later at Shepheard's,'' he said. ''Wait for me on the terrace if you finish your interrogation before I arrive.''

''And where are you going?''

''To the bazaars, to pursue the course I mentioned.''

''I will go with you.''

''That would be ill-advised, Peabody. The negotiations I mean to pursue are of the most delicate nature. My informants will be reluctant to talk at all; the presence of a third party, even you, might silence them.''

His argument could not be gainsaid. Emerson had a rare, I might even say unique, rapprochement with

Egyptians of all varieties and social classes, stemming from his eloquence in invective, his formidable strength, his colloquial command of the language, and—it pains me to admit—his complete contempt for the Christian religion. To be sure, Emerson was tolerantly and equally contemptuous of Islam, Buddhism, Judaism, and all other faiths, but his Egyptian friends were only concerned about the religion they equate with foreign domination over their country. Other archaeologists claimed to have good relations with their workers—Petrie, I am sorry to say, was always boasting about it—but their attitude was always tempered with the condescension of the "superior race" toward a lesser breed. Emerson made no such distinctions. To him a man was not an Englishman or a "native," but only a man.

I see that I have digressed. I do not apologize. The complex nobility of Emerson's character is worthy of an even longer digression.

However, I felt certain there was another reason why he preferred I should not accompany him. In his bachelor days, before I met him and civilized him, Emerson had a widespread acquaintance in certain circles he was not anxious for me to know about. Respecting his scruples and his right to privacy, I never attempted to intrude into this part of his past.

Feeling that I was entitled to the same consideration from him, I did not feel it necessary to inform him that I had business of my own in the old section, and that if he expected me to sit meekly on the terrace of Shepheard's until he condescended to appear, he was sadly mistaken. First, however, there were my inquiries at the hotel to be made, so I allowed the carriage driver to follow Emerson's directions.

However, Mr. Baehler was a sad disappointment. He absolutely refused to allow me to examine the hotel registers for the previous winter. Upon my persisting, he finally agreed to consult them himself, and he assured me that Mr. Ronald Fraser had not been a guest at the hotel during that period. I was disappointed, but not downhearted; Ronald might have stayed at another hostelry.

I then asked the name of the safragi who had been on duty at the time of Kalenischeff's murder. As I had expected from a man of Mr. Baehler's efficiency, he knew the names and duties of every employee in the hotel, but again I met with a check. The person in question, whose assignment had been the third-floor wing, was no longer in the employ of the hotel.

"He had a bit of good luck," Baehler said with a smile. "An aged relative died and left him a large sum of money. He has retired to his village and I hear he is living like a pasha."

"And what village is that?" I asked.

Baehler shrugged. "I don't remember. It is far to the south, near Assuan. But really, Mrs. Emerson, if it is information concerning the murder you want, you are wasting your time looking for him. The police questioned him at length."

"I see. I understand the police have fixed on some anonymous beggar as the killer, and that Miss Debenham is no longer under suspicion."

"So I believe. If you will excuse me, Mrs. Emerson, I am expecting a large party—"

"One more thing, Mr. Baehler, and I will detain you no longer. The name of the safragi who was on duty in our part of the hotel while we were here."

"I hope you don't suspect him of wrongdoing," Baehler exclaimed. "He is a responsible man who has been with us for years."

I reassured him, and upon learning that the man in

question was even now at his station, I dismissed Mr. Baehler with thanks, and went upstairs.

I remembered the safragi well—a lean, grizzled man of middle age, with a quiet voice and pleasant features marred only when he smiled by a set of brown, broken teeth.

The fellow's smile was without guile, however, and he answered my questions readily. Alas, he could not remember anything unusual about the porters who had delivered our parcels. There had been a number of deliveries from a number of different shops; some of the men were known to him, some were not.

I thanked and rewarded him and left him to the peaceful nap my arrival had interrupted. I was convinced he was unwitting. His demeanor was that of an innocent man, and besides, if he had been aware of the identity of the delivery man, he would have been pensioned off, like the other safragi—who was, I felt sure, the same one who had claimed to have seen Donald inside the hotel. Sethos rewarded his loyal assistants liberally.

Since some of my inquiries had proved abortive, I found myself with plenty of time to carry out my other business, and I determined to proceed with it rather than pause for luncheon. Emerson would be occupied for several more hours, and if I hurried, I could be back at the hotel before he got there.

I was crossing the lobby when the concierge intercepted me. "Mrs. Emerson! This letter was left for you."

"How extraordinary," I said, examining the superscripture, which was in an unfamiliar hand. There was no question of a mistake, however, for the name was my own, and in full: Amelia Peabody Emerson. "Who was the person who left it?"

"I did not recognize the gentleman, madam. He is not a guest at the hotel."

I thanked the concierge and hastened to open the sealed envelope. The message within was brief, but the few lines set my pulses leaping. "Have important information. Will be at the Café Orientale between one-thirty and two." It was signed "T. Gregson."

I had almost forgotten the famous private detective—as perhaps you have also, dear Reader. Apparently he had seen me enter the hotel. But why had he written a note instead of speaking to me personally?

I consulted my watch. The timing could not have been better. I could visit the shop of Aziz before keeping the appointment with Gregson.

Do not suppose, Reader, that I was unconscious of the peculiarity of the arrangement. There was a chance I might be walking into a trap. Mr. Gregson could not be Sethos; his eyes were not black, but a soft velvety brown. Yet he might be an ally of that enigmatic villain, or someone else might have used his name in order to lure me into his toils.

This seemed, on the whole, unlikely. I knew the Café Orientale; it was on the Muski, in a respectable neighborhood much frequented by the foreign community. And if my suspicion was correct—if Sethos himself lay in wait for me—I was ready for him. I was alert and on guard, I had my parasol and my belt of tools.

However, I felt it advisable to take one precaution. Going into the writing room, I inscribed a brief note to Emerson, telling him where I was going and assuring him, in closing, that if I did not return he was to console himself with the knowledge that our deep and tender love had enriched my life and, I trusted, his own.

Upon rereading this, I found it a trifle pessimistic, so I added a postscript. "My dear Emerson, I do not sup-

pose that the M.C. will slaughter me out of hand, since
t would be more in character for him to hold me prisoner in order to arouse in you the anguish of uncertainty
as to my fate. I feel confident that if I cannot effect my
own escape, you will eventually find and free me. This
is not farewell, then, but only *au revoir*, from your most
devoted, et cetera, et cetera.''

I left the envelope at the desk with instructions to
give it to Emerson no earlier than 5 P.M. if I had not
collected it myself before then.

Feeling in need of exercise to work off the excited
anticipation that poured through my veins, I did not take
a carriage but set off on foot toward the shop. Aziz was
a singularly unpleasant little man, but he was the sole
survivor of a family that had been intimately connected
with the Master Criminal. His father and his brother had
been involved in the illegal antiquities trade; both had
met terrible ends the previous year, though admittedly
not at the hands of Sethos. Aziz had inherited his father's stock of antiquities and perhaps (as I hoped) his
father's connection with the genius of crime. It was
worth a try, at any rate.

Aziz was out in front of his shop, calling to passers-
by to come in and view his wares. He recognized me
immediately; his fixed tradesman's smile turned into a
look of consternation, and he darted inside.

It was a tawdry place, its shelves and showcases filled
with cheap tourist goods and fake antiquities, many of
them made in Birmingham. Aziz was nowhere to be
seen. The clerk behind the showcase was staring at the
swaying curtain through which his employer had presumably fled. There were no customers; most of the
tourists were at luncheon, and the shop would soon be
closing for the afternoon.

"Tell Mr. Aziz I wish to see him," I said loudly. "I

won't leave until he comes out, so he may as well do it now."

I knew Aziz was in the back room and could hear every word I said. It took him a few minutes to make up his cowardly mind, but finally he emerged, smiling broadly. The lines in his face looked like cracks in plaster, one had the feeling that if the smile stretched another half inch, the whole façade would crumble and drop off.

He greeted me with bows and cries of delight. He was so happy I had honored his establishment. What could he show me? He had received a shipment of embroidered brocades from Damascus, woven with gold threads—

I did not much care for Mr. Aziz, so I did not attempt to spare his feelings. "I want to talk to you about Sethos," I said.

Mr. Aziz turned pale. "No, sitt," he whispered. "No, please, sitt—"

"You know me, Mr. Aziz. I have nothing else to do this afternoon. I can wait."

Aziz's lips curled into a wolfish snarl. Turning on his gaping clerk, he clapped his hands. "Out," he snapped.

When the clerk had gone, Aziz locked the door and pulled the curtain. "What have I done to you, sitt, that you wish my death?" he demanded tragically. "Those who betray this—this person—die. If I knew anything of this—this person—which I do not—I swear it, sitt, on my father's grave—the mere fact that you were heard to mention his name in my shop would be the end of me."

"But if you know nothing about him, you are in no danger," I said.

Aziz brightened a trifle. "That is true."

"What do they say of him in the bazaars? You do

not endanger yourself by repeating what all men know.''

According to Aziz, no one really knew anything, for Sethos' men did not gossip about him. He was known only by his actions, and even these were obscure, for his reputation was such that every successful crime in Cairo was laid at his door. Aziz believed he was not a man at all, but an efreet. It was said that not even his own men knew his true identity. He communicated with them by means of messages left in designated places; and those few who had seen him face to face were well aware that the face he wore that day was not the one in which he would next be seen.

Once started, Aziz rather warmed to his theme, and rambled on at length, repeating the legends that had accrued to this mysterious person. They were no more than that for the most part—wild, fantastic tales that were fast becoming part of the folklore of the under-world.

''Very well,'' I said, glancing at my watch. ''I believe, Mr. Aziz, that you have told me all you know. Sethos would never enlist a man like you; you are too great a coward, and you talk too much.''

He let me out and locked the door after me. Looking back, I saw his face, shining with perspiration, peering fearfully at me through a crack in the curtain.

I hoped Emerson had done better, but feared he had been no more successful than I. By a combination of cleverness and terror, Sethos seemed to have done an excellent job of covering his tracks. If I had not had the meeting with Mr. Gregson to look forward to, I would have been somewhat discouraged.

It was thirty-five minutes past one when I arrived at the Café Orientale. Mr. Gregson was nowhere to be seen, so I seated myself at a table near the door, ignoring the curious stares of the other patrons. They were all men. I believe there is some nonsensical convention against ladies patronizing cafés. Either Mr. Gregson was unaware of this unspoken rule, or he paid me the compliment of realizing that I was supremely indifferent to such things.

I summoned the waiter with a rap of my parasol and a crisp command in Arabic, and ordered coffee. Mr. Gregson arrived before the coffee. I had forgotten what a fine-looking man he was. The smile that illumined his face softened his austere features.

"You came!" he exclaimed.

"You asked me to, didn't you?"

"Yes, but I scarcely dared hope . . . No, that is not true. I know the ardent spirit that moves you. I knew you would rush in where lesser women fear to tread."

"I did not rush, Mr. Gregson, I walked—into a respectable café filled with people. The only danger I faced was that of social ostracism, and that has never been a matter of concern to me."

"Ah," said Gregson, "but I am going to ask you to accompany me into an area that is not so free of peril. I tell you frankly, Mrs. Emerson—"

He broke off as the waiter came with my order. Curtly he ordered, *"Kahweh mingheir sukkar."*

"You speak Arabic?" I asked.

"Only enough to order food and complain that the price is too high."

The waiter returned. Mr. Gregson raised his cup. "To the spirit of adventure," he said gravely.

"Cheers," I replied, raising my own cup. "And now, Mr. Gregson, you were telling me frankly . . ."

"That the mission I am about to propose is one in which you may reasonably refuse to join me. But I think I have—persuaded, shall we say?—one of Sethos' henchmen to talk to us. How much the fellow knows I cannot tell, but he is reputed to be as close to that genius of crime as anyone, and I believe it is an opportunity not to be missed. I would not bring you into this, except that the man insisted you be present. He seems to have confidence in your ability to protect him—"

"Say no more," I exclaimed, rising to my feet. "Let us go at once!"

"You do not hesitate," Gregson said, looking at me curiously. "I confess that in your position I would be highly suspicious of such a request."

"Well, as to that, it is quite understandable that the fellow should select me as a confidante. You are a stranger; whereas, if I may say so, my reputation for square dealing is well known. The man may even be someone I know personally! Come, Mr. Gregson, we mustn't delay an instant."

As we penetrated deeper into the heart of the old city, the narrow winding streets took on the character of a maze, composed of dirty crumbling walls and shuttered windows. The latticed balconies jutting out from the upper stories of the tall old houses cut off the sunlight, so that we walked through a dusty shade. There were few Europeans or English among the pedestrians, some of whom stumbled in a drugged daze, their eyes fixed on vacancy.

Since the streets (if they could be called that) turned and twisted, I was able to keep a watchful eye to the rear. Mr. Gregson noted my glances. "You are uneasy," he said seriously. "I should not have brought you. If you would rather return—"

"Keep walking," I hissed.

"What is it?"

"We are being followed."

"What?"

"Keep walking, I say. Don't turn your head."

"Surely you are mistaken."

"No. There is a man behind us whom I have seen twice before—once outside Shepheard's, and again loitering near the café. A slight fellow wearing a white *gibbeh* and a blue turban."

"But, Mrs. Emerson, that description would fit half the men in Cairo!"

"He has been careful to keep the sleeve of his *gibbeh* across the lower part of his face. I am certain he is following us—and I intend to capture him. Follow me!"

Turning abruptly, I rushed at the spy, my parasol raised.

My sudden attack caught both men by surprise. Gregson let out a grunt of alarm, and the pursuer stopped short, raising his arms in an attempt to shield his head. In vain—I was too quick for him! I brought my parasol crashing down on the crown of his head. His eyes rolled up, his knees buckled, and he sank to the ground in a flurry of fluttering white cotton.

"I have him," I cried, seating myself on the fallen man's chest. "Here, Mr. Gregson—come at once, I have captured the spy!"

The street had cleared as if by magic. I knew there were watchers hidden in the doorways and peering out from behind the shuttered windows, but the spectators had prudently removed themselves from the scene of action. Gregson edged toward me, with none of the enthusiastic congratulations I had expected.

Then a muffled voice murmured pathetically, "Sitt Hakim—oh, sitt, you have broken my head, I think."

I knew that voice. With a trembling hand I lifted the folds of fabric that hid my captive's face.

It was Selim, Abdullah's son—the beloved young

Benjamin of that loyal family. And I had struck him down!

"What the devil are you doing here, Selim?" I demanded. "No, don't tell me. Emerson sent you. You came up with us on the same train, in another carriage—you have been spying on me ever since Emerson and I parted outside the Administration Building!"

"Not spying, sitt," the boy protested. "Guarding you, protecting you! The Father of Curses honored me with this mission, and I have failed—I am disgraced—my heart is broken—and so is my head, sitt. I am dying. Take my farewells to the Father of Curses and to my honored father, and to my brothers Ali and Hassan and—"

I stood up and reached a hand to Selim. "Get up, you foolish boy. You are not hurt; the folds of your turban muffled the blow and I don't believe the skin is even broken. Let me have a look."

In fact, Selim's injury consisted of nothing more than a rising lump on his cranium. I took a box of ointment from the medicine kit in my tool collection and applied it to the lump, after which I wrapped Selim's head with bandages before replacing his turban. It rode rather high on his head because of the bandages, but that could not be helped.

Mr. Gregson watched in absolute silence. There was a curious absence of expression on his face.

"I beg your pardon, Mr. Gregson," I said. "We can continue now. Do you mind if Selim comes along, or would you rather I sent him away?"

Gregson hesitated. Before he could reply, Selim let out a howl of woe. "No, sitt, no. Do not send me away! I will not return to the Father of Curses without you. I would rather run away. I would rather join the army. I would rather take poison and die!"

"Be still," I said angrily. "Mr. Gregson?"

"I am afraid this delay has caused us to miss the appointment," Gregson said. "You had better take your lachrymose guard back to his master."

"Please, sitt, please." Selim, who was indeed weeping copiously, took hold of my arm. "Emerson Effendi will curse me and take my soul. Come with me, or I will cut out my tongue with my knife so that I need not confess my failure; I will put out my eyes lest I see his terrible frown. I will—"

"Good Gad," I exclaimed. "There is no help for it, Mr. Gregson. Won't you come with me and meet my husband? He will be extremely interested in any information you can give."

"Not today," Gregson said quietly. "If I go at once, I may be able to reach the person I spoke of and make another appointment. Perhaps I can also persuade him to allow the Professor to accompany us next time."

"Excellent," I said. "How will you let us know?"

"I will send a messenger to you. You may leave word for me at Shepheard's, if you have news; I stop there every day or so to pick up my mail."

"Very well." I held out my hand. Mr. Gregson took it in both of his. They were white, well-tended hands, but the callouses on his palms and the strength of his long fingers proved that here was a man of action as well as a gentleman.

"We will soon meet again," he said.

"I hope so. And I hope at that time to have the pleasure of introducing you to my husband."

"Yes, quite. Until then."

He strode off and, turning a corner, disappeared from sight. With Selim trailing disconsolately at my heels, I began to retrace my steps.

In fact, it required the combined concentration of my-

self and Selim to find our way. I had not taken note of
the turns and zigzags, since I expected to have Mr.
Gregson as escort on the return journey, and Selim had
been too preoccupied with keeping us in sight to pay
attention to where he was going. Eventually, however,
we reached a part of the city that was familiar to me,
and from there it was only a short distance to the Muski.
I hired a carriage and ordered Selim to take a seat beside
me.

"Now then, Selim," I said. "I don't want to put you
in a difficult position with the professor, but I don't see
how we are going to get round what happened if we tell
the truth."

The boy raised his drooping head. "Oh, sitt," he said
tremulously. "I will do anything you say."

"I never lie to the professor, Selim."

Selim looked distraught. "However," I said, "there
is no reason why we cannot bend the truth a little. We
will have to account for that lump on your head."

"I could remove the bandages, sitt," Selim said eagerly. "You were very generous with the bandages. I
do not need them."

"No, you must not do that. What I propose is this.
You will tell Professor Emerson everything that happened up to the moment when I discovered you. Then
say simply that someone fell upon you and attacked
you, striking you with a heavy object."

"Someone did," said Selim.

"Precisely. It is not a falsehood. Omit the name of
your attacker; let the professor think it was an ordinary
thief. Upon hearing the altercation, I ran to your rescue."

"It is good, sitt," Selim exclaimed.

"Because of your injury I felt it necessary to return
with you," I continued. "The blow on the head left you

dizzy and confused; if the professor asks you any awkward questions, you can just say you don't remember."

The lad's soft brown eyes shone with admiration.
"Sitt, you are my mother and my father! You are the
kindest and wisest of women!"

"You know how I hate flattery, Selim. Your praise
is unnecessary; just do as I say and everything will work
out. Er—you might lean back and try to look faint.
There is the hotel, and I see Emerson storming up and
down on the terrace."

Selim drooped and moaned so exquisitely that the
sight of him quite distracted Emerson from the scolding
he had meant to give me. "Good Gad," he shouted,
peering into the carriage. "What has happened? Is he
dead? Selim, my boy—"

"I am not dead but I am dying," Selim groaned.
"Honored Father of Curses, give my respects to my
father, to my brothers Ali and Hassan and—"

I jabbed him surreptitiously with my parasol. Selim
sat up with a start. "Perhaps I am not dying. I think I
will recover."

Emerson climbed into the carriage and slammed the
door. "To the railroad station," he directed the driver.

"But, Emerson," I began. "Don't you want to
know—"

"I do indeed, Peabody. You can tell me as we go.
We will just catch the afternoon express if we hurry."

He plucked off Selim's turban. The boy gave a dismal
yelp, and Emerson said coolly, "I recognize your hand-
iwork, Peabody. One-half pennyworth of blood to this
intolerable deal of bandages, eh? Tell me all about it,
from the beginning."

The tale was long in the telling, for I had to begin
with my meeting with Mr. Gregson, and at first Emerson
interrupted me every few words. "You must be out of

your mind, Peabody," he bellowed. "To follow that fellow into the heart of the old city on the strength of a cock-and-bull story . . . Who is he, anyway? You don't even know him!"

I persevered, and by the time we reached the station I had told the modified version of the truth Selim and I had agreed upon. Emerson's only comment was a gruff "Humph." Tossing the driver a few coins, he helped Selim out of the carriage with a gentleness his scowling countenance belied, and hurried us toward the train. There was a little altercation when we took Selim with us into a first-class carriage; but Emerson silenced the conductor with a handful of money and a few firm comments, and the other passengers departed, muttering— but not very loudly.

"Ah," said Emerson in a pleased voice. "Very good. We have the carriage to ourselves. We can discuss this remarkable story of yours at leisure."

"First," I said, hoping to distract him, "tell me what you learned in the *sûk*."

He had—if I could believe him—discovered more than I. One acquaintance, whom Emerson chose not to identify by name, claimed he knew the murderer of Kalenischeff. The killer was a professional assassin, for hire by anyone who had the price. It was rumored that he sometimes carried out assignments for Sethos, but he was not an official member of the gang. The man had left Cairo shortly after Kalenischeff's death, and no one knew where he was to be found.

"But," said Emerson, his eyes narrowing, "I am on his trail, Peabody. Eventually he will return, for Cairo is where he does his business. And when he does, word will be brought to me."

"But that may take weeks—months," I exclaimed.

"If you think you can do better, Peabody, you have

my permission to try,'' Emerson said. Then he clapped
his hand to his mouth. "No. No! I did not say that. I
meant—"

"Never mind, my dear Emerson. My comment was
not intended as criticism. Only you could have learned
as much."

"Humph," said Emerson. "What have you been up
to, Peabody? You never flatter me unless you have
something to hide."

"That is unjust, Emerson. I have often—"

"Indeed? I cannot remember when—"

"I have the greatest respect—"

"You constantly deceive and—"

"I—"

"You—"

Selim let out a groan and collapsed against Emerson's
broad shoulder. Taking a flask from my belt, I admin-
istered a sip of brandy, and Selim declared he felt much
better.

I handed the flask to Emerson, who absently took a
drink. "Now then, Peabody," he said affably. "What
else did you learn?"

I told him about the safragis and described my visit
to Mr. Aziz. Emerson shook his head. "That was a
waste of time, Peabody. I could have told you Aziz was
not a member of the organization. He has not the intelligence or the—er—intestinal fortitude."

"Precisely what I said to Aziz, Emerson. So it appears we are not much farther along."

"We have made a start, at any rate. I did not anticipate bringing our inquiries to a successful conclusion
in one day."

"Quite right, Emerson. You always cut straight to the

heart of the matter. And,'' I added hopefully, ''perhaps during our absence Sethos has done something, such as attacking the compound, which will give us more information.''

·

Twelve

·

At Emerson's request the train stopped at Dahshoor long enough to let us disembark. We trudged off along the path, Emerson supporting Selim with such vigor that the boy's feet scarcely touched the ground. After a short time Selim declared breathlessly that he was fully recovered and capable of walking by himself.

"Good lad," said Emerson, with a hearty slap on the back.

Alternately rubbing his back and his head, Selim followed us. "He may have saved your life, Amelia," said Emerson. "You didn't happen to see the man who attacked him?"

"It all happened so quickly," I said truthfully.

"The attacker may have been a common thief, you know. We need not see emissaries of Sethos everywhere."

"I think you are right, Emerson."

Before we reached the house we knew something was amiss. The gates were wide open and the place was buzzing like a beehive. The men had gathered in a group, all talking at once. Enid sat in a chair by the door, her face hidden in her hands; Donald paced up and down, patting her shoulder each time he passed her.

"What the devil," Emerson began.

"It is Ramses, of course," I said. "I expect he has gone off again."

As soon as we appeared, the entire assemblage rushed toward us and a dozen voices strove to be the first to tell the news. Emerson bellowed, "Silence!" Silence duly ensued. "Well?" said Emerson, looking at Donald.

"It is my fault," Enid cried. "The poor dear little boy wanted to give me a lesson in Egyptian; but I—" She gave Donald a betraying glance.

"No, it is my fault," Donald said. "He was my responsibility; but I—" He looked at Enid.

Emerson rounded on me and shook a finger under my nose. "Now you see, Amelia, what comes of this love nonsense. People afflicted by that illness have no sense of responsibility, no sense of duty—"

"Be calm, Emerson," I implored. "Let Donald speak."

"He is gone, that is all," Donald said, shrugging helplessly. "We noted his absence about an hour ago, but precisely how long ago he left I cannot say."

"Is he on foot or on donkeyback?" I inquired.

"Neither," Donald said grimly. "The little—er—fellow borrowed a horse—not any horse, but the cherished steed of the mayor, the same one you hired the other day. I say borrow, but I ought to add that the mayor was unaware of the fact. He has threatened to nail Ramses to the door of his house if anything happens to that animal."

"He cannot control such a large horse," Enid exclaimed, wringing her hands. "How he managed to mount and get away without being seen—"

"Ramses has a knack with animals," I said. "Never mind that. I assume no one saw him leave and therefore we have no idea as to which direction he took?"

"That is correct," said Donald.

Emerson clapped his hand to his brow. "How could he do this? He left no message, no letter?"

"Oh yes," Donald said. "He left a letter."

"Then why have you not gone after him?" Emerson cried, snatching the grimy paper Donald held out.

"Because," said Donald, "the letter is written in hieroglyphic."

And indeed it was. I stood on tiptoe and read over Emerson's shoulder. Ramses' hieroglyphic hand was extremely elegant, in striking contrast to his English handwriting, which was practically illegible. I doubted, however, that it was for that reason he had chosen to employ the former language.

"Mazghunah," Emerson exclaimed. "He has gone to Mazghunah! 'For the purpose of speaking with the wab-priest. . . .' That is a rather unorthodox use of the present participle, I must say."

"You may be sure Ramses can and will justify the usage if you are foolish enough to ask him," I said. "Well, Emerson, shall we go after him?"

"How can you ask, Amelia? Of course we will go after him, and as quickly as we can. When I think of what may have befallen him, alone in the desert—a little child on a horse he cannot handle, pursued by unknown villains. . . . Oh, good Gad!" Emerson ran toward the stable.

*   *   *

A lurid sunset glorified the west as our patient little donkeys trotted south along the path we knew so well. Emerson was as incapable as I of whipping an animal, but he urged his steed forward with impassioned pleas.

"So far so good," I remarked, in the hope of comforting him. "Ramses would have followed this same path; we have not seen his fallen body, so it is probably safe to assume he managed to control the horse."

"Oh, curse it," was Emerson's only response.

We entered the village from the north, passing the ruins of the American mission, which had been the scene of some of our most thrilling adventures the year before. It was silent and abandoned; the makeshift steeple of the church had collapsed and the surrounding houses were uninhabited. I had no doubt that the villagers shunned the spot as haunted and accursed.

As we approached the well, we saw a crowd of people. One and all stood in silent fascination, facing the house of the priest, their heads tilted as they listened. Faint and far away, yet distinctly audible, the wavering notes rose and fell—the cry of the muezzin reciting the call to prayer. A strange sound in a Christian village, with never a mosque in sight! Most curious of all was the fact that the sound came from inside the house of the priest.

There was a brief, waiting silence. Then the *adan* was repeated, but more loudly, and in a different voice. The first had been tenor, this was a gruff baritone. It broke off after a few words, to be followed immediately by yet a third voice, distinguished by a perceptible lisp. It sounded as if the priest of Dronkeh were entertaining, or interviewing, all the local muezzins.

The crowd parted like the Red Sea before Emerson's impetuous rush. Without waiting to knock, he flung the door open.

The last rays of the dying sun cut like a flaming
sword through the gloom within. They fell full upon the
form of Walter "Ramses" Peabody Emerson, seated
cross-legged on the divan, his head thrown back, his
Adam's apple bobbing up and down as from his parted
lips came the wailing rise and fall of the call to prayer.

The priest, who had been sitting in the shadow,
started up. Ramses—being Ramses—finished all four of
the initial statements of the ritual ("God is most great,
et cetera") before remarking, "Good evening, Mama.
Good evening, Papa. Did you have a productive day in
Cairo?"

Emerson accepted Father Todorus' offer of a cup of
cognac. I declined. I required all my wits to deal with
Ramses.

"May I ask," I inquired, taking a seat beside him,
"what you are doing?"

I hated to ask, for I felt sure he would tell me, at
tedious length; but I was so bewildered by the uncanny
performance I was not quite myself. It was obvious that
not only the last, but *all* the other muezzin calls had
come from the scrawny throat of my son. Emerson continued to sip his cognac, his bulging eyes fixed on
Ramses' Adam's apple.

Ramses cleared his throat. "When you and Papa discussed the unfortunate captivity of Father Todorus here,
I found myself in complete agreement with your conclusion that he had been imprisoned somewhere within
the environs of Cairo. Your further conclusion, that it
would not be possible to narrow this down, was one
with which I was reluctantly forced to disagree. For in
my opinion—"

"Ramses."

"Yes, Mama?"

"I would be indebted to you if you would endeavor to restrict your use of that phrase."

"What phrase, Mama?"

" 'In my opinion.' "

The cognac had restored Emerson's powers of speech. He said hoarsely, "I am inclined to agree with your mama, Ramses, but let us leave that for the moment. Please proceed with your explanation."

"Yes, Papa. For in my . . . That is, I felt that although Father Todorus had been unable to *see* out of the windows, he had probably been able to *hear* out of them. Indeed, one of your own statements corroborated that assumption. Now while the agglomerate of sounds that might be called the 'voice of the city' is generally indistinctive—I refer to such sounds as the braying of donkeys, the calls of water sellers and vendors, the whining pleas of beggars, the—"

"I observe with concern, Ramses, that you seem to be developing a literary, not to say poetic, turn of phrase. Writing verses and keeping a journal are excellent methods of expurgating these tendencies. Incorporating them into an explanatory narrative is not."

"Ah," said Ramses thoughtfully.

"Please continue, Ramses," said his father. "And, my dearest son—be brief!"

"Yes, Papa. There is one variety of auditory phenomena that is, in contrast to those I have mentioned (and others I was not allowed to mention), distinctive and differentiated. I refer, of course, to the calls of the muezzins of the mosques of Cairo. It occurred to me that Father Todorus, who had probably heard these calls ad nauseam, so to speak, day after day, might be able to distinguish between them and perhaps even recall their relative loudness and softness. I came, therefore, to attempt the experiment. By reproducing—"

"Oh, good Gad!" I cried out. "Ramses—have you been sitting here for over three hours repeating the *adan* in different voices and different tones? Emerson—as you know, I seldom succumb to weakness, but I must confess I feel—I feel rather faint."

"Have some cognac," said Emerson, handing me the cup. "Was the experiment a success, my son?"

"To some extent, Papa. I believe I have narrowed the area down to one approximately a quarter of a mile square."

"I cannot believe this," I murmured, half to myself—entirely to myself as it turned out, for none of the others was listening.

"It was very interesting," said Father Todorus, nodding like a wind-up toy. "When I closed my eyes I could imagine myself in that house of Satan, listening, as I had done so often, to the calling of the heathen."

"I cannot believe this," I repeated. "Ramses. How did you learn to differentiate these calls? There are three hundred mosques in Cairo!"

"But only thirty or forty within the area I considered most likely," said Ramses. "To wit, the old city, with its dark and secret byways and its crumbling ancient mansions and its—" He caught my eye. "I became interested in the matter last spring," he went on, more prosaically. "When we were in Cairo before leaving for England. We were there for several weeks, and I had ample opportunity to—"

"I understand," said Emerson. "A most ingenious idea, upon my word. Don't you agree, Peabody?"

My cup was empty. I thought of asking for more, but my iron will rose triumphant over distress and disbelief. "I believe we should go home now," I said. "Father Todorus must be tired."

Father Todorus made polite protestations, but it was evident he would be glad to see the last of us. His manner toward Ramses as he bade him farewell was a blend of respect and terror.

As we emerged from the priest's house, one of the villagers came up leading the mare and, with a deep salaam, handed the reins to Ramses.

Ramses' excursion into grand theft had momentarily slipped my mind. I remembered reading that in the American West, horse thieves were usually hanged.

Perhaps Ramses remembered this too. In the act of mounting he hesitated and then turned to me. With his most winning smile he said, "Would you like to ride Mazeppa, Mama?"

"A very proper thought, Ramses," said Emerson approvingly. "I am glad to see you show your dear mama the consideration she deserves."

The mayor shared the opinion of the American cowboy with regard to horse thieves. I was obliged to propitiate him by hiring the horse, at a staggering fee, for the duration of our stay at Dahshoor. Leaving the mare with her owner, for we had no stabling facilities worthy of such a paragon, I returned to the house.

My annoyance was not assuaged by the sight of Ramses and his father deep in consultation over a map of Cairo that was spread across the table, on which our evening meal had already been set out. One end of the map was in the gravy. Ramses was jabbing at the paper with his forefinger and saying, "The most audible of the muezzins was the gentleman from the mosque of Gâmia 'Seiyidna Hosein. By a process of elimination and repetition I feel we can eliminate everything outside a region roughly seven hundred and fifty—"

Very firmly and quietly I suggested that the map be removed and the dishes rearranged. We sat down to the excellent (though tepid) meal Hamid had prepared. A distinct air of constraint was to be felt, and for a time all ate in silence. Then Emerson, whose motives are always admirable but whose notion of tact is distinctly peculiar, said brightly, "I trust the matter of the mare was settled to your satisfaction, Peabody."

"It was settled to the satisfaction of the mayor, Emerson. We have hired the mare for the season, at a price of one hundred shekels."

Emerson choked on a mouthful of stew and had to retire behind his table napkin. However, he did not complain about the price. Instead he suggested, "Perhaps we should purchase the animal outright. For you, Peabody, I mean; wouldn't you like to have her for your own? She is a pretty creature—"

"No, thank you, Emerson. The next thing, Ramses would be demanding that we ship her back to England with us."

"You are quite mistaken, Mama; such an idea had not occurred to me. It would be more convenient to keep Mazeppa here, so that I can ride her when we come out each—"

The sentence ended in a gasp and a start, as Emerson, who had realized that any further reference to the mare, especially from his son, would not improve my mood, kicked Ramses in the shin. No one spoke for a while. Donald had not said a word the entire time; I attributed his silence to remorse at his failure to carry out his duty, but as I was soon to learn, there was another reason. He had been thinking. As Emerson says—somewhat unjustly, I believe—the process is difficult for Englishmen, and requires all their concentration.

Not until we had slaked the first pangs of hunger and

were nibbling on slices of fruit did the young man rise from his chair and clear his throat. "I have come to a decision," he announced. "That is, Enid and I have come to a decision."

He took the hand the girl offered him, squared his shoulders, and went on, "We wish to be married at once. Professor, will you perform the service this evening?"

The sheer lunacy of the request startled me so that I dropped my napkin. It fell on top of the cat Bastet, who was crouched under the table, hoping (correctly) that Ramses would slip tidbits to her. This upset her a great deal, and the rest of the conversation was punctuated with growls and thumps as Bastet wrestled with the napkin.

Emerson's jaw dropped. He started to speak, or perhaps to laugh. Then a thought seemed to occur to him, for his eyes narrowed and his hand crept to his chin. "That would certainly solve some of our difficulties," he said musingly, stroking the dimple. "Mrs. Emerson's obsession with chaperonage and propriety . . ."

"Emerson!" I exclaimed. "How can you entertain such a notion for a split second? My dear Ronald—excuse me, Donald—my dear Enid—whatever gave you the idea that Professor Emerson is licensed to marry people?"

"Why, I don't know," Donald said, looking confused. "The captain of a ship has such privileges; I thought the leader of an expedition in a foreign country—"

"You thought wrong," I said.

Enid lowered her eyes. Yet I had a feeling she had known the truth all along—and had not cared. I should not wish it to be supposed that I ever approve of immorality, but I must confess that my opinion of the girl rose.

"Sit down, Donald," I said. "You look so very indecisive standing there scratching your ear. Let us discuss this rationally. I thoroughly approve of your decision, which will, of course, have to wait until the proper formalities have been carried out. May I ask what led you to it?"

Donald continued to hold Enid's hand. She smiled at him with (I could not help thinking) the gentle encouragement of a teacher toward a rather backward child.

"Enid has convinced me," Donald said. "We cannot continue to hide like criminals who have something to be ashamed of. Surely she is in no danger from the police; only a madman could entertain the notion of her guilt."

"That is in fact the case," I said. "We learned today that the police have abandoned any idea that she killed Kalenischeff. You, however—"

"I," said Donald, lifting his chin, "will face my accusers like a man. They cannot prove I killed the fellow—though I was often tempted to punch him senseless as I followed him and Enid around Cairo and saw him smirk and leer at her."

"That is the sort of statement I strongly advise you not to make to anyone else," said Emerson. "However, I agree with you that there is little evidence against you. But you have not explained this sudden surge of gallantry. Was it love, that noble emotion, that strengthened your moral sinews?"

His satirical tone was lost on Donald, who replied simply. "Yes, sir, it was. Besides, reluctant as I am to face the truth, Enid has convinced me that it was Ronald who tried to kill me this morning."

"Well, of course it was," Emerson said. "It has been

evident from the first that the difficulties you two have
encountered are purely domestic in nature. Your
brother, Mr. Fraser, appears to be a thoroughly unprin-
cipled person. It was he, was it not, who forged the
signature and persuaded you to accept the blame? Stupid, Mr. Fraser—very stupid indeed. For that act had
consequences far more dangerous to you than mere dis-
honor. Your brother hoped that despair would lead you
to death by accident or self-destruction, thus giving him
control of your estate. I suspect he has an additional
motive which has to do with the affections of Miss Debenham here. I also suspect that had Miss Debenham
been content to accept Donald's disgrace and disappearance, not to mention the hand in marriage of
Ronald, Donald (curse it, these names are very confus-
ing)—Ronald, I mean, would have gone no further. By
vigorously pursuing the search for Donald and denying
his guilt, she endangered Ronald's position and he was
forced to take more direct action.

"He hired Kalenischeff, not to lead Miss Debenham
to Donald, but to mislead her. But Kalenischeff would
have betrayed Ronald for a price, and Ronald had to
stop him. It is not difficult to hire assassins in Cairo.
Kalenischeff was lured to Miss Debenham's room, not
only because he was more vulnerable to attack there,
but because Ronald hoped to incriminate his 'delicate
darling,' as he had the audacity to call her, and keep
her from pressing her search. I suspect, Miss Debenham,
that he resented your contemptuous treatment of him
and his proposal of marriage, and you may thank heaven
you did not change your mind, for, once in his power,
you would have paid for your contumely in tears and
anguish. He is a vicious and vindictive man."

"Amazing, Professor," Donald exclaimed. "You are
right in every particular; you have even made me see

painful truths I was unwilling to admit to myself. How did you know all that?"

"Only an idiot would fail to see it," Emerson grunted.

"Or a brother, blinded by fraternal affection," I said, more charitably.

"Or," said Emerson, fixing me with a hideous scowl, "an individual obsessed by master criminals."

When we sought our couch in the desert, we did not go alone. To Emerson's poorly concealed fury, Donald had insisted Enid occupy the other tent. "Now, of all times," he had said, pressing the girl's hand, "it is important that not the slightest shadow of reproach rest upon Enid."

"Humph," said Emerson.

I was against the idea myself, though not entirely for the same reason. Emerson's analysis of the case had been cogent, as his analyses always were. That is not to say it was correct. I felt in my bones that my two young friends were entwined in the invisible strands of Sethos' filthy web. My arguments had little effect, however. Donald supported Emerson (men always stick together), and Enid supported Donald. The only one who showed an ounce of sense was Ramses. His offer to stand guard outside Enid's tent was unanimously rejected, but when he offered the cat in his stead, Enid laughed and said she would be delighted to have a nice cuddly kitty curl up with her.

I looked at the great brindled cat. Her topaz eyes had narrowed to slits and her lip curled, as if she were smiling contemptuously at the ludicrously inappropriate description. It seemed even more ludicrous when Ramses took her off into a corner, squatted down, facing her, and began mumbling at her. It was enough to make one's blood run cold to see them staring into one another's eyes, the cat quiet and intent, her head tilted and her tail twitching.

Whatever Ramses said had the desired effect. Bastet accompanied us when we left the house. Donald had declared his intention of escorting his beloved and seeing her safely to her tent. They followed at a discreet distance, whispering in the starlight. It was a perfect night for lovers—as indeed most nights in Egypt are—and I would have been content to walk in dreamy silence, with Emerson's hand holding mine. However, Emerson was being stubborn.

"If they are determined to go to Cairo and give themselves up tomorrow, it is essential that some responsible person accompany them," I insisted.

"Absolutely not, Peabody. We will be shorthanded as it is once they have gone—although *she* was never much use, and *he* is too distracted by *her* to carry out his duties. I don't know why you keep encouraging people like that. You always have a few of those vapid young persons hanging about, interfering with our work and complicating our lives. I have nothing against them, and I wish them well, but I will be glad to see the last of them."

I let Emerson rant, which he did, scarcely pausing to draw breath, until we had reached our tent. I stopped to call a pleasant good night to the two shadowy forms behind us. Emerson took my hand and pulled me inside. For a long time thereafter, the only sounds that broke the stillness were the far-off cries of jackals.

When I woke in the pre-dawn darkness, it was not, for once, a burglar or an assassin who had disturbed my slumber. I had dreamed again—a dream so vivid and distinct that I had to stretch out my hand to Emerson in order to reassure myself that I was really in the tent with my husband at my side. The contours of those familiar features under my groping fingers brought a great sense of relief. Emerson snorted and mumbled but did not wake up.

I could have wished just then that he did not sleep so soundly. I felt a ridiculous need for consultation—even, though I am reluctant to confess it, for comforting. It was not so much the scenario of the dream that made me tremble in the darkness, but, if I may so express it, the psychic atmosphere that had prevailed. Anyone who has wakened shrieking from a nightmare will know what I mean, for in dreams the most innocuous objects can arouse extraordinary sensations of apprehension. I yearned to discuss my sensations with Emerson and hear his reassuring "Balderdash, Peabody!"

My better nature prevailed, as I hope it always does, and, creeping closer to his side, I sought once again to woo Morpheus. The fickle god would not be seduced, though I tried a variety of sleeping positions. Through all my tossing and turning Emerson lay like a log, his arms folded across his breast.

At last I abandoned the attempt. As yet no light penetrated the heavy canvas of the walls, but an indefinable freshness in the air told me that dawn could not be far off. Rising, I lighted a lamp and got dressed. As those who have attempted to perform this feat in the narrow confines of a tent can testify, it is impossible to do it gracefully or quietly, yet Emerson continued to sleep, undisturbed by the light or by my inadvertent stumbles over his limbs, or even by the jingling of my tool belt as I buckled it on. I had to pound gently on his chest and apply a variety of tactile stimuli to his face and

form before his regular breathing changed its rhythm.
A smile tugged at the corners of his mouth. Without
opening his eyes he put out his arm and pulled me down
upon him.

As I believe I have mentioned, Emerson dislikes the
encumbrance of sleeping garments. The vigor of his
movement brought my belt and its fringe of hard, sharp-
edged objects in sudden contact with a vulnerable portion of his anatomy, and the benevolent aspect of his
countenance underwent a dreadful change. I clapped my
hand over his mouth before the shriek bubbling in his
throat could emerge.

"Don't cry out, Emerson. You will waken Enid and
frighten the poor girl out of her wits."

After a while the rigidity of Emerson's muscular
chest subsided, and his bulging eyes resumed their normal aspect. I deemed it safe to remove my hand.

"Peabody," he said.

"Yes, my dear Emerson?"

"Are we surrounded by hostile Bedouin on the verge
of a murderous attack?"

"Why no, Emerson, I don't think so."

"Did a shadowy figure creep into the tent, brandishing a knife?"

"No."

"A mummified hand, perhaps? Slipping through the
gap between the tent wall and the canvas floor, groping
for your throat?"

"Emerson, you are particularly annoying when you
try to be sarcastic. There is nothing wrong. At least
nothing of the sort you mention. It is almost morning,
and I . . . I could not sleep."

I removed my elbows from his chest and sat up. I
said no more; but Emerson then demonstrated the ster-
ling qualities that have won him the wholehearted af-

fection of a woman who, I venture to assert, insists upon the highest standards in a spouse.

Once again his sinewy arms reached out and drew me into a close embrace—not quite so close, and with some degree of caution. "Tell me about it, Peabody," he said.

"It sounds foolish," I murmured, resting my head against his breast.

"I love you when you are foolish, Peabody. It is a rare event—if by foolish you mean gentle and yielding, timid and fearful. . . ."

"Stop that, Emerson," I said firmly, taking his hand. "I am not fearful; only puzzled. I had the most peculiar dream."

"That is also a rare event. Proceed."

"I found myself in a strange room, Emerson. It was decorated in the most luxurious and voluptuous fashion—rosy-pink draperies covering the walls and windows, a soft couch strewn with silken pillows, antique rugs, and a tiny tinkling fountain. Upon a low table of ebony and mother-of-pearl was a tray with fruit and wine, silver bowls and crystal glasses. A dreaming silence filled the chamber, broken only by the melodious murmur of the fountain.

"I lay upon the couch. I felt myself to be wide awake, and my dreaming self was as bewildered by my surroundings as I myself would have been. My eyes were drawn to a fringed and embroidered curtain that concealed a door. How I knew this I cannot say; but I did, and I also knew something was approaching—that the door would soon open, the curtain lift—that I would see . . ."

"Go on, Peabody."

"That was when I woke, Emerson—woke in a cold sweat of terror, trembling in every limb. You know, my dear, that I have no patience with the superstition that dreams are portents of things to come, but I cannot help but believe there is some deeper meaning in this dream.''

I could not see Emerson's face, but I felt a hardening of the arms that held me. ''Are you sure,'' he inquired, ''that the emotion you felt was terror?''

''That is a strange question, Emerson.''

''It was a strange dream, Peabody.'' He sat up and put me gently from him, holding me by the shoulders and looking deep into my eyes. ''Who was it, Peabody? Who was approaching the door?''

''I don't know.''

''Hmmm.'' He continued to gaze at me with that peculiar intensity. Then he said quietly, ''I believe I can identify the origin of your dream, Peabody. Your description sounds like the one Father Todorus gave of his prison.''

''Why, of course,'' I exclaimed. ''You are quite right, Emerson. No doubt that explains it. Even my emotions were the same as those the poor old man must have felt.''

''I am glad to have relieved your apprehension. Have I done so, Peabody?''

''Yes, Emerson, and I thank you. Only—only I still have a sensation of approaching doom—that something lies in wait on the threshold of our lives—''

''That is a sensation to which you should be accustomed,'' said Emerson, in his old sardonic manner. ''Never mind, Peabody, we will face the danger together, you and I—side by side, back to back, shoulder to shoulder.''

''With Ramses running around getting in the way,'' I said, emulating his light tone. ''Emerson, I apologize for disturbing you with my nonsense. Do you dress now and I will go out and light the spirit stove and make some tea.''

I handed him his trousers, knowing he could never find them without a prolonged and profane search. Emerson's broad shoulders lifted in a shrug, and he accepted the offering.

I crawled to the entrance of the tent. The flap had been secured by a simple slip knot, running through a ring in the canvas floor. Unloosening this, I saw a slit of daylight outside. It was morning, though still very early. Rising, I pushed the flap aside and went out.

Immediately I felt myself falling. I had tripped over some object that lay before the tent. My outstretched hands struck the hard ground, but I felt the obstruction under my shins. Not until I stumbled to my feet did I see what it was.

Donald Fraser lay on his back. His limbs had been arranged, his hands were folded on his breast. A blackened hole like a third eye marked the center of his forehead; his blue eyes were wide open and their surfaces were blurred by a faint dusting of sand.

I did not scream, as an ordinary woman might have done, but a loud, shrill cry of surprise did escape my lips. It brought Emerson rushing out of the tent with such precipitation that the most strenuous efforts on my part were required to prevent both of us from falling onto the corpse a second time. An oath broke from Emerson; but before he could enlarge upon the theme, he was distracted by a third person who came running toward us.

''The assassin,'' Emerson exclaimed, freeing himself from my grasp and raising his fist. As he recognized the newcomer his arm fell nervelessly to his side and I my-

self staggered under the shock of the impression. I
looked from Donald, alive and on his feet, to Donald
recumbent and slain; and then, somewhat belatedly, the
truth dawned on me.

"It is Ronald, not Donald," I exclaimed. "What is
he doing here? What is either of them doing here?"

Donald had seen his brother. The rays of the sun
warmed the dead man's face with a false flush of life,
but there could be no doubt in anyone's mind that Ronald was no more. With a cry that sent a thrill of sympathy through my veins, Donald dropped to his knees
beside the body.

"Don't touch him," Emerson said sharply. "There
is nothing anyone can do for him now. He has been
dead for hours; the rigidity of the limbs is well advanced."

Donald might not have heeded this sensible advice,
but the sound of someone approaching reminded him of
a more important duty. He rose and ran to meet Enid,
taking her in his arms and holding her head against his
breast. "Don't look," he said in broken tones. "It is
Ronald—my poor brother, dead, foully slain!"

The cat Bastet was at Enid's heels. After a curious
but cursory inspection of the body she sat down and
began washing herself. I was tempted to speak severely
to her about her failings as a watch cat, but upon reflection I decided she could not be blamed for failing
to warn us of the killer's presence, if, as I assumed, she
had been shut in Enid's tent. Her primary responsibility
had been to watch over the girl and that aim had been
achieved, though how much of the credit was due to
the cat Bastet only she (the cat) and heaven knew.

Emerson went into the tent and returned with a blanket, which he threw over the dead man. "A suspicion
of murder does indeed arise," he said grimly. "Aside

from the fact that I see no weapon in his hand, he must
have been carried to this spot after the deed was done.
I am a sound sleeper, but I rather think a pistol shot
five feet from my ear would have awakened me. Come,
come, Donald, pull yourself together. Your grief is
somewhat absurd, considering the fact that your brother
has done his best to ruin you. Explain your presence."

Holding Enid in the curve of his arm, Donald turned.
With his free hand he dashed the tears from his eyes.
"I do not apologize for my womanly weakness," he
muttered. "At such a time resentment is forgotten and
a thousand tender memories of childhood soften the recent past. Professor, surely my brother's death casts a
doubt upon his culpability. He cannot have taken his
own life."

"Precisely," Emerson said.

Enid, more quick-witted than her lover, instantly understood Emerson's meaning. "How dare you, Professor! Are you suggesting that Donald murdered his
brother?"

"What?" Donald cried. "Enid, my darling, you don't
believe—"

"No, my darling, of course not. But he—"

Emerson let out a roar. "If I hear one more maudlin
phrase or sentimental endearment, I will abandon you
to your fate! You are in a pretty fix, Mr. Donald Fraser,
and I have a feeling we may be short on time. Answer
me without delay. What brought you here at this hour?"

"I have been here all night," Donald said.

"I see." Emerson's critical fown softened. "Well,
Mr. Fraser, I must say that demonstrates better sense
than I had expected from you. Miss Debenham can testify that you were with her—"

"Sir," Donald exclaimed, his cheeks flushed with indignation. "You are casting aspersions upon the no-blest, the purest girl who ever—"

Enid's face was as rosy as his. "Oh, Donald, you dear, adorable idiot . . . He *was* with me, Professor. I shall swear to it in any court."

Donald protested, of course, and it took several roars from Emerson to silence the pair. To summarize the confused and impassioned statements that were eventually produced, it seemed that Donald had spent the night stretched out on a rug before the entrance to his beloved's sleeping quarters. She had not been aware of his presence, and neither had heard anything out of the way.

Emerson gave the young man a look of blistering contempt. "It is this cursed public-school spirit," he muttered. "Of all the pernicious, fatuous attitudes . . . What of Ramses, you irresponsible young fool?"

"He promised me solemnly he would not leave the house during the night. I felt I could take his word—"

"Oh yes," I said hollowly. "But, Donald, the night is spent."

Across the desert, from out of the sunrise, galloped a splendid horse, with a small figure perched on its back.

Ramses tried to bring the mare to a spectacular, rearing stop. The feat was of course quite beyond his strength; he rolled off the animal's back and hit the ground with a thump. Rising to hands and knees, he began, "Good morning, Mama. Good morning, Papa. Good—"

Emerson hoisted him to his feet. "Eschew the formalities, my son," he said.

"Yes, Papa. Thank you for reminding me that time is indeed of the essence. A party of officials has just disembarked from a government steamer. It will not take them long to learn where we are to be found, and

from the constitution of the group and the solemnity of
their demeanor I deduce that some serious matter—''

"Good Gad," I exclaimed. "We should have anticipated this, Emerson. The murderer—whose name, or
epithet, rather, I need not mention—wishes to have
Donald arrested for his brother's death. Of course he
would notify the police."

The latest catastrophe had struck Donald dumb. He
stood staring helplessly as Emerson ran his hands over
the young man's body. "He has no weapon," he remarked.

"The weapon," I cried. "Without it the police cannot
prove—''

"That is not necessarily true, Mama," said the voice
of Ramses, from somewhere nearby.

At first I could not tell where he had got to. Turning,
I discovered that he had crept to the shrouded figure
and lifted the blanket. After a brief and emotionless
stare he let the covering fall again and stood up. "The
situation is as I surmised," he said. "Papa, failure to
find the pistol that fired the fatal shot may not save Mr.
Donald Fraser, for the prosecution will claim it could
easily be concealed in the sand. I would not be surprised, however, if it were not found nearby, in a place
easily discovered by the most cursory search."

With a cry, Enid ran toward her tent. I knew what
was in her mind and hastened to aid her; for although
Ramses was right (drat him) in saying that the *absence*
of the weapon would not clear Donald, the *discovery*
of it would certainly strengthen the case against him.

When I reached her, Enid was crawling on the
ground, brushing sand and pebbles aside in her frantic
search. However, it was Ramses who found the pistol
wedged in a crevice in the rock some twenty feet from
the tent. Emerson hastily took it from him.

"We ought, by rights, to turn it over to the authorities," he said.

"Give it to me," I said. "I will conceal it in my sponge-bag."

"Whatever you do had best be done quickly," remarked Ramses. "For here they come."

The party was an imposing one—several constables, Major Ramsay, and no less a personage than Sir Eldon Gorst, the Adviser on police matters in the Ministry of the Interior. The latter was the first to speak. Dismounting from his donkey, he approached me, his face grave. "Mrs. Emerson! It is always a pleasure to see you; I wish our meeting could have taken place under more pleasant circumstances. Professor—"

"Hallo, Gorst," said Emerson. "Get it over with, will you? I have a great deal of work to do. The body is over there."

"So it is true," Sir Eldon said heavily. "I could scarcely believe . . . You know Major Ramsay, I think?"

"Yes," I said, nodding frostily at the major. "We have only just made the tragic discovery ourselves. May I ask how you happened to have been notified—hours ago, one presumes, since it would take you some time to get here?"

Sir Eldon started to speak, but was anticipated by the major. "The source was unimpeachable," he said, scowling.

"It must have been, to send you out on what might have been a wild-goose chase," said Emerson. "Curse it, I insist upon knowing who dumped a corpse on my doorstep. I am not a man to be trifled with, Ramsay."

"Damn it, Professor," Ramsay began.

"My dear fellow, there are ladies present," Sir Eldon exclaimed. "Speaking of ladies—I am correct, madam, am I not, in assuming that you are Miss Enid Debenham, whose prolonged absence has caused such concern to my office?"

"I am she."

"And I," said Donald, "am Donald Fraser. I expect, Sir Eldon, that you have been looking for me too."

Sir Eldon bowed. It was clear that his unknown informant had told him, not only about the death of Ronald, but the presence of Donald. "It is my duty to inform you," he began.

"For once I agree with Professor Emerson," growled the major. "Let's get this over with."

He gestured. One of the constables stepped forward. There was a click, and a soft moan from Enid, and Donald stood handcuffed before us.

Thirteen

Enid insisted upon accompanying Donald to Cairo. Sir Eldon tried to dissuade her, but Major Ramsay, who had no gentlemanly instincts, said she might as well come along, since she would have to give a statement and he had a lot of questions to ask her. I of course assured her I would follow as soon as possible. Instead of protesting, as I expected, Emerson only gave me an odd look and said nothing.

One of the constables was left behind to search for the weapon. As I departed from my tent with my sponge-bag over my arm, I saw him disconsolately surveying the vast and tumbled terrain.

We had to bustle in order to catch the morning train. I say we, for to my surprise I discovered that Emerson meant to come with me. I was about to express my approval and my pleasure when Emerson put an end to both by pointing out that we would have to take Ramses too. He was quite correct; leaving Ramses at Dahshoor was too fraught with terrible possibilities to be contemplated. He had Abdullah and the other men completely under his thumb. It need hardly be said that Bastet also accompanied us, for Ramses refused to be parted from her for any length of time.

I could not make out what Emerson was planning. For him to abandon his work was almost unheard of, yet he had not even given Abdullah directions as to how to proceed, only told him to declare a holiday.

As soon as we had taken our seats on the train, I began my inquiries. I thought it better not to ask Emerson point-blank what was on his mind, but instead attempted to work up to it by subtle indirection.

"I trust," I began, "that the events of this morning have altered your appraisal of the situation and brought you around to my way of thinking."

"I doubt it," Emerson said curtly.

"Your belief that Donald's difficulties are purely domestic in nature—I believe you used that phrase—was obviously erroneous. Unless you think Donald killed his brother?"

"It seems unlikely," said Ramses, who had recovered his breath after being yanked into the compartment and thrust into a seat. "Mr. Donald Fraser is not distinguished by great intellectual capacity—indeed, I cannot help but wonder what a lady of Miss Debenham's superior qualities could possibly see in him—but there is no reason why he should go to the trouble of carrying the body a long distance from the scene of the murder in order to place it conspicuously in front of your tent."

"Humph," said Emerson, tacitly acknowledging the truth of Ramses' analysis.

"Furthermore," Ramses continued, "if the pistol was his, it must have been procured in the last day or two, since he did not have it with him when he came, and I do not see how—"

"Did you have the effrontery to search the young man's belongings?" I demanded indignantly.

"He had no belongings," Ramses replied calmly. "Except for the opium and pipe which you took from him. Nor was there any hiding place in his room, except under the cot, which I investigated at an early—"

"Never mind," Emerson said, anticipating my protest. "We will take it as read that Donald did not kill his brother. Some other person ... Oh, curse it, I may as well admit it. We are back to your friend Sethos, Amelia."

"I knew that from the first, Emerson."

"Bah," said Emerson. "Here is something I'll wager you don't know. I have come to the conclusion that Sethos has played the same trick he played on us once before—that at some point he has actually introduced himself to us. In disguise, I hardly need say—"

"Quite right, Papa," cried Ramses. "You anticipate my very words. And I know who he is. The gentleman Mama met in Cairo, the self-styled private investigator!"

"Don't be silly, Ramses," I said. "You have not even met Mr. Gregson."

Ramses became red in the face with frustration. "But, Mama, I have tried over and over to tell you—Tobias Gregson is the name of the police officer in the detective stories by Arthur Conan Doyle. I put it to you that it would be typical of the strange sense of humor of the man known as Sethos to select as a pseudonym the name of the character Mr. Sherlock Holmes—the most famous private investigator in modern fiction—despised as a bungler and a fool. What do you know of this man, in fact? Did he show you his papers? Did he refer you to the police in order to verify his semi-official standing? Did he—"

"I will not permit that accusatory tone, Ramses," I exclaimed. "Don't dare talk to me like a schoolmaster lecturing a dull student. Mr. Gregson was working under cover. Furthermore—er—furthermore, he has brown eyes."

Emerson started as if he had been stung. "I am shocked, Amelia, that you should go around staring into the eyes of strange men."

"I have good reason to notice the color of a suspect's eyes," I replied stoutly. "As for Mr. Gregson, I hope and believe you will meet him shortly. He is not Sethos. But I know who is. Mrs. Axhammer, the elderly American lady who visited us at Dahshoor!"

I expected Emerson to say "Bah," or "Humbug," or something equally insulting. His response offended me even more. He burst into a peal of laughter. "Come, now, Peabody, that is too absurd. On what basis—"

"Several. She was careful to wear a veil, but it did not conceal the lively sparkle of dark eyes. When on one occasion the veil was displaced, I observed that her teeth were firm and white and that her chin, though close-shaven, showed signs of stubble!"

"I have known old ladies with full mustaches and beards," said Emerson, grinning. "You are both wrong. I know who Sethos really is. His lordship, Viscount Everly!"

He gave me no time for rebuttal, but went on, "Ronald was in his entourage. It was while the presumed viscount and his friends were shooting at Dahshoor that both the incidents involving firearms occurred. It was his horse that bolted, endangering Ramses—"

"Pure coincidence," I said. "Sethos cannot be his lordship. He is Mrs. Axhammer."

"The viscount," Emerson growled.

"Mr. Gregson," piped Ramses.

His high-pitched voice contrasted so oddly with his father's baritone grumble that Emerson and I both burst out laughing. Ramses contemplated us haughtily down the length of his nose. "I fail to see the humor in the situation," he said.

"You are quite right, my boy," said Emerson, smiling. "I suppose we must agree to disagree. Time will tell which of us is correct."

"If we are not all wrong," I said more seriously. "I cannot get it out of my head, Emerson—your reminder that the god Set was red-haired. But I will wager that I am the first to come face to face with his evil emissary."

"You had damned well better not be," said Emerson, and refused to apologize, even though he had promised me he would try not to swear in front of Ramses.

When we entered the lobby of Shepheard's, the first person we saw was Enid. She sat reading a newspaper, apparently oblivious to the curious stares and whispers of the other guests, but the moment we appeared she jumped up and hastened to meet us.

"You came," she whispered, seizing my hand. "I was afraid you would not. Thank you, thank you!"

"I said I would come," I replied. "When I say I will do something, Enid, you may be certain I will do it."

Ramses studied her from under lowered brows; and indeed she little resembled the demure archaeologist of Dahshoor. She was wearing an extravagantly frivolous gown, all ruffles and puffs and lace, and her lips and cheeks were rouged. I daresay she wore no more paint than usual, but owing to the pallor of her face, the red patches stood out with garish effect.

Retaining her tight grasp on my hand, she reached out her other hand to Ramses. "Don't you know your old friend in this costume?" she asked, with a brave attempt at a smile.

"I hope you do not suppose that a superficial alteration of that nature could deceive my trained eye," Ramses replied in evident chagrin. "I was merely endeavoring to decide whether I prefer this persona to the other. On the whole—"

It had taken only a few days to teach Enid that if someone did not interrupt Ramses, he would go on talking indefinitely. "No matter what my outward appearance, Ramses, my feelings will never change. I am your true friend, and I hope I may consider you mine."

Ramses was moved. A casual observer might not have realized it, for the only outward expression of his feelings was a rapid blink of his eyelids. He replied in his most dignified manner, "Thank you. You may indeed rely upon my friendship, and if at any time in the future you have need of my services, they are at your disposal, although I sincerely trust that you will never regret your decision to accept the hand of a person who, though not entirely devoid of admirable qualities, is not—"

I suppressed Ramses. At least he had made Enid smile; turning to me, she said, "Perhaps you think me bold to sit here in full view of all the gossips. But I will not skulk in my room as if I had done something to be ashamed of. Donald and I are victims, not villains."

"I am entirely of your opinion," I replied warmly. "Mr. Baehler gave you your rooms back? I was concerned about that, since it is the height of the season, and Shepheard's is always crowded."

"I had booked them for a month and paid in advance. Besides," Enid added, with a wry smile, "I imagine he would have difficulty finding someone who was willing to inhabit them just now. I confess I do not look forward to sleeping in that bed. If you are remaining in Cairo for a few days, perhaps Ramses—"

"I would be more than happy," declared Ramses.

I exchanged glances with Emerson. "We will think about it, Enid. In the meantime—"

"In the meantime, I hope you will be my guests for luncheon," Enid said. "I have not quite enough courage to walk into the dining salon alone."

Naturally we agreed. I excused myself long enough to retrieve and destroy the letter I had left for Emerson the day before, and then joined the others. We had hardly taken our seats when Mr. Baehler came to the table. He apologized for disturbing our meal. "But this message was just left for you, and since it is marked 'Urgent,' I thought—"

"Ah," I said, reaching for the letter. "You were quite right to bring it at once, Mr. Baehler."

"It is directed to Professor Emerson," Baehler said.

"How extraordinary," I exclaimed.

"What do you mean, extraordinary?" Emerson demanded. "I have many acquaintances in Cairo who . . ." He perused the letter. "Extraordinary," he muttered.

Baehler departed, and Emerson handed me the letter. It was, as I had suspected, from Mr. Gregson. "Professor," it read. "I will be at the Café Orientale at twelve noon sharp. Do not fail me. Matters are approaching a climax, and if you wish to avert the peril threatening a person near and dear to you, you must hear what I have learned."

"I knew it," I said triumphantly. "That proves you

are mistaken, Ramses; if Mr. Gregson had any designs on me, he would not invite your father to be present. We must go at once; it is almost twelve."

Emerson pressed me back into my chair. "You are not mentioned in the invitation, Amelia," he said.

"But, Emerson—"

"It is a trap," squeaked Ramses. "There is some diabolical mystery in this; I beg you, Mama—"

"Please, Amelia, don't leave me." Enid added her entreaties to those of the others. "I had counted on your support later this afternoon, when I go to police headquarters to give my statement."

"I tell you, Mama, it is a trap," Ramses insisted.

"If it is, I am forewarned and shall be forearmed," Emerson declared. "Amelia, you must guard Miss Debenham. She will be especially vulnerable when she leaves the hotel. This could be a ruse, to lure us away and leave her unprotected."

"I had not thought of that," I admitted. "Very well, Emerson; your argument has convinced me."

"I thought it might," Emerson said, rising.

"Don't go alone, Emerson," I begged.

"Of course not. Ramses will go with me."

That was not what I had had in mind, but before I could say so, Ramses and his father had left us.

"I would feel very bad if I thought my selfish needs had caused you to neglect a more important duty," Enid said anxiously. "Do you believe they are going into danger?"

"No. Were that the case, I am afraid I would choose to neglect you instead. For you know, Enid, that my dear Emerson and I are joined by bonds of affection of the strongest kind. I would be the first to rush to his side if peril threatened him."

"Or Ramses."

"Oh yes, or Ramses, of course. The fact that I can sit here and quietly sip my soup"—which I proceeded to do, the waiter having brought the first course as we conversed—"testifies to my perfect confidence in Mr. Gregson. Just think, Enid, when Emerson returns he may have in his possession the evidence that will clear Donald."

Enid's eager questions prompted me to explain more fully about Mr. Gregson's involvement in the case. She had not heard the full story, and as she listened she began to look grave.

"Of course I am only an ignorant girl, with little experience in such things," she said hesitantly. "But I have never heard of this Mr. Gregson. He said he was a famous detective?"

"Famous in his own circles, I presume he meant," I replied. "People in that line of work have reason to remain inconspicuous."

"No doubt that is true," Enid said.

The dining salon was filling rapidly. We had been among the first ones there, since Enid's appointment with the police was for one o'clock. I watched the entering guests, wondering if "Mrs. Axhammer" would dare to make an appearance. She did not, but before long I saw another familiar form—that of Viscount Everly. He was alone, and for the first time since I had met him he was wearing proper morning dress instead of a bizarre costume. His eyes met mine, and after a moment of hesitation, he squared his shoulders and approached.

"Er—" he began.

"Don't dither, young man," I said. "If you have any sensible remark to make, make it."

"Well, ma'am, it's deuced difficult to do that with you looking at a chap as if he'd stolen your handbag," said the viscount plaintively. "It puts a chap off, you know."

"I am attempting, your lordship, to ascertain the color of your eyes."

The young man shied back, but not before I had discovered what I wanted to know. His eyes were an indeterminate shade of muddy brownish-gray, with flecks of green. . . . It would have been hard to say what color they were, but at least I was certain they were not black.

Enid stared at me in bewilderment, but I did not explain. I must confess I sometimes enjoy little mystifications of that nature. "Sit down, your lordship," I said. "I presume you wish to offer your condolences to Miss Debenham on the death of her kinsman?"

"He said he was her affianced husband," said Everly, taking a chair.

"He was mistaken," Enid said shortly.

"Well, er—in any case—deuced sorry, you know. He was a fine chap—splendid shot—held his whiskey. . . . No, forget that."

"Had you known him long?" I asked.

"Never met the fellow before I came to Cairo. Seemed a good sort. Ran into him at the Turf Club."

"And how did you know he was dead?"

I meant to catch him off guard, but he replied with prompt and ingenuous candor. "Why, it's all over the city, you know. And besides, I was the one who told Gorst yesterday that he was missing and that I feared foul play."

"You!" I exclaimed.

"Why, yes." The viscount leaned forward and planted his elbows on the table, pulling the cloth askew and setting my wineglass rocking. He caught it before more than a few drops had spilled. "See that?" he exclaimed proudly. "Quick as a conjurer! What was I talking about?"

"You informed the police yesterday . . ."

"Oh, right. It was last evening that he disappeared, you see. Smack out of his room at Mena House, while we were waiting for him to join us for dinner. Sent a waiter up to fetch him when he didn't turn up; room in a shambles, tables overturned, drawers pulled out— deuced exciting! Well, it was sure there'd been a struggle, and he didn't come back, and . . . I happened to run into Sir Eldon later, and mentioned it to him. Thought it was the least I could do."

As I listened to his semi-coherent statement and studied his lax, undistinguished features, I could not imagine what had prompted Emerson to suspect him of being a genius of crime. Nor could Emerson accuse me of being careless and taking foolish chances in speaking with him; for what could even a desperate and brilliant criminal do to me in a crowded dining salon in the most popular hotel in Cairo?

I was soon to find out.

There were no preliminary warning symptoms, such as giddiness or nausea. The only thing I remember is seeing his lordship, still seated in his chair, suddenly rush away from me at the speed of an express train, until he was no larger than a bumblebee. I felt my chin strike the table and felt nothing more.

I dreamed the same strange dream. Every detail matched the first—the soft couch on which I reclined, the walls draped with rosy silk, the marble floor, the tinkling fountain. Knowing I would soon wake at Emerson's side, I lay in drowsy content enjoying the voluptuous beauty of my surroundings. The ceiling above me was swathed in folds of soft fabric like the roof of a sultan's tent; from it hung silver lamps that shed a soft and tender light upon the scene. Lazily I turned my head. It was there, just as I had seen it before—the low table of ebony and mother-of-pearl, the bowl filled with oranges and nectarines, grapes and plums. Only the wine decanter and crystal goblets were missing.

Musingly I pondered the possible significance of such a recurring dream. Further study of the subject suggested itself. I resolved to take advantage of the prolongation of this vision to explore the ambiance more thoroughly, so I swung my feet off the couch and stood up.

A wave of giddiness sent me reeling back onto the cushions. But it was not that unpleasant sensation so much as the cool marble against the soles of my bare feet that brought the shocking truth home to me. This was not a dream. I was here, in the flesh—and someone had had the audacity to remove my boots!

And my tools! They were the first things I reached for; the dizziness had passed, and I was fully alert and capable of reasoning logically. Logic quickly informed me of the full horror of my situation. How he had abducted me in broad daylight from a crowded hotel I did not know, but I had no doubt of his identity. Only Sethos could be so bold; only he could carry out such a daring plot. And he was—he must be—the vapid viscount! The little trick with the wineglass, so deftly performed, had given him an opportunity to drug my wine. Emerson had been right and I had been wrong. The only consolation was that Ramses had been wrong too.

My heart was beating rather more rapidly than was comfortable, but the emotion that tingled through me was not so much fear as intense determination, mingled, I confess, with a burning curiosity. Was I at last to come face to face with the enigmatic personage whose exploits had aroused in me both repugnance and a certain unwilling admiration? There is, all critics agree, a dark grandeur in Milton's Satan; his local emissary could not but inspire a degree of the same respect.

Without moving from my seat, I took stock of the situation. Now I understood the absence of the crystal glasses and decanter I had seen in my dream. There was not a single object in the room that could be used as a weapon. My tools and my parasol had been taken, my pistol had been removed from its holster; even the heavy boots were gone from my feet. I saw no mirrors, no vases, no glass objects of any kind, whose shattered shards could be used to strike at an enemy or slash a vein. A grim smile, worthy of Emerson himself, crossed my lips. If Sethos feared I would attempt self-destruction in order to cheat him of his revenge, he underestimated me.

The drug had left me extremely thirsty, but I was afraid to taste the delectable fruit or drink the water from the fountain, though a delicate silver cup had been provided. Rising cautiously to my feet, I was pleased to find that I experienced no recurrence of the giddiness. A hasty circuit of the chamber revealed what I had expected. The windows, concealed behind filmy draperies, were shuttered and bolted. The shutters were beautifully carved wooden affairs, pierced in a delicate pattern to admit air, but when I applied my eye to one of the larger holes I could see only a narrow sliver of daylight, owing to the cunning curvature of the aperture. No hinges were visible; evidently they were on the outside of the shutters.

The only other exit from the room was a heavy door behind a curtain of fringed damask. Its inner surface was unmarked by hinges or keyholes or handles. I put my shoulder against it but it did not yield so much as a fraction of an inch.

Returning to the couch, I pondered my new discoveries and was forced to conclude that they offered little hope. The room had been designed for a prisoner, and I was sure I knew what kind of prisoner. That the villain should insult me by putting me into a room of the harem made me grind my teeth in rage. Nor was my ire assuaged when I discovered, spread upon the couch, such a costume as was worn by favored concubines of wealthy voluptuaries—the flowing, semi-transparent *shintiyan*, or trousers, and the *anteree*, or vest, that leaves half the bosom exposed. A respectable woman would wear a robe over these garments even in the privacy of her house, but none had been supplied. I tossed *shintiyan* and *anteree* contemptuously onto the floor.

At the moment there appeared to be nothing more I could do. The lamps were too high for me to reach, the door and windows were unassailable. I could probably twist the filmy fabric of the trousers into a rope, but a rope was of no use to me except to hang myself. Yet the situation was not entirely hopeless. In his consummate arrogance, Sethos had not bothered to change his headquarters. Not that I expected anything would come of Ramses' ridiculous idea of locating the place by means of the muezzins' calls, but I knew Emerson would raze the city of Cairo to its foundations before he gave up the search. There was hope as well in the information Mr. Gregson had discovered. Perhaps even now he and Emerson were on their way to release me!

I cannot say the time dragged, for I was fully occupied in considering and dismissing ideas for escape (mostly, I confess, the latter). I had no intention of sitting supinely waiting to be rescued. When I heard the faint sound at the curtained door I was instantly on my

feet and speeding across the room. I had no great ex-
pectation that my attempt would succeed, for I had only
my bare hands with which to strike at the person who
was about to enter, and I was also ignorant of whether
the door opened in or out, to right or to left. Still, one
must do one's best. Clasping my hands together in the
manner demonstrated to me by an Arab thug of my
acquaintance, I took up my position by the door.

I did not see the door open, or hear it; the hinges had
been well oiled. A faint draft of air was the only warning I had. It was followed by the abrupt displacement
of the heavy curtain as a man passed through. I was
ready. I brought my clenched hands down with bruising
force on the back of his neck.

At least that was where I had planned to strike him.
My fists landed in the middle of his back and fell numb
and tingling to my side. The fellow was almost seven
feet tall, and his muscles felt like granite.

He was an astonishing and formidable figure, one that
might have stepped straight out of the pages of *The
Arabian Nights*. His sole article of attire was a pair of
knee-length drawers, bound at the waist by a wide crimson sash into which he had thrust a pair of long, curving
swords, one on each side. Otherwise his body was bare,
from the crown of his shaven head to his midriff and
from his knees to the soles of his enormous feet. Every
inch of his exposed skin gleamed with oil and bulged
with muscle. His arms were as big around as my waist.

He glanced at me with mild curiosity. I suppose my
blow must have felt to him like the brush of a butterfly's
wing. As he advanced slowly toward me I retreated, step
by step, until the backs of my calves struck the couch
and I sat down rather more abruptly than I had intended.
That seemed to be what the apparition desired I should
do. He halted, and then drew himself up into military

rigidity as the curtain once more lifted to admit his master.

I knew him—yet he was no one I had ever seen before. A black beard and mustache masked the lower part of his face; but unlike the hirsute adornments he had worn in his disguise as Father Girgis, this beard was short and neatly trimmed. Tinted glasses concealed his eyes, and I had no doubt that his black, waving locks were false. He wore riding boots and breeches and a white silk shirt with full sleeves, a costume that set off his narrow waist and broad shoulders, and made me wonder how he could ever have played the role of the hollow-chested, feeble-looking young nobleman.

With a peremptory gesture he dismissed the guard. The giant dropped to the floor in a deep salaam and then went out.

"Good afternoon, Amelia," said Sethos. "I hope I may call you that?"

"You may not," I replied.

"Defiant as ever," he murmured. "It does not surprise me to find your spirit undaunted and your courage high; but are you not in the least curious as to how I brought you here?"

"Curiosity is a quality I hope I will never lose," I said. "But at the moment the question of how I came here interests me less than the more important question of how I will get away."

"Allow me to satisfy the former question, then," came the suave reply. "But first, let us make ourselves comfortable."

He clapped his hands. The giant reappeared, carrying a tray that looked like a doll's platter in his huge hands. He placed it on the table and withdrew. Sethos poured wine into the crystal glasses.

"I know you must be thirsty," he remarked, "for the

drug I was forced to use has that effect, and I observe you have not tasted the fruit or used the cup. I admire your caution, but it was unnecessary; the water and the fruit are untainted, as is the wine.''

"I had expected cognac," I remarked ironically.

Sethos burst out laughing, displaying a set of handsome white teeth. "So you appreciated my little joke with the good father? Since some ignorant persons persist in regarding my divine patron as the Egyptian Satan, I feel I ought to live up to the reputation he enjoys. Tempting the smug and the pious, and observing the ludicrous haste with which they tumble from virtue, gives me a great deal of innocent pleasure."

"I am not amused," I assured him. "It was a childish, unworthy gesture."

"One day, my dear, you will learn to laugh with me at the follies of mankind. But I beg you will assuage your thirst."

The sight of the pale liquid in the glass he offered made my throat feel drier than ever, but I folded my arms and shook my head. "Thank you, no. I never drink with assassins and kidnappers."

"You don't trust me? See here." He raised the glass to his lips and drank deeply before offering it again. I took it; ostentatiously turning it so that my lips would not touch the spot his had rested upon, I quenched my thirst. The wine had a dry, tingling taste that was most refreshing.

"Now," Sethos went on, seating himself on a cushion, "shall I tell you how I captured you?"

"It is obvious," I said with a shrug. "You slipped something into my glass of wine when you caught it to prevent it from spilling. My collapse alarmed my companion; assisted by you, she had me carried to her room. Her balcony gives onto a courtyard, from which it would not be difficult to transport a trunk or a bag of laundry to a waiting carriage. Is Miss Debenham also a prisoner, or have you added another murder to your long list?''

Sethos was offended. ''I do not murder women,'' he said haughtily.

''You only have them abducted, accused of murder—''

''The young woman was never in danger of being executed or even imprisoned,'' Sethos said. ''Nor has she been harmed. A touch of chloroform, from which she has long since recovered . . .''

''Then she must know you are the viscount—or you were—or perhaps I should say that the viscount was you. . . .''

''It does not matter. That persona is of no use to me now; it has been discarded. You never suspected me?''

''Emerson did,'' I cried. ''You cannot deceive Emerson; he is on your trail, and you will not escape his vengeance!''

''Emerson,'' Sethos repeated, with a sardonic smile. ''Never mind him; what about you?''

''I thought you were Mrs. Axhammer,'' I admitted. ''And Ramses—you remember Ramses—''

''Only too well.''

''Ramses—after all, he is only a little boy—suspected the detective, Mr. Gregson.''

''I was Gregson.''

''What!''

''I was also Mrs. Axhammer. I was all three!''

As the meaning of his words struck home, my spirits plummeted into the depths. I was as close to despair as I have ever been, even when I thought myself buried alive in the Black Pyramid. For I had counted on Gregson to assist Emerson in tracking Sethos to his lair. . . .

Galvanized, I bounded to my feet. "Emerson," I shrieked. "He was to meet you—Gregson—what have you done with my husband?"

"Damn Emerson," was the irritated reply. "Why must you keep mentioning him? I haven't done anything to him. The appointment was a ruse, to get him out of the way. I never went near the Café Orientale, and I hope he is still sitting there swilling coffee and reeling from the conversation of that abominably loquacious offspring of yours."

"I don't know why I should believe you."

"I don't know why you should not." Sethos rose to his feet. Slowly and thoughtfully, he said, "Radcliffe Emerson is one of the few men in the world who could be a serious threat to me. An ordinary, unimaginative villain would have him exterminated; but that is not my way. Besides, I rather enjoy a challenge, and appreciate a worthy adversary. The only advantages I have over Emerson are, first, his preoccupation with his archaeological research, from which he is not easily distracted, and, second, his atrocious temper, which leads him to act without thinking."

"Yet," I said wonderingly, "you have destroyed the first of those advantages by abducting me; for if I am not restored to Emerson unharmed, every ounce of his considerable energy and intelligence will be bent on finding you. As for his temper, it is a terrifying thing to encounter when it is aroused. You, sir, have aroused it."

"Quite true. Don't suppose I was unaware of the risks. Since I proceeded with my plan, you must believe I considered the result worth those risks."

As he spoke, he advanced slowly toward me. I stepped back, circling the couch, until I could retreat no farther. Sethos came on, lightly as a panther stalking its prey.

I set my back against the wall, prepared to defend myself to the last. "Do your worst, you monster," I cried. "You have taken away my parasol and stripped off my tools; but never think you can break the spirit of a Peabody! Torture me, murder me—"

"Torture? Murder?" He gasped for breath, his hands tearing at the open throat of his shirt. "Madam! Amelia! You misunderstand me totally. Why, I killed a man yesterday and left him lying before your tent only because he dared hazard your safety by shooting at the man who was with you!"

Before I could take in this remarkable speech, much less respond to it, he had flung himself—not at my throat—but at my feet. "Most magnificent of women, I adore you with all my heart and soul! I brought you here, not to harm you, but to shower upon you the ardent devotion of a soul hopelessly caught in your spell!" And he buried his flushed face in the folds of my trousers.

Fourteen

Though the astonishing turn of events surprised me considerably, it did not offer any reassurance for the future, and my indomitable will quickly conquered my amazement. Sethos continued to breathe heavily onto my left knee. His shirt collar had slipped back, exposing the nape of his neck. The trick had failed the first time; all the more reason why I should give it another try. Clasping my hands tightly together, I struck.

The results were most gratifying. Sethos let out a grunt and released his hold. His knees slipped on the polished marble and his head hit the floor as he fell forward. His head would have struck my feet had I remained motionless, but even as he toppled, I was running for the door.

I had forgotten the cursed thing had no handle. I pushed at it in vain. Turning at bay, I saw Sethos advancing toward me. His tinted glasses had fallen off.

His black eyes—his brown eyes—or were they gray? Whatever color they were, they were blazing with homicidal lust—or perhaps, considering his recent declaration, it was another kind of lust. To be honest, I did not really care which. Desperately I ran my hands over my trousers, hoping against hope some small tool had been overlooked—my penknife, my scissors, even a box of matches. He was almost upon me when a burst of inspiration illumined the darkness of despair. The belt itself! It was two inches wide and fashioned of thick though flexible leather, with a heavy steel buckle. Whipping it off, I whirled it vigorously.

"Back!" I shouted. "Stand back, or I will mark you in such a fashion that you will always bear one unmistakable stigma no disguise can hide!"

Sethos leaped back with agile grace. A smile twitched at the corners of his mouth. "That," he remarked, "is what made me love you, Amelia. You are so magnificently disdainful of common sense and discretion. The man who shares your life will never be bored.

"Please put that down and be reasonable. Even if you could strike me unconscious you could not leave the house."

"I could try," I retorted, continuing to whirl my belt, which made a sharp singing sound, like that of an angry insect.

"You could try. But you would fail; and if my men thought you had killed me or seriously injured me, they might harm you. Will you be more amenable if I promise on my solemn oath that I will not touch you or approach you again until you ask me to?"

"That will never happen," I assured him.

"Who knows? Life is full of unexpected happenings; that is what makes it endurable. If you won't take my word, look at it this way: You know me to be—well, let us not say vain—let us just say I have a good opinion of myself. Does it not seem more in keeping with what you know of my character that I would derive a peculiar pleasure from winning your affection—turning hate to love, contempt to admiration—rather than resorting to the brute force lesser men might employ? I despise such crudeness. And," he added, with another smile, "I am sure your arm must be getting tired."

"Not at all," I said stoutly. "I can keep this up all afternoon. However, your argument has its merits." I did not mention another, more persuasive argument, and I must say he was courteous enough not to refer to it with so much as a fleeting glance—the fact that my trousers, deprived of a large part of their support, were responding to the inexorable law of gravity.

"Very well," I said. "It appears to be an impasse, Mr. Sethos. I will take your word, but mind you, I give no promise in return."

I had not used his name before. Upon hearing it, his eyebrows lifted and he laughed. "So you have discovered my favorite pseudonym! Leave off the honorific, if you please; it sounds a trifle absurd, and dispels the confidential air I would like to see between us."

"No, thank you," I replied. "I prefer to maintain as much formality between us as the unusual circumstances permit."

"But, hang it," he cried, half laughing and half angry, "how can I begin my wooing with soft phrases and tender words if I must refer to you as Mrs. Emerson?"

"I feel sure a little difficulty of that nature will only be a challenge to you."

He held out his hand. With a shrug I gave him the belt.

"Thank you, Mrs. Emerson," he said gravely. "And

now I must ask that you assume those garments I have had laid out for you.''

''How dare you, sir!''

''As a simple matter of self-defense, Mrs. Emerson. Heaven knows what other hard or prickly objects you have concealed about your person. There is room for a set of carving knives in those trousers.'' Correctly interpreting my mutinous expression, he added, ''Aside from removing the arsenal you carried on your belt, and your boots, neither I nor my assistants searched you. It was a mark of the peculiar respect I feel for you, but if you force me . . .''

''Again your arguments are persuasive, sir. I trust you will show me the additional courtesy of leaving me alone while I carry out your command?''

''Certainly. Rap on the door when you are ready. But don't try my patience too long.'' Then he said, in a language I recognized as French, though it was slurred and oddly accented, ''Let down your tresses, oh my beloved, that their perfumed splendor may be the only barrier between your ecstasy and mine.''

I believe I succeeded in concealing my surprise at this extremely personal comment, for I thought it better to pretend I had not understood. Yet a strange sensation ran through me—a tingling warmth, if there can be such a thing. The extraordinary powers of the man were not limited to those of the mind; his body was that of an athlete, and his voice—that remarkable, flexible, and sonorous instrument—could change as suddenly and as completely as could his appearance.

He left me then, and I did not delay in following his orders. Do not believe, dear Reader, that I would have acquiesced so meekly had I not had an ulterior motive. Little did the villain know he had played into my hands! It was a pity that I could only attain my ends by such a doubtful stratagem, but by ordering me to remove my garments he had given me an excuse to dispose of certain of those garments in a manner he could not expect. He had said he would not return until I summoned him, but not knowing whether he would keep to his word, I had to work quickly.

Removing my trousers, I unwound the flannel belt I always wear when in Egypt and tore off a strip. How often had my dear Emerson teased me about this article of clothing! It was an invaluable protection against catarrh, as was proved by the fact that I had never suffered from that complaint. (In fact, Emerson had never suffered from it, either, though he absolutely refused to wear a flannel belt. However, Emerson is a law unto himself.) The belt had proved useful on a number of occasions; now it might be my salvation. Fortunately I had purchased a new supply before leaving England, and the bright pink color had not been faded by repeated washings.

It was with some reluctance that I removed from around my neck the chain from which hung my lapis scarab bearing the cartouche of Thutmose the Third. It had been Emerson's bridal gift; to part with it now, when it was my only memento of him, was hard indeed. But my hands were firm as I knotted the chain onto the end of the flannel strip. How fitting it would be if the gift of marital affection should save me from a fate that is (supposed to be) worse than death.

Returning to the window with my bit of flannel, I extracted one of my hairpins. Though a good three inches in length, these devices were useless as weapons because of their flexibility. However, this very quality was what I counted on now. Selecting the largest of the apertures in the shutter, I pushed the flannel and its scarab appendage into the hole as far as I could reach with my finger. The hairpin then came into play. There was a moment of suspense when the flannel jammed in the outer opening and would not move; after poking and prodding it, I finally felt it give way, and triumph filled me as I pushed the rest of the strip through and knotted the end to prevent it from falling out.

I felt certain the shutters covered a window that opened onto the open air. From that shutter now dangled a bright pink strip of flannel with a lapis scarab at its end. If, as I hoped, the window gave onto a public thoroughfare, someone was certain to notice my marker eventually.

I ripped the rest of the flannel into strips and knotted the ends together. Not even Sethos would notice that one strip was missing, and he could amuse himself by speculating on what I had meant to do with the cloth.

Once stripped down to my combinations—a one-piece, knee-length cotton garment trimmed with lace and little pink bows—I picked up the filmy objects Sethos had supplied. They were not quite so indecent as I had thought; the bodice was low-cut and sleeveless, but not translucent, for the fabric was covered with heavy embroidery and beadwork. But the trousers! There was enough fabric in them to have covered the tall windows in my drawing room at home, but they concealed very little. I put them on over my combinations.

"Let down thy hair, oh my beloved. . . ." It was halfway down already. My hair is heavy and coarse, and the rough handling I had received had not improved the neatness of my coiffure. I had no intention of appearing to respond to Sethos' impertinent request, particularly since I meant to retain my hairpins if I could. One never knows when a hairpin may come in handy. However, it was not easy to rearrange my tresses without the help of a comb or brush and I was still struggling with them when there was a rap on the door.

"Oh, curse it," I said, quite as Emerson might have done.

The door opened and Sethos put his head through the curtain. He stepped aside; the bald-pated giant entered with another tray, this one loaded with plates and dishes.

Sethos looked me over and then remarked coolly, "I hope you don't mind my saying, Mrs. Emerson, that the effect is not quite what I had expected. Never mind, it is a start. That unusual garment you are wearing is sufficiently form-fitting to assure me you are not concealing a pistol or a stiletto."

Having arranged the dishes on the table, the giant retired. Scarcely had he vanished behind the curtain before a series of thuds and knocks broke out. "Don't get your hopes up," said Sethos with a smile. "It is not a rescue party you hear, but my servant engaging in a bit of carpentry. I ordered a bar to be placed on this side of the door, as a token of my respectful intentions and my high esteem. Aren't you going to thank me?"

"What, thank my jailor for refraining from assaulting me?"

Sethos laughed and shook his head. "You are incomparable, my dear—Mrs. Emerson. Please sit down and let us dine."

He lifted a silver cover. The delicious aroma of chicken and spices reminded me that I was extremely hungry, my luncheon having been rudely interrupted. I would require all my strength in the hours to come; so I sat down on a cushion and helped myself. I refused wine, however.

"Don't worry," said Sethos, with one of his peculiar smiles. "I do not intend to weaken your resistance by rendering you intoxicated. It may take weeks, even months, but eventually you will learn to love me for myself.''

"Months! You can't keep me shut up in one room so long. I need exercise, fresh air—''

"Never fear. This is only a temporary stopover. To-morrow we leave for one of my country estates. I have prepared it especially for you and I know you will appreciate it. There are gardens filled with shade trees and exotic blooms, winding paths and crystal fountains, where you will be free to wander as you will.''

This was a piece of news, and no mistake! I should have expected it, but it cast a decided shadow over my hope of escape. I knew Emerson would find me sooner or later if I remained in Cairo; but even Emerson would find it difficult to search every inch of Egypt. Nor had Sethos said we were to remain in Egypt. His villa might be anywhere in the Near East—or the world!

The longer I could delay our departure, the better for me, but I could not think of any way of doing that. To pretend illness would not deceive Sethos; to pretend a sudden, overwhelming affection would be even less convincing, supposing I could bring myself to simulate that emotion. However, it would do no harm to simulate tolerance at least, and encourage him to talk in the hope that he might inadvertently betray some information I could use.

"Who are you really?" I asked. "Is this your true appearance?''

Sethos smiled. ''That is another of the qualities I love in you, Amelia—I beg your pardon, Mrs. Emerson. You are not subtle. Much as I yearn to confide in you, greatly as I burn to come to you as myself, caution compels me to preserve my incognito until we are truly united. This face you see is only one of a thousand I can assume if I wish. I am, if I may say so, a master in the art of

disguise. Permit me the indulgence of boasting a little—
of making myself appear admirable in the opinion of
one I adore—"

"Pray continue," I said, helping myself to a salad.
"The subject interests me a great deal."

"But it is not a subject in which you could excel.
You are my antithesis, direct where I am subtle, forth-
right where I am cunning and indirect. You go straight
to your goal, banging people over the head with your
parasol, and I glide as slyly and sinuously as a serpent.
The art of disguise is essential in my business, not only
for practical reasons but because it casts an aura of the
supernatural over my actions. Many of my ignorant assistants believe I change my appearance by magical
means. Whereas in reality it is only a matter of grease
paint and hair dye, wigs and beards and costumes, and
a more subtle yet equally important alteration of demeanor. Gestures, carriage, the tone of the voice—these
change a man's appearance more effectively than any
physical trick. I can make myself an inch or two taller
by means of special shoes and boots; but I make myself
appear shorter by holding myself in a certain way. If
you had examined the viscount with a critical measuring
eye, you would have seen that he was taller than his
stooping posture suggested; that his bowed shoulders
were not so narrow as they seemed; that his hesitant
speech and foolish mannerisms suggested a physical
weakness his actual proportions did not support."

"But his eyes," I exclaimed—for I was genuinely
fascinated. "Surely the priest of Dronkeh had black
eyes; and Ramses assured me—"

"Ramses has a great deal to learn," Sethos said.
"There are ways of changing the color of the eyes. Certain drugs enlarge the pupils. Paint applied to the eyelids
and lashes make the iris appear darker or lighter, es-

pecially if one is fortunate enough to have eyes of an ambiguous shade between brown and gray. Someday I will show you my bag of tricks, Amelia; in each of my hideaways I have a laboratory fitted out with my equipment, including a few items I developed myself. It may amuse you to experiment with them; though in your case it would be difficult to conceal those sparkling, steely orbs or dim their brilliance. . . ."

He gazed into them as he spoke, his voice dropping to a soft murmur.

"I would rather hear rational discourse than empty compliments," I said—though I was conscious of a perceptible quickening of my pulse.

He drew back. "Forgive me. I will keep my word, though you make it very difficult. . . . I will answer any questions you may have—except one."

"Your real identity, I suppose. Well, Mr. Sethos, I have a dozen others. Why do you lead such a life? With your abilities you could succeed in any one of a number of lawful professions."

Thoughtfully he replied, "Someday I will tell you my history, and then you will understand the motives that impelled me into this admittedly curious way of life. But one I may confess now. It is not for monetary gain alone that I rob the dead and the living. The finest objects I acquire never reach the sordid stalls of the marketplace. I am a lover of beauty; and the most beautiful objects I take, I keep for myself."

His meaning was unmistakable, for he gazed again into my eyes with an expression of intense interest. I burst out laughing. "That is a very pretty speech, Mr. Sethos, but I am afraid you have undermined your claim to be a connoisseur by abducting me. Emerson is the only man—"

"Please do me the favor of refraining from mention-

ing that person every few sentences," he interrupted
fiercely. "You are right, though; the professor and I are
more alike than he would care to admit, and his appreciation of your charms is only one of the things we
share."

"I can't stop mentioning him, because he is constantly in my thoughts."

His eyes fell. "You have the power to hurt me," he
muttered. "Your laughter wounded me deeply."

"I really don't think I owe you an apology, Mr. Sethos. If I have wounded your *amour-propre*, you have
done me a more serious injury. This is the first time I
have been abducted by a man who claimed to have been
moved to madness by my beauty, so I don't know the
correct way to behave."

My little attempt at humor was not well received.
Sethos looked down at me. "How could you have
missed the attentions I paid you?" he demanded tragically. "How could you have supposed, as you apparently did, that I intended to harm you? Why, scarcely a
day has passed since your return to Egypt that I have
not managed to speak to you or at least admire you from
afar. Not only was I the three individuals you mentioned—I was a tourist, a snake-charmer in the Muski,
even a digger in your own excavations. Everything I
have done was designed to demonstrate my deep passion—"

"Such as whisking Ramses off the top of the Great
Pyramid?"

"That was a scheme that went awry," Sethos admitted. "I was—as you have probably guessed—the American gentleman who spoke to you atop the pyramid. My
intention was to stage a daring rescue of that appalling
child and restore him to your arms. However, I was
foiled by Donald Fraser, curse him."

"I see. And on another occasion, when your horse ran away with Ramses—"

"The same rascal interfered to spoil my plans." Sethos' lips curled back in a wolfish snarl. "He at least will have occasion to regret his interference. I had determined to slaughter his even more rascally brother the moment I learned he had fired a shot that might have struck you. Ronald was a tiresome fellow anyway, and so stupidly single-minded, I was afraid he would continue to endanger you by making further attempts on Donald. So I did away with him, and it gave me a particular satisfaction to incriminate Donald when I did so. Surely you must have understood why I went to the trouble of carrying his body all that distance and laying it at your feet? I returned the communion vessels because, in a newspaper interview I read, you expressed your disapprobation of that particular theft. I sent you flowers—you know the meaning of red roses in the language of love—and a golden ring bearing my name! How could you have overlooked their significance?"

"Good Gad," I exclaimed. "So that is what was troubling Emerson! Poor dear man, he must have thought—"

"Emerson again!" Sethos flung up his hands.

My poor dear Emerson! (I continued my soliloquy in my thoughts, since it did not seem sensible to irritate my companion further.) Emerson had correctly interpreted the signs I had missed. It was not surprising that I should have done so, for my inherent modesty had clouded my normally clear intelligence. My thoughts were in a whirl, for a new and terrible thought had invaded my calm. Was it possible that Emerson believed—that he suspected—that he entertained for a single instant the slightest doubt of the wholehearted sincerity of my devotion? Was he—in short—jealous?

Impossible, my heart cried out. Surely Emerson could no more question my affection than I could doubt his. But if he did—if he could—then my disappearance must raise doubts. . . . It was a thought more terrible than any fear of imminent annihilation. I believe my lips actually quivered for a moment. But only for a moment; the necessity of escape became more pressing than ever.

Incredibly, I had almost forgotten my position in the interest of the conversation, and another fear wormed its way into my mind. The man had a superhuman power of fascination. I had been chatting with him easily, fearlessly. Could time bring about the result he confidently expected?

Again my heart responded with a fervent "Impossible!" But a doubt lingered. . . .

"Tell me," I said resolutely, "about the Fraser brothers. How did you become involved with Ronald?"

"Through normal business channels," Sethos said readily. "I have in my employ several of the most reliable assassins in Cairo. He approached one of them and his request was, in due course, passed on to me. He had hired Kalenischeff (whose reputation was known to everyone except the naive officials of the police department) to distract Miss Debenham when she came to Cairo bent on tracking down Donald Fraser and convincing him to tell the truth about Ronald. Ronald could not permit that; only his brother's woolly-witted loyalty stood between him and prison, disgrace and destitution. And he had good reason to fear that Donald might yield to the persuasion of the young and wealthy woman he secretly adored. Hence Kalenischeff, who led the girl astray instead of helping her.

"Kalenischeff, however, was not trustworthy. I had dismissed him from my employ some months earlier for that very reason. It would have been more discreet of me to have had him killed, but I am not so prone to needless slaughter as you suppose. He was in no position to betray my identity—I take care that no one shall be in that position—but if he had told all he knew, he could have crippled some of my operations.

"I kept an eye on him, therefore; and when I learned from Ronald Fraser that Kalenischeff was about to betray both of us, I was happy to accede to his request that Kalenischeff be disposed of. The wretch had decided to make a clean sweep, collect as much money as possible, and leave Egypt for good. He knew the Department of Antiquities would pay a tidy sum for information about me."

"And Miss Debenham offered an even larger sum if he would help her find Donald and tell Donald of his brother's treachery."

"Precisely. The girl proved resistant to the drug we used and made the mistake of running away. As I told you, she was never in real danger; the weak muscles of a woman—even yours, my dear—could not have struck a blow like the one that destroyed Kalenischeff."

"But Donald—poor Donald! You must clear him. That was an unworthy act, Mr. Sethos."

"If it will please you," Sethos said softly, "I will see to it that Fraser goes free." He reached for my hand. I pulled it away. He shrugged and sighed and smiled, and leaned back.

"Not even a touch of the hand in return for my confessing to murder? So be it. I told you I was a patient man.

"The rest of the business should be clear to you now. Ronald never knew my real identity. As Viscount Everly I encouraged him to join my little group because I wanted to watch the fellow. I knew, of course, that Miss Debenham had fled to you, just as I knew you had taken

Donald Fraser under your wing. I was not surprised, since it is your habit to adopt every unfortunate innocent you come across—by force, if necessary.''

''It is the duty of a Christian to help the unfortunate.''

''It is a Moslem's duty too. Strange, how the so-called great religions all insist on the same weak virtues. Even the ancient Egyptians boasted of having given food to the hungry and clothing to the naked.''

''It is a sublime and universal truth,'' I replied. ''What you view as weakness is the quality that makes us one with the Divine. 'And the *greatest* of these is love.' Or,'' I hastily amended, ''as the word is sometimes translated, charity.''

''A poor, feeble translation,'' said Sethos softly. His eyes held mine with hypnotic power; I felt myself sinking deep into their velvety depths. Then he lowered his gaze, and I let out a quick, involuntary sigh. His lashes were as long and thick and curling as those of a pretty girl. I wondered if they were his own.

''I have always avoided the softer sentiments,'' Sethos went on reflectively. ''My feelings for you came on me like a hurricane, a great natural force I was powerless to resist. I would have resisted them if I could. Even now I have a strange foreboding—''

''You have them too!'' I exclaimed.

His lashes lifted; laughter warmed his brown—his gray—his chameleon eyes, before they darkened into somber pensiveness. ''I used to view such premonitions as the expression of an instinct developed by those who have reason to fear danger. But now I wonder if there is not some higher fate that guides our destinies. Not a benevolent deity; no one who studies the cruelty of man can believe in a god who permits such atrocities. Only a vast, impersonal something, with a perverted sense of humor! It would be strange, would it not, if the solitary weakness of a lifetime should be my downfall? I sense that this may be so. You could redeem me, Amelia—you and you alone. Only imagine what I might do for the world if my powers were turned to good instead of evil. Help me, Amelia. Give me your hand—lead me out of darkness into light. . . .''

It was a thrilling moment. I felt that at long last I understood this strange, brilliant, and tormented man. I was moved—nay, I was inspired. My lips parted. My breast heaved. My hand reached out . . .

Our fingertips had not quite touched when the sounds of violence made both of us start from our seats. The curtains swayed wildly as the door opened and slammed back against the wall. There was only one person of my acquaintance who opened a door in that manner! I pressed my hand to my palpitating bosom.

It was Emerson! It was he! But what a sight he was! His hair stood on end, his best dress shirt was in shreds; one sleeve had been ripped away from the seam and huddled on his forearm like a ragged gauntlet. His face was disfigured by reddening patches, and one eye was half-closed. Blood dripped from his scraped knuckles, and in either hand he held a naked sword. Never in my life had I beheld a spectacle that moved me more! I felt that my pounding heart must burst the confines of my breast.

Before the curtain had fallen back into place, Emerson whirled round. He let out a startled remark, dropped one of the swords, and slammed the door shut but not before a sinuous and tawny form had streaked through the opening. Emerson dropped the bar into place just as the panels began to reverberate under a fierce assault. Then he turned again. His gaze went straight to me.

"Amelia," he exclaimed. "For God's sake, put on some clothes!"

"Emerson," I replied, with equal passion. "Watch out!"

Emerson ducked and a heavy silver bowl crashed into the door, skimming his disheveled head. The cat Bastet sauntered toward Sethos. Her loud rasping purr blended with the dying echoes of the sound of the bowl striking the door. Sethos staggered as the cat twined affectionately around his ankles—she was, as I believe I have mentioned, a large and muscular animal. Agilely he leaped away, and the cat Bastet, deeply affronted, headed for the table and the stuffed chicken.

After a casual glance around to assure himself that Sethos had no other missiles convenient to hand, Emerson looked again at me. "Has he harmed you, Peabody? Has he dared . . . Has he . . . Good Gad, Peabody, seeing you in that outrageous costume has filled me with apprehensions I scarcely—"

"Have no fear, Emerson! He has not . . . He did not . . ."

"Ah!" Emerson's chest swelled, completing the ruin of his best shirt. He shook the tatters of his sleeve from his arm and flexed his muscles. "In that case," he said, "I will only tear *one* of his legs off."

He started toward Sethos, who retreated as delicately as Bastet might have done, his hands hanging limp and loosely flexed.

"Emerson," I said.

"Please don't distract me, Peabody."

"He is unarmed, Emerson. Your scimitar—"

"Scimitar? Oh." Emerson stared curiously at the weapon. "I took it from that fellow out there," he explained. "Never saw such a hard head on a human being. He was up and at me again almost at once. I expect, though, that they have overpowered him by this time.''

Indeed, the pounding on the door had ceased. "You did not come alone then?'' I asked.

"Certainly not. Ramses—''

"Emerson!''

"And a regiment of police officers.'' He transferred his gaze to Sethos. "Your evil career is ended, you swine. But I shan't admit the police until I have dealt with you. I promised myself that satisfaction, and I think I deserve it.''

Sethos straightened to his full height. He was not as tall as Emerson, or as brawny, but they made a magnificent pair as they faced one another in mutual animosity.

"Good, Professor,'' he said in a low, drawling voice. "I promise myself some satisfaction too, for I have yearned to come to grips with you. Give me the other sword, and we'll fight for her like men.''

"Emerson,'' I cried in some anxiety, for I knew my husband's temperament only too well. "Emerson, you don't know how to fence!''

"No, I don't,'' Emerson admitted. "But you know, Peabody, there can't be much to it—whacking at one another in turn, and—''

"Emerson, I insist . . . No. No, my dearest Emerson— I beg you, I implore you. . . .''

A pleased smile spread over Emerson's face. "Well, Peabody, since you put it that way. . . .'' And to my horror he flung the sword away. It skipped across the smooth marble floor in a series of musical ringing sounds. Even before it struck the floor, Sethos moved— not toward that sword, but toward the first, which Emerson had dropped at the door. Snatching it up, he swung on Emerson.

"Now, Professor, we are more evenly matched,'' he

snarled. "I know something of boxing, but I prefer not
to meet *you* in that arena. Pick up the sword—I give
you that much."

Emerson shrugged. "It wouldn't be much use to
me," he remarked. "However . . ." And with the cat-
like quickness he could sometimes summon, he
snatched the wine decanter and brought it crashing
down on the edge of the table. Bastet, who had been
eating the chicken, soared up with a yowl of protest;
the decanter shattered; and the table collapsed, spilling
food and broken glass. The air glittered with crystal
shards, like drops of clear hail.

Emerson ripped the silken covering from the couch
and wrapped it round his left arm. "Now then," he said.
"Come on, you bas—excuse me, Peabody—you villain."

They circled one another in taut silence. Sethos
lunged. With a quick twist of his body, Emerson
stepped inside the other man's guard and jabbed at his
face with the broken bottle. Sethos jumped back. His
next move was a slash, from left to right; Emerson beat
it back with a blow across Sethos' forearm. The blade
whistled past his side. Sethos retreated again, giving
Emerson a chance to snatch up the silver tray. It served
as a makeshift shield; with its aid he took the offensive,
striking the sword back each time it approached, and
jabbing with the decanter.

In my opinion there is never any excuse for violence.
It is the last resort of people and nations who are too
stupid to think of a sensible way of settling their dif-
ferences. The sight of two pugilists beating one another
to a pulp sickens me; the idea of little boys being taught
to "fight like men" revolts and repels me. Was I
therefore filled with disgust at the bloody battle that
raged between these two men of intellect and ability?

No.

The sight of Emerson's muscles rippling under his
bronzed skin—of the ferocious smile that bared his
strong white teeth—of the grace and vigor of his movements—roused an answering joyful ferocity in my
bosom. My breath came in gasps, my cheeks burned.
For a few moments I was not a civilized, sensible
woman; I was a primitive female crouched in her cave
as two savage male beasts fought to possess her.

It was a most curious and interesting sensation.

A wicked feint and even quicker riposte struck the
make-shift shield aside. Sethos' blade bit deep into Emerson's arm. He gave a grunt of annoyance rather than
pain and lunged forward. Only Sethos' sideways turn of
the head saved his eyes; the glass scored a row of ragged cuts down his cheek. Wounded and in need of a
respite, the combatants broke apart, both dripping blood,
both panting, both glaring.

"This is ridiculous!" I cried.

Neither man paid the least attention, but my fit of
temporary insanity had ended abruptly at the sight of
the blood spurting from Emerson's wound. Masculine
pride is all very well, and I hoped Emerson was enjoying himself, but I was cursed if I was going to stand by
and see him cut to ribbons just so he could have the
satisfaction of dying to defend my honor.

I ran toward the door. Emerson did not take his eyes
off Sethos, but he saw me. "Peabody," he gasped. "If
you open—that door—I will—I will—oof!" I heard
Sethos' blade ring on the silver platter. I snatched up
the scimitar Emerson had flung away and turned for an
appraisal of the situation.

It was far from reassuring. Even as I turned, the final
blow was struck. Too late, I thought wildly—too late
to admit the helpers waiting outside, too late even to

reach my stricken spouse and stand side by side with
him, sword in hand! Sethos' blade came down on the
platter again and knocked it out of Emerson's grasp. As
the sword hung motionless from the impact for a split
second, Emerson dropped the decanter and caught his
opponent's arm in both hands.

They stood frozen in matching strength, Sethos' efforts to free his arm and Emerson's efforts to hold it
producing a temporary equilibrium. Slowly Sethos' arm
bent. The sword quivered in his straining hand. Beads
of sweat broke out on Emerson's brow. The rose-pink
wrappings on his arm were crimson now, but his grip
never weakened.

Then the end came. The sword fell from Sethos' fingers, and Emerson's hand, slippery with blood, lost its
hold. Quick as ever, Emerson reached for the fallen
sword. Sethos, just as quick, leaped back against the
wall. He looked at me. ''Amelia—farewell!'' he cried—
and vanished.

Emerson bounded forward with a series of oaths that
exceeded anything I had ever heard him utter. The slab
of marble through which Sethos had vanished closed
again, in Emerson's face. ''Damn!'' said Emerson, beating on the slab with the scimitar and then with his fist.
''Damn, damn, damn, damn!''

After a while I said, ''Emerson.''

''Damn, damn . . . Yes, Peabody? Damn!'' said Emerson.

''Shall I open the door now, Emerson?''

''Curse the cursed fellow,'' Emerson bellowed, var-
ying the tone of his remarks. ''One day—one day, I
swear . . .'' He stopped kicking the marble and stared at
me. ''What did you say, Peabody? Did I hear you correctly? Did you ask my permission to open the door?''

''Yes, you heard me, Emerson. But oh, my dear Em-

erson, I think we should let them in; you are wounded,
my dear, and—"

"Do you really want to let them in, Peabody?"

"No, Emerson. At least—not just yet."

"How could you possibly suppose, even for a second,
that I cared for anyone but you?"

"Well, Peabody, if you hadn't kept referring to that
man in such admiring terms—"

"I never stopped thinking of you for a moment, Emerson. I never lost hope that you would find me."

"Had it not been for your quick wit in stringing your
bits of flannel out the window, we would not have succeeded, Peabody. We began searching in the area
Ramses' research had indicated, but it was somewhat
extensive."

"Where did you learn to do that, Emerson?"

"This, Peabody?"

"No—no, not . . . Oh, Emerson. Oh, my dear Emerson!"

"I was referring, some minutes ago, to your skill in
fighting with broken bottles, Emerson. I had no idea you
could do that."

"Oh, that. One picks up odds and ends, here and
there. . . . Something is sitting on my back, Peabody. Or
are you—"

"No, Emerson. I believe it is the cat Bastet. I suppose
she has finished the chicken and is indicating she is
ready to leave. Shall I remove her?"

"Not if it would necessitate your moving from your
present agreeable position, Peabody. The sensation is
unusual but not unpleasant. . . . Without the cat Bastet,

we might not have reached you so soon. Apparently your idea that Sethos had tempted her with tidbits when he delivered the communion vessels was right on the mark. She remembered him well; he dropped his handkerchief in Miss Debenham's room, and his scent was strong on it. Bastet picked it up at once in the street outside this house.''

"How very interesting! But without the signal of my flannel belt—''

"That was the decisive factor, Peabody.''

"You were never out of my thoughts, Emerson.''

"Nor you from mine, Peabody. I imagined that fellow holding you in his arms—I thought I would go mad with rage.''

"He was very courteous. He explained that he wanted to win my love, not force his upon me.''

"Curse the rascal!''

"He did have a strange charm, Emerson. Not that he would have succeeded with me, but I imagine many women—''

"I don't care for the tenor of the conversation, Peabody. Stop talking.''

Before we admitted the police, who were making agitated assaults upon the door, it was necessary to tidy ourselves up a bit. After a refreshing splash in the fountain I reassumed my dear familiar clothes. Fortunately there was a great deal of fabric at hand, so I was able to bind up the cut in Emerson's arm, though I promised myself I would tend to it properly as soon as we got to the hotel. We then unbarred the door.

The anteroom was filled with constables, led by Major Ramsay. He beamed with almost amiable pleasure when he beheld us unharmed, though he was not at all happy to learn of Sethos' escape. After we had satisfied his curiosity as to the events (most of them, at least) which had preceded our opening the door, I asked curiously, "Where is Ramses?"

"He is somewhere about," Ramsay replied.

Ramses came running out of an adjoining room, his face alight with a boyish enthusiasm seldom seen upon that saturnine countenance. "Mama," he cried. "Mama, look here!"

He swept his hand across his mouth and then curled his lips back, displaying a set of brown, rotten teeth, like those of an old Egyptian beggar. "They are a trifle large," he explained indistinctly, "but in time—"

"Take them out at once," I exclaimed in disgust.

Ramses complied, all the more readily because the dentures were in fact considerably oversized for his mouth. "There are wonderful things in there," he exclaimed, his eyes shining. "Paints for the face and hands, pads to fit in the cheeks, wigs and beards and . . . Oh, Mama, may I have them? Please, Mama?"

It was hard for a mother to disappoint a little lad, to wipe the shining joy from his face. "I think not, Ramses," I said. "The police will want those things as evidence."

(However, it appears they did not; for since we returned to England, the servants have complained of seeing strange individuals wandering around the house and the grounds. One apparition is that of a little golden-haired girl, and Rose is convinced we have a ghost.)

So ended our second encounter with the strange and mysterious personage known as Sethos. The second, and perhaps the last—for several days after that battle of Titans we received a letter. It was delivered to us at

Dahshoor, whither we had returned after seeing Ronald—or Donald, rather—and his bride-to-be cleared of all charges and rejoicing in their approaching nuptials. As Emerson had pithily expressed it, "Now that nonsense is over, thank heaven, and I can get back to work."

But was it over? An unseen messenger had delivered the letter, eluding our watchful men, gliding like a ghost through the barred gates of the compound. We found it on the doorstep one morning at dawn. Actually, it was Ramses who found it, since he was usually the first one to arise, but it was Emerson's deep voice that intoned the message aloud.

" 'You might have redeemed me,' " it began.

Emerson stopped. "It seems to be directed to you, Peabody," he said drily.

"Read on, Emerson. There are not now and have never been any secrets between us."

"Humph," said Emerson. He proceeded. " 'From this time on, when the unhappy world reels under the miseries of the blows I shall deal it, remember that its suffering is on your head. My Amelia—my beloved . . .' Curse the fellow's impertinence! I have half a mind to rip this paper to shreds!"

"You may do with it what you like after you have finished reading it, Emerson."

"Bah," said Emerson. "Very well, then. . . . 'Henceforth you and yours are safe from my avenging hand. You may refrain from assaulting elderly ladies whom you suspect of being Sethos in disguise; you may leave unpulled the luxuriant beards of suspicious gentlemen. You will see me no more. I am leaving Egypt forever. Think of me sometimes, Amelia, as I will think constantly of you. What could we not have achieved together!' "

"I wonder if he means it," I said, as Emerson methodically converted the letter into confetti.

"Humph," said Emerson.

"I really wish you had not destroyed that letter, Emerson. It was not very sensible."

Emerson's hands stopped moving. "What did you say, Peabody?"

"You are making a mess on my nice clean doorstep, and the time may come—I hope it does not, but it may—when we might want a specimen of Sethos' handwriting."

"Peabody," said Emerson, looking at me strangely.

"Yes, Emerson?"

"That is the first time in three days you have criticized or reprimanded me."

"Indeed? Well, I am sorry, Emerson, but if you persist in—"

"No, no, you don't understand." Emerson grasped me by the shoulders and gazed into my eyes. "I was beginning to fear you had turned into one of those boring females who can only say, 'Yes, my dear,' and 'Just as you like, my dear.' You know very well, Peabody, that our little discussions are the spice of life—"

"The pepper in the soup of marriage."

"Very aptly put, Peabody. If you become meek and acquiescent, I will put an advertisement in the *Times* telling Sethos to drop by and collect you. Promise me you will never stop scolding, Peabody."

Ramses and the cat were both watching with intense interest, but for once I did not care. I put my arms around Emerson's neck. "My dear Emerson," I said, "I think I can safely promise that."

AN ARCHEOLOGIST DIGS UP MURDER IN THE ALAN GRAHAM MYSTERIES BY

MALCOLM SHUMAN

THE MERIWETHER MURDER
0-380-79424-1/$5.99 US/$7.99 Can

ASSASSIN'S BLOOD
0-380-80485-9/$5.99 US/$7.99 Can

PAST DYING
0-380-80486-7/$5.99 US/$7.99 Can